The Sun Child

Other Books by J. M. Failde

The Vampires of Malvania Series

The Crow Lord

The Sun Child

A Krampus Story

For Teen Readers

Where Did the Wind Go?

The Sun Child

J. M. FAILDE

B

BOOKLOGIX®
Alpharetta, Georgia

This is a work of fiction. Names, characters, businesses, places, and events are either the products of the author's imagination or are used in a fictitious manner. Any resemblance to actual persons, living or dead, or actual events is purely coincidental.

Copyright © 2024 by J. M. Failde

All rights reserved. No part of this book may be reproduced or transmitted in any form or by any means, electronic or mechanical, including photocopying, recording, or any information storage and retrieval system, without permission in writing from the author.

ISBN: 978-1-6653-0904-2 – Paperback
ISBN: 978-1-6653-0905-9 – Hardcover
eISBN: 978-1-6653-0906-6 – eBook

These ISBNs are the property of BookLogix for the express purpose of sales and distribution of this title. The content of this book is the property of the copyright holder only. BookLogix does not hold any ownership of the content of this book and is not liable in any way for the materials contained within. The views and opinions expressed in this book are the property of the Author/Copyright holder, and do not necessarily reflect those of BookLogix.

Library of Congress Control Number: 2024911589

∞This paper meets the requirements of ANSI/NISO Z39.48-1992
(Permanence of Paper)

Illustrations, cover, and layout design by Anto Marr.

061024

To all the people who thought Beast was much hotter
before he turned back into a human.

CONTENT WARNING

This book contains dark and mature language, themes, and content that may not be suitable for all readers, including violence, blood, abuse, attempted sexual assault, and explicit sex. Reader discretion is advised.

MALVANIA

1

"*Crawl to me.*"

Her knees buckled to the floor of their own will, slamming into the rough stone below her. She dropped too fast to even think of breaking the thrall, but the moment the small rocks bit into her flesh, the spell shattered around her mind.

But that didn't mean Hektor could know.

Begrudgingly, Lila played the role of Hektor Reinick's pet, as he sat on the floor of the dais in the Viper Morada's great hall. His legs spread wide, a thick, wicked smile slashing his face, he beckoned her like a fucking dog.

She placed her hands on the floor, moving slowly toward him, keeping the blank expression as she knew that was what he would want.

"*Little Mouse,*" he cooed, and the words made her stomach sick. His voice twisted the words that once made her heart sore. That once filled her with warmth. He took it and sullied it with his disgusting lips. She almost broke the act, almost snapped, picturing her nails digging into his eyes, her hands at his throat. But, even as she neared him, even as his hand cupped her cheek, rubbed her lip, even as he bit into her neck, she did nothing.

Lila Bran was stronger than their torment. She was here to make them pay. She was here to hurt them in any way she could. And to do that, she'd be their pet. She'd be their plaything. She'd be their murine.

And when the opportunity arose, when the fire in her engulfed the Morada in flames, that was when Lila would strike.

The moment she arrived at the Viper Morada three months ago, Hektor tore the leathers off her very back. She still remembered how the cloth felt tearing from her arms, her legs, her breasts, as he *pulled* it away from her. She remembered the choked sound she made as the collar snagged on her throat—of the embarrassed flush that reached her cheeks the moment she stood nude before the Viper siblings, of the sharp snap against her skin as the material tore around her.

"What a pretty little murine. Your skin," Hektor cooed, grazing his finger along her bare shoulder, "You're like a blank canvas for me to mark all over again." His nail dug into her shoulder, a long, thin cut opening the skin. "This bare neck needs a necklace worthy of its beauty." Too fast for Lila to react, Hektor grabbed her neck, squeezing till a small gasp escaped her lips. His fingers dug into her throat, bruising her skin as his grin widened. "Welcome home."

She spit at him. Probably unwise, but worth it.

Ciro snickered as Hektor grabbed her chin, angling it toward him. His sickly yellow eyes gleamed a shade that reminded Lila of bile. "Where did all my marks go? Tell me," he commanded, and she felt the lick of his thrall all around her.

But Hektor was weak. She felt the pull at first, but was able to shove it away immediately.

"Tell him," Ciro commanded, seeing her moment of hesitation. And before she even realized she was speaking, Lila said, "Ambrose." Then, prouder, "He removed your venom and cured my wounds. All of them."

"Fuck. That damned crow," Hektor cursed.

Even now, the siblings still believed him to be dead, killed by Lila's hand. And he has remained in the shadows since, as the Crow Court feigned mourning and loss. "*The Crow Lord is dead*," they'd said, and though she knew it wasn't true, it gutted her each and every time it was brought up.

Lila felt the remnants of Ciro's thrall on her, an unwelcome hand caressing her mind. She felt . . . dirty. He shouldn't be allowed in. If he could do this, what else could he do?

Maybe this wasn't a good idea, she thought. On the battlefield, she was able to withstand both of their thralls. But then, Ambrose had been there. She played along, just to keep them in the dark of how far she had come.

Ambrose had tested Lila, forced her to break from a thrall that had been as powerful as he could make it. And through some intense convincing, she was able to do just that.

Lila theorized Hektor *couldn't* push his thrall to those same high levels. But Ciro, once again, proved he could, and the thought that at any moment she may not be able to break out of one made her knees shake.

Ciro stepped close behind her, caging her between himself and Hektor. Lila was sure this must've been some kind of sick, twisted fantasy of theirs, but before she could say as much, Hektor spoke up.

"What do you think, Ciro? Should we just have her as our little sex doll, prancing around the Morada, naked and ready at our beck and call?" He flicked her nipple, causing her to flinch back—right into Ciro.

The horned Viper smirked. "I'd like to keep *some* mystery." He snapped his fingers at Rebekkah, who had been standing silently, watching from the corner of the room, horrified. "Bring me what we prepared for her."

For the briefest moment, Rebekkah's eyes met Lila's. Regret, sorrow, and guilt swirled in those dark golden orbs, just before she scurried out of the room.

"Plus, brother," Ciro's tone turned to ice as his hands landed on Lila's shoulders. "How many times have I told you? Now that she is back with us, she's *mine*. Not *ours*." His hand shot forward quicker than Lila could see. Ciro grabbed his brother's hand, and bent the index finger so far back, Lila heard the bone crack under Hektor's skin. The same finger—Lila realized—he had used to flick her with. "You do *not* touch, unless I say you can. You can look all you want, but she is *mine* to claim. *Mine to cleanse.*"

Before Hektor could retort, before Rebekkah could return, and before Lila could even think, Ciro threw her over his shoulder, bottom on full display to anyone he passed, and stalked away. His hand rested precariously high, at the base of her thighs, and she feared squirming would grant him even closer access.

He stalked into what was once his parents' room, past

the bedroom and into the adjoining bathroom, and tossed her into a steaming bath. The water splashed over the sides onto the floor as the heat from it stung her body.

"Clean that fucker off of you. I don't want to smell *him* anywhere on what's mine." Ciro tossed a thick sponge into the water next to her and pointed at the soap on the ledge of the tub.

Lila hesitated.

"Now, or I'll get in there and do it myself."

She realized he wasn't enthralling her. He wanted her to do this by her own will. He wanted her to give in without forcing her. To give in to *him*.

Ciro stepped forward, and Lila quickly grabbed the sponge. Ambrose was more than just on her skin, she could do this, and still keep him with her. He was her mind, her heart, the very air she breathed. Removing his scent did not remove *him*.

Lila lathered the sponge and began to swipe at her body as Ciro stepped back to his original position, and folded his arms across his massive chest, watching. She avoided the space between her thighs, and tried hard not to think about it. But he was unrelenting. "You missed a spot. That's where I smell him the most."

Lila flushed. She *liked* smelling like Ambrose there. She wanted him to have the dominance over whatever stupid game this was. Ciro would *never* own her—not in the way Ambrose did. But if she wanted to stop Ciro from *taking* what wasn't his, she knew she needed to comply. She turned her back to the viper and scrubbed quickly.

"*Harder*," Ciro commanded, his voice thick with the thrall now. She could hear the smirk over his lips. Her grip on the sponge tightened as it scrubbed between her legs, and as it rubbed against her clit, she got the brief memory of Ambrose's perfect fingers sliding between her thighs, a wave of unsolicited pleasure purred through her.

Ciro grunted in amusement behind her as her body shivered, just once, and Lila knew he assumed it was for him. "Asshole," she muttered and released the sponge. He was wrong. No matter what the Reinicks made her do, even if they made her peel her skin off, Ambrose would *always* be there. In every touch, every breath.

Once bathed and dried, Lila only waited a moment before Ciro allowed Rebekkah into his room. She carried a fabric so thin and light, it looked more like the drape of a window, but she soon realized it was some kind of gown... or frock or... were they expecting her to wear *that*?

Rebekkah tossed the loose fabric over her head. The dress—if she could call it that—was indeed flowy and thin. So thin, Lila could see every curve and freckle of her body, and her pink nipples practically illuminated under the white fabric of the thing. The skirt was long enough to trip on, and at her waist in the front, two pieces of fabric were just thick enough to cover her breasts, before meeting around the base of her neck, leaving her back fully exposed.

"Ahh, lovely," Ciro cooed as he drank her in. "I bet Hektor will go absolutely mad seeing her like this, don't you think, Bek?"

Once again, her eyes met Lila's. "He's going to be begging you for permission to touch her," she said as her eyes said something completely different. Her eyes were begging, pleading. Lila saw "I'm sorry," and "run."

That was three months ago. Three months of walking the halls of the Viper Morada practically nude. Three months of being ogled at by Hektor, who relished on small touches. He'd grope her breasts as she turned a corner, he'd slap her ass as she walked past him in a hall. She could feel him watching her as she slept, as she changed, as she bathed.

But he kept his distance like a beast stalking his prey. She knew he was a pot ready to boil over, and at any minute he would scald her with his forced touch.

But Ciro... Ciro was a different kind of animal.

He *never* touched her. Not once. Time and time again he would force her to lay next to him in his bed, but his skin would never so much as graze hers.

And though she felt this should be reassuring, it was... concerning. She felt his obsession for her in the way he watched her, in the way he didn't let anyone else touch her. Not one vampire in the Viper Morada had spared a second glance at her, let alone anything else. And Ciro was the sole vampire to drink from her before earlier tonight, in the great hall. She felt Hektor's venom course through her blood like a sludge injected right into her veins. Her knees were scratched, her palms bloodied.

But the wounds didn't stop there. Her wrists and ankles were marred with bruises and bite marks from Ciro, his favorite places to drink from. He relished in her blood, moaning at each drag he took from her. And though she sometimes saw his hardening cock in his pants, he never took it further.

Like Hektor, she wondered when Ciro would boil over. She feared that when it happened, he would be so much worse.

Lila heard the footsteps make their way down the long

stone hallway and her heart leaped. Would it be one of the brothers, there to torture her some more, or would it be Rebekkah, bringing her a moment of solace? She held her breath. She'd been sent back to her room after Hektor filled himself, and hadn't seen a soul in the hours that have passed as she tended to her own wounds.

"Murine," the voice was like ice, sending shivers as sharp as blades down her back. "Come out."

Ciro Reinick stood in her open doorway. They had removed the door—though it didn't do much before—the moment she arrived back in her cell of a room.

Lila stood, lifting her chin defiantly—well, as much as she could in her state—then walked to him.

"We're leaving," he said. "Just for the day. We'll be back before nightfall."

This hadn't been the first time they'd disappeared, and each instance was a breath of relief. The Morada without them was just another dark, dingey castle. The Morada *with* them was hell on earth.

Lila nodded.

"I want you to behave, pet." Ciro chucked his fingers under her chin, forcing her eyes to meet his. "Can you do that for me?"

Ambrose's words sprang to her mind. *"Now, are you going to be good for me?"* Another night, another time, white lace, and a dark wooden desk.

Lila cleared her throat. "Yes."

She felt Ciro's thumb rub against her cheek, just for a moment, and then he pulled away.

"Good. Hektor and Rebekkah might be back sooner than I am." Ciro turned and began to walk down the hallway that was once the murine quarters—but was now just hers. He paused midstep, and turned over his shoulder.

"If they should return before me, stay in your room. No matter what. Am I understood?"

Lila felt herself gulp. The idea of being . . . alone with Hektor was appalling. She knew Rebekkah would be there, and surely, if Ciro wasn't around, Rebekkah may even help Lila. But she couldn't rely on that.

The idea of *needing* Ciro around to ensure her safety also greatly unsettled her. Lords, she missed her freedom. She missed kicking and stabbing and—

"Murine, I asked you a question."

"Yes. I'll stay in my room."

Ciro's gaze wandered down her body once again, still in that same, idiotic dress, the bottom hem now tattered and torn. She felt the heat of his gaze, as his eyes lingered everywhere they shouldn't, then she watched as Ciro licked his lips before his eyes met hers once more.

"Good." And with that, the horned viper turned and stalked from the corridor. After minutes alone, she knew the siblings were gone from the tower.

She was alone.

I have to do this.

Ambrose Draven could still smell her in the dark, cold halls of the manor in the Crow Court. Lilacs from her baths, leather from the armor she wore, and wood from her stake. He loved her smell—couldn't get enough of it as it permeated his office. But now that she was gone, it teased him—a sick reminder that he *let* her go.

But he had to, didn't he?

I have to do this, she had said. And she was right, he knew it. He knew she needed closure, and she was so much stronger now than she had been when she wandered into his manor.

The vampire's thoughts raced as he remembered her on that first night, scraped up, slick with sweat, and . . . gorgeous.

She took his undead breath away the moment his eyes landed on her and her long lilac hair. And his heart lurched when she saw the Reinick bite marks all over her. He wanted to replace them with his.

At first, Ambrose confused his feelings. He knew he was fiercely attracted to the woman, and he assumed lust guided his whims, his words. But it wasn't his lust that made a bargain with Lila Bran. It wasn't his lust that fell in love with her.

His fist pounded on his desk, splinters of wood shooting out, pricking his skin before instantly healing. He remembered her bent over this very desk as he teased her ruthlessly, and he wished he had taken her, then and there.

Ambrose wasn't sure when he realized he loved her—perhaps it was during their first training session, or on the night before Sanktus Pernox when he discovered his deep need to protect her, to keep her safe from any kind of harm, emotional or physical—but he now knew it had always been there.

Before her, he didn't think vampires could love anymore. No matter how encapsulated love and vampires always seemed to be, the vampires of Malvania confused love for other things. Lust, yes. Companionship, of course. Longing, definitely. And above all, hunger.

But *love* wasn't a common occurrence in a vampire's eternity. Love was rare. Love was painful. Love was death.

Yet . . . that girl—*that goddess of a woman*—proved him wrong with a bat of those long lashes, with the curve of her soft lips, and with the strength of her utter resilience.

Ambrose Draven loved Lila Bran. *Why?* Why hadn't he realized it *sooner*?

And now, she was gone. It had been the beginning of Yule when she left—was taken—and now the spring equinox was in a few days.

The Reinicks and Drusilla had schemed wisely. She sent a number of her strigoi to the Maggot Mansion, playing at war, but the real fight was in the Crow Court—the real fight had been between Lila and Ambrose, as he chased her through his lands, hungry for her, ready to devour her in a way he'd never expected.

He still remembered the taste of her fear-induced blood on his lips, the gush of flesh around his teeth. He still remembered her cries of pain that *he* caused. And a sick part of him *craved* more. He'd wake, in a fit of sweat and screams, from dreams where he'd drank her whole, where he hadn't stopped when she burst with power.

He knew she forgave him but, for that, he hadn't quite yet forgiven himself.

Lila had been gone for a longer time than she had been with him and that thought alone sent him spiraling many nights since her departure. He had left her, trapped, enslaved as he'd once been, with their enemy. He had allowed her to be in the same position he'd been in for nearly fifteen long years of his life before he was a vampire, when he was still a man with a family from a world far away from this one. From a world of color and culture and *life*—not the world of pyres and man killing man. A world of monsters before vampires ever even came to be.

Ambrose?

Immediately, his taut shoulders eased. On cue, Lila had called to his mind, just before sunrise, as she had every night through the Concord since she'd been with the Vipers.

Yes, love. I'm here. He paused. *How was tonight?*

He heard her sigh. *Typical. Ciro still believes I'm fully under his control—and truthfully, it is getting harder to resist it. There are . . . moments. Moments in which I can feel him raise the dial on his thrall.*

Ambrose clenched his jaw. He would rip Ciro's godforsaken head off. *And Hektor?*

His thralls are still nothing in comparison. They only work when they catch me off guard.

He felt a sliver of hesitation from Lila. Like she wasn't saying everything.

She continued, *But he is getting a bit more handsy.*

His nails dug into his palms, drawing small droplets of blood so black, it resembled ink. *Want me to remind him that the only hands allowed to touch your gorgeous body belong to the monster of Malvania? I'll fly over right now and show him that my hands are yours alone.*

Lila snickered. *What about my hands, Crow Lord? Aren't I allowed to touch myself?*

Ambrose choked, his eyes growing wide, as Lila laughed in his mind. *Those pretty little fingers can go wherever they please. I'd just hope they're thinking of me as they do.*

He could hear the mirth in her tone as she sighed. *Lords, what I would give to see the look on your face right now.*

You can, Ambrose thought, regaining his composure. *If you came home . . .*

She hesitated. *Soon. You know I want to be there, with you and the rest of the Crow Court. But—*

But you need to prove yourself, I know, Little Crow. I couldn't help but try.

There was silence for a long moment, but he felt her, there in his mind like a soft warmth.

How are you? she asked.

He huffed. *Oh, you know. Peachy.*

Ambrose, she scolded.

Damn right miserable, darling. I'm growing more and more desperate for you with each passing moment. I think of you, night and day. I smell you in the halls, I hear you in my coffin—those sweet moans and giggles like ghosts from our last morning together haunt me. My arms feel empty without you in them, my fingers feel tangled in the phantom strands of your hair. My soul has never felt colder.

He could feel just how awestruck—and how utterly guilty—his words had left her.

And on top of that, my balls have never been in more pain.

The tension he'd built snapped, and she giggled again. *I promise to mend that as soon as I return.*

And you do promise, right? To return?

Of course, she thought back to him without a lick of hesitation. *I cannot wait to be home. I cannot wait to be wrapped in your arms again.*

He sensed her truth through the Concord. *And I cannot wait to meticulously wash that body of yours, cleansing away the Viper filth.* He felt her heat at the thought, a warm tickle in his mind. *Ah, would you like some more ideas of what I will do to you when you return? For those pretty little fingers to go where they please?*

He loved riling her up, loved that even through their minds, he could have her orgasm to the thought of him—the thought of *them*. He decided, when she returned, he wanted to watch her work herself till she begged him to take over.

You silver-tongued devil, she snipped back.

Thinking about my tongue now, are we? Remember how it made you scream at the top of—

Stop! She squeaked through a laugh. He could feel how flustered she was becoming and he loved it.

All right, all right. Use that rush of energy I've given you and train. Remember, they're weakening you with each bite.

Oh, I know. I feel weaker than I was when I got here, but nowhere close to how I'd been before. I guess all those damned squats were worth something.

He smirked. *And you still have your stake concealed?*

Yep, they're none the wiser.

Excellent. Ambrose had been taking these stolen moments to train Lila, keeping her body as active as possible.

Ambrose leaned back in his chair. *Remember, Little Crow, if you need me—*

Call. *I know.* Lila paused for a moment. *I love you, Ambrose. And I cannot wait to show you how much I have missed you.*

Ambrose smiled. *We may need to leave the Crow Court for a few days till we satiate ourselves. I wouldn't want half of our people to hear you scream my name in absolute ecstasy.*

A few days? Lila scoffed. *Let's call it a month. And don't forget, you'd have the entire manor in rubbles if we stayed there.*

You're right. When it comes to you, I am absolutely feral, darling.

He could imagine Lila huffing a breath and rolling her eyes.

Be safe, my love, he commanded. *And, Lila?*

Yes?

I love you too.

He felt her like a caress, and then their connection through the Concord slipped close. But he felt her, there in his heart. She was with him.

She would always be with him.

3

A shrill scream jerked Lila awake from her already fitful sleep. As soon as the Reinicks had left, she kept her word to Ambrose and trained her heart out. Her limbs had grown weak once more in her months back under the Viper's venom, but she tried her best to keep her muscles as strengthened as they could be. Squats, push-ups, sit-ups, and even pull-ups, if she could find a spot, were now her daily solace from this hell hole.

Unlike her time in the Crow Court, however, her body showed little improvement. Every time Ciro drank from her, it felt like an entire week's worth of exercise was for nothing.

And what was worse, everything was so much harder to accomplish. She went from banging out one hundred squats a night, to barely maintaining thirty.

Damn the viper venom, she thought.

After a few rigorous rounds of stabbing the wall and bed with her stake, Lila's body was ready to give out on her. She washed up in the small basin in her room, and collapsed into the bed.

Sleep didn't come — not really.

It was hard to sleep when, at any point, Lila knew she could be attacked. The brothers were silent, deadly beasts, and she had no clue as to when they'd return.

But when she heard the shrill scream echo through the stone walls of the Viper Morada, Lila knew they were back. And worse, they brought trouble.

She shot out of bed, her back stiff from the hay-made bed, and her muscles still sore from the work out. But, the scream shot through her, first like a fever dream and then brought her to fully alert, fully awake, and her body tensed as she prepared for any possibility, though her body was in no shape for another fight. With them, she never knew what to expect, but she knew it was never good.

As soon as Lila made it to the threshold of her room, she knew something was off. There was a sharp, metallic tang in the air, and the scream had multiplied into a choir of wailing.

"Lilaaaa . . ."

She knew she shouldn't leave her room. Not only had Ciro directly commanded her not to, but who knew what would await her.

"Lila, pet, come join the fun . . ."

Her feet moved before her mind could process. Cold stone froze Lila's toes with each step, as Drusilla's voice carved its way into her very being.

She wasn't sure where she was being led to, all she knew was that she *had* to follow. Had to follow and *see*. Lila climbed the four steps and placed her palm on the damp wooden door that led out of the murine quarters.

"Hurry, doll, or you'll miss all the fun . . ."

The Sun Child

Lila quickened her step. Through the darkened corridors and chilly hallways she went, until she arrived at the two massive doors that lead to the main hall of the Viper Morada.

Through Lila's time as a murine in the manor, she abhorrently avoided the main hall at all costs. Back when Lord and Lady Reinick were still around, they would hold massive revels for all the vampires in the land. Slues of murine would be brought in from neighboring villages. Ciro made sure Lila and her brother remained in their tiny crypt during those nights, but the screams they would hear echoing through the stone would keep them wide awake for much longer than the night itself.

She remembered, once, Hektor dragged her upstairs during one of them. He kept a territorial grip on her waist the entire night, growling at any vampire who dared even look at her. But that didn't stop him from forcing her to join the murine games.

Shackles and cages decorated the halls during the murine feasts. Lila remembered the cuffs placed around her ankles, her wrists, as she was shackled to a wall, unable to escape as Hektor drank from her.

That was around the time he discovered how much he loved drinking her blood from her thighs.

Since then, Ciro had kept a close eye on Lila, making sure Hektor never stole her away again, and though she'd always been thankful, she knew it was for selfish, greedy reasons — not chivalry.

But now, thanks to Drusilla, she felt such a strong desire to be where the murine were. To be where the Reinicks were. To be in the center of it all.

As her hand pressed against the final door, a tiny voice in her head yelled *danger, danger*. But the forest-green fog clouding her mind was blinding. It was all she could see.

Until she only saw red.

A scream bubbled from Lila's throat before her eyes could focus on any of the countless bodies before her. She threw herself against the door, to run back the way she came, but it was too late. Vampires were on either side of it, blood coating their chins and chests, their eyes glowing a gold so brilliant, they looked like fireflies in the dark of night.

But Lila couldn't focus on any of them, she couldn't see their faces—only their sharp fangs and those glowing orbs that made her sick.

One of the faceless vampires grabbed her arm, pulling her to them in a sharp tug. With their free hand, the vampire angled Lila's face toward the room.

Immediately, the sick feeling in her stomach turned into a disease. She felt the bile rise in her throat, stinging and burning, and threatening to burst.

All around her were bodies. Human bodies, torn to shreds and bits. An arm over here, a head being tossed around over there—some of the bodies were still screaming, still shaking, still trying to get away. But the vampires of the Viper Morada wouldn't let them.

The vampire behind her shoved Lila to a dais in the center of the room, on which lay Ciro, Hektor, and Drusilla. She felt the blood, both cold and hot, squish under her bare feet the moment she was pushed across the room, oozing under her sole, between her toes. She didn't want to think about which of these poor souls it belonged to. Or rather, how many of them it belonged to.

Drusilla lounged against pillows, other vampires surrounding her as they fed on murine, while others shared from each other's soaked bodies as they groped on one another. But Drusilla's sick hazel eyes were a violent shade of green as they landed on Lila.

"Pet, you came," Drusilla smirked, her ruby lips splitting as the blood shimmered on her pearly white teeth.

Lila nearly vomited right then.

"Do you like what I've done with the place?" Drusilla wove a long hand with even longer nails around the room. Murine cried in cages—were shackled to walls as vampires cut them up and lapped at the wounds, were torn apart across the floor.

The screams from the humans melded with the moans of the vampires. Monsters were feasting on flesh, fucking over corpses, covered in blood.

Lila spotted Hektor then, his ravenous eyes on her as he fucked into a screaming woman and tore open her neck.

He smirked at her as their eyes met, and she knew . . .

I'm pretending she's you.

As he thrust into the human woman harder, Lila took a step back, turning back to the door but was stopped again. The vampire holding Lila, a creature with the same venomous green eyes as those from the Arachnid Estate, snickered behind her as their claws dug into Lila's arm. They looked about ready to prance the moment Drusilla gave the word, their teeth at the ready, mere inches from Lila's neck.

But it seemed the hag of the Arachnid Estate had other plans for her. She beckoned the vampire to release Lila, and with an aggressive shove, Lila was on her knees in front of the dais.

"Come, doll," Drusilla beckoned. Like before, the thick sage fog clouded her mind, and before she knew it, Lila was crawling up the steps of the dais. Drusilla patted the pillow beside her and Lila's body instinctively curled into the crook of the hag's arm, body pressed to body. "Lovely Ciro gave me *special* permission to sample you tonight. How do you feel about that?"

Lila didn't move. She liked being against Drusilla's body, it was so warm, and soft, and—

Vile.

Blinking furiously, Lila tried to fight the thrall on her. She shoved away from the woman, but it was too late and she was already far too close. Drusilla threw herself atop Lila, pinning her down below her.

"I like this dress, Ciro. Did you have it custom made?" Drusilla's eyes sparkled as she addressed the man watching them, her clawed hand gliding under the strap at Lila's shoulder.

Lila struggled underneath, but her hands were bound by Drusilla's, her wrists grasped in one hand as though it were an iron band.

Ciro grunted. "I did."

"I might need to borrow your seamstress," Drusilla smirked as she ran a taloned finger over Lila's body, making a sharp slit just under her collarbone. Small droplets of warm blood immediately welled.

Deadly silence echoed louder than the screams all throughout the room. It was a silence Lila felt down to her very bones. And she knew, every vampires' eye was on her at that moment. Everyone in that room would be ready to *have her*, their bloodlust stronger than it had been all evening.

"Get off!" Lila bucked against Drusilla, kneeing her in the gut with as much force as she could muster in this angle. Drusilla gasped, her grip loosening just enough for Lila to wiggle out from under her.

But once again, the vampire was faster. Drusilla wrapped a hand as cold as stone around Lila's arm and dragged her back. She didn't leave time for a witty remark as she pulled Lila's body into hers and licked at the wound.

Drusilla moaned against Lila's skin. "Lords, you are

truly one of a kind. How you have not drained her completely, Reinick, is beyond me."

Everything and everyone in the room faded from Lila's mind as she struggled to free herself. She had to get out. *Now.*

She pushed against Drusilla's shoulders as she straddled the vampire, but all it did was push the thin red strap of her crimson silk dress off her shoulder.

"You're a feisty little one, aren't you?"

And before the words had even fully fallen from her lips, Drusilla pulled Lila's hair to the side and snapped into the curve of her neck.

Immediately, Lila felt all her muscles go taut. Drusilla squeezed Lila's body to her own, breast to breast, as a thin layer of blood seeped through the fabric of both of their dresses from the wound at Lila's collar.

A small whimper escaped Lila's lips as Drusilla took another drag before finally letting go.

The hag's eyes were wild with bloodlust, her pupils dilated to where Lila could only see the blacks of her eyes. At that moment, Drusilla truly looked like a black widow about to snap its mate's head tangled in her web. And Lila was caught. Her taut limbs wouldn't move, all the fight left her body while it raged in her mind. She slunk into Drusilla's arms, completely paralyzed save her for eyes and the small wheezes of breath she was able to release.

"Aw, the *Little Mouse* can't move? What fun we could have with her now . . ."

Lila's bones chilled as Hektor spoke. She heard the sick slide of skin as he shoved the woman he was with away. She tumbled down the dais and landed hard on the stone floor, a trail of blood dripping from her torn neck down her chest. Lila realized the girl's eyes weren't moving . . . they looked hollow, cold. Lifeless.

Hektor crawled into Lila's line of sight. His shirt was gone and his pants hung low on his waist. But even more terrifying was the girl's blood still dripping down his chin. The girl he just *murdered*. His gold eyes looked up behind Lila, and in them was a sense of desperation, pleading. Lila realized he was looking at Ciro, silently asking him if he could, in fact, *have fun with her now.*

She could just barely see Ciro out of the corner of her eye, her head tilted away from. But, she could just make out his jaw clenching, and his eyes meeting hers.

Lila tried to *will* her body to move, tried to get away, but nothing worked. She considered calling Ambrose through the Concord but . . .

But if she did, he would be throwing himself into a den full of vampires who'd be ready to kill him the moment they sensed him.

And while she knew he'd stop at nothing to take down what would essentially be two manors on his own, she couldn't bring herself to reach out to him. No. She'd come to the Viper Morada for a reason. She had to handle this herself.

She'd been through worse, this would be nothing. But the invisible restraints paralyzing her body made her heart feel as though it were going to give out. Everything became too much, too quickly. Her lungs wouldn't expand enough and she wasn't breathing nearly enough air.

It was as though Lila forgot how to breathe, and all at once, her entire body was *begging* to move, to stir. She tried to bend her finger. She tried to wiggle her toe, her nose, to purse her lips, to scratch the itch on her cheek. But her body *wouldn't listen.*

Drusilla, still under Lila, shifted back into her original spot against the pillows. She turned Lila around in her arms, and pulled Lila between her legs, Lila's back to Drusilla's chest.

Before she heard Ciro respond to his brother, Drusilla groaned, "Oh, let him have some fun, Reinick. The boy just wants to play with his food." Lila could feel Drusilla's wicked grin and hot breath spread over Lila's neck as she tried desperately to avoid the heat of Hektor's glare roaming over her body.

After a silent beat, Ciro sighed out of sight. "Fine. But Hektor..."

Hektor looked up, past Lila.

"Know your limits." Ciro's words were like ice. A command, a threat, and—for Lila—a death sentence.

I can handle this, she reminded herself.

But... Lila could do nothing but watch as Hektor's lips cracked into a terrifying grin. He looked like a little boy who'd just been gifted the entire world for Yule.

And then his eyes latched onto her.

He crawled to her, on hands and knees. As one hand landed on the floor beside Drusilla's ankles, she lifted a heeled foot and pressed it into Hektor's strong shoulder.

"Slow there, serpent. Let's share her."

Lila felt Drusilla's nails graze the skin at her shoulder, shift the hair from her neck, leaving it bare.

"I'd rather not. But as the guest of honor in a Viper Morada revel, I suppose I don't mind."

A rock clogged in Lila's throat as the pit of her stomach felt like it was trying to run away from her. Not only would they cause her double the pain now, but the two of them drinking from her would surely cause a bloodlust frenzy. Vampires were creatures of passion, and that passion melded when it came to hunger, sex, and pain.

And now Lila would be right in the middle of it.

I can handle this, she reminded herself again and again. Ciro wouldn't let Hektor go too far. He was too selfish for that. It may get bad, but not worse. She *could* handle this. She didn't need to call on Ambrose and endanger him. She could handle this.

Could she?

I can handle this!

She felt Drusilla's lips smile again as they hovered over her neck, as Hektor smirked at her. There was a glimmer of lust in his eyes, and she felt that heat radiate from Drusilla as well now.

Hektor reached for Drusilla's foot still on his shoulder and kissed her ankle as he lowered it. He crawled forward, shifting his gaze to Lila.

"I have been *dying* to have you again, *Little Mouse*." The nickname twisted Lila's stomach again. It was taunting and it made Lila's blood boil. "Oh, so warm today. I wonder how hot you are on the inside." He smirked, and then lowered to Lila's eye level. "Well, Drusilla. *Buen provecho.*" Hektor's smile revealed sharp fangs as Drusilla bit into Lila's neck again.

Lila yelped and in a flash, the pain spread to her thigh, where Hektor had lowered himself to drink from *his favorite spot*. Lila could only watch as he held her thighs apart, biting into one as his nail dug into the other, gripping them, *claiming* them. He closed his eyes, and she felt his tongue as it lapped up every single drop of her.

She was already feeling lightheaded as the two were *literally* sucking the life from her. The fight in her mind finally gave out, matching her paralyzed body.

Behind her, Drusilla moaned as her hands began to roam over Lila's body, searching for Hektor.

The frenzy had taken over, and she was sure the demons wanted more.

Hektor tore himself from her thigh as Drusilla finally found the waistband of his dark leather pants. She pulled him, and Hektor obliged, climbing up Lila and Drusilla's body. His hands were on Lila and Drusilla both, shifting Drusilla's dress up as fingers grazed Lila's skin, over her hips, her breasts. His venom-colored eyes bore into Lila, watching in apt attention as she tried to look *anywhere* but him.

Around them, the revel was still going on. The eyes that had once been on her were now on the other humans in the room. Screams were still echoing as she made eye contact with a few survivors.

Lila imagined this is what Hell must look like. She didn't know much about the older religions, but Hell was often brought up by the vampires—often described in their history. And she knew in her very soul, the hellfire she had heard only snippets of must have looked exactly as this room did now. Bodies tossed about, dead and near-dead, humans begging for mercy, blood as thick as butter spread throughout the floor.

But worst of all, was the lack of hope this room permeated. There was no way out of this. No way for safety to weasel its way in.

As Drusilla took another pull of Lila's blood, she pulled Hektor's cock free from his pants and he hungrily chuckled as Lila's eyes widened as much as the Arachnid venom would allow.

"Do you finally want my cock inside of you, Little Mouse?"

Drusilla didn't seem to care what was happening, she just needed to feel *something* as she lapped at Lila's throat.

Lila's heart stopped beating as she tried with all her might to just *fucking move*.

But not even a flinch would escape her.

"Hektor," Ciro's voice warned.

And for once, that voice was like a miracle. She praised that voice in that moment, for it was keeping the leash on the monster. She still couldn't see him, but she knew he was there. And though she hated it—hated him—Ciro was her only assurance right now that she *would* survive this. And if she could survive, she could handle anything else that might happen.

Hektor sneered but heeded his brother. His focus once again shifted to Drusilla as he shoved her dress farther up her thighs, bunching it at her waist. He pulled Drusilla down toward him, pressing her thighs open as she latched her teeth back into Lila's neck once more.

Lila figured they must've looked like a monster of limbs, as Hektor angled himself at the apex of Drusilla's thighs. He raised himself to his knees as Drusilla lay flat on the dais with Lila above her. He was going to fuck her with Lila right in the middle of them like the cheese in their fucked-up sandwich.

Hektor hoisted one of Drusilla's thighs in his hand, while his other grabbed for Lila's ankle. She felt his grip tighten around her frail bones and she desperately wanted to use the moment to kick him in the face. But when she couldn't so much as twitch, Hektor just smiled at her. It was like a shock of cold water, as fangs coated in her blood shone back at her, his chin still covered in blood. It was a smile of nightmares, of her worst fears. The smile of a predator.

Her gut roiled, and all she could hope on was Ciro. Lords, what a sick and twisted situation she'd gotten herself into, that her one hope for mere *safety* was in the form of one of her greatest nightmares.

With eyes still locked on Lila, Hektor plunged into Drusilla.

Lila felt Drusilla's moan on her neck as her hands continued trailing up Lila's body.

"Harder, love," she said between licks of blood.

Hektor rammed into her again, his eyes glued to Lila's. When Lila fought to look anywhere but him once more, Hektor yanked her ankle, digging his teeth into it and drawing even more blood. She didn't know how she wasn't dead yet. The ankle bites always hurt Lila most, and she screamed at the immediate pain, which only sent Hektor wilder.

"Fuck, Lila, you feel so good."

She expected Drusilla to stop him, but clearly, she was using the fucker too. And Ciro—he was still watching, monitoring . . . wasn't he? Ciro wouldn't let any more than *this* happen to her.

What if he'd left? What if there *was* no sliver of hope there to protect her now? What if . . . What if she were next? What if Hektor acted on his desires and raped Lila?

Fear rolled through her, simmering in her gut. She needed to get away. She needed to do *something*.

Lila didn't want to be here anymore. She wanted to be elsewhere.

She wanted to be with Ambrose.

She wanted to be home.

Lila imagined herself then, in her bed at the Crow Court. Pollock nesting on her pillows by her head. Ambrose was there, comforting, warm. She lay on top of his leathery wing, as he read her a fairy tale of a far-off kingdom—a kingdom in the ocean—and a princess who was in love with a man of the sea. He would tuck the loose strands of her lilac hair behind her ear, and kiss her forehead as she nodded off to sleep. Ambrose would tuck her in, lying beside her till morning. His warmth would be her warmth and their hearts would beat in tandem as they cuddled together. Safe.

But as Hektor grunted in pleasure, pulling out of Drusilla and spilling himself all over Lila's crotch, her illusion of *home* shattered.

"Urgh!" Drusilla painfully broke away from Lila's neck and kicked that same heeled foot into Hektor's chest, hard enough to send him tumbling back down the dais. "You can't even please a woman, you selfish snake!" Drusilla shoved Lila off of her, and she rolled to the side, her back now to Drusilla and Hektor. "Find me someone else to fuck—someone who knows what they're doing."

And just like that, the vampire forgot about her.

Which was fine by Lila, she was ready to go to sleep and never wake up.

A black polished shoe stopped just in her line of sight. And then a man bent down and eased her back up. Ciro.

"If you're done, I'm taking her now . . ."

Anywhere is safer than here.

"Brother, please, I—" Hektor began, but Ciro was *done sharing*. Lila could see the flair in his eyes as he punched his brother so hard, Lila heard the crush of bone as Hektor's nose caved in.

Ciro stood, easily lifting Lila into his arms. The rush of movement sent Lila's head spinning, and as she felt blood ooze from her ankle, her neck, her collar, and her thigh, Lila's vision completely faded to black.

4

"You're doing excellent," Ambrose mused, patting Marcus on the shoulder as he stood over the boy in the dining room.

"You're reading so much faster!" Constance cheered.

Marcus looked sheepishly at the young girl, a small grin spread on his lips.

Together, Constance and Ambrose had taken up the task of teaching Marcus how to read, along with some basic knowledge of math, science, history, and anything he may need. It filled Ambrose's heart every time the young boy learned something new, to take care of the one Lila had loved so much.

"Thank you, Lord Draven."

But, lords, Marcus was even meeker than Lila had been when she first arrived at the Crow Court.

"I've told you, Marcus—Ambrose is fine."

Constance rolled her eyes. "Everyone calls you Lord Draven, *Lord Draven*. You're only trying to make him call you that because you want him to be your future brother-in-law." A coy smile spread on the girl's lips. Ambrose needed to remind himself the cute little girl he'd saved from the Arachnid Estate was becoming a little woman every day. She looked like a tiny adult, with the baby fat still in her cheeks. But now, with Marcus in the manor, Ambrose found Constance *trying* to look more and more like a lady.

Lords, he wasn't sure what he would do with *two* teenagers running around the place.

Ambrose groaned as he took his seat at the head of the table. "Remind me to send you back to Maronai till you come of age."

Constance harrumphed and crossed her arms over her chest, eliciting a small giggle to slip through Marcus's lips. Immediately, Constance's pale cheeks turned a light shade of pink. He quickly covered his mouth with his hands, hiding his smile, and a new kind of ache formed in Ambrose's chest. The boy was *so* young. And he lived his entire life in fear for himself and for the only person who'd protected him. And now he was alone, here, while she was suffering even more torture.

It reminded Ambrose of his early years as a slave, when he was still with his younger brother—though, in truth, he often thought of him. He'd been sold off before Ambrose—just . . . there one day, and gone the next. Where had he gone? Had he survived long enough to see adulthood? How was he treated? Ambrose wondered if many of these thoughts ran through Marcus's mind. He'd noticed the guilt cloud over the boy's features at the mention of Lila. It seemed as though Marcus wasn't allowing himself to smile, to laugh, to be comfortable—not till his sister was home and safe.

Ambrose's grip tightened on the armrest of his seat. *Lila Bran. That damned, gorgeous, hellfire of a woman.* He wasn't sure if he was cursing her drive for closure or praising her bravery. But he knew he fucking missed her. And, evidently, so did the rest of her family.

"Lor—Ambrose," Marcus corrected, his voice small and meek, like Lila's was. "Have you heard from my sister?"

Ambrose leaned back in his chair. "I spoke to her yesterday. The Reinicks were leaving her unattended for a while, so she should've had some time to herself."

Marcus looked relieved. He knew what a few hours of solace meant to Lila. It's what it once meant to him.

But now, Ambrose swore he'd keep him safe, no matter the cost.

"She sends her love. To both of you, and Kaz—"

Pollock squawked on the back of the seat above him.

"I was getting to you, fiend. *And* Pollock."

A small, happy chirp came from the bird as he hopped back and forth on his feet.

Ambrose breathed a laugh as he stood. "Now, I must attend to other matters. Constance, can you take over the rest of his lessons for the day?"

Constance nodded and scooched her chair closer to Marcus. The same shade of pink Ambrose had just seen on Constance's cheeks now illuminated from Marcus's as the girl neared him.

"Here," he said, pulling out a book from under the table. It was Lila's book of fairy tales. "I think this will be helpful to practice from." Ambrose handed them the book, and they immediately flipped it open.

As Constance pointed to the words, Marcus began sounding out the letters, making complete sentences, then paragraphs, and as the two entered their own world of words and stories, Ambrose slipped out of the dining room.

Every time he entered his main hall, he was reminded of images of Lila. Lila, running down the staircase in the evenings. Lila, in his arms when he first carried her inside, bleeding all over the place. Lila, sneaking into his office when she didn't think he was watching. He saw ghosts of her everywhere—and every time, he wished they were more than ghosts. He wished they were *her*.

"Ah, Master Ambrose, I was looking for you." Kaz walked through the back doors leading in from the garden. "The reports have come back. Master Maronai and Master Nostro have reported an influx of strigoi sightings in their cities and towns farthest from their manors. They're slowly infiltrating."

Kazimir handed Ambrose a folder of papers. *Great*, Ambrose thought as he heaved a sigh. Flipping through them, he saw a slew of information: population reports, death tolls, strigoi sightings in the three manors. As he flipped to the last page, Kaz continued, "While Maronai and Nostro obviously know, the entirety of Malvania still seems to be under the impression you are dead. Which hasn't been boding well for the citizens of the Crow Court."

"Has there been hysteria?"

"Nearly. It has been so long since the fall of a manor, no one knows what it means for them. The people of the Crow Court are worried a new lord will come to power, and others fear division between the already existing manors."

"Which is unfortunate for those in the south," Ambrose guessed.

"Correct. Our reports from the Southern Tail are looking grim. People are moving north or east, some even slipping into the Arachnid Estate. Maronai states he doesn't mind, but people are doing whatever is needed to get as far from the Viper Morada border as possible."

The Sun Child

"And Drusilla? Has she been spotted?"

Kaz nodded. "Unfortunately for Miss Bran, she was spotted with the brothers just yesterday, presumably on their way back to the manor."

Ambrose clenched his fist, feeling the bite of his nails against his palm. Though she wasn't a lord, Drusilla was much older than either of the Reinick brothers—and far smarter. He wouldn't be surprised if she had the brothers wrapped around her claws. She and Ciro *could* go head-to-head and it may be a fair fight, but against Hektor? She would destroy him. To have not just the brothers but now Drusilla as well in the Morada, Lila would need to be extra careful.

After gulping his frustration, Ambrose clenched his jaw and asked the question he'd been dreading. "Do any of our people know what Drusilla and the brothers were doing while they were away from the Morada? Lila told me they had been leaving more and more frequently."

Kaz's face fell, causing Ambrose to immediately stiffen. "I think we should discuss this in your office, sir."

Fuck.

The two hurried through the hall, past the stairs, and into Ambrose's office. The room was surrounded by crows, all perched in their unique spots, but their caws all but stopped the moment Ambrose entered the room. He paced the floor as Kaz sat down in the seat across his desk.

Before speaking, Kaz took a deep breath. "Obviously, sir, it isn't good."

Ambrose folded his arms over his chest, mostly to hide the twitches in his fingers. Lila was *there*, in the thick of it. He didn't know what he was about to hear, but he was ready to jump from this window and fly to the Morada at *that moment* to get her out of there. Even if it meant flying in daylight. Even if it meant ruining all of Lila's plans. Even if it meant destroying himself in the process. He would do it to make her safe.

"Go on," he choked out.

Kaz, in habit it seemed, started to organize Ambrose's desks. "It seems Drusilla Reclus is going with the Reinick siblings to different murine settlements around the Morada. They've already hit three of their major cities."

"And what are they doing, killing them? Are they idiots? They'll eliminate their food supply."

"Well, they are taking some back to the Morada. Very few. The rest, however..."

Fear settled in Ambrose's bones. The Reinicks *were* idiots, he didn't question it. But Drusilla wasn't. She was tactfully smart. She had waged wars, fought battles, and demolished civilizations during the Mass Death. She helped *create* the original eight vampire manors, and helped destroy the four that fell.

She was power hungry and wanted her own. It was why she was on this quest now.

"What?" Ambrose bit out, harsher than he had intended.

Kaz's white mustache wiggled—something he often did when nervous—and then he finally spoke. "They are turning the rest into new strigoi. She's already tripled the amount Lila healed during your battle. And that isn't accounting for the numerous she had hidden away. More and more are being changed by her strigoi, and the remaining fear, since the Crow Court was hit, they will be Drusilla's next targets."

Ambrose needed to hit something.

"And no reports of Lila healing any new strigoi?" he asked through gritted teeth.

"No reports of Lila at all. She has been kept under lock and key. Our crows haven't even spotted a glimpse of her as they spy on the manor."

Fuck, fuck, fuck. Ambrose knew she was okay—or, mostly okay. But not having the visual confirmation hurt, driving him mad.

"Kaz, tell me something—anything—that will keep me from flying there *right now*," Ambrose heard the begging in his own voice. He wasn't a begging man—or, at least he had never been one before Lila—but right now, he was afraid his heart wouldn't be able to handle much more of this.

Though he wasn't facing him, Ambrose felt Kaz's emotions behind him. Distress, sorrow, concern, fear. His heart rate accelerated after Ambrose's last question, and before the man even opened his mouth, Ambrose knew what he was going to say.

"I'm sorry, sir. I have nothing."

And just like that, all of Ambrose's hope abandoned him.

It was funny. Lila had taught Ambrose to hope again. She warmed his heart, his life, and with that came her love. Her love *was* hope. It was inspiring and uplifting, and it made him feel like he could do *anything,* be *anything.*

And, for her, he wanted to be *better.*

With a quick and solemn nod, Ambrose muttered, "Thank you," dismissing Kazimir all together. Without waiting for the man to leave the room, Ambrose hurried out into the hall.

Lila? he tried. It was rare she was able to respond, which was why he had waited for her to establish the Concord link every morning.

Lila, please. I just need a single word to know you're all right.

Still, nothing.

Ambrose hurried through the manor, down the stairs into the basement, through the dungeons, and into his training room. He threw his shirt and grabbed two daggers from the wall.

His knuckles whitened as he felt the bend of the metal in his grip, but he wasted no time. He lashed out against the training dummies around him, slashing and gutting all of them in a furious whirlwind of blows. He punched and kicked with all his might, created craters in the bags, sand spilling all across the floor. When it wasn't enough, he turned to the stone wall.

Anger seethed through him, like a tidal wave he couldn't control, he couldn't taper. It bubbled and boiled till it felt like his skin would peel from his bones, and the scream of frustration would rumble through his lungs, his throat, his mouth.

Lila was *alone*. And he'd let her go, he'd let her become a slave, a blood bag. He'd let her become the very thing she feared most of all, and the very thing Ambrose had detested about his society. And worst of all, he'd let her go as the taste of her blood still sang on his teeth, still coated his tongue. He'd chased her as a monster, and he felt the thrill of a predator hunting prey, a thrill he hadn't felt since he earned the title of monster of Malvania.

By the time his long white strands stuck to his forehead in sweat, his knuckles had been oozing black blood, and he could see small specks of bone peeking through skin. At some point the afternoon had become the evening, and eventually the night.

Again, he cursed, and dropped the daggers on the floor. Ambrose shook out his hands, the wounds healing instantly, and ran them through his damp hair.

His exertion of energy did nothing to quiet his mind, his worry.

Ambrose spent all of two moments pacing the room, before he stared at the recessed fighting pit in the center. The same spot he spent countless nights with Lila, training her to be the best damned version of herself she could be.

He *knew* she could take care of herself.

He knew she could do whatever she set her mind to.

But this was more than that. This was about his sanity. This was about wanting to make sure she wasn't being drained alive.

In truth, he just wanted to see her.

Or that's what he told himself. He knew it to be true, but another draw had been guiding him.

He wanted to taste her again.

So, Ambrose Draven made a very bad decision.

He shifted into his monstrous form, stretching his muscles from being confined for so long, and with a burst of his wings, he flew through the halls, the stairways, and out of his manor into the night sky.

Lila, I'm coming.

And then he went in search of his sunlight.

5

Lila's eyes flashed open and her body leaped up before her mind was fully awake.

Blood.

Paralyzed.

Trapped.

Lila looked for Hektor, for Drusilla, for any of the vampires in the main hall as her head spun violently. Immediately, her legs gave out under her, and she flopped back onto her straw mattress.

Her straw mattress. Lila was in her room and she was— well, not *safe*, but she was okay. Her room was dark, save for a small candle lit near her bed, and when she looked down at herself she was actually ... dressed. She wore a red nightgown that reached her knees, with long, flowy sleeves that cuffed at her wrists. Lila clutched the chest of the gown, happier than she'd expect to be in opaque fabric once again.

"Finally," a voice said from the corner. Lila jumped out of her skin, a small yelp escaping her lips as she turned to find Rebekkah sitting in a chair near her bed. She curled a piece of her dark red hair in her long fingers, wearing a black robe as elegant as any gown. "I have been waiting all day for you to wake up."

"Rebekkah . . . how—where—" The spinning of Lila's head didn't ease. She closed her eyes, trying to focus on one thing, one question. Thankfully, Rebekkah understood her.

"I don't have all the details. I was locked in my room throughout the revel. Ciro took the key and didn't let me out till just before sunset. All I know is you passed out from blood loss. Hektor and Drusilla did quite a number on you. Then Ciro took you, bathed you, and brought you back here."

The idea of Ciro's hands on her while she slept made her skin crawl.

"I know he removed Drusilla's venom, as is evident by the fact you can move. But you've been unconscious for two nights now. My brothers and that she-devil left the Morada again. They said they'd be gone for the night, so they told me to watch over you. When I came in and found you, naked and bruised and bitten all over . . ." she hesitated.

A pang of guilt shook her heart. *Two nights? I haven't checked in with Ambrose. He must be worried sick.* Then, *Naked in bed for two full days? With Hektor and Ciro around?* Disgust rolled in the pit of her stomach, and she didn't allow herself to think of it further. She would just lock that little thought away for as long as possible.

"I'm guessing then you're to thank for the nightgown?"

Rebekkah bit her lip. "I—Yes. I hate seeing you frolic around in that pathetic thing they forced on you."

Lila smiled. She could tell, no matter how unusual this was for her, Rebekkah was at least *trying*.

"Thank you. I mean it."

A small blush colored Rebekkah's warm cheeks. "Well, Mousey, don't thank me too much. I haven't been able to assist you at all. My brothers—"

"Are treating you just as horribly." The things she has heard them say to Rebekkah can freeze an ocean. They torture her in a different kind of way than they do Lila. Venomous words, starving her after locking her in her room for nights on end. And that didn't even cover the rage they took out on her.

Rebekkah sighed. "Well, as much as I hate to say it, I was planning to have us stick together. But Drusilla is smart. She knows how to tame a revolution against her."

It was true. Lila saw Rebekkah less now that they were both in the Morada than she had when they were apart. This had probably been the first actual conversation they've had in months.

"When did Drusilla get here?" Lila asked. Seeing her at the party—lords, that was *three* nights ago now—was the first she had since their confrontation at the Crow Court.

"Basically since we arrived back. She's been skulking around, going to our nearby towns and villages."

"And . . . that revel?"

Rebekkah solemnly nodded, the yellow in her eyes dimmer than Lila had ever seen them. "Spring equinox. Just an excuse to fuck and eat, in my opinion." She flattened the wrinkles on her lap and stood. "I'm going to go find you some food. That should give you strength. Stay here, and don't stand up."

Rebekkah was still a commanding brat, but Lila was happy to have her on her side—if Lila could call it that. It was a stark difference from their relationship just a few months back. Before she met—

Lila. His voice echoed through her mind, immediately sending a wash of comforting shivers down her spine. *Lila, the window.*

Just then, Lila heard a *tap, tap, tap*. She turned her head toward the only access to the outside her room had. On the far wall, at the very top, sat a thin window—too small to escape from, but big enough to see the ground it sat above. It was the only way Lila knew if it was night or day—at least, when it wasn't covered by the thick black-out curtain her nor Marcus had been able to reach. But lucky for her, tonight, it was pulled open.

A gasp escaped Lila as her lips impulsively spread into a wide grin. On the other side of the window, a white crow pecked at the glass.

Darling . . .

Ambrose! Lila jumped up and ran to it. She stood as close as she could, hopping up and down to try to see him better. *How are you—why are you—I'm so happy to see you!* She squealed into his mind.

He snickered. *I'm happy to see you too. The brothers?*

Gone! You came at the perfect time, it's just me and Rebekkah here.

The crow hopped back and forth, and Lila giggled, picturing Ambrose in his monstrous form doing the same little dance. *Can you come out? I don't want to put you in danger—*

I can! I'll be right there!

Lila ran from the room, ignoring the way her head swam with each movement. As she raced up the few stairs leading out of the murine hall, Rebekkah opened the door.

For a moment, Lila halted in her tracks. Reverting back to the little mouse she had been for so long when she saw the sister viper of the Morada.

Rebekkah raised an eyebrow. "I thought I told you to stay put?"

Lila gulped. If she told her, would Rebekkah stop her from seeing Ambrose? Would she sound an alarm? Attack Ambrose? Attack her?

No, Lila reminded herself. *Rebekkah is different now. We are different.*

Taking a deep breath, Lila met Rebekkah's eyes. "I-It's Ambrose. He's here."

Lila watched Rebekkah's face for any signs of anger or doubt, but all she saw was what looked like . . . relief.

"He's alive," she stated more than asked. "Does this mean you're leaving?"

Lila shook her head and the disappointment on Rebekkah's face—disappointment *for* Lila—was palpable. "It would be better if Ciro, Hektor, and Drusilla continue to believe he's dead. Plus, I still—"

"Need to fucking kill them," Rebekkah said blandly. Lila studied her for a moment, searching, unsure how to respond. "Listen, Mousey. I-I've already said how blinded I was. How much of a fool I was. But I will never *stop* saying it. I've spent my life thinking my brothers were . . . *everything*. My parents were shit, as you know. And they together created three little monsters. But, I don't know—maybe I'm broken, because I do *not* want to be like them. And while I don't believe I can ever do anything to redeem my past actions, I won't stop trying." She gently took Lila's hands, and looked at her own feet. "I don't deserve forgiveness, but let me try to earn it. They stopped being my brothers the moment they laid their hands on me, and I finally woke up and saw all they did to you—all *I* did to you—and I know now that they have everything coming to them. Drusilla too, that wench. I just—"

"Bek," Lila squeezed her hands. "You have already earned that forgiveness in more ways than one. You should *never* feel the need to compare yourself to them. You are so much more than they will ever be."

Rebekkah smiled, and then scrunched her nose. "Well, thanks for the girl talk. I can't believe I'm saying this, but I'm thankful to have you in my life, Mousey," she let go of her hands and stepped aside. "Now, it seems like that big oaf is waiting for you so go. I'll come get you soon and help you cover his scent so my brothers don't notice anything when they return."

Lila impulsively threw her arms around Rebekkah's shoulders. "Thank you." And without another glance, she ran out of the room.

She ran to Ambrose.

As soon as she was outside, Lila's eyes locked with his. Dark, mysterious, and all-encompassing just as she had remembered. She had seen those eyes in the darkest of nights, and now, seeing them in the moonlight, she felt like her heart stopped beating.

Ambrose's hair was disheveled, probably from his flight, he was without a shirt—which immediately did funny things to Lila's stomach—and his trousers were torn past his knees. He was also barefoot, standing in the early spring snow below his feet. Lila tilted her head, before her eyes met his again, questioning his appearance.

But all thoughts died when she saw his face. He had the goofiest grin Lila had ever seen on him, and it immediately brought a warm smile to her face. Lila started running to him, and in less than a blink of an eye, Ambrose had met her. His arms crashed around her as he immediately took her into a wonderfully suffocating embrace.

Lila, Lila, Lila, Lila, Lila, she could hear through the Concord as she threw her arms around his neck and squeezed him to her. Before she noticed it, she felt wet drops on her cheeks and realized she'd begun to cry. Ambrose tightened his grip around her waist, spinning her around so much, they toppled into the soft snow below them.

"Lords, Lila. I've missed you, I've missed saying your name. I've missed your smell, your feel, the way you fit in my arms so perfectly." He petted the top of her head then, brushing kisses all over it.

"Ambrose—"

"*Fuck.* I've missed that too." Immediately, he took her chin and pressed his lips to hers. The way his hand felt against her skin sent goosebumps all throughout her body. The callouses brushing her cheek as it found its way through her hair made her realize how starved for his touch she had been.

His lips were hard, chapped, but greedy as they kissed her, and it only took a moment for her to open her mouth and suck on his bottom lip, begging him for more. Ambrose groaned into her throat as he opened his lips, pushing his tongue into her mouth.

He's here. He's real.

Lila kissed him as she had never kissed him before, with all the love she could muster. He moved, flipping her on her back so he could cage her under him as he continued taking her mouth. The snow below her was cold against her back, but nothing could compare to the warmth she felt around this god of a man. She ran her hands down his neck, over his bare chest, feeling every bulge and groove of muscle—you know, to *make sure* he was real. She ran her thumb over the massive crow tattooed on his chest and felt his heart fluttering under her palm. Her heart felt like it was going to burst from her chest, her lungs would explode, and—

Ambrose pulled away. "Breathe, Little Crow." He smirked, and she knew he was also remembering when he said the same thing the night of Sanktus Pernox in the Arachnid Estate. His eyes were drinking her in, as hers were him.

He had bags under his eyes, but he was still so goddamn beautiful, it was alarming.

"I've missed you so much," she whispered, placing a hand on his cheek. Ambrose gulped and leaned into it.

"You have *no* idea how much I've missed you, your voice. Say my name again. Please, Lila." His eyes were begging, as though it would physically hurt him if she didn't.

"Ambrose. Ambrose, Ambrose, Ambrose," and then softer, "I love you, Ambrose."

His lips were on hers once more, and this time, the kiss was more than greed—it was desire and heat and love and everything that made them, *them*. It was the kind of kiss Lila thought she might have been born for.

Ambrose's hands moved, trailing down the long column of her neck and over her chest. He paused over her heart, smiling against her lips as it fluttered in tune with his.

And then his hand trailed down.

It grazed over her breast, the pad of his finger stopping at her nipple. The moment he pressed into that small bud, *all* of Lila's body reacted. Her stomach dipped, and that same funny feeling she had grown so accustomed to in the

Crow Court had finally woken up after all these months away. She immediately felt her core heat and dampen, ready to be touched by Ambrose.

She wanted him. Even if it was in the snow. Even if it was outside. Even if it was in the Viper Morada. She. Wanted. Him.

Lila moaned into his mouth, and immediately wrapped her legs around the small of Ambrose's back, and used her thighs to pull him closer. The moment she felt his hard length grind against her center, they groaned into each other as they kissed.

Ambrose pulled apart, trailing kisses down Lila's cheek, her jaw, and all along her neck. He immediately found the spot she liked so much, and sucked till Lila was moaning his name.

She bucked her hips, rubbing herself against the bulge, trying to get as much friction as she could. The moment her clit ran over his cock, Lila felt like she'd combust.

"So. Fucking. Warm," he uttered, still kissing her neck. He thrust against her then, as his hand tightened on her breast, then he bent lower and sucked it into his mouth, despite the nightgown completely in the way.

Lila yelped and grabbed his face, returning his lips to hers. She bucked into him, cursing his stupid pants for being between them as she pressed the sensitive bud against him. She wanted his skin on hers—*in* her.

"Ambrose." She kissed him. "I want you."

"I want you too," he said against her lips, but continued kissing her.

"No, I want you *now*."

His lips hesitated, but his hips dipped one more delicious time, the hard bulge driving right through her center, sending another whimper from her lips.

Ambrose moved his hand from her breast, and rested it next to her, before placing his forehead onto hers. "More than anything, I wish I could. But you mean more to me than a quick fuck outside." He brought his palm to her cheek, rubbing her bottom lip with his thumb. "I want to take my time when we make love for the first time. I want to ravage you and savor you all at once—not one or the other." Her heart did a funny flip. *This* was the reason she loved this man. "So, though my cock feels like it might explode and my balls will be aching for days, being here with you is intoxicating enough."

Lila giggled at his words, and though she was desperate for him, she knew his point was valid, for she wanted to cherish their time just as much—preferably without the fear of the Reinicks coming home at any moment.

"Plus," Ambrose started with a wicked smirk spreading his lips, "If I make you any more hot and bothered, you might just create a new ocean." He nodded his head to the snow around her.

But it was no longer snow. Her warmth had melted it, and Lila was lying in a small pool of water, the back of her red nightgown soaked.

"You became a puddle for me."

She immediately blushed and laughed.

He grinned, his fangs poking through his lips. "Ah, I miss that sound too. Almost more than your moans."

A wave of heat flushed her. "If you don't want me to jump on your cock right now, you need to keep that tongue in check, *Lord Draven*," she teased.

"Hmm. I can think of far better things my tongue *should* be doing right now."

Again, Lila felt the heat in her core, and a bit more snow around them melted.

"Just because I don't think we should fuck in the Viper Morada, doesn't mean I have any issue feasting on that sweet little pussy of yours." His eyes changed to the feral shade of red. The same shade when he chased her through the woods, when he cornered her in the alcove of rocks, when he drove his teeth into her.

And for some twisted reason, Lila felt herself grow more wet from the memories.

"If you do that," she breathed. "I don't think I'll be able to handle *not* having you."

Ambrose blinked, his white lashes long and—beautiful. Like everything else about him.

She watched as Ambrose swallowed hard and blinked very slowly, and then he eased himself off of her. Lila immediately missed his warmth and presence, but as he helped her sit up, she loved cradling into him.

Her mind finally settling from what felt like rabid intoxication, she finally realized the fact that *Ambrose* was *here*, and *here* was a very dangerous place to be. "Wait. What are you doing here?"

"I—" he shook his head. "When I didn't hear from you for two nights, I needed to come. Honestly, I don't know when I decided—I mostly just acted."

"And why are you . . . shirtless?" she asked, grazing her fingers over his abs. "Not that I'm upset about it."

He snickered, but clenched the muscles there and she saw his cock bob in response to her touch. "I flew here. In my true form. I was training, and just came . . . I honestly didn't even think to put a shirt on."

"What a rake you are," Lila giggled.

"Only for you, darling." He wrapped his arm around her and pulled her into his lap before nuzzling into her hair. "I never want to let you go."

Lila nuzzled him back, cuddling into the crook of his perfect neck. "For now, you don't have to."

They sat there together, in silence, just embracing their togetherness of the moment. She paid close attention to how his skin felt against hers, to the sounds of his breath each time he inhaled, and to the warm feeling of his eyes on her. It was pure and utter bliss.

"If you *ever*," he began, chucking his finger under her chin and pulling her face to look at him, "don't respond to me through the Concord for more than a day, I'm coming right back here, laying waste to this hellhole, and dragging you home. Bound, if I have to."

Lila smirked and wiggled her eyebrows. "Bound? You promise?"

He snickered. "Who's the rake now, love?"

Another beat passed between them. Ambrose was looking between her eyes and she realized he was finally studying her. He had been too caught up in the frenzy of their kisses to really *look* before, but she was sure he now saw everything she didn't want him to see. The dress she wore should be mostly covering the new bite marks from Drusilla and Hektor, but she was sure she had grown thinner, gaunter, and she had no idea what the bags under her eyes looked like.

She probably looked more dead than the undead vampire she was sitting on.

"Are you okay?" His voice was low, as though he were telling her a secret.

She didn't want to lie, but she also didn't want to worry him too much. She didn't think he would leave her if she did.

"Better now that you're here."

In truth, Lila was forgetting *why* she wanted to be here.

Her desire to prove herself hadn't been going as quickly as she liked, nor as well as she hoped. She didn't believe she was the meek mouse she once was, but being back here had definitely regressed all her progress. And now, being in Ambrose's arms, she wanted nothing more than to just go back home with him.

But then all these months would've been for nothing, and the Reinicks and Drusilla would know Ambrose was alive, which would eliminate any kind of surprise attack they could pull in the future. And, she wanted to sabotage them more. She wanted to sow doubt between Hektor and Ciro. Maybe, if she were lucky, they would attack each other so she didn't have to.

"I can feel your mind working, love. Talk to me."

Lila gulped. "I want to go back with you . . ."

"But?"

She took his hand and squeezed it. "But I don't think I'm done here yet. Soon. But not yet."

Ambrose nodded. "I thought as much. I didn't come here to drag you back against your will. I just came to make sure you were all right."

And I am, she said through the Concord, *because I got to see you.* She cupped his cheek once more.

They stayed huddled together for what felt like an hour, and in that time, neither of them grew cold, despite the snow falling around them.

As Lila was curling a gleaming strand of Ambrose's hair around her fingers, he stiffened. *Someone's coming.*

"Lila!" Rebekkah shouted just seconds later, just as she exited the manor. "Draven." She nodded at him, and though he hesitated a moment, he returned the gesture. "I'm sorry to interrupt. My brothers are returning and we need to wash his scent from you. *Quickly.*"

Ambrose jumped up, Lila in his arms. *I hate that our time was so short*, he said in her mind. *But I'm glad I came. Promise you won't be gone for much longer?*

I promise.

Ambrose pulled her flush against him and pressed a hard kiss to her lips. She felt everything in it as he mentally said, *I love you, Lila.*

I love you too, and I'm sorry I can't go with you.

He brushed his lips against hers. "It's okay, sunshine. We'll be together again soon."

Ambrose gently placed her feet on the ground. She took one step away from him before turning and pulling his head down to meet hers, kissing him again.

"You are my everything, Ambrose," she whispered, and she saw the shivers it sent through him, felt the warmth it brought to his cheeks as he blushed.

"Say that again when we're alone," he huffed a laugh and kissed her chastely on the cheek. "Now go, before those bastards get back and I have to kill them." He turned her around and gave a light spank on her ass—which did much more to her core than she'd expect.

Lila started walking away, toward Rebekkah, who'd been patiently waiting for her, not saying a word though Lila was sure she'd heard everything.

She turned over her shoulder, looking back at Ambrose once more, his smile was sad, but he waved his hand, encouraging her on. *I'll speak to you after daybreak, when they're asleep.*

Lila smiled back at him, and she knew it matched the sad cadence of his. Walking away from him right now was one of the hardest things she'd ever have to do. And she'd tried—and succeeded—to stab him before.

I'll be waiting, she thought back. Finally, she felt cold.

Colder than the snow, colder than the outside. Her warmth had dimmed and she felt less like sunshine and more like an endless night awaiting the dawn as she stepped back into the Viper Morada.

6

Watching her go, *again*, had been the third hardest thing Ambrose Draven ever had to do. The first was letting her go three months ago, just after biting her neck open. The second had been when they first met, after their bargain was made, and he let the devils steal her away again. And while it had caused an ache inside of him he couldn't quite place then, he knew exactly what it was now, all too well. Just like then, he didn't *want* to let her go, but he had to. He wanted her to know the depths of her power too.

And, for the record, the fourth had been rejecting her advances just an hour ago. Lords, how he *wished* he would've ripped that crimson gown from her body and plummeted into her. Her voice would sound fucking amazing as it echoed through the snowy trees. He wished he could've used the snow to peak her nipples even more just before licking it off of them.

Fuck. Her nipples. He was so damned desperate to see his favorite shade of pink again.

But Ambrose Draven was a gentleman.

Well, for Lila Bran he'd be a gentleman. He'd properly wait to have her, and once they did, he'd take her *everywhere*.

The garden, the office, his room, her room, the dining room, the foyer, the fucking *sky* if it were up to him.

So no, Ambrose Draven did not want to take her for the first time outside of the *fucking* Morada. He wanted to keep every scream and moan and yelp and whimper that came from her sweet mouth *all* to himself. He wanted to have hours upon hours—*days*—for themselves. To worship her. To blow her mind.

If it were up to him, by the time they were done, neither of them would be able to speak because their voices would be too hoarse, nor move because their limbs would be too weak. And, then, he would carry her to his bathing room and wash every centimeter of her body before he did it all over again.

But, now, watching Lila disappear through that godforsaken doorway, had him second guessing every decision he'd ever made.

And an unwelcome morbid thought crossed his mind.

What if that was the last time I see her?

Ambrose clenched his fists again, resisting every urge to not break down the door—the whole manor if need be—and take her back.

Another part of him regretted not giving her what she wanted. *Next time*, he decided. *Next time I see her, if she wants me, I will have her. I will show her* how *much I love her.*

With that promise, Ambrose took a step back from the Morada. He shifted into his true form, flared his wings out, and with a powerful flap, he burst into the night sky.

The Sun Child

The Crow Court was silent by the time Ambrose arrived home. The sun was just about ready to peek its way into the world, but the night was still a cobalt blue that made the stars shine even brighter.

He didn't fly to the front entrance, nor did he fly directly into his room. Ambrose hovered, for just a moment, above the balcony outside Lila's bedroom. And before he could think any better of it, he landed on the cold stone underfoot. He wasn't sure why his absent mind chose her room over his, but now that he was here, it was as though an invisible string was tugging him forward, tugging him inside.

Ambrose followed the pull.

As he swung the door open, he saw how dim everything looked inside. He had stood in this room countless times before and every time she was within, it would radiate. Without her, it was just another guest room.

But Lila had made this room her own and he could still feel the ghost of her energy in the walls, the pillows, the sheets.

He walked inside, shutting the door behind him and closing the blackout curtains in preparation for sunrise. It even *smelled* like her still, and he took a deep inhale—an inhale he didn't want to release. As he walked toward the center of the room, her bed, he saw himself in the mirror. Or rather, the lack of him. It was as though he weren't actually there, in her space, just as she wasn't there either. He could fantasize they were away together, maybe somewhere by the ocean. He'd love to see her stand by the waves, watching her as she listened to the sounds and rumbles of the water smashing into the shore. He knew she would love it.

Ambrose tentatively sat at the edge of her bed, running his hand along the comforter. He still remembered her first day in the Crow Court, when he removed the venom from her body. She had been so strong, enduring the pain of the removal and the emotional turmoil of the fact they'd been with her *always*. When she fainted from pain, it was the first time he'd seen peace on her face. Her features softened, the furrow between her brows disappeared, and she looked . . .

Beautiful.

Ethereal.

Like the stars cannot compete.

Ambrose smiled at his past words. What an understatement that had been, but there were no words that would captivate her beauty, just as there were no words to captivate his love for her. He could write songs and poems until she tires of hearing them, and still it would not be enough.

She was . . . *everything.*

Dropping his head, Ambrose rolled under the covers of her bed. It was smaller than his, and in his natural form, it barely fit his wings and his feet were hanging off the edge a bit, but it smelled like her. It felt like her.

As he settled in, a bundle of feathers squished against him under his arm and a loud caw broke the silence.

"Shit," Ambrose groaned, sitting up.

Under him, Pollock sat nestled, peering up at him, sadly cooing.

Please don't make me leave.

Ambrose smirked at the bird and lifted him carefully into his palms. He placed Pollock on the pillow next to him, and settled back in.

"You can stay. It's her room after all, and she'd want you here."

The crow stood abruptly, hopping over to Ambrose and cuddling into his neck before nesting against him.

Ambrose heaved a heavy sigh, and as he scratched Pollock's head, he said, "I miss her too, Pol. We'll have her back soon."

And right then, Ambrose wanted to believe that. As he drifted to sleep, his mind dreamed of him and Lila on a beach as she danced in the waves and dragged him in with her. The water would be cold, but they'd keep each other warm. Their bodies would be covered in sand but that wouldn't stop them from making love and having the night of their lives.

7

Rebekkah helped Lila remove every trace of Ambrose from her body. The red nightgown, though it belonged to Rebekkah, was burned. Her body had been scrubbed raw until Rebekkah said she couldn't smell him anymore. Then Rebekkah gave Lila a new dress, one in black this time, and together they walked back to Lila's room.

"You'll want to remember to keep your emotions in check when they return too. Right now, you look downright smitten. Not to mention, you're radiating heat. They'll know Draven was here the moment they walk into the Morada."

Lila smirked before sighing, trying to school her face into indifference. But she was just so happy from the time she had with Ambrose. Seeing him again, feeling him, hearing him—it was exactly what she needed.

"And how's your head?"

"Hmm?" Lila hummed, still in a daze.

"You haven't eaten anything, and you had a terrible amount of blood loss last night. Or have you forgotten?" Rebekkah raised an eyebrow, crossing her arms.

And on cue, Lila's head swam. "Oh. Right." She huffed a laugh, "Honestly, I forgot."

Rebekkah smirked, "Well, lucky for you, Mousey, I already brought food. Light foods, toast and crackers. Cheese. It should help."

They got to Lila's door, where they both stopped. "Thanks, Bek."

Rebekkah scrunched her nose again. "Hearing you call me that makes me want to gag."

Lila startled back, before Rebekkah's expression changed and she laughed.

"But I also like it. Eat up and get some more rest." She lightly shoved Lila through the doorway, ushering her to her bed. And Rebekkah was right, a plate of food sat at the edge, calling Lila's name.

After saying goodbye to Rebekkah, she sat in her bed, and ate all the cheese first. With her strength slowly returning, Lila lay on her bed, tray of food now on the floor. The sun had already been up, but Lila wasn't tired. In fact, she was more awake than she had been in a long time.

Ambrose? she tried. But when no return came, she figured he must be asleep. *Sweet dreams,* she told him, sending him a kiss through the Concord—even if she didn't think it worked that way.

Her chest warmed, thinking of him and their night together. The way the moon shone in his eyes, brightening his gorgeous hair, illuminating him like the god he was.

Her whole body started to warm.

Then, an idea hit her.

Lila's warmth—it was connected to her emotions.

The moment the realization hit her, it felt as though everything had fallen into place, everything made sense and connected. Her time in the Viper Morada, it was hard getting warm because of the lack of joy. Her time in the Crow Court was too easy—scorchingly so. Her emotions ebbed and flowed, and with it, the heat and warmth she radiated.

Lila jolted up in bed, testing her theory. She thought of Ambrose, of his lips on hers. Immediately, she felt her body warm, her heart, her fingertips, everything.

Love and lust and joy—they all brought about the comforting warmth Ambrose had spoken of so many times. It was her love for Ambrose that healed him and all the other strigoi around. It was her love that healed *her* after Ambrose had nearly killed her.

So if those emotions brought on a comforting, healing warmth, what did emotions such as fear and rage bring on?

Lila tried to imagine it. She first pictured Ciro enthralling her to kiss him as she stood over his dead parents.

A small prickle of energy crackled along her fingers.

She needed something more raw, more . . . traumatizing.

And that led to one person.

Hektor.

Lila swallowed and stood up, pacing her room from her newfound discovery. She imagined Hektor, pinning her to the floor just as he threw Marcus off her, biting into her thigh. She imagined Hektor, smacking her ass as she walked by him. She imagined Hektor, groping at her breasts as he drank from her. Hektor, as he drank murine after murine and forced her to watch. Hektor, who ogled at her when she was still a teenager. Hektor, who stood at her door every month, when her period would come, licking his lips. Hektor, as he fucked Drusilla but stared into Lila's eyes.

Hektor, who had turned her brother.

Something in Lila's chest had clicked into place, and she felt like such a fool for not realizing—not *utilizing*—it sooner. Just like her love, her rage could be weaponized. Just like her love, her rage was a weapon.

Lila opened her eyes, rage seeping from her pores. She hadn't even noticed the uneaten bread on the food tray had been toasted black, the sheet to her bedding singed at the edges, the hay within smoking. She yelped and quickly patted out the smoke.

The heat she had created singed, burned, and melted the room around her. *That* was what her anger did. It *burned*.

Lila opened and closed her fist, adjusting to this new development. She had known she had power. She knew she could keep her and her brother alive in the coldest of nights.

But *this* . . . this was *real* power. Power she could use to defend herself and others. To *save* herself and others. She could turn strigoi back. She could heal whomever her warmth touched. And she could burn all of her enemies.

Lila was more than just a warm murine the Reinicks possessed. She was the fucking sun.

Hours passed, and Lila didn't sleep a wink. She continued to test her powers throughout the day, finding it got stronger around midday. All her wounds healed as she thought of those she loved, and more items around the room boiled and singed as she thought of the brothers. She had a difficult time focusing on *what* she was affecting around her—it almost felt more like a radius than any one solid object. Which explained why her burst of energy affected all the nearby strigoi back in the Crow Court battle.

But, Lila figured, if she could manage to affect *one* item—or person—she may just be able to use her power as a weapon. She wondered if, like sunlight, *she* could burn vampires.

She couldn't wait to test this theory on Hektor or Ciro.

So long as it actually *did* kill them.

It was just after sunset when she heard the loud and vivacious sounds of laughter and screams. Lila knew it meant the brothers and Drusilla were back. She hardened herself, prepared for anything, just as Hektor burst through her open doorway, a smile as wicked as sin spread on his lips.

Blood was coating his face and hands, giving him an even more deranged look as his eyes traced over Lila.

"What on earth are you wearing?" The smile fell to an almost-comedic frown. "That's not what we dress you in. And last I saw you, you wore nothing—which is what you *should* be in now!"

Just as Hektor dashed into the room, a blur of red smashed against him, shoving him into the wall.

"*I* gave it to her," Rebekkah hissed, as she pinned Hektor against the stone. Her forearm pressed into his neck, while her other hand held his wrist. Both of them snarled their teeth at one another like a pair of rabid wolves.

"Why? Want to get locked up again?" Hektor spit. "We can just leave you up there, no food. How long can you last this time? A week? Two?"

"*Fuck* you." She shoved against his neck.

But if Lila assumed right, they'd been starving Rebekkah

on and off again which would naturally make her so much weaker than—

Hektor shoved her hard, and his sister crashed to the floor. Her head jerked back, and Lila knew if the girl was human, Rebekkah's neck would be broken. The blood he drank from Lila and all the other murine at the Reinick revel the other night had clearly made him so much stronger. He was oozing pride, and Lila knew whenever he got like this, it usually came with reckless behavior. Behavior, though, that brother Ciro—actual Lord of the Viper Morada— would highly disapprove of. May even reprimand him. May even kill him. So, taking the opportunity she was presented, Lila took a wary step back. Like a fool.

Predictably, Hektor was on her in the blink of an eye, his predatory instincts kicking in. He roughly grabbed her wrists and pulled her toward him. She let herself fall right into him.

"Ciro won't like you touching what's his," she hissed, egging him on. "Don't forget he's your Lord."

Hektor snarled, immediately satisfying Lila's plan. She knew whatever he was about to retaliate with would be horrible, but at least she could play the long game. At least she could use these terrible moments to sow doubt.

"I can do whatever I want," he grunted.

"Can you? It seems Ciro has you on a pretty tight leash. I think you're more of his pet than even I am."

Hektor backhanded her. But Lila had been ready for it. Though it still stung, and her head whipped to the side, she had gritted her teeth the moment after speaking. She used that slap to fuel her heat.

"You need to be reminded who's the pet and who's the master? Let's get you into something more . . . comfortable." Hektor smiled widely as he ripped the high neckline of the nightgown right down the center to Lila's sternum.

"*NO!*" Rebekkah yelled, jumping back up to her feet, and crashing into Hektor, knocking him to the floor with her. She quickly shifted into her true form, splaying her wings out, and growling at her brother. "You. Will. Stop. Being. A. *Fucking*. Pig!" With each word, Rebekkah slashed her claws over Hektor, scratching up his face, his arms.

She pummeled and pummeled, but Lila knew it wouldn't be enough. She had seen Hektor's jaw get punched clean off his face before regenerating. This would be nothing. And it seemed Rebekkah knew this too as she spun around to Lila and yelled, "Go!"

Lila didn't hesitate. She dashed out of the room, pumping her fists just as Ambrose had taught her to do, and ran down the hallway. She didn't know where she was going, she just knew Hektor equaled danger right now. Maybe Ciro, for he was a semblance of safety, and perhaps she could use the opportunity to weave even more discord between the brothers.

The soles of her feet smashed into the cold stone below her, tiny, jagged edges scraping against her smooth flesh. She cursed her lack of training when her thighs immediately lit up, burning from the sensation. She had gotten past this in her efforts, yet here she was again.

Weak.

But not defenseless.

Lila ran through the Morada, toward the great hall where the main exit waited, and hopefully where Ciro resided. But, just as she burst through the door, deep regret settled into her bones. Ciro sat in an ornate chair on the center dais, Drusilla standing by his side, whispering into his ear. Both of them had smug expressions on their faces, covered in blood. With Drusilla here, there was little she could do. With Drusilla here, it was three against one. Lila tried to double back, but the moment she took the smallest step, she bumped directly into Hektor's chest.

"Little Mouse tried to get away," he smirked. Lila jumped back from him, deeper into the room.

"He was trying to rape me," she said. "Trying to take me for his own." She ushered to the torn dress, revealing the plane between her breasts.

Ciro's eyebrow rose, a spark of fury aimed at his brother. Then Drusilla placed her hand on his arm and the fury dissipated.

Fuck.

As Hektor followed her in, he dragged Rebekkah in behind him. His hand was wrapping in her hair, pulling, as she fought against his grip.

Then Ciro stood. "What do we have here?"

"Rebekkah thought she could do as she pleased." He pointed at Lila. "That is not what we left her in." His voice was practically a growl. Over a *dress*.

Lila turned to Ciro, Drusilla still behind him. While Ciro schooled his expression into utter indifference, Drusilla's lips tilted into a smile.

"Well, we can't have that." She stepped off the dais. "She is a pet, so why do we dress her like one of us?"

Hektor snickered, then threw Rebekkah forward at Drusilla's feet. Immediately, Drusilla pressed one of her heels into the back of Rebekkah's head, pushing her down.

"Tell us, sister. Why give the murine clothes?" Ciro asked calmly.

Lila seethed. They were treating their sibling like an animal. Their own flesh and blood. She thought of Marcus, and the idea of treating him so much less than made her stomach sick.

"You're letting her do this to a Reinick? To your own blood?" she hissed, keeping her eyes locked on Ciro.

Drusilla grinded her heel deeper against Rebekkah's head.

"As far as I'm concerned," Ciro said in a sigh—as if he were bored and nothing else—"blood means nothing but food for a king. Remember, *pet*, I killed my own father for a title. Sibling or not, if my word is not obeyed, I *will* act." His eyes found Hektor's, for the briefest moment.

But Lila had had enough. She went to lunge at Drusilla, but just as she kicked off, Hektor wrapped his arms around her waist. She crashed into him as he roughly squeezed her to him, one hand dropping to her hip and pressing her ass into him. She started to fight, but the moment she felt his *small*, hard cock against her, she wanted to do anything in her power to *not* feel it.

She readied herself to summon her scalding heat, but just as she felt the first spike of body heat, Rebekkah shoved Drusilla away from her and stood.

"You leave her, naked and bloodied. You treat her *worse* than a pet."

"And since when did you care?" Hektor snickered again, pressing his cheek against Lila's. "Last we checked, she was food for you too."

Rebekkah opened her mouth to speak, but before she could, Drusilla backhanded her so hard, she went flying across the room.

"I'm thinking Bek has grown sentimental on us," Ciro hummed. His hands were in his pocket as he raised his eyebrow at his sister's beaten body. "Maybe we should leave her here, make her think about who she puts her alliance with."

"Treat her like a murine, and maybe she'll finally remember how different we are from them," Drusilla sang. Her pride oozed off of her, making Lila sick.

"And in the meantime," Hektor groaned against Lila's flesh, "we'll return our pet to her . . . natural form." He gripped the fabric at her hip, bunching it in his fist, and pulled. Again, Lila was stripped bare, the pull of fabric reddening her skin. "Ah, that's better." He cupped her breast and squeezed, humming from his throat.

Lila saw red. She bucked against him, clawing his arms, head butting his face—but nothing worked.

"Watch yourself," Ciro said, in such a minute, pathetic way. She caught Ciro's gaze from his spot on the dais, and he just watched. Bristling, but still. He did *nothing*.

"*Coward*," she cursed under her breath, knowing he'd hear.

"Leave her alone." Rebekkah stood slowly. Her limbs looked odd and . . . broken. "Leave her *alone!*" She leaped forward, claws bared. She tackled Hektor and Lila, digging her claws into his flesh immediately. As soon as the three crashed to the floor, Lila scurried back and away. But the fight before her was utter madness. Hektor shifted into his true form, and fought, smashing Rebekkah's jaw with the heel of his palm.

Lila tried to back as far away as possible, but icy hands fell on her shoulders.

"Where are you going, dear?" Drusilla whispered, holding Lila in place. Then, louder, "Throw the princess in her tower already!"

Ciro moved forward, pulling his sister off Hektor. She fought against his grip, but didn't budge. Hektor stood and brushed himself off, as though he were removing dust.

"Take her," Ciro commanded, pushing Rebekkah at Hektor.

Lila and Rebekkah both fought against the people holding them—but it was no use. Rebekkah was taken from the room, kicking and screaming. Hektor backhanded her just as she disappeared from Lila's sight.

"What are you doing to her?" Lila seethed, looking up at Ciro as Drusilla's claws began pinching her skin.

He looked down his nose at Lila, keeping his eyes locked on hers and no lower.

"She's your fucking sister. And you treat her like *that*? For giving me a *dress*?"

"For doing as she pleases," Ciro bristled. "*I* am the lord of this house. *I* make the rules, set the commands."

Lila snatched her shoulder from Drusilla, and stood up, not caring she was nude, not caring she was in a room with two of the deadliest vampires she knew—or rather, the two vampires who could actually be a threat to her. Ambrose was the deadliest, but she didn't have to fear him.

She stomped up to Ciro. "*You* are a tool. You're being used by that hag, and made to be a puppet when you *could* be making the Morada better. Has it even occurred to you that the Viper Morada is the only manor that still owns murine? That it is the only family to still live in the past? To still treat their *only* food source worse than insects? And you are the youngest generation! It makes no sense for you to be so archaic! You say you set the rules, the commands, yet you let Hektor do as he pleases with me!"

Then softer, looking into those yellow eyes. "Aren't I yours to take? Aren't I yours to touch? Why do you let Hektor have what is *rightfully* yours?" Inside, Lila was vomiting as each syllable uttered. She lied through her teeth, feeling sick at the notion of *ever* being anyone but

Ambrose's. But she needed to say it. She needed Ciro to be mad at Hektor.

Lila felt Drusilla's presence behind her, just as her icy hand wrapped around Lila's throat.

With the claws around her, Lila felt her fight kick back in. "*She* is making an army out of *your* food. Who will be left when she's done? All those people she and Hektor murdered the other night at the revel? They're lives were forfeit for nothing but gluttony, greed, and lust," she spat.

Drusilla's hand tightened, and Lila coughed out the only remaining air in her throat.

"You want to see what we're doing with *our* murine, Little Bug?" Drusilla spoke against Lila's ear, grazing it with a sharp fang. "Ciro, let's show her. Show her what *you* have created. She disobeys you, acts like she is better than you. But she is *your pet*. You *own* her. And she will learn to behave or I think she may need to be put down, as any unruly pet should."

With a sharp shove, Drusilla pushed Lila into Ciro's arms, who immediately locked her in an embrace. "You're right. I've been too soft with her since her return. She needs . . . reminding of *who* she belongs to."

Lila's blood turned to ice in her veins. She struggled against his grip, but his arms only squeezed harder—constricting her like a snake.

Drusilla snickered. "She's been a bad girl. And bad girls deserve punishment."

8

Dressed in the same thin, see-through fabric as before, Lila was wrapped in Ciro's arms as he flew from the Morada. Behind him, Drusilla and Hektor accompanied, smiling wickedly all the way.

She kept hoping Ciro would accidentally drop her so she wouldn't have to be in his arms a moment more. She knew they had something vile planned for her . . . she just didn't know what.

"I am not anyone's puppet," Ciro seethed. His voice was so low, and directly in her ear, she knew he meant it only for her to hear. "Except—maybe yours." Fingers dug into her arms, her thighs. "You make me lose myself, my ambitions, my goals. When I see you, I want *nothing but you*. I want to own you, and dominate you. But more than that, I want you to *want me* to do those things."

Lila didn't make eye contact, she refused, but she saw as he gulped, as he . . . trembled.

"I own murine *for* our use. You live in our lands, you *chose* this."

"We didn't choose any of this! We are living with the hands we were dealt!" Lila balked.

"Then move. Like you said, the other manors don't own murine. Why stay?"

"You don't let us! You threaten us, take us every month! Do you know how difficult it is to get by on *nothing*?!"

"No," he said simply. "Nor do I care. We found you, we *saved* you. Before us, you were stealing away into other towns, taking whatever crumbs you could find to feed your stupid brother and pathetic father."

Lila slapped him. Hard.

"You didn't save me. You *damned me*."

"Is that what you call clothing you, feeding you, giving you a place to sleep, keeping you safe from Hektor?"

"It's what I call treating me like cattle! It's what I call tormenting and torturing me every fucking day of my existence. It's what I call trying to have your way with me every chance you get, until one of these days, Hektor *is* going to rape me, and you'll let him. He's only gotten worse and you've *let him*. If you think you *saved* me, you truly are more delusional than I thought."

"And is that what Draven did?" Every word he spewed dripped a venom thicker than that of his bite. "He *saved* you? Or was he just a different cock for you to enrapture? A different breeder you could tease along until you finally allowed him to touch you? You already have my cock, and my fucking brother's, but you just needed Draven's too? You little attention whore. You've got a list of men desperate to beg for you on their knees. Maybe, now that Draven's dead, you can fill that hole in your cunt with me instead."

Lila gaped, but before she could retort, Ciro flared out his arms, dropping her. She yelped before landing on the hard ground right below her. She hadn't noticed they reached their destination during their argument.

Ciro looked down at her, and then wrapped a hand around her neck, holding just tight enough to make her wheeze.

"In the meantime, *Little Mouse*, I want you to see what I'm creating. What I'm creating *for us*."

He turned her, forcing her to look out. It was still night out, the stars had been covered by clouds, and everything just looked . . . dark.

The four of them stood on the top of a small hill, facing a town that began at the foot of it. Immediately, Lila went pale. She knew this town. She knew it like she knew her mother's scent, her father's voice. She knew this town because it was *hers*. Her hometown sat quiet, defenseless, in front of her. The small shops may have had different signs, been painted different colors, but it was just as she remembered it.

The illusion shattered as she saw one pale strigoi stalking through the town center. Lila's eyes went wide, her heart pumped. Another strigoi was crawling down a house, toward an open window. She wrestled against Ciro's hand at her neck. More strigoi were flooding into sight, like cockroaches in the dark.

"*Watch*," Ciro commanded, and she felt the familiar fog of his thrall wrap around her mind.

Then she heard the first scream.

Next to her, Hektor stepped forward. "Can we join in on the fun?" He was practically shaking, his eyes glowing from bloodlust.

"Hmm," Drusilla hummed on her other side. "We can have *some* fun. We don't need every murine to change. We have . . . enough." Her eyes met Lila's and she smirked.

They were changing people . . . *humans* in Lila's hometown

into strigoi? For their *army?!* Guilt stabbed into Lila's gut. They were doing all of this because of *her*. Because *she* had lived here, grown up here. It wasn't home, and it hadn't been for a long time, but it was *hers*.

She fought against the thrall, trying to avert her gaze.

"Let's go take a closer look, shall we?" Ciro uttered from behind her. Immediately, Hektor flew up and dove between houses, grabbing a mother running out of her house, child in arm, and dug his teeth into her neck. She screamed and dropped the child. As soon as he fell, a strigoi grabbed him.

Horror twisted Lila's gut.

"No," she muttered. "Please, don't make me."

"This is your punishment, remember? Once it's over, maybe you'll remember who you belong to." Ciro's voice was so cold, colder than she'd ever heard it before. As he pushed her down the hill and into the stone streets, blood splashed all around Lila. Blood and screams. The entire town had awoken by now, and were running for their lives. Running out of buildings, running *into* buildings, grabbing each other and trying all they could to stay safe.

But none of it mattered, not as the strigoi cleaved their way through the town, either turning every living being into one of them or drinking them dry. Drusilla joined in the madness, dashing into a house just before a plethora of wails and shrieks burst from the open door.

Lila couldn't handle it anymore. She needed to *do something*.

She thought of her fear, how fucking *afraid* she was for these people, for her. And she used it.

Ciro yelped, pulling his hand from Lila's neck. She saw a flash of his palm, the flesh boiling. Then, with more of her fear and anger entwining, she *pushed*. A gust of heat flared from her skin, and she could hear the sizzle of Ciro's flesh before he screamed.

Ambrose's words rang through her ears. *Will you continue to dwell on the past? Will you allow those who have wronged you to continue controlling your actions? Or will you let go? Will you let go and be* better? *Will you show them they were wrong about you, that you are more than just their murine?*

"What are you doing?" he demanded.

"Being *better!*" Lila pushed another wave at him, forcing him to take a few steps from her, and dashed into the night.

She ran behind houses, between shops and alleys, away from Ciro. Lila played her hand earlier than she expected, and now she needed to get away. If she used her fear to singe everyone around her, she feared it may hurt the humans currently fighting for their lives. So, she thought of a different approach.

Lila knew each and every turn to take, knew how many steps it would be, so when she got to the center of the town square, she stood strong and confident.

Love, Lila thought, *Ambrose, Marcus, Mother, Father, Constance, Pollock, Kaz, Sandra, Rebekkah*. These were the people Lila loved. She thought of them and her love for them, what they meant to her. Warmth started seeping from her body, radiating like the sun. She would cure these strigoi, she would save this town.

But not much happened. People were dropping or changing all around her, in every corner. It was as though her warmth was barely reaching them.

She focused harder, trying to push down the fear and rage erupting around her.

Ambrose.

She focused on her lust, trying desperately to grab for

something, anything. As she thought of his tongue lapping her up on the rooftop of the Crow Court, she tried to give into her desires. Tried so hard to feel what she felt then.

But the image of Hektor biting into a mother's neck, of a strigoi grabbing the child, of Ciro genuinely thinking he was doing any of this *for her*, crawled into her brain. And any flame in her core was immediately extinguished.

Just as Lila was about to try again, Hektor appeared before her—blood-soaked and eager. He walked toward her and didn't stop till his chest bumped hers.

"What are you doing?" he asked coyly. "Why are you here alone?"

Fuck, Lila thought.

She tried to take a step back, but he followed.

"I heard my brother while we were flying here." He scoffed, "He thinks he was speaking low enough for me not to hear, but I heard every word."

He took another step closer, pushing Lila back, as he drove a hand through his unruly brown hair.

"The thing is, my brother's an idiot. He doesn't see what he has." Another step.

"And what's that?" Lila clenched her jaw, afraid of the answer.

"Well, for starters, he has you. I don't know what this nonsense is about reminding you of who your true owner is. You are *his*, and he can do anything he likes to you." He took another step, and Lila felt cold stone brush against her back. There was nowhere else to go. "I don't understand why he doesn't just *take* what he wants."

Lila tried to act brave. "I'm sure if it were you, you'd—"

"Baby, I would've fucked you a long time ago. I would have you as my personal sex doll to fuck whenever *I* pleased. And you would fucking love it. You'd be begging for my cock again and again and again." He placed a finger under her chin and forced her to face him.

"That tiny thing? I'd—"

He slapped her cheek and then immediately pressed into her, caging her in. It was too much, too suffocating.

"You want to test it now?" Hektor quickly grabbed the underside of her knee with one hand, and lifted it onto his wrist. He positioned himself between her thighs and Lila felt just how hard he already was as he pressed himself roughly against the apex of her thighs.

"Ciro'll kill you for this."

"He's too much of a pussy to do anything to me. I can take you right now if I want. Fuck, how I've imagined it. I've dreamed of stealing away into your room and fucking you senseless, gagging you so Ciro would never hear."

Lila tried to push him off, but with his free hand, Hektor grabbed her wrists.

"You know I like when you fight. It turns me on more."

Lila spat at his face, but he just licked his lips.

"I can do that too. Want to spit on my cock next before I shove it down these pretty lips of yours?" He raised her thigh higher, making her lose balance and fall into him. "You know, my favorite fantasy of us is when I'm fucking you so hard, you can't help but scream. I have to cover your mouth just so Ciro won't hear us, won't find out what I'm doing *without his permission*," he seethes. "I fantasize about coming inside of you till you're so full of me, it leaks down your thighs. And when my cock is filthy from our mixed juices, I force you on your knees and fuck your mouth, just to shut you up."

Hektor's lips crashed into Lila's, painfully and disgustingly. His teeth pulled at her bottom lip, forcing her mouth open. Blood. She could taste her own blood.

He drove his tongue into her mouth, exploring, hungry, and greedy. He sucked her tongue into his mouth, but Lila pulled back.

"*Kiss me,*" he tried to enthrall, but not even a hint of the fog clouded her mind. She pushed and kicked and punched but he didn't budge. He drove his tongue into her mouth again, and Lila bit down—hard.

Hektor yelled, but Lila didn't let go. She'd rip it right out if she could.

Rage filled her, fear shook her, and Lila felt like she'd burn the world. She grabbed Hektor's face and pushed him back with all her might, trying to get him off of her. As soon as her hands touched his flesh, she felt it bubbling under her palms. Bubbling and boiling.

Hektor reared back away from Lila, and finally let her go. He cupped his face and Lila used that moment of reprieve to *run*. She pumped her arms and legs as fast as she could. She was in the southernmost region of the Viper Morada, but that didn't stop her heart from wanting to go to the Crow Court—from wanting to go to Ambrose.

But just as she considered Concording him, a hand clamped on her wrist.

"Where are you going, Little Bug? You don't like the show?" Drusilla smiled at her.

Blood. Her face and chin were covered in blood.

Drusilla looked down at Lila's lips, and her eyes shone a green so emerald, it rivaled Darius's.

Drusilla yanked Lila's head to her, licking her bottom lip slowly.

"Lords, I love the taste of you."

Lila jerked the heel of her palm into Drusilla's chin, shoving her face away.

"Get the fuck off me," Lila hissed and then dashed

away again. But these vampires were relentless. Ciro dropped from nowhere, blocked her path, his eyes flaring with so much fury, Lila could practically feel her body consumed in it.

"Hektor! He—" but Lila didn't get a chance to finish. She saw the glimpse of his charred hand, just as the back of it smashed against her cheek once more. The impact was so hard, it rattled Lila's brain and for a moment she saw stars.

When the second impact came, she didn't see anything at all.

9

Lila's head swam. It felt heavy and clouded and—

She jumped up, despite the pain. When her eyes finally adjusted, she saw she was back in her room—her *cell*—in the Viper Morada. Again. Morning had come and based on the limited light in the room, it seemed it was around noon. She was lying in her bed, under the covers . . . almost as if nothing had happened.

When she reached up to her lips, the blood had been cleaned, but the two small puncture wounds were faintly there.

Lila was still shaking. All the fear from her night coiled inside of her and she couldn't stop. As she pulled the blanket closer, she tried to remind herself of another night her fear nearly got the better of her.

Ambrose's large wings cocooned her in the Arachnid Estate the night before Sanktus Pernox. He held her till she stopped crying, till her limbs weren't shaking. She had been so warm then. So comfortable. So . . . happy.

Lila felt her heart pang at the thought of him. Yes she just saw him, but it wasn't enough. She just missed him *so much*. She longed to see his face, to hear that low, golden voice — especially now. To hear him laugh. To hear him moan her name. Lords, she loved making him moan. Loved making the monster of Malvania simper with need *for her*.

She kicked her legs and groaned.

She just wanted to be wrapped up in his arms, safe.

They had just professed their love for one another, and they couldn't even use their own voices to do so.

"I love you, Ambrose. I love you, I love you, I love you." There. At least now it was out in the world and not just festering in her mind.

She tried to shut her eyes again, tried to go back to sleep to ignore her wants and fears. But after a few moments, she was still wide awake and her heart still ached. Her lips had been tainted by another and it hurt her very being to think of it.

Every time her eyes closed, she saw Hektor there, against her. Kissing her. Trying to take her.

But she wouldn't let him. She already belonged to another — body, soul, and heart.

Lila needed comfort. She needed distraction. If not, she feared she may just combust. If her shaking limbs were any sign, it seemed like she was nearly at a breaking point.

Maybe . . . maybe she just needed to talk to Ambrose. See if he was awake by some chance.

There had been many days like these in her three months. Days when she almost gave up her quest to prove herself. Days she almost begged him to come get her. Those days were harder than most — and much more frequent than she'd ever admit. But on those days, she'd been able to call to him, and he had been there, in her mind, and though it didn't quite quench her thirst, it did what it needed to.

Ambrose? Are you awake?

Moments ticked by. It had to be nearing the afternoon. He was probably asleep.

Yes, Little Crow? The voice in Lila's mind was thick. It sounded like he'd just woken up. And then, more urgently, *Why are you awake? Are you okay?*

Yes, yes. I'm fine, she thought quickly.

And you're awake because?

Lila blushed, hesitating. This damned vampire drove her to utopia with his tongue on her clit, yet she still felt embarrassed telling him how she felt. Not to mention, she didn't want to tell him about her horrible night.

Not her town, not Rebekkah's confinement, not Drusilla, not Ciro, and definitely not Hektor. If she had, she didn't think Ambrose would be able to stop himself from coming to steal her.

It didn't matter that her eyes were still stained from the bloodshed she saw.

It didn't matter that she still felt Hektor's touch on her skin.

What mattered was *him*.

Because . . . I miss you.

She heard his chuckle tickle her mind. *And do you know how absolutely mad I'm being driven waiting for you? Lords, Lila. I miss you. You're all I think about.*

Lila smiled and suddenly felt warm all over. *I want to go to you. I want to go home.*

Do you mean that? Or are you lamenting again?

She hesitated. *Both. I do want to go home. But not yet. I just—*

I know, love. I know.

There was a heavy silence. She still felt him there, somehow. But neither said anything.

I have an idea, Ambrose mused. Lila heard his coy smile and it sent shivers down her body.

Yes?

You're all alone, correct?

Mhm. In my room.

Tell me, love. Do you want a distraction from thinking?

The damn vampire knew her too well. Even when he couldn't read her emotions with his powers, he still somehow read her as though she were an open book.

Desperately.

He chuckled, the hum of his laugh trailing down to her core. *I want you to take those pretty hands of yours and play with your nipples.*

Really?

No questions, darling. Do as I say. You're going to be a good girl, right?

Lila blushed. *Yes. I'll be a good girl.*

She dragged her hands up her body, feeling the thin fabric roll under her skin. How she *wished* she could have worn this for Ambrose. He would love it moments before he tore it off of her. She would love to pad around in the Crow Court for him. Love to tease him endlessly with the slip of a nipple, the curve of her ass, every time he saw her.

But the idea had been tainted. This dress was like a shackle to hell.

Are your hands there? Ambrose asked. His voice did funny things to her stomach and though she wasn't physically hearing it, it still had the same effect.

Yes. She groped herself, squeezing and pulling how she knew Ambrose liked. She fiddled with one nipple between her fingers before pulling on it roughly.

Mmm. Good. Now—

Wait. What are you doing with your hands?

Ambrose choked. *What do you mean?*

If I'm doing this, you have to also. I want you to touch yourself, Ambrose Draven, to the thought of me.

Darling, he scoffed. *I have done that every night since you've been gone. Sometimes, I don't leave my room because the thought of you is all consuming.*

Lila warmed, feeling a familiar wave of heat centralize between her thighs. However, it was stronger than ever before, hotter, tingly, and more intensifying. She felt like lava coming to life. *You have no idea how much I've wanted to touch myself. How much I've wanted to think of you and just . . . but the Reinicks. If they found out, they'd—*

You don't have to explain, darling. I would rather you be safe than horny.

Lila giggled. He knew how to lighten her mood so easily.

Well, you want control? Tell me, love. What should I do to myself?

Lila grabbed her breast hard, squeezing it to the point it turned a shade reminiscent of her hair. *I want you to grab your cock and think of my mouth on it. Remember how my tongue felt as it glided up your shaft. How it felt when I sucked down your head.*

Lords. Remind me to make you talk dirty next time I see you. Stroke. Now.

Lila, he pleaded. She could imagine the red glowing in his eyes, his cheeks hot to the touch with desire as he watched her touch herself. But she knew he was doing it.

When his voice returned, it was hoarse. *Leave one hand teasing your nipple but drag the other slowly down your body. Slowly.* She did as he told her. Her nails grazed against the plain of her stomach as her other hand pulled and toyed with her hard nipple. *Tell me when you're there.*

With the apex of her thighs exposed, Lila thought back, *Ready*.

Good girl. Now take those fingers and run it through the soft, warm folds of your pussy. As he said these things to her, Ambrose's voice became more and more rushed. Desperate. *Are you wet, Little Crow?*

Mhm. Ah—Ambrose. Let me—

Not yet. Tell me how wet you are.

Lila hesitated, she hadn't realized how turned on she had become. Her body acted as though it were starved for him, and now it was reacting so quickly. *M-my fingers are slick.*

Do you feel yourself dripping?

She let herself feel her body. *Yes. Ambrose—please.*

Please what, love?

Let me touch myself.

Ambrose groaned into her mind. *Fuck. Okay. I want you to stick your middle finger inside.*

Lila moaned into her pillow, muffling the sound, as she drove her finger inside herself.

How warm is it?

Lords, it's so hot.

What I'd give to be buried inside of you right now. Ambrose sounded desperate, his voice shaking.

You have yet to know that heat, Lord Draven, she teased, knowing just how wild it'd drive him.

Fuck, I need to feel you.

Are you still stroking? she asked.

Yes.

I want you to think of how hot and wet I'd feel on your cock. I want you to feel me riding you. To feel yourself inside of me.

Fuck, Lila. He paused for a moment, then, *Slip another finger in.*

She did and immediately moaned his name, curving her fingers to hit the exact spot she liked.

Get your fingers nice and wet for me, love. And when you're good and ready, take them and draw circles on your clit.

Lila yelped as she did so, rocking against her own hand as her damp fingers pressed against the bud between her thighs. The pressure was insane and it made her rock her hips farther against her.

I'm turning over. She turned, laying on her stomach and used the bed as leverage for her hand. The farther down she pushed, the more beautiful pressure on her clit. *Ambrose, I'm close.*

So am I, love. Tell me what else you want me to do.

I want you to think of my hand as yours, and your hand as mine. I want you to think of me stroking that huge cock of yours, and your fingers to be the ones circling my clit.

Fuck, yes.

Squeeze harder, Ambrose.

Ah—Lila. Rub your clit, baby.

Lila did. She swirled quicker and harder, feeling herself on the edge of a precipice she hadn't felt in three long months. She bucked into the mattress below her. *Ambrose!*

Love, she heard the smile in his voice before she even heard the words, *I want you to stop.*

What? Her fingers hesitated, confused.

I want you to grab the stake I gave to you. Is it near?

The stake? Lila slipped her fingers from her core and raised herself on her elbows. *Why do you want me to grab that?*

He snickered again. *You'll see. Do you have it yet?*

She reached under the mattress of her bed and pulled the wooden weapon from its hiding place within the hay. The wood was smooth in her palm, the design mesmerizing her just as much as it had the first time she saw it.

This weapon had been Ambrose's once upon a time,

and then he gave it to her. She felt her strength tied to this weapon, her very being.

I have it, she said, having the slightest of inclinations as to where this was going and flipping back over on her back.

The smile was still in his voice, *I want you to take it between your thighs and grind the pretty little clit against it for me.*

Though she had the feeling, his words still shook her, still made her toes curl. Her immediate thought led to splinters in the worst place ever—but she knew Ambrose's craftsmanship was better than that. The weapon had been waxed and sealed, and was as smooth as her own skin. Probably.

Lila? he questioned. *Are you doing as I say?*

She tentatively placed the handle of the stake between her thighs.

Yes. It-it's there.

Good, darling. Now, I want you to move those hips. Move them like you were grinding against my cock.

A wave of heat spread through Lila's body and she swore she felt even wetter than before. She slowly rocked her hips, grinding the weapon between her thighs.

Her clit rubbed against the corner of the handle in the perfect way and Lila let slip a moan into the room.

Fuck, it's good.

I knew you'd like it, Ambrose said. *When you're good and ready, I want you to go faster.*

Lila waited a moment, savoring the slow, torturous friction against her, and then she did as she was told.

Ah! Ambrose—It's so . . . she trailed off, too encompassed by the feeling building inside of her.

You're such a good girl, you're taking my orders so well.

The praise sent what felt like another shock wave to her

system. She rocked against the stake, feeling it press against the bud growing more and more sensitive once again.

Will you take my cock this well?

Ambrose, your mouth—my lords.

She once again heard the smirk in his hoarse voice. *Last I checked, you loved my mouth. Especially when it was feasting on you under the stars.*

Lila moaned once again at the memory.

I want you to try something for me, he said.

Lila didn't hesitate. She knew she'd like whatever he'd ask of her. *Anything.*

I want you to press the stake into you. Not all the way, but I want you to feel as though I were about to fuck you senseless.

Her back arched as she dipped the stake lower, immediately following his orders. She pressed it to her core, swirling the edges of it at her entrance. She held the sharp end in her palm, and rocked against the wood, letting it drive into her just a little bit farther each time.

Do you remember my cock at your entrance that morning?

Lila felt her entire body heat, her cheeks felt like they were on fire. She thought the stake might catch fire if she got any hotter.

I can't stop thinking about it, she admitted. *How close we were.*

Imagine how I feel. I got the briefest glimpse of heaven before it was yanked away from me. Lords, you were so fucking hot and tight. I can't wait to pick up where we left off.

Lila dipped the stake just a tiny bit farther, bucking against it as her clit rubbed against the edge.

Ambrose, I want you to fuck me till I forget everything. I want you to take me and never let go.

Darling, I can promise you, even if you want me to let go, I never could. Once I have you, I won't ever stop. You may get sick of me, but I will keep going. I will make you orgasm till your body gives out, and then I will give you more.

She imagined what he promised her, and it made the heat coil in her belly. Her toes curled and her body shook violently.

Fuck. Yes. Rub your cock, Ambrose. I want you to fill me with your cum until my body is just as much you as it is me.

She felt him with her, right on the edge, ready to dive over.

Fuck, Lila. I love you.

And that was what did her in. She came on her stake— *his* stake—as he said those three words that made her heart full, feeling her slick wetness.

Her entire body felt like it was vibrating and as she pulled the stake away, it was hot to the touch.

Heavy breathing filled her mind. *Lila?* His voice was so hoarse and Lila just couldn't get enough of it. *Did you finish?*

She had a hard time even thinking of words. *Yes.*

Her nipples were sore from how much she pulled on them, her clit throbbed, her entrance was slightly sore, and she still shook from the euphoria. *Did you?*

Lords, yes. And I made a proper mess in my coffin thanks to you, he chuckled.

She giggled then wiped the stake off on the edge of the bed sheets and tucked it back into its hiding place.

As she rolled back on her side, she said, *Can you stay with me today? Keep the Concord up?*

A beat passed and Ambrose's tender voice filled her mind. *Of course, love. I'd like nothing more.*

Lila smiled to herself. She knew she could rely on him, no matter what the situation, no matter what emotion she needed from him—he was there *for her*.

She cuddled into the thin blanket and stared at the wall,

picturing him there next to her. *I'd like to pretend . . . that I'm with you. At home. I want to pretend it hasn't been three months, or that the other day was the first I'd seen your face since. I want to pretend I'm not at the Morada and that we're not apart, but together. In the same room, the same bed. Under the same blanket—preferably under your wing.*

She heard him snicker. *We can do that. Though, as I think I've made clear, if you were here we would be doing anything but sleeping.*

You rake. You just had me coming at the thought of you and you're already having dirty thoughts again?

Darling, when it comes to you, every thought I have is dirty.

Lila blushed and snickered into the blanket. *Well, after we have the most mind-blowing sex imaginable—*

I like where this is going already, Ambrose cooed.

I'd make a small burrow for myself right in your arms and never leave.

And I'd hold you like my very undead life depended on it. You'd be so warm pressed against me.

So warm, we wouldn't even need blankets. Just each other . . . and wings, she giggled. *We're going to need a coffin big enough to fit your monstrous form and me.*

Darling, I had one made within a week of your departure. I haven't slept in it yet. I'm waiting till our first day together again.

Lila's heart fluttered in her chest, but not even a moment later, a pang shot through her as well. Lords, she missed him. She missed being with him. And more and more, she was feeling like she'd made a huge mistake by coming to the Morada for her "redemption." She knew sowing the discord between Ciro and Hektor was working. But at what cost? *We're pretending I'm already back, remember?*

Ah, of course. Then I'm sure we've already sullied our new coffin and will shortly need a new-new one.

Of course, of course. I'm in it now. As soon as the words left Lila's mind, she truly did feel heavy with sleep. Her eyelids had already closed, and as she cuddled into the blanket—pretending it was Ambrose—she felt like sleep just might take her.

If we were in it, I would kiss your cheek, your eyelids, your forehead. I would shower you with kisses until you fell asleep. I would whisper my confession of love like a lullaby.

Interest peaked, Lila mumbled back, *Why don't you?*

She heard a breath of laughter. *All right, get ready to fall in love all over again.*

10

After she'd asked him to keep speaking through the Concord, Ambrose slunk from his coffin into her room. He lay in Lila's bedroom once again. Pollock had gone to roost with the other crows the night before, so he had the room to himself. Only, it felt like she was right there with him.

It drove him absolutely feral when she did as he asked and took his stake to her wet cunt. Lords, how he wished he could see it. He wished he could see *her*. But he felt like if she were with him, nothing but pure restraint would've stopped him from ravaging her, from driving his teeth into her neck as he fucked into her.

He needed to calm down. To shake off the violence of his affection. Their time together just the night before wasn't enough. It was never enough when it came to her. He wished he could be fully consumed by her at all times. Like Icarus to the sun.

But he could make sure this was enough—at least, for

her. He could make the most of their time together, as sparse as it was.

Ambrose knew something was wrong, but she seemed so damned . . . tired. And he didn't want to force anything out of her, especially if she was looking for comfort right now—not a solution.

He searched his heart and whispered the first thing he thought. *I love your eyes. I know I've said this, but you have no idea the colors that shine through them. How they warm as you do, how the yellows and golds brighten and beam when I make you come, how the greens peek through when you laugh, or the copper that glows when you're sad or upset—*

You can see all of that?

Ambrose huffed another laugh. *Remember what I said, darling. Your face speaks volumes before you even open those pretty lips. And those eyes—*lords, *those eyes. I can stare at them for eternity and never get enough.*

He heard Lila hum and it tickled his mind. *I like the sound of that.*

Smiling, Ambrose hooked his arm behind his head, resting against the pillow. Her voice was growing more and more sleepy and the lilt did funny things to his heart.

I love the way you sound. Your voice is the sound to my soul. Every little moan you make sends me absolutely wild. Every laugh makes me feel like I can lift mountains. And every cry shatters my heart in a million pieces.

I have never, in my immortal life, loved like I love you, Lila Bran. You have lit up my soul from within, and brought warmth and joy and life *back to the Crow Court.*

Lila bashfully said his name like a caress, *Ambrose . . .*

Let me finish, love. I've told you some of my past. I have been scorned, kicked, beaten, shoved—made to believe I was a monster. Ambrose clenched his jaw, remembering his life, the blood on his hands, the lives he's taken with his own teeth—most importantly, the taste of Lila on his tongue, and the feel of her flesh ripping under his nails, his fangs. Guilt and want wrapped themselves around him, constricting his throat, but he powered on. *And though I believe myself still a monster, I know I am a monster for you, by your side. Like the shadow made by your sunlight. I am desperate and needy and completely obsessed with you.*

A moment passed and Lila made no response.

Have I rendered you speechless, love? he grinned. Still, no response came. Smiling sardonically, Ambrose clucked his teeth. *I guess I'll have to repeat those words when I see you. Goodnight, love, and sweet dreams.*

Ambrose kept the line of the Concord open, thinking of Lila, asleep, on the other side. How he wished he could see her. She always looked so peaceful as she slept, and he loved the small noises she made that sounded reminiscent of a tiny forest creature. He smiled to himself just imagining it.

Soon, he thought to himself. *Soon, I'll be with her as she sleeps again.*

11

As Lila awoke that evening, her eyelids fluttered, her heart felt warm, and her body felt... actually rested. It may have just been the best sleep she'd had in the three months since she's been in the Morada.

Ambrose? she called. She felt the remnants of the Concord still open, but when no response came, she knew he must be asleep.

Lords, he probably looked like a god right now. She imagined him shirtless in bed, sprawled out with nothing but a sliver of blanket covering his—

She felt something slither along her leg just before it coiled around her calf. Immediately, Lila closed the connection with the Concord. She abruptly sat up in bed and tossed the covers off her.

Slithering up her leg was a yellow-eyed viper. Its scales were a number of shades of brown, all pointed to look like the scales of a dragon.

Hektor.

He flicked his tongue against Lila's knee as he passed, his tail coiling around Lila's flesh. The rough scales felt like tiny rocks grazing her skin and she wanted so desperately to smack him away, but she knew if she did, he'd only bite her. And he struck so quickly while in this form.

The first night she was at the Crow Court flashed through her mind. She still remembered the pain that rocked her entire body when Ambrose had to remove Hektor's venom. His was the worst of them—like removing tar from her bloodstream.

"*Little Moussse*," he hissed, slithering up her thigh. "*I can sssmell what'sss between your thighsss.*" He slithered closer and Lila felt paralyzed—not from a thrall or Drusilla's venom. But from fear. "*Did you touch yoursssself to the thought of me?*" The snake coiled just before the apex of her thighs, flicking its tongue out once again.

In the blink of an eye, the snake became a man, and Hektor caged her under him as his hands and knees rested on either side of her.

Lila almost shrieked at the sight of him—half of his face looked as though he had stuck it in a pot of boiling water. It was bubbling and oozing white liquid, a shade too pink to be considered normal. The same marks marred his chin and neck and Lila realized—that was where she had touched him in her village. That was where she used her power to push him away.

The burns didn't heal.

Hektor raised an eyebrow. "How do you like your handy work? I think it makes me look . . . mysterious." He neared her, and she pressed herself as far back into the bed as she could. "Neat little trick, pet. But, boy, was Drusilla upset. She has a little . . . punishment waiting for you."

Another jerking movement had Lila whimpering as

Hektor threw his hand past her and reached under her bed. He smirked as she winced, agonizing over her own fear.

"Not only do I smell your delicious cum, but I smell . . ." He seemed to dig around what he was searching for, before "Ah," and yanked her stake free of the mattress. "This. Kinky, pet. Using this to get off? You could've just snuck into my bedroom. I would've let you use my cock all day long. In fact, you don't even have to ask." He jerked forward again, purposefully scaring her.

She tried her best not to flinch, but that only made him angry. He sat back, crushing her thighs under him, and grabbed Lila's cheeks between his fingers. Her lips puckered, and though she immediately tried to fight his grip, it was useless.

"Taste yourself," he mumbled, bringing the edge of the stake that drove her to bliss that afternoon to her lips. When she didn't move, he pushed it past her teeth and rubbed the wood against her tongue. "Do you like the taste of yourself?" Hektor pulled it from her lips and brought it to his own. He dragged his tongue along the corner, swirling it at the edge before he groaned against it.

"Fuck," he said. "*This* is what you taste like?" He sucked on the edge of it, clamping his teeth into the wood. "I knew you were sweet, but . . ."

When his eyes closed, still sucking the wood, Lila sprang into action.

She focused her fear into the tops of her thighs, scalding where Hektor sat on her. Just as he impulsively rose for the briefest moment, she refocused that fear into her palms and *pushed*. She pushed him back, and he lost balance, his back flattening on the bed. Then Lila leaped off the mattress, propelling herself forward, and sprinting at full speed.

If she could get to Ciro, even Drusilla, she knew she'd at least be safe from Hektor's vile sexual assaults. Hopefully. She was afraid one more minute alone with him, and Hektor may take her, no matter how unwilling she was. Maybe even more because of it.

She dashed through the halls of the Morada yet again, feeling like it was becoming a common occurrence. Footsteps pounded on the stone behind her, but she dared not look back. She knew Hektor was near but the moment of hesitation would mean he'd reach her.

Lila felt as she did the night Ambrose finally took her from here. When she had seen Ciro's parents dead on the floor, when he tried to make her kiss him, when Hektor chased her down and bit into her thigh.

It felt the same now as it did then. *She* felt the same now as she did then. Weak, useless, and so utterly . . . human.

Just outside the large oak doors to the great hall, Hektor—in his monstrous form—leaped on top of her, shoving her down to the floor. Lila immediately screamed, hoping someone would hear her and actually help. She screamed and screamed, and Hektor tried to pull her under him, but she didn't stop fighting against him.

The door was thrown open and an icy glare shot down her spine. Ciro was there, and just as she'd hoped, Hektor stopped in his tracks.

"I said bring her here, not attack her," Ciro said coldly.

Lila clawed at the stone floor, pulling herself forward, toward the lesser of two evils.

She heard a snicker behind her as Hektor sat up on his knees. "I thought I'd have some fun first. After all, she did *this* to my face. I felt I had the right to punish her myself."

Ciro practically hissed. "You have *no* right. Remember that, *brother*."

The tension was palpable. Since being here, she could do little more than weave her words like poison. No—like *venom*. They pumped her with their weakening sickness each time they bit her, and she filled their minds with thoughts of power—who was the stronger brother? Who had more power here? Who owned her?

If she could think of something, she could use this tension. Prove *her* strength and break theirs.

She grabbed onto Ciro's pant leg. "Ciro! He—"

But it was broken the moment Drusilla groaned from deeper in the room. "When will you boys shut up? It's power trip after power trip with you two."

His back may have been to Drusilla, but Lila saw Ciro roll his eyes and clench his fist. His sleeves had been rolled up to his elbow, and the tattoo of a black widow on his forearm reminded her of Drusilla's snake coiling down her arm. Of their bargain. Or, *bargains* it seemed.

"Bring her in already," Drusilla demanded.

With the breath of a sigh, Ciro reached down and hauled Lila up by her arm. He dragged her after him, her feet barely keeping in time with his steps.

"Where do you want her?"

He was asking her like she owned the place. Like *she* were lord of the manor, not him. When had he grown so complacent? So obedient?

Maybe, she'd been focusing on the wrong power struggle all along. Maybe, instead of sowing doubt between Hektor and Ciro, she should've been focusing on the dynamic between the brothers and Drusilla all along

Drusilla stood up from where she lounged, and Lila immediately knew something was very, *very* wrong. She pulled at where Ciro held her, trying to remove his hand from her but his grip only tightened. She felt more of that singed skin and saw the mark she'd left on Ciro's hand had remained as well.

This was why she was being punished. Not because of Ambrose, not because of her pleasure last night, but because of *this*. Her powers. Her powers to hurt them and damage Drusilla's cause.

Ciro seemed to see the realization in Lila's eyes, and something *almost* akin to pity crossed his features in a flash. Almost.

"Outside, I think. The snow will add to her wounds wonderfully."

Wounds? Lila didn't have any wounds.

Not yet.

Hektor came up on her other side, grabbing her arm, and pulled her along with Ciro. He carried something in his free hand, but it was covered in a dark wrapping and he seemed to be hiding it behind his body.

"A little bug needs two vampires, the Reinick lords, to carry her?" Drusilla crossed her arms over her chest, pouted her red lips, and curved a blond eyebrow before walking before the three of them.

"Well, apparently she's got a burning touch. So, if she tried it again, one of us can be back up while the other gets burned," Hektor explained, almost more to himself than anyone else.

"Or she'll burn you both," Drusilla said flatly.

Lila didn't fight as they dragged her out of the Morada and across the snowy ground. It was already past the spring equinox, yet the snow fell heavily.

And as they rounded a corner, more than the snow sent shivers across Lila's skin.

Tons of vampires were outside, wearing thick coats and training. Many of those vampires were strigoi, fighting each other like animals in the wild, fighting over pieces of bones and flesh.

As they got closer to the crowds of vampires, Ciro pushed Lila to her knees and stopped behind her.

"Fellow vampires of the Viper Morada and the Reclus army," Drusilla called. "For months we have wondered what this *human* did to our allies, the strigoi morte, fighting with us at the Crow Court. For months we have watched and studied, but for months we came up empty. But that is no more. My assumptions were proven correct last night." Drusilla took a step closer to Lila, kicking snow into her face. "This *human* is the Sun Child. Our biggest threat. Yet, she is here—by fate—in our possession."

The Sun Child. Lila looked up at Drusilla, at Ciro . . . even at the other vampire. She'd heard that term before, but she thought it was just a reference to her powers, how sun-like her warmth had been. She knew she was descended from the original vampire's first wife. But why did it all sound so . . . official? So important?

Ciro stepped forward. "She marred my brother and me, and as lord of the house, I cannot let this go unpunished. But after—" he paused, his eyes meeting Lila's. "After, she is *ours*. Wholly and truly ours . . . to use and command as we please. She will no longer only be our pet. She will be our *weapon*."

Lila's eyes went wide. How—

Hektor lurched her back, dragging her in the snow.

"What are—" But the words struggled to come out. She fought and kicked and used her heat to singe his knuckles. But he didn't let go.

Hektor threw her down, knocking her into the ground just in front of a large wooden beam, before lifting each of her hands and binding them high above her with a rope so rough, it immediately irritated the flesh at the smalls of her wrists.

She bucked against them, pulling at them as hard as she could. Lila felt her skin break within seconds.

"Let me go!"

Her back was to the crowd and at the angle she was in, she could barely see Drusilla or the brothers.

She tried to focus her power on the ropes, saw the small coil of smoke as she began to burn through. Her hands shook, as panic started to overtake her.

Then, with a crack of lightning through the air, something slashed against Lila's back. She immediately felt her flesh rip open as she screamed. The heat was all new to her, as another crack broke against her back.

Whipped. She was being whipped and torn apart. Torn *open* in front of a number of blood-thirsty vampires. She screamed again, louder this time.

The moment she thought to call out for Ambrose, another whip cracked against her back.

Three.

Three raging marks. The pain was blinding—worse than that of the venom removal. And the snow dropping into her now-open wounds felt like knives being stabbed into her flesh. She sobbed, feeling snot and tears cover her face, as another whip crashed against her.

"Pl-please," she mumbled, but either they didn't hear her or they didn't care. Another whip slashed her back open.

"One more, bug," Drusilla cooed. Lila heard the tightening of leather around Drusilla's palm, and another crack split her in half.

Someone untied her from the post, Lila didn't see who. Her eyes were too filled with tears.

She felt so breakable. Like glass cracked on the floor.

All the development her body had endured—all her *mind* had endured. The *healing* when she was at the Crow Court, the growth and strength—it was all for nothing.

In the next moment, Lila was being dragged across the snow, and placed in front of a fire. The fire made the flayed skin on her back feel as though they were melting off of her, revealing only muscle and tissue.

Her eyes cleared just enough for her to see Hektor smiling at her. Smiling, and holding her stake. *Ambrose's* stake. He twirled it between his fingers and without so much as a word, threw it into the flames.

"No!" Lila lurched forward, throwing her fist into the fire. That weapon was the *only* thing that made Lila feel safe or strong. It was her only connection to Ambrose. It was what made her . . . what made her okay.

Someone was hauling her back by her ankles, her hand burning in the flames. But she didn't care, she kept trying to reach it, kept trying to grab it, but it was wood. It was already burning away. All of Ambrose's hard work from carving it to waxing it had just been destroyed.

A ragged cry tore through her as the vampires and strigoi of the court before her continued laughing and jeering, approaching with hunger shining in their eyes. Lila would have none of it.

"Don't worry, bug," Drusilla's voice cooed behind her, and Lila felt a wave of fog wrap around her mind.

"You'll soon forget all about Ambrose Draven," Ciro whispered as another kind of fog clouded her. They were both enthralling her. At the same time.

"Now, pet," Drusilla said.

Ciro finished, *"Submit."*

And as soon as the words left their lips, Hektor stepped

forward, the item he'd been carrying before in his hands. He tossed off the black sheet and below sat a golden collar. A collar meant for *her*.

"*Stay still, pet.*" She didn't even know who was speaking, but her body didn't move an inch as Hektor reached forward and put the collar around her neck.

Rage overtook all of Lila's thoughts. Rage, and the heat of the fire. *Fuck this*, Lila thought, breaking their attempt at a thrall.

She thrust her fist back blindly, knocking the collar from Hektor's hands, jumped up, and kicked him hard in the chest. The imprint of her foot left a gaping hole surrounded by black-singed edges on his shirt. "Touch me again and I'll melt your fucking face off next," she spat.

Hektor smirked but retreated a step back, and Ciro and Drusilla kept their distance as heat sang through Lila's bones. Lila felt her skin prickle, the hair on her arms stood on their ends and a thin layer of dew covered her flesh. An aura of heat surrounded her, radiated from her, and Lila watched as the snow all around melted instantly, leaving nothing but the muddy ground beneath her toes.

"What are you standing around for?" Drusilla called from behind her. "Get her!"

The crowd of vampires before her barely stirred, maybe a few stepped forward, but only the strigoi headed their mistress. They crawled through the mud, clicking and clacking their pronged jaws, but Lila wasn't afraid of them anymore. So, facing the crowd before her, Lila stepped forward to meet them.

"Fuck you," another step. "You do *not* own me," another step. Lila didn't stop, she neared the crowd, taking her power with her.

The heat grew, sizzling off of her—so hot, she could see

the haze warp the air around her. And by the time the first strigoi jumped at her, claws and fangs bared to kill, Lila did nothing but watch as its skin melted off its bones, as its clothes singed and burst in flames, as its eyes popped from its head and dripped down its charring white skin.

Pop.

The noise sickened her, but before her body could gag, another strigoi was melting—then another and another, and soon the vampires were in the mix, melting and burning and oozing to the muddy ground beneath her. She couldn't distinguish the melted skin from the melted snow, the oozing black blood from muddy dirt that squelched with each step.

With just a few steps, Lila had wiped out a chunk of the Viper Morada's nobility, a chunk of those wicked and loyal to the Lord of the manor—but with them, she had also killed strigoi.

Strigoi who were once people, vampire or not.

The realization immediately sent ice down to her very being. Dread filled her like a raging sea, threatening to break out. Innocent people. People who didn't want to be strigoi in the first place. What if . . . the strigoi had been murine? What if they'd been people from her town Drusilla had changed just the other night?

Lila couldn't breathe, her lungs wouldn't loosen, and her throat was too tight, like she'd swallowed a rock. Like a scream could burst through her, but it was lodged within.

She'd protected herself, but at what cost?

The bodies melding with mud splashed on her thighs, her arms, as Lila collapsed into herself.

Breathe, Little Mouse, she remembered Ambrose saying to her once. *Breathe.*

But she couldn't.

She'd killed people. She'd killed people who'd been like her.

The last thing Lila saw was the black ooze and brown mud coating her fingers as she fisted the ground, and Hektor's marred hands circling her throat. The last thing she felt was the cold bite of metal compressing her throat even more, as a silent yelp escaped her lips. The last thing she heard was the click of the lock.

And then, Lila was no more.

12

Ambrose woke up alone. He'd been waking up alone every evening since Lila left—save for his one or two days with Pollock. But waking up that evening was different. He had felt Lila there with him the day before. He had felt her in his mind, and he expected she'd be there when he awoke, and so when she wasn't, it felt like a whole new wave of despair crashed through him.

He just wanted her back, permanently. Ambrose felt the urge to chain her to the bed and never let her go more with each passing night. And with each passing moment, it seemed more and more likely Lila *had* actually bewitched him. He felt . . . obsessed. Sick, almost, with need.

His need felt so similar to those first few months as a vampire so many years ago. When bloodlust ran his mind rampant. Only now, his lust was a blurred line of hunger and love for Lila. Just to be in her presence was enough—he didn't even have to touch her—but if he could, he was afraid he would be like an animal. Lords, what he'd give to hear those sweet little moans and gasps she breathed when he *did* touch her.

As the moon grew brighter and dusk turned to night, Ambrose dragged himself through the motions. He washed up and threw on a loose, black shirt and black leather pants. He didn't bother equipping a blade and he rolled his sleeves to his elbows, walking barefoot on the plush rugs and cold stone engulfing the floors of the manor.

Everyone was already in the large dining room, ready for the usual morning breakfast meeting, but Ambrose barely heard any of them as they discussed the manor's welfare.

Blood had been distributed, and as some drank quietly, others seemed fidgety, restless. He took a sip of his own cup before him, the blood tasting stale on his tongue. Nothing like Lila's sweet flavor.

Fuck. This was bad. The hunger for her was growing.

Usually, breakfast was reserved for things of the manor, if anything needed repairs, shipments of the day to and from the towns of the Crow Court, and the like, but this evening was different.

"I have news," Kaz said, turning to him. "Would you like to discuss in private or shall I share with everyone?"

Ambrose put the gross blood back on the table and leaned back in his seat. Nodding, he said, "Go on. It's time everyone was up to date on matters."

"Very well, sir." Kaz stood, tucked in his seat, and walked around the table. "I had the crows scout our neighboring villages last night. All along the border of the Viper Morada, more and more strigoi attacks are occurring. It seems like, with the fall of the Crow Lord, the Reinicks and Reclus are growing braver with each passing night. They're coming more inland as the nights pass, and reports say attacks have begun along our southern coasts just as of last week. We can assume the north of the Crow Court is safe for now, but who knows for how much longer?"

Ambrose sat up. "Shall we start evacuating our people?"

Kaz nodded. "I believe it would be in our best interest. Since the strigoi venom infects vampires and humans alike, it may benefit to evacuate all our lands in the south. Lord Maronai has offered refuge for any civilians of the Crow Court as well."

Ambrose leaned his elbows against the table, rubbing at his chin. "All right. Send the southernmost communities north, toward Catacomb City. The capital should be able to foster everyone for the time being and there should be enough blood storage for the vampires to survive years without consumption of our human population. For our coastal cities, send everyone east of *Bonne Mère,* to Darius. They should be able to reach the Arachnid Estate territories rather quickly."

Kaz continued to pace, but nodded nonetheless. "There is more, Lord Draven."

Ambrose lifted his hand, indicating him to continue.

"It seems just within the last hour, there has been movement from our enemies. The Reinicks and Drusilla have left the Morada, with Miss Bran in tow."

Ambrose immediately stiffened.

"They seem to be heading toward the Maggot Mansion. With your permission, we think it would behoove us to inform Lord Nostro as soon as possible."

"Send word," Ambrose ordered. "How are they traveling?" Normally, to get from the Morada to the Mansion, land travel was expected—land travel *through* the Crow Court. And if they believe Ambrose to be dead...

"Straight through, sir. We thought they may choose to

voyage by sea, around the Crow Court, but with your supposed death, it seems they may be trying to terrorize our land. For all we know, they may even try to claim it." Kaz paused, fidgeting with the cuffs on his sleeves. "Our projection shows they'll travel just north of us, through Asterim."

Lila would be passing just by him. Did she still want him to sit by and do nothing?

Little Crow, he called.

When a moment passed and there was still no return, he tried again. *Lila, answer me.*

But nothing, yet again.

He cracked his knuckles. "Pollock," he called.

The bird came soaring down from the iron chandelier hanging in the room and perched on the back of the Crow Lord's seat.

"Find them, and keep an eye on Lila. But fly high and out of sight."

The bird squawked as he bobbed his head, and then soared from the room.

"What is your plan, sir?"

Ambrose drummed his fingers against the wood as all looked at him. Constance and Marcus sat silent the entire time, but at the mention of Lila, he caught them both stiffening. Kaz waited for orders, as did the vampires surrounding them at the table. Even Robin, his gardener, seemed ready to take his shovel and hoes to battle if the Crow Lord only asked.

Ambrose looked up, meeting Kaz's eyes. "What do you think would be the best course of action from here, Kaz?"

He straightened and smirked, his mustache twitching. "You know me, sir. I'm all for defending what is ours."

Ambrose smirked in turn. "That's why I asked you." He knew Kaz would express what Ambrose desired. And right now, that desire was to get those fuckers off his land and bring his woman home.

Once the room cleared, and everyone left to either their daily routines or their stations, Ambrose and Kaz moved to his study.

With a large map of the Crow Court between them, Kaz sat on the other side of the desk.

"It is just the siblings, Drusilla, about a dozen strigoi, and only five or so members of the Viper Morada. And, of course, Miss Bran."

And just like that, the *thought* of her brought warmth to his chest. Fuck, he was in trouble.

Kaz smirked.

"I'm afraid *I'm* unworthy of her," Ambrose admitted.

The man across from him scoffed. But it was the truth. The invisible bloodshed on his hands still made him feel . . . tainted. Lila was so good, so pure. And he was a monster, after all. And this sick desire he couldn't shake was only proving it more and more.

"Ever the self-loathing. How many actions will it take to undo those of when you didn't even know yourself? When will you forgive yourself?"

Now Ambrose shrugged.

"Master Draven, I've said it once, and I'll say it again. You have made our civilization what it is today. *You* are the reason it works. *You* are the reason Lila will have a safe place to come home to. The other manors—they don't believe in the murine because of *you*. Lord and Lady Reinick kept the treaties, but they tested the boundaries as much as they could. It isn't surprising Ciro broke it the moment he stole that power. *They* are at fault, not you. You are more than deserving of happiness, and I think Miss Bran is well enough equipped to decide if you are worthy of her affection or not, and she has already chosen." With a gruffled sigh, Kaz studied the map between them, tapping at small icons for towns and villages. "So stop wallowing and be proactive. What's your plan?" he asked, meeting Ambrose's eyes.

Without responding, Ambrose sat back in his chair, the plush velvet under him reminding him of a very different office encounter he had with Lila just a few months ago. He still had her white thong in the desk drawer.

He closed his eyes, and focused. In an instant, he felt every crow residing in the Crow Court. He felt them as if he *were* them. He saw through their eyes, he felt their flight. But none were the crow he needed.

Pollock.

Ambrose focused his mind on Lila's bird, focused on the desires of the bird.

Find Lila. Find friend.

There he was.

Ambrose's eyes went from seeing the black behind his closed lids to seeing a vast forest below him. *His* forest.

Pollock was soaring near the clouds, flapping his wings as he scanned the ground below him.

Find friend, save friend.

Ambrose felt Pollock's need and he reciprocated.

Lila, hear me. But there was still no response. The Concord was off—it was never *off*. There were times she couldn't respond, or if she'd be asleep, but the connection was *always* there. Now, it was just gone. It was almost as though it was blocked. Like, there had never been one in the first place. He couldn't feel her, couldn't reach her. Worry grew in the pit of his stomach.

Pollock spotted a shimmer of silver sparkle from the ground. The shimmer coalesced into a shape, and that shape became the carriage party carrying the Reinicks and Drusilla. The large carriage had its windows drawn, but around slithered a number of strigoi—just about a dozen. Some ran ahead while others continued to attempt to bite at the horses' legs.

Pollock's eyes focused further. All around were more people on horseback. Ambrose counted the courtiers of the Viper Morada, but then he—or rather, Pollock—saw his favorite color.

Lilac flashed before their eyes, and a weight immediately and simultaneously lifted and dropped. Ambrose couldn't tell what was his emotion and what was Pollock's, but he knew they both felt a mix of anger, fear, sorrow, and want.

Lila rode on a chestnut-colored horse, with Ciro behind her. His hand was wrapped precariously around her waist. Hektor rode next to them, chatting with his brother and eyeing Lila. But Pollock couldn't look anywhere else once his eyes landed on her. He flew just a little closer.

Keep your distance. We don't want them to spot you.

Begrudgingly, Pollock kept his altitude, but his eyes stayed locked to Lila.

He couldn't see much, just her hair. The angle blocked her face from his, but she seemed to be lolling back and forth, the only thing keeping her upright was the arm around her waist . . . unwelcome as it might be.

His heart was pounding—or maybe it was Pollock's—but there she was. Alive.

Lila, please. Yet still nothing. Maybe she'd been asleep, maybe she couldn't hear him in her dreams.

But it felt like more than that. And he *knew* she could. He'd invaded her dreams when they first made their bargain.

Stay on them, Ambrose ordered before coming back to himself. The feeling of falling rushed over him as he pulled his mind from the crow, and grounded himself back into the office in the Crow Court.

Ambrose opened his eyes, adjusting to the room around him. "It's exactly as you said. We have only a few hours, perhaps. Maybe less. You will take the kids and go to the Arachnid Estate—it's getting too dangerous for them here and Darius will protect you. I'll intercept the Reinicks, and I'll get Lila back. I'll bring her home."

13

Glimpses. That was all Lila felt for so long.

A brush of fur on her arm.

The bruising grip of a rough palm dragged down her thigh, nails biting.

A rush of wind through her hair.

A leathery touch of a wing against her fingers.

The salty taste of tears coating her lips. Cheeks wet.

A metallic smell of blood invading her senses.

A sharp sting of something piercing her neck, lips sucking at her skin.

The nothingness in her chest hollowing further. Emptiness was all she knew.

And then she would slip back into nothing.

14

The last time Ambrose had been here, in Asterim, he'd allowed the Reinicks to take Lila away, he'd pretended she was nothing more than their murine. Regret filled every fiber of his being at the memory, and he swore he would never allow that to happen again. He *would* be leaving here with her, but for now, he was alone, the town empty, as he awaited the Reinicks to drag his beloved through the familiar streets.

As Ambrose flapped his wings downward, pushing his monstrous self into the night sky above the town and onto the roof of the nearest building, the empty village sang with crickets.

He would face them all—Hektor, Drusilla, Ciro, the strigoi, the other ruthless vampires of the Viper Morada. He would fight them all for her. In silence, he crept closer to the town square, watching all around, waiting for that glimpse of lilac, that brush of warmth that caressed his skin, his soul, anytime she entered a room.

But at the first sight of the entourage of vampires, of that color he loved so dearly, all warmth had been sapped from the very air he breathed.

Lila's head lolled back, onto Ciro's shoulder, who only smiled and tightened his grip on her waist, and Ambrose completely lost his mind.

Just as emotion overtook him, he heard the faraway—or maybe it was near and urgent—sound of a scream of words.

But Ambrose didn't care.

The Crow Lord felt every fiber of his being grow taut, his hair stood on end, his vision tunneled, black surrounding everything—except for Lila. As his eyes focused on her, taking her in, the strange fabric she wore for a dress, the arm wrapped around her waist, Ambrose saw the love of his immortal life collared and chained by a golden metal wrapped around Ciro's fist.

His mind emptied of everything—everything but pure rage. His body moved. His wings tucked in and he dove from the rooftop toward Ciro and Lila. Toward his sunlight and the eclipse threatening to block it.

The moment he landed, he grabbed the face of the closest enemy—one of the Morada nobility—and tore his arms from their sockets as he saw Lila had cuts and bruises all along her body, under the sheer dress. It was a thin white material—so thin it revealed *everything*.

Furor surged forth at her exposure, and Ambrose dug his claws into flesh, and ripped the head off the flailing, screaming noble's body—his eyes never leaving Lila. He could see the inflamed scratches and bites, the red claw marks, from here, as the two pieces of cloth "covering" her breast met at the thick gold collar encompassing her neck.

His eyes focused, seeing Ciro's burned hand *too* close to

Lila's breasts. Ambrose dashed forward, pulling another noble off her horse, and slamming her to the ground as he moved closer to Ciro and Lila. Blood was smeared on Lila's ribs, just below her breast, and another under her collar bone. His hands dove into the noble's chest, pulled apart her ribs, and revealed her beating heart. He stabbed into it with a stake on his thigh.

After he took another step, six of the twelve strigoi jumped on his back. They forced his body down to the ground, tearing into the hard flesh of his back, and the leathery film of his wings. Claws ripped through them and Ambrose yelled, but didn't stop clawing his way to Lila.

Her legs were on full display as the pieces broke into four long panels, two on her front and two on her back, slit along the sides. Her thighs were covered in scratches, bites, and bruises, and her feet were bare and blistered.

Ambrose saw nothing but her. So just as soon as the strigoi appeared, they were gone. Ambrose threw them off, driving stakes into them, ripping heads off and hearts out. He could hear their cries, feel their blood coat his face, feel their flesh tear under his nails. But *nothing* would stop him from getting to Lila. The six strigoi were dead in less than a moment, and all the while, his eyes never strayed from Lila.

She had been dismounted, and was seated on the ground, her legs bent underneath her. Ciro stood to one side holding the thin golden chain attached to her collar as if she were their fucking pet.

"Take one more step, Draven, and you'll regret it," Ciro smirked.

Hektor dropped from his horse, the carriage behind him. Absently, Ambrose noticed the door swung wide open. Hektor stepped forward, with a smirk spread to reveal sharp fangs, beckoning Lila to him. Her head swayed and turned to him. "Come, pet." And then she *fucking crawled to him.*

Ambrose couldn't think beyond what he was seeing. The only words racing through his mind were her name, over and over again. *Lila Lila Lila Lila Lila Lila Lila.*

Small droplets of blood emerged on the skin of her knees from the hard ground below her. And her eyes—her sunshine eyes—were so cold and distant and just *gone* as they looked up at the fucking bastard above her. It froze Ambrose's heart.

She wasn't just enthralled. She was being controlled. Owned.

Ambrose couldn't breathe. He couldn't see anyone but her and the fuckers next to her. He couldn't hear anything over the race of his undead heart and the faint ringing in his ears. Even as the rest of the strigoi lunged at him.

Hektor placed a hand against Lila's cheek as she kneeled next to him, stroking her lips with his thumb. "Ah, such a good pet." Hektor flashed his fangs in another wicked grin. "Isn't she so much better on her knees, Draven?"

Ambrose lost his goddamn mind.

Before he could even process what he was doing, the Crow Lord lunged forward—three steps, four, five. He snapped necks and pulled apart bisected jaws with little more than a thought. He plunged his fist into the face of another strigoi, over and over till there was nothing left but brain matter on his knuckles and blood on the ground. He knew his actions wouldn't keep them down, but it would be long enough for him to get to Lila.

Ambrose was in front of Hektor in less than a heartbeat, his giant claws at the bastard's throat, as the six strigoi

The Sun Child

around them all fell, near death. Hektor didn't even have a second to react, his hand was halfway up to Ambrose's wrist, but it never made it. Ambrose dug his nails into the flesh of the bastard's neck, piercing skin and tissue and muscles and bone, until he had Hektor's trachea gripped in his fist.

And then he pulled.

Ambrose tore Hektor's throat open, ripping out his stupid fucking voice. It would heal over time, but he couldn't hear him speak more about Lila.

Faintly, he heard Ciro say, "Kill him," but his eyes didn't stray from the fucker before him. Hektor's eyes were so wide, they looked like they'd burst from their sockets, as he frantically gripped at his throat. Black blood sprayed all over Ambrose, but he didn't care at all. He grabbed both sides of Hektor's face, ready to pull it free from his neck, but something pinched on his tricep. Ambrose ignored it and just began pulling, stretching Hektor's skin as he wailed, but then Ambrose felt another blunt pinch around his bicep.

Finally, he looked down to see Lila biting down, holding onto his arm—nearly the size of her body—and barely bruising the hard skin below her teeth.

Ambrose let go of Hektor's head, grabbed her, and lunged back, using his broken wings to propel him farther. The moment he took a step away, Hektor covered his bleeding throat with both hands, and slumped down, bleeding all over the town square.

"Lila, love," he whispered, turning his gaze back to her, as she was still biting at his arm. There was no reaction. He patted her head, brushing her hair between his fingers. "What the *fuck* did you do to her, Reinick?"

Ciro took a singular step forward, his tousled hair, slim fit clothing, and trimmed beard exemplifying every ounce of self-important pretension the vampire clearly held for himself. All the while, his "pet" was shivering from the cold, shoeless, underwearless—basically nude for all intents and purposes—and he didn't even seem to notice, let alone care.

"She's gone. Lila was a *bad girl*, and she needed to be taught a lesson. She's been just a shell for us to enthrall as we please."

Ambrose clenched his fists, his nails biting into the meat of his palms. His entire body was taut, incredibly worked up and ready to explode, even as Lila still fought him, but he held her arms down. She was so fucking cold to the touch. Her lips were chapped and her fingers from where she slapped him and her toes from where she kicked him felt like tiny pieces of ice. She was freezing. It was as if all her warmth, all her sunshine, had been torn away from her and she was left to be as cold as them. As cold as an undead vampire.

As he studied her, Ambrose noticed the welded seam on the collar. The only way off would be to break it. "What. Did. You. Do?" His voice was like a thousand sharp icicles pointed right at Ciro.

But the bastard smiled. "Whatever we wished."

Ambrose flew. He couldn't keep anything straight, but he needed to kill him. He needed to rip his tongue from his mouth and his head from his body. He needed to burn Ciro's hands and rip his flesh off, inch by inch. Ambrose needed Ciro to be in pain, he needed Ciro to die, to cease existing. His hands buried into Ciro's chest before he could stop himself, before he realized he lunged with Lila.

He saw her crash to the ground as he lurched to a stop. But her expression didn't change. Like a doll being tossed around, she threw herself against Ambrose's legs again, clawing with all her little might to attack him, to stop him.

Ambrose pushed Ciro down, and stomped on his chest, holding him in place with the weight of his foot above him, as he lifted Lila up, her feet dangling from the ground.

"Hektor!" Ciro yelled. "Help me!" He tried to push Ambrose's foot from his chest, but to no avail. Hektor, meanwhile, only stared between the two of them. And after a pregnant pause, Hektor hissed out, "Sorry, brother," and ran into the woods, disappearing in less than a moment.

Lila still squirmed and slashed at Ambrose's face, cutting a line in his cheek, but he only brought her closer.

Lila Lila.

He couldn't take seeing her collared any more, knew it had something to do with her state. He opened his giant maw, as wide as it would go, and brought his lips to her throat, snapping his jaw against the gold around her neck.

Snap!

The noise cracked throughout the town center as the gold pieces fell from her throat. Being so close to her neck . . . it reminded him of when he'd been forced to chase her. Sent wild from bloodlust to hunt her down like an animal, biting into her neck with a ferocious need. Her blood coating his tongue, her skin under his lips. He felt the pull to do it again, to taste her again. He could almost feel the give of her flesh under his fangs, wishing the golden collar had been her beautiful, racing pulse.

He snapped his jaws shut at the realization of his thoughts. What the fuck was he doing? Ambrose slowly pulled away—everything felt slow.

His eyes were inches from hers when she seemed to finally come back to herself, the dull brown bursting like a ray of golden light as her gaze finally connected with his.

Her chapped lips trembled. "A—" she paused, trying again. "Am—"

Ambrose. The Concord burst open and he felt her there, through the link they shared, as though a curtain had been tossed open on a dark room, the sun beaming through the window to light the void. Warmth spread through his bones at her presence, even though she was still cold to the touch.

"Lila," he began, but his voice got caught in his throat. She was in his arms, she was back, she was safe. But he tightened his grip anyway, pulling her flush to him. She touched his chest, placed her palm over his heart, and studied him. But her lips were just trembling *so much*.

Tears dripped from her eyes. She lifted a finger to her cheek, touching the wet trail and analyzed it. For a moment, her eyebrows scrunched, but then her eyes grew wide, and in the next instant, the tears were pouring down her cheeks and a whimper escaped her lips.

"Lila, I—" he tried again, but she threw her arms around his neck and wailed. All of her cold limbs shook as she cried into his shoulder. Her chest felt like it was bursting with each short, haggard breath she took and it only broke Ambrose's heart further.

For the first time ever, Ambrose Draven was paralyzed. He didn't know what to do, what to say. His hands had their own ideas as they viciously squeezed her closer, and his usual silver tongue felt like lead.

He held her, but he couldn't do anything for her.

Then, a growl erupted from under his foot. And he remembered something he *could* do. His grip on Lila loosened and she wailed harder.

"Lila," Ambrose's voice changed, inside somewhere, he knew he didn't recognize this voice anymore. He hadn't heard it in nearly two hundred years.

She looked up at him, and the sunbeams in her eyes reflected pure gold, as her entire face reddened.

"Don't let me go," she mumbled. But he had to. In order to *do something*, he had to.

A brush of wind neared him. He saw auburn hair. "L-Lord Draven." Rebekkah. He'd give her to Rebekkah. "They kept me locked in the carriage. I got out as soon as we saw you. I defeated all the Viper nobility, but Drusilla—"

"I don't give a damn about her right now. Please, Rebekkah, take her." His voice was ice, it was steel. Distantly, he asked himself why was he giving Lila to someone else, another *Reinick*, when he finally got her back in his arms?

It was like Ambrose was trapped within himself, and a monster had taken over his body. The monster was in control now, and Ambrose could do nothing but watch.

And all the monster of Malvania could think was, *I'll fucking kill him for hurting her.*

15

Lila couldn't think, couldn't breathe, as she sobbed into Ambrose's shoulder. He was here, he was real, and he would keep her safe. She could feel each of her limbs trembling, and she couldn't tell if it was from the cold or from how afraid she was.

She couldn't remember a single thing. And that terrified her. What had they done to her while she was in the collar? What had they made her do?

What if... what if Hektor touched her? What if Ciro had?

Lila's cries grew ravenous. All she wanted to do was bury herself into Ambrose, into the man she loved.

But he wasn't holding her anymore, he was... looking past her, down at Ciro.

"Draven," Rebekkah said more sternly. Lila hadn't even registered that she was there until that moment. She was standing in her monstrous form, snarling at her brother as well. "You *need* to hear this. All of this was a diversion from my brothers. A fucking trap. Drusilla and an entire battalion of her strigoi are in your manor *right now*."

Lila's heart dropped.

The manor is in peril? she asked through the Concord.

She didn't really know if he'd reply, until she heard a gruff, *The entire population of Asterim is there* right now...

Lila gasped. If the humans were in the manor, they were probably all being changed into strigoi morte.

We have to—

"I. Don't. *Care*," Ambrose seethed, his eyes still on the prone Reinick below them. Ambrose's skin felt hot to the touch, but it wasn't the usual warmth Lila knew. This was different. And his voice. No longer was it dripping liquid gold. Now, it was pure ice. "Get Lila out of her, *now*," he said to Rebekkah.

Something wasn't right.

She pulled away from him to look into his face. But a small squeak escaped her lips as she did. Ambrose's jaw was clenched so tight, it looked like it might break. And his eyes... they were so, so incredibly bloody red. Though the same color as his usual rubies, it looked so different with the rage flaming behind them. His entire monstrous form was twisted in rage and it might just have been the scariest sight Lila had ever seen.

But she wasn't afraid of him.

She was worried.

"Ambrose," she said. Her voice was hoarse and cracked on the syllables, coming out in barely a whisper.

But it was enough. Ambrose's eyes fell to hers.

"Go with her, love." Though slightly softer, it was still a command.

She looked at Rebekkah, who shrugged and held her arm out for her.

"Get the *fuck* off me, Draven," Ciro grunted from under

them. "And you, *sister*," he said like a curse. "Fucking traitor! I am your *lord*. Get him off of me!"

Rebekkah ignored him as, in the same moment, Lila was practically thrown into her arms. Without so much as letting Lila get another word in, Rebekkah flapped her wings and they burst into the sky.

"Bek," Lila croaked. "I want to . . . I want to make sure he's okay."

Rebekkah glanced back at Ambrose, before meeting Lila's gaze. "Very well. But I must warn you, Mousey, I've never seen Ambrose like this, but I've only heard stories from my parents. I don't believe he is himself right now. Not in the way you know him. He's—"

"The monster of Malvania."

Rebekkah clenched her jaw, and Lila saw a rush of thoughts sweep across her expression before she stilled and nodded. She softly landed on the roof of a nearby building, but kept her arm around Lila's waist, ready to fly off with her at a moment's notice.

"I am not afraid of him, Bek. Any part of him. Nothing he can do will change that."

"Even when he chased you after being turned into a strigoi?"

Lila nodded. "Even then. I still love him."

Something in Rebekkah softened then.

As Lila turned her gaze downward, she saw Ambrose and Ciro fighting like animals in a den.

Ciro was already torn apart, his eye had been swollen shut and was trying desperately to heal itself, but Ambrose didn't give it the chance as he threw punch after punch. Ciro finally managed to dodge a singular blow and jumped back, just out of Ambrose's reach, and shifted into the giant horned viper Lila had seen only a handful of times. The black serpent slithered away so fast, but he clearly didn't realize his size would be a disadvantage.

Ambrose lifted both hands above his head and, with more force than Lila had ever seen, thrust them down into the snake's scales. Lila could practically hear the gush of thick flesh as Ambrose's claws dug into meat as he pulled Ciro back. Ambrose dragged him across the town square, every muscle rippling and straining from the weight. Ciro fought with all his strength, but it didn't seem to be enough, all he could do was snap his fangs at Ambrose, try to slither around him and constrict him. But Ambrose was having none of it.

He yanked Ciro toward a massive post in the dead center of town and with an incredible show of force, he lifted the tail end of Ciro up above the post, and pushed it down. The post broke through the viper, pinning him to that spot. Ciro hissed so loud, it sounded more like a sharp howl of wind hissing by a cracked doorway. He whipped around, and snapped his fangs at Ambrose, but Ambrose was faster and seemed to expect the attack. He threw his fists forward, catching the snake's jaws in each of his hands.

Lila grimaced at the sight, the raw anger and bloodlust in both of them, and she knew she was about to see Ambrose kill someone. It was different than watching him stop strigoi. This was . . . someone she *knew*. Someone she hated. And though she had always claimed she wanted him dead, in a strange twist of fate, he had been her only protection these months. It was jarring, to switch her view of him from relative safety to enemy. And, she also knew, whatever he knew happened to her while she wore the collar would die with him.

But it didn't matter, because Ambrose had made his own decision.

He spread Ciro's jaw down, his knee high enough to force the lower jaw under his foot, and then stomped down. With both hands now, he stretched his arms up as high as they would go, stretching Ciro's jaw uncomfortably wide, but not enough to break it.

Ciro looked like he was trying to force his jaw shut, trying to snap it on Ambrose.

Ambrose! Lila called through the Concord. *He's going to kill you!*

No, he will not.

The voice was cold, determined, and utterly confident.

His head turned around and his eyes shot up, gaze locking with hers even though they were so far.

He was the monster of Malvania. But he was *her* monster.

Ambrose looked back into the open maw of the viper before him.

"I told you, if you hurt her, I'd fucking kill you." Ciro thrashed in his grip, but Ambrose's hold was unrelenting. "Now—fucking die."

A burst of black erupted from Ambrose's chest, and a massive murder of crows dove into the mouth of the snake.

Ciro tried to shift back, arms would appear, then a few ringlets of brown hair, but if he fully shifted back, his jaw would split completely apart.

The crows dove into Ciro, and Lila could only imagine how gruesomely they were tearing him open from the inside out. A few burst from scales at his center, then more from his back.

The sound alone made Lila want to vomit, but she watched. She would not turn away, even as the flap of crow wings were nearly deafening. Rebekkah squeezed her side, but from the corner of her eyes, Lila saw that Bek wouldn't look away either. She'd watch her brother, corrupt Lord of the Viper Morada, die just as Lila would watch her tormentor die.

The snake flailed wildly as crows tried to fight their way out of him and Ambrose let go of his jaw. The moment Ambrose's grip was released, Ciro thrashed even wilder, slamming his own body into the ground so hard, it rumbled the buildings below Lila and Rebekkah.

And then he made a fatal mistake.

The viper thrashed upward, leaving his underside fully revealed—revealed and angled toward Ambrose.

Ambrose lurched forward, grabbing Ciro and slamming his fist into the right side of him. Blood gushed onto Ambrose's arm, but as he pulled it back out, Ciro immediately stilled.

There, in Ambrose's hand, was a black, gory heart, and it was still pumping. Ambrose tightened his grip on it, squishing it between his massive palm, but from the sheath on his lower back, he pulled out a plain wooden stake.

This was the moment Lila had been waiting for, yet her heart stopped completely. She wouldn't so much as take a breath, and her insides felt ready to implode. She didn't know how to feel. Happy this monster was finally being stopped, by the love of her life no less? Or was it concern for Ambrose, who didn't seem to be himself?

Lila didn't have any more time to consider her feelings as Ambrose drove the stake through Ciro Reinick's black heart.

16

Ambrose wasn't sure if it was his tunneled vision causing him to only see all black or the gush of vampire blood coating every inch of his face.

He had killed the lord of another vampire manor, Ciro Reinick. He had ripped his heart out and stabbed it with a wooden stake.

And he barely remembered doing any of it even though it'd just happened.

The giant snake slumped to the ground with a loud thud, the corpse before him was shriveling up before turning to something like ash. It made him want to vomit. It wasn't so much the act of killing Ciro that had him like this, but rather the fact that he was beyond his own control. Ambrose had tried so hard, and for two full centuries, he had kept the monster within him tamed. He kept his rage in check, holding back the vampire's fangs. But when he was like this, nothing mattered—not himself, not the people around him, no wounds hurt, and no damage caused was too much.

It was like being changed into the strigoi all over again. It was why he'd been so afraid of himself all those years ago, when human life was nothing more than substance to him, when he could lay waste to an entire city and not care in the slightest.

But he'd evolved since then, found his humanity once more, made the Crow Court, established actual peace between vampire and human. He was still a monster, yes, but a monster with more purpose than solely bloodshed.

Ambrose heard footfalls from behind him and swiftly turned. Cold, thin arms were thrown around his center and a small thing of a woman was holding him.

It wasn't till then that he realized she'd been calling his name through the Concord since the moment he pulled her tormentor's heart out.

"Lila?" Her name felt thick on his tongue. And suddenly, every morsel of his being wanted to run away and hide... from her. Ambrose had never wanted her to see that side of him, never to know what he was truly capable of. She'd seen, and felt, enough when he became a strigoi. And, sure, he did this to someone who'd hurt her... but now she knew exactly what he *could* do to someone. What he *could* do to her. What he *almost* did while being a strigoi. He clenched his fist at the memory plaguing his mind once more.

He wouldn't run from her, no matter how desperately he wanted to. If she looked at him any differently, he would just have to live with it. He could live with it.

And as he looked down at that perfect head of lilac hair, her face buried in his lower abdomen, he could see the emotions sweeping through her. Violent colors clashed all around her as she felt... she just felt *so much*. Fear, joy, sorrow, confusion, relief—it was all so overwhelming just seeing it, he couldn't imagine the turmoil going through her.

He wished he could rip the sorrow and the fear from her, wished he could take it on himself if it meant she'd be freed of it. Rage began to shake his body again, he felt it rise in his chest, the need for violence. It was *for* her. His nails dug into his palms, and thank lords for his rapid healing or his hands would have permanent crescent moon scars all along his flesh.

Maybe she was afraid of him.

He skipped saying her name, afraid he'd choke if he did. "Are you hurt?" His voice was so distant, so cold, and he didn't know where his usual easy cadence went.

Are you? She didn't look up. Was she refusing to meet his gaze?

"No," he said aloud.

She peeked up at him through those long lashes he loved so much, assessing his body, clearly seeing the scratches along his arms, the tears in his wings. And he could feel his heart melt as each second passed by, but still he wouldn't allow himself to embrace her. He was afraid to relax would mean to let go of the monster inside that would surely tear her apart. He didn't so much as pry his fist apart.

"Draven," Rebekkah called. "I'm sorry to interrupt, but decisions need to be made now if you have any hope of stopping that fucking hag and my brother from taking your land."

Ambrose didn't move, but he shot his gaze at Rebekkah, tucking away the monster of Malvania a little further with the welcomed distraction.

Just then, Ambrose dove into the eyes of a crow. He watched the manor. Strigoi were literally *climbing* his walls, tearing apart *his* people, and changing anyone they didn't kill. He hopped into another bird, seeing *his* dining room, as Drusilla sat in *his* seat, draining the blood of a woman on *his* table. Her smile was filled with red as she looked up and spotted the crow. A moment later, the link had been disconnected.

"Fuck," Ambrose cursed, seething.

He looked through more eyes, and more. His rooms had been destroyed, his office in chaos, the garden looked like it'd been stampeded, bodies—alive, dead, and undead—were everywhere. And each time, crows were being killed.

Get out, get out now! He told them. He felt the flaps of wings and the urgency as they swarmed from the manor.

Finally, Ambrose looked in Lila's old bedroom. And his heart stilled as his blood sang in a fire he'd never felt before.

With his throat still bloody and his face sweaty, Hektor scurried through Lila's room, through her drawers. Heaps of clothes were tossed around, her bed had been slashed open, and a pillow was lying precariously on the floor.

The crow Ambrose watched through seemed to be hiding within one of these piles of clothes. And Ambrose immediately knew it was Pollock. He watched the intruder, full of rage himself, readying himself to attack.

Pollock, no. Stay hidden until it is safe to fly away.

Ambrose felt Pollock's reluctancy.

Do it for Lila. She's here. She's safe. And she wants to see you safe.

Finally, he felt Pollock concede. But as Hektor pulled Lila's under garments from her drawers, he wished he could swap places with Pollock and rip every limb from the man's body as slowly as possible.

Pollock hopped out of the pile he was under, and flapped his wings as hard as possible to get away as Hektor buried his face in Lila's clothes, using the vampire's gross and distracted moment for his escape. As Pollock soared out of the room and past the manor, Ambrose saw a group of strigoi inbound to Asterim—toward them.

"The manor has been overrun. Strigoi are everywhere, and quickly approaching. We need to leave."

Fly to the Arachnid Estate. Watch over Constance, Kaz, and Marcus. I need your eyes, Pol. I'll get Lila out of here. I'll get her to safety, he told Pollock and then unlinked himself.

The feeling of falling rushed him, and as he returned to himself, he felt his arms had wrapped around Lila. She was watching him, concern filling her features.

But right now he needed to get her out of there. They could talk later. He turned to Rebekkah, "We need to leave, now. We're going to Nostro's."

She balked. "That's far. Wouldn't the Arachnid Estate be closer?"

"We've sent the kids to Darius with Kaz—"

"Marcus! Is he all right?" Lila asked, and he could see the fear in her eyes.

"He is. He and Constance are both fine. They miss you terribly." She sighed in relief. "But going to them now may be more dangerous for them if any strigoi were to follow. Plus," he looked down at Lila, who'd been watching him warily, and caressed the tattooed feather on her collarbone—the mark of a bargain, "I have business with the Lord of the Maggot Mansion, and if all goes according to plan, it may benefit us more to stay with Nostro, regroup, go to Darius's, and then come back."

"All right," Rebekkah swallowed hard. "But if strigoi are coming, our first priority should be to get out of here."

Without so much as a word, Ambrose went to scoop Lila into his arms, still finding her as cold as ice. But the moment his hand touched her back, she flinched and bit her lip. And that was when Ambrose *really*, finally looked at her. He didn't know how much more of this storm of rage and heartbreak he could take.

"You never answered my question . . ." he realized. She'd never said if she was hurt. And she was. How had she even been standing a moment ago? How had he not noticed?

Other than the bite marks he saw earlier in his blinded rage, other than the revealing piece of cloth she wore wrapped around her body, and other than the heavy collar they forced around her neck, making her their pet, Lila had so many other wounds.

Long slashes yet again ran down the length of her back. But unlike the angry tears the Reinicks gave her before she came to his manor, these were thin, deep, and almost precise. Ambrose recognized them immediately, for he had them often in his human life. These were lashing marks. They had whipped her. And based on the cuts and bruises on her wrists, they'd bound her to do so.

"Who did this to you?"

Her eyes shot up to his. "Ambrose—"

"Give me a name, Lila. Because if it was Ciro, I swear I'll bring him back just to kill him again. Who fucking hurt you?"

She flinched again and he knew his voice was still harsher than he meant it to be—but he was just so damn *angry*.

She shook her head, only slightly. "It wasn't Ciro. Drusilla whipped my back, and Hektor . . ." She slowly lifted her hand to her neck. "Hektor helped. Then . . ." she paused, began again. "They put the collar on me, and then—" her voice wobbled. "And then I don't remember anything. Not until you broke it off of me."

Ambrose didn't speak. He couldn't. His jaw was clenching so hard he thought his teeth would shatter. He was afraid of what he'd say, what he'd do, if he unclenched them.

"Ambrose . . . I-I don't . . . I don't remember *anything*. I don't know what they did to me while I wore that thing. I don't—I don't know." He saw the panic in her eyes, the fear growing and growing with each heartbeat. He wanted to hold her. To tell her everything would be all right.

But instead, he just stood there like an idiot.

Lila swallowed a lump in her throat and met his eyes again, her arms hugging herself. She was still shivering. But before Ambrose moved to warm her, she said, "I don't want to be in *this* anymore." She picked at the sheer fabric on her thigh.

"I'm sorry I didn't bring a spare outfit for you. If I had known—"

"It's fine."

Ambrose stood there awkwardly for a moment, and he glanced around Asterim's square for a clothing boutique. *I'll pay the owner back later*, he thought, as he smashed the wooden door open. He grabbed a bag and blindly stuffed as much as he could inside, shoes, underwear, dresses, pants, jackets. He grabbed a coat off a hanger and met Lila back outside, placing it gently around her shoulders. She carefully slipped her arms into it, and Ambrose helped button it up as her trembling fingers did one in the time he did three.

"Lila!" Rebekkah called from nearby. She had wandered off to give them a moment, but by the shrill cadence of her voice, Ambrose knew—something was coming.

"We should go. Once we clean your wounds, I have more you can change into. But we need to get out of here."

The Sun Child

Lila nodded and as Ambrose went to lift her again, she took a staggering step back.

"I can walk," she claimed. But as Ambrose looked down at her torn, bare feet, he raised an eyebrow.

"We don't have time, Lila. Not only can you barely stand on your own, your feet will thank you later." And without another word, he carefully lifted her into his arms. He wrapped one large arm around her, so she sat in the crook of his elbow, careful not to touch any part of her back.

She clutched onto him, averting her eyes anytime they wandered up.

Ambrose sensed the shock she was in, the shock that she was *here*, that everything just happened. But he also saw discomfort.

I make her uncomfortable, he thought briefly.

Though he should've, Ambrose didn't say another word as they flew from Asterim and into the lavender fields on the outskirts of town.

17

Lila hadn't felt truly cold in so long. In fact, she couldn't even remember the last time her body had this kind of reaction. And it was the start of spring, the snow should have all but disappeared, and the weather was warming more and more as each night passed. But the chill Lila felt was bone deep, and her limbs were shivering even as she wore the coat, Ambrose had given her, and as her body pressed against him. Even as she knew the temperature outside didn't match the tundra she felt in her skin.

She tried to conjure the familiar warmth within. Thinking of how she was finally safe and okay. Ambrose was hurt. Rebekkah was hurt. *She* was hurt. Healing them would help, especially if the strigoi caught up to them.

But not a lick of warmth came to her.

She felt . . . tainted. And she couldn't remember if it was because someone *had* tainted her, or if the collar just zapped away all her power.

The Sun Child

After a while of flying, Rebekkah and Ambrose landed in the thick of trees, keeping to the ground for coverage. It was nearing the early morning hours when the crows finally reported to Ambrose the strigoi had stopped following them, and a few hours later when they found a cave for them to rest during the day. And all throughout, as Ambrose held her, Lila felt further from herself than she ever had.

She didn't know how to act with Ambrose. Why was everything so damned awkward? Why was his embrace so distant, and his words so cold? Why was she cold?

Lila had a million questions running through her mind, but she felt like she couldn't voice any of them. Not as Ambrose seemed wound so tightly, like he'd burst if the wind blew too hard. He was still clenching his jaw and hadn't said a word to her since they left the field.

She had even tried speaking to him through the Concord, she felt the link between them established, but there was nothing. No response.

By then, the night was already beginning to lighten—shortly before dawn—and Rebekkah slunk into the deeper part of the cave, mentioning to Lila she needed to be alone. Needed to process the night's events.

It was late, Lila didn't think she could sleep if she wanted to. Not with her mind racing a mile a minute.

Finally in frustration, she turned to him. "Put me down."

Ambrose eased her down to the ground, and then stood straight. His hands were still clasped into tight fists, his veins protruding everywhere.

"What's wro—"

"I'm going to take a walk," Ambrose claimed. Then without another word, he turned and walked from the cave. Lila was left dumbfounded. And then anxiety set in, and she felt over exposed in the coat and dress she wore.

Lila had no idea what happened to her in the time she wore the Reinicks' collar, and Ambrose knew that. Was... was Ambrose thinking the same thing she was? She wondered if the same fear crossed his mind, and if it was true, how would he react?

Lila chased after him. The sun was maybe an hour or two away from rising, she needed to find him. She needed to know.

She swiftly followed behind him, and if he knew, he didn't let on. It almost seemed like he was beelining to a specific location, he walked as though he had a purpose. The trees around them were thick and tall, and Lila heard small critters in every direction. But as the muddy ground squished between her toes, Lila felt the chill of the night sap into her skin more and more.

She tried to focus on her memories, the brief glimpses of feeling whenever she gained the smallest semblance of consciousness while wearing the collar. Something that would definitively tell her she was wrong. But as she remembered the fingertips on her thigh, the brush against her arm, she truly could not remember. She hadn't even known how much time had passed.

Finally, Ambrose stopped in his tracks just before a flowing river. The moon illuminated off the water, making it shimmer a pearly blue.

"I needed a moment *alone*," he said, without turning.

His words were like a punch to the gut, but she stood straight and walked to him.

"And I needed a moment with you. You've barely even looked at me since you broke the collar off."

Ambrose grunted, though she wondered if it was really meant to be a sigh.

"It's because every time I do, I'm reminded of the pain

you've endured without me knowing. Every time I look at you, I see you crawling on your knees toward them with that blank expression in your eyes."

Lila flinched. "They did that . . . in front of you?" What would they have done then when Ambrose wasn't before them?

"Yes," he ground out.

Look at me, she said through the Concord, but again Ambrose ignored it. He didn't bother turning around.

"Why are you being like this?"

"Why did you follow me?" he rebutted.

"To talk to you! You've only looked at me like . . . like I'm *tainted*! Are you afraid Hektor touched me when I wore the collar?"

"Yes."

There was no hesitation in his voice, and it broke Lila's heart. If she weren't already so cold, she knew he would've just chilled her to the bone.

"So," she breathed, clenching her fists tightly, "you don't want me if I've been fucked by another?"

Ambrose turned so quickly, it sent her staggering back. His eyebrows were drawn together and his mouth hung open. "What?"

But Lila didn't repeat herself. He'd heard her.

"You really—" he paused, taking a breath. "You think I would—" Ambrose put his two giant, monstrous hands on her shoulders. "I will *never* stop wanting you, Lila Bran. *Nothing* will ever change that. What I'm furious about is the idea that Hektor may have *raped* you while you wore that fucking thing. That Ciro may have . . ."

Hearing the word cracked something inside of her. Lila stopped breathing. Fear threatened to close her throat, as she struggled to swallow. Hektor had grown impossibly more threatening. So much so that Rebekkah slipped Lila a tonic to prevent pregnancy when she first arrived back in the Morada.

As she cleaned Lila's bite mark of the day—at her thigh once again—Rebekkah gave Lila what seemed like a steaming cup of tea. "Drink."

When Lila did, the herbs within tasted beyond gross.

"It's unpleasant. But it'll keep you safe . . . from pregnancy for a year."

A very real weight pressed against Lila's chest, her stomach. The chance that someone would . . . that Hektor *would . . . Even Rebekkah saw how much more likely it was now that she was back in their clutches.*

"Thank you," she said as Rebekkah went back to cleaning the wound and Lila downed the rest of the cup in a single gulp.

Now, she wondered how much she needed that tonic without even remembering it.

"It kills me you can't remember, but if either of them did *anything*, I don't want you to remember. And maybe that's selfish but—" Ambrose cursed and Lila saw he was shaking just as much as she was, but she knew it wasn't from how cold he was. It was rage. "The fact that you watched me butcher Ciro alive, that you saw me when I couldn't control myself, that I've been holding the monster in since Asterim and I am too afraid to say or do anything that might let it out, including hold you. I want to rip apart the world right now, and I am *so fucking afraid* that rage will come out on you. Because I am *not* in control right now, Lila."

Lila gaped at him. "You think that would bother me?"

"I felt it. Your emotions. You were . . . so afraid. And after the attack on the Crow Court, after . . . hurting you . . . as a strigoi—I just can't—"

She stepped closer into him, but Ambrose stiffened still. Gently, she placed her hand on his chest. "Not of you, you big oaf. *Never* of you." Suddenly, Lila needed him. Needed him to *know* how much she loved him, regardless of what he was. She *needed* him to love her. "You're afraid to let the monster out? The monster I am so deeply, deeply in love with?" She took the smallest step back, and shrugged out of the coat, carefully throwing it onto the dry grass. Then she pressed herself against him. "Then do it. Let the monster take me."

Ambrose watched her for a moment, and then crashed to his knees. In his monstrous form, the top of his head was just below her chin, and his mouth was right at her breasts.

"I only want you, Ambrose. Monster and all. If you need to lose control, lose it on me. If you need to yell, yell for me. If you need to *kill*, kill for *me*. But know, even in death, all I will ever want is you." She held his face between her hands, making sure he understood each and every word she said.

He threw his arms around her middle and squeezed her so tightly, it was almost painful. At least he didn't have to clench his fists anymore.

"Lila," he whispered. And her name on his lips caused a tingle to course through her back. A tingle that turned warm. "I haven't been able to shift back. I can't . . . calm myself enough to focus."

His voice was like an admission. He'd been wound so tight, he could barely move without fear of exploding.

Lila leaned forward, pressing her breast to his lips. "Let go, then. Use me."

The ghost of his teeth hovered over her nipple and she felt an immediate slickness coat the apex of her thighs. Ambrose inhaled deeply before looking up at her through long lashes. The lost, hard expression had shifted to something hot with desire. Something ravenous.

And suddenly, every thought and fear and concern Lila had was gone. All she knew, right then and there, was that she wanted Ambrose to fuck her until everything in the Morada was out of her mind.

"I want you to rip this dress off of me, Ambrose. And I want you to make me yours, *now*."

Ambrose pressed his face against Lila's chest, running his hands over her curves, her sides. He flicked out his tongue, languidly running it over her nipple over the fabric.

"I—" he took a deep breath and aggressively grabbed her breast to the point of pain. She whimpered, but the sharpness of it all felt so damn good. In the same heartbeat, he pushed the dress off her shoulder. It fell to her arm, her entire breast revealed to the chilly night air, her peaked nipple exposed for Ambrose.

"I don't think I could be nice right now," he breathed, his words coming out in harsh grunts as his sole focus was on her revealed nipples.

Lila lifted a hand, and pushed the other strap of the dress from her shoulder, exposing herself further, as Ambrose cupped her breasts and kissed her. "I don't want you to be."

18

Ambrose tore the dress from Lila as soon as the words spilled from her lips. Good riddance. She'd have to make sure to destroy it later.

He reached a hand behind her neck, and pulled her to him, kissing her for the first time since seeing her again. And he wasted no time, dipping his tongue into her mouth and swirling it with hers, driving the hungry need that had been building inside of her. He drank her in, desperate, needy, and it fueled her to do the same. She bit his lips, sucked his tongue into her mouth, as warmth bubbled between her legs, as though she were boiling from the inside.

As they kissed, she felt his size shift, his lips and tongue and teeth fitting her mouth, and he rose to his feet, the leathery wings at his back disappeared. He'd shifted back into his human form.

But before she could throw her arms around him, he pulled her to the ground and flipped her onto her stomach. Ambrose's hand tightened on the back of her neck as he pushed her farther down into the mud and hiked her hips up with his free hand. He caressed her ass for a moment and then his fingers were at her entrance in less than a heartbeat as he had her fully displayed before him.

"Fuck. Look at you," he praised, rubbing her lips between his forefinger and thumb. "I've dreamt about this pussy every fucking night."

He slipped a finger inside of her and it was like a dam burst in her chest as a moan rocked through her body. She didn't know how badly she'd needed him all this time, but now her body was *fully* aware.

More. She needed more.

As if on cue, he slipped another finger inside of her and her hips rocked against them, forcing them deeper.

"So fucking needy, love."

"For you, yes," she moaned.

As Ambrose hovered over her, she felt soft kisses run down her back, where the lashes still burned. And as he pumped his hand into her, she felt the dichotomy of the gentle kisses and the rough finger fuck rock her to her core.

"I need you," she breathed, and Ambrose immediately pulled his fingers from her—leaving her missing the pressure—and straightened.

She tilted her head back to see him as he shimmied out of his pants, tossing them to where her coat lay. His hard cock immediately made Lila's mouth water and core drench. She was ready for him.

But as he caught her watching, he smirked, and slapped her ass so hard, it brought tears to her eyes.

Then he did it again.

"Ambrose!" she moaned.

"This is *mine* to smack. Mine to bite. Mine to fuck." He

bit her cheek then, and eased a finger slick from her pussy into her ass. It was tight and uncomfortable but the pressure had her near buckling. Then he pulled out again, and slapped her pussy. It nearly made her convulse as the sharp sting struck against her needy clit.

Fuck, fuck, fuck.

"Yours. All yours. Use me," she repeated. She wanted to be his, she wanted the monster of Malvania to fuck her till he came all over her, claiming every aspect of her being.

Ambrose pressed the head of his hard cock against her folds, sliding against her, up and down.

"It feels like you're splitting me in half," she breathed as another slow drag pulled his cock from her hole to her clit, where he paused.

"Grind your pussy on me. Show me how much you want this."

Lila wanted his cock inside of her so bad, she'd do anything. She grinded her hips back and forth against him, feeling every vein on her pulsing bud, she lingered on his head, driving herself into it.

"Fuck, you feel so good."

He pulled away from her, and then repositioned at her entrance.

The anticipation was nearly choking Lila. She couldn't wait to feel him, to have him, to—

"Are you sure you want me to do this?" he breathed, and it was so soft and strained, she knew he didn't actually want to ask her. He wanted to fuck her just as badly, and she was sure denying him now would kill him, as it would her. But *this* was why she loved him. And if he could only see what she saw, he'd know he wasn't a monster at all. No matter how much control he may lose, her safety and comfort still came first.

"I love you, Ambrose Draven. Now, let the monster out and fuck me till I can't stand straight."

He smirked against her ear. "Oh, love. I'll fuck you till you simply can't stand."

Ambrose plunged into her.

Lila screamed as he pushed his head into her, stretching her with each small thrust as she tensed around him, her inner walls felt like they were squeezing around him, fighting him to stay back. It was unlike anything she had felt, unlike filling herself with her fingers, his fingers, unlike grinding the stake.

"Fuck, you're huge," she gasped.

"You're taking me so well, love," he groaned out. "You're doing so good. Just relax, a little bit more, and I'll be able to fit inside." Lila took a deep breath as Ambrose circled her clit. Then he went just a little deeper, thrusting back and forth until she squeezed around him.

He chuckled as he grabbed her ass. "My Little Crow is so fucking needy. I love it. I love you." He pushed into her again. "And lords, you're so tight and hot. You feel so *fucking good* around my cock—and you've only taken the head."

He filled her so much more than she'd ever imagined. She had never felt anything this good, despite the sliver of pain, in her life.

Ambrose's praise had her rocking back against his cock, taking him a little deeper. He was thrusting slowly, mixing that fleeting pain into nothing but pleasure, when he met a sharp resistance. Slowly, he pushed past it, and Lila inhaled at the sharp pain.

Ambrose immediately paused, stiffening.

But she needed him to keep going, not to stop. "What—"

"You're a virgin." It wasn't a question. "Or, you were until just now."

Then . . . Hektor didn't rape her. A weight lifted and she released a breath from deep in her lungs that she'd been holding onto since the collar. It was hers to give.

It was *hers*. And she knew just what to do with it.

"It's-it's yours. Take it. Take *me*."

Ambrose didn't respond, instead, he pulled himself from her, leaving her feeling empty with need and desire. She wanted him to continue filling her up, to explore parts of her that had never been touched, wanted—

"Fuck, you're a *virgin*. For *me*." His voice was so hoarse and gravelly, it nearly sounded like it would break.

He lowered himself behind her, and pulled her hips back toward his face. Immediately his tongue dove inside of her and a violent moan escaped her. "Your blood—" he breathed. "You're bleeding for *me*." Ambrose pushed his tongue inside of her again, lapping at her pussy, fucking her with his tongue instead of his cock.

"Ah, Ambrose," she tried to speak, to tell him that if he continued that, she'd finish before he got to fuck her again. But her words stopped all together as his tongue drove into her.

She felt the orgasm building in her belly, felt herself dripping down her thighs, on his face, and she knew it was about to happen. She felt his nose press against her rear, and his face smothered between her legs as his hot breath added to the incredible warmth already excluding between her thighs.

But just as her body grew taut, ready to burst, every muscle in her body stiffening, Ambrose sat up again and crawled over her, pushed her hips down to the ground, straddled her thighs, and then drove himself into her to the hilt.

Lila screamed so loud, she was sure Rebekkah would

hear her, as he thrust into her, hard and fast. A moment of guilt flashed through her mind, but it felt too damn good to matter. She'd apologize to Bek later.

She'd given her virginity to Ambrose, the fullness so foreign to her, but *lords*, did she love every thrust, every twitch, every squeeze inside of her. His balls dragged on her upper thighs, and each thrust had him pushing into her ass cheeks. "Lords, you're so fucking perfect." Ambrose fucked her like her life depended on it. And right now, she thought it did. Her legs were squeezed together, and the new tightness of this position was pulling the breath from her lungs with each rock of his hips into her.

She pushed herself up onto her elbows, just as he wrapped a hand around her throat, angling her face back to lock eyes with him. "Eyes on me, darling."

Don't stop, she pleaded through the Concord as her eyes nearly threatened to roll in the back of her head as she looked up at him. *Please don't stop.*

Never.

His grip tightened around her neck just a bit and his gaze was unwavering. Ambrose watched her as he fucked into her so hard, Lila's vision almost doubled. She could feel him so deep in this position, and it felt so damn good as he aggressively dove into her with each and every thrust, quickening his pace like a savage animal. Too good. She didn't think she'd survive this orgasm. Her legs stiffened under him, toes straightening.

"Ambrose," she moaned.

His hand at her throat tightened, constricting her already limited breath. "Come for me, baby," he demanded, his eyes like shimmering rubies. His words were all the encouragement she needed.

She came all over his cock as it pumped into her, as she

screamed his name into the night with his hand tight around her neck.

Ambrose timed each of his thrusts to her waves of ecstasy, slowing only as the earth-shattering orgasm ebbed.

When she could finally breathe again, he eased out of her and slapped his still-hard cock onto her ass.

He grunted, "So. Fucking. Perfect."

19

Lila was fucking gorgeous. Perfect. Ethereal. And he wasn't done with her yet. Somehow, the position he fucked her in was both so animalistic yet so intimate as he watched her come undone by his cock, eyes locked together as he hovered over her, hand wrapped around her throat, her pulse. Seeing her eyes as she came for him would've sent him to another plane of existence if he weren't so obsessed with giving her everything she wanted.

She was so tight and hot, it wasn't like anything he'd imagined in his dirtiest fantasies. And he still wanted more.

As Ambrose eased back, he saw her dripping all over herself, her cunt sopping wet *for him*. He still tasted her virgin blood on his tongue and wanted more. She'd let *him* take her first, have her first, and he would cherish that honor. But feasting on Lila could wait, all he wanted to do now was fuck her again.

The monster wasn't satiated. Not yet.

He stood, his cock still painfully hard, and lifted *his* shaking woman into his arms carefully. He kissed her as he walked both of them into the river, kissed her as he cleaned the mud from her breasts, her cheek pushed into the dirt, the plane of her stomach. He kissed her as he dunked his hand into the water and rubbed between her thighs. He kissed her as soft whimpers escaped her lips each time he stroked her clit.

"Can you swim?" he asked, already guessing the answer.

"I don't think I can do anything right now, but definitely not that."

He chuckled and held her closer, her wet body warm against his. "There's still more I want to do to you," he whispered into her ear, and he loved the goose flesh that rose on her skin.

As Ambrose fucked her, he'd felt her warmth return in burst. He wasn't sure she'd noticed it yet but the cold water contrasted her warm skin so wonderfully and her shivering had stopped.

So, he kissed her again and then dunked both of them into the water.

Bubbles flew from Lila's lips before he stood upright again, both of them dripping messes now.

As Ambrose flipped his hair back and away from his face, Lila's hair lay flat against her eyes as she tried to push it back, pulling another chuckle from Ambrose. He dunked her again, dipping her head back and pulling her up with ease. Now her hair was all back and she wiggled in his arms, trying to splash him.

"Feels good, doesn't it?" he asked, raising an eyebrow.

She rolled her eyes before begrudgingly smiling and nodding.

"One day, I'll properly teach you how to swim. But tonight, I like you holding onto me too much to let go."

There was that blush he missed so much.

"Plus. I'm going to fuck you again, and I'd rather you not try to swim away from me."

Lila startled. "A-again?!"

"Over and over, if I can." He pulled her just a little down his body, poking her backside with his cock. Just to remind her he was still, very much, hard.

Ambrose wadded over to a massive rock, protruding from the river just enough to create a small seat as his thighs were half submerged in the water. He sat Lila on his lap, her back flush to his chest.

And then his hands started to wander.

"Lords, I love looking at you. I love touching you. And now I love fucking you. Though, that was never a question." He cupped her breasts, pawing them between his large hands. She leaned her head back against his shoulder, letting him do as he pleased.

Her pink nipples kept calling his attention, and he knew he wanted to toy with them. He'd missed them so much. He rubbed one between his fingers, before pulling at it hard.

"You know, there are toys for these," he breathed against her neck.

"Toys?"

"Little clamps," he said, squeezing and pulling both nipples simultaneously, "that latch to your nipples, and with a small chain, I can pull them as much as I please."

Lila whimpered as he pulled again.

"Doesn't that sound fun?" He licked the column of her neck.

"Mhm," Lila breathed, nodding vigorously. She was wet again, he could smell it—and he had barely even started.

"There are more toys too." His hand slowly traveled down the front of her, inching near her center again. "Clamps that grab onto this," he flicked her clit, sending her bucking back into him. "Small balls I can shove into your pussy"—he pushed a finger inside of her, cupping it to scoop against the spot that always drove her wild—"or your ass, if you're willing to try. There are even toys I can use while I fuck you." He returned to rubbing small circles around the needy bud. "How does that sound? Do you want to try?"

"I want to try it all with you."

He smiled. "Good girl."

She moaned at his words, once again bucking against him and humping his hand.

"I'll buy you all the toys when we're back in the manor. So you'll have to wait and be a good girl till then. Can you do that for me?"

Lila nodded and he could tell she was already beyond words.

"Good. Then I'll give you a present now instead."

Lila tried to turn around, but Ambrose stopped her. He removed his hand from between her thighs and grabbed her waist, lifting her above his cock, and then he plunged back into her to the hilt.

He almost erupted inside of her as he pulled her down, sheathing his cock completely in her incredibly tight pussy. She screamed as her walls clamped around him and it was like music to his ears. She was so fucking wet already, as he hit a new spot that felt so damn good.

"Do you like that, Lila? Do you like when I fuck you?"

"Lords, I love it. I love it, I love it, I love it." She had nothing to hold onto but his thighs and she dug her nails into them.

He only pulled her down harder.

"Ah!"

Ambrose pushed into her, dropping one hand from her waist, back to her clit, where he rubbed her harder.

"Ride me, Little Crow, ride me like the good girl you are."

Lila looked like she was about to lose it, but Ambrose couldn't stop himself. Not when she felt this good taking him, not when she felt this wonderful around his cock. She lifted her ass and moved her hips, riding him as he'd demanded.

"*Fuck,*" he breathed.

He felt like he'd explode from just the thought of all this happening, of him thrusting himself into her hot pussy. Of her riding his cock as though she'd been starved for it. But just as he nearly came, he stopped thrusting and focused on his fingers circling her clit.

He wasn't worthy of finishing. Not yet.

"Lila, love," he breathed against her neck, pressing his fingers firmly against the sensitive bud, before picking up his speed on those small circles she liked so much. "Moan for me."

Lila did, she moaned his name, she moaned "yes" over and over. He slipped the hand at her waist up her body, cupping her breasts, squeezing her throat, and slipping his two middle fingers between her lips. She sucked them into her mouth, whimpering around them as she wrapped her tongue around each digit.

I feel so full, she rasped through the Concord, and he licked her neck as his fingers squeezed her clit before massaging it again. Then he felt her body tighten, her back arch against him, just as a new wave of liquid heat burst around his cock again.

Lila slumped against him, but Ambrose wasn't done.

The Sun Child

The wet, hot rush made him nearly burst, but he still wasn't worthy. He picked up the pace once more, gripped her hips with both hands, thrusting into her with everything he had. Hard, fast, and even deeper than before.

He hadn't given her anytime to come down from her orgasm, and immediately began building the next. Lila was moaning and whimpering and screaming but it *still* wasn't enough. He wanted to give her *everything*.

He threw his arms around her waist, just under her breasts, and squeezed him to her, fucking her with everything he had.

"Ah! I—I'm—" But her words failed her as she bit out another moan. *I'm going to come again!* she gasped through the Concord.

I love you, I love you, I love you. He pushed all his love to her through the Concord, and he felt it all reciprocated right back.

Ambrose, I want you to come inside me.

His chest fluttered in time with her inner walls, and his cock flinched. Fuck, it was all he wanted to too. But his conscience was getting the better of him. *But, what about—*

I've taken a tonic. I'm safe for a year. Do it, please!

Ambrose had every intention of meeting her demands. Her wish was his command. But not yet.

He bounced her up and down his cock, forcing her to take each and every inch of him.

"Come for me first."

"Together," Lila demanded.

Together, then.

Ambrose would burst at any second. She was just so tight around him, he felt like he would completely lose himself the moment he finished.

She bounced her ass against him, moving in sync as her slickness overtook them both.

They were both at the edge as Ambrose thrust into her as hard as he could, pulling her down at the same moment.

In tandem, they both yelled, and Ambrose felt himself explode into Lila as she burst around him. Their juices mixed and dripped down his length and between their thighs as they both took ragged breaths.

Lila slumped against him, and he rested his forehead against her shoulder.

Neither were able to speak and their entire bodies vibrated with everything they'd just done as they sat there till the sun was threatening to rise.

"Lila, are you—are you okay?" He struggled to catch his breath. He hadn't come that hard. Ever.

She weakly nodded. "Better than okay. Perfect." She smiled up at him. "But really, really sore. I think you accomplished your goal—I don't think I can walk."

Ambrose huffed a laugh and as he pulled out of her, they both moaned a final time. He ran his hand in the water, and drizzled it onto her thighs, her core, cleaning what he could. She spasmed each time, and each time it made him want to do it all over again.

Ambrose carried Lila to the shore, and after the two had cleaned themselves off, he held her in his arms, watching her.

"Is the monster satiated?" she asked.

Lords. He would never have enough of her. But he was sure if he did fuck her again, he'd continue for days and they'd never make it to the Maggot Mansion.

"For now, love." Ambrose kissed her forehead, and helped her dry her hair before helping her into the coat.

Once he was in pants and boots again, he lifted the sheer fabric that'd been thrown to the floor. As he looked at it, held it, he felt every vile emotion rising in him again. What they'd done to her, what they *could* have done to her.

The sheer embarrassment she faced while being forced to wear this for them. If looks could kill, his gaze would've incinerated it right there.

Lila eyed it, clearly appalled. She walked up to him, grabbing the cloth from his hands, and met his eyes.

"They do not own me," she mumbled, just as she ripped it in half, turned around, and threw it in the river.

Immediately, the rage dissipated. Ambrose wrapped his arm around her waist as they watched it flow downstream and out of sight.

"They never did, Little Crow. They never did."

20

Lila had so much to tell him. As they walked—well, Lila limped after the seventh time Ambrose offered to carry her—back to the small cave, she went into detail of everything that occurred between her and Rebekkah at the Viper Morada, leaving out the most gruesome of details about Hektor and the night of the revel, the night they took her to her home. She had just gotten him back, and was too afraid to lose him again to anger so soon.

But she did tell him of her powers—of the healing warmth and the burning heat.

"The heat leaves scars on vampires?"

"Did you notice the burns on Hektor's face and hands? Or the one on Ciro's palm?"

Ambrose looked blankly at her for a moment. "To be honest, love, I didn't notice anything *but* you." Then his eyebrows came close together for a moment, a tick in his jaw pronounced. He gritted out, "I do remember Ciro's hand, now."

The cave was dim, and Rebekkah seemed asleep already, so Ambrose continued the conversation through their Concord link. *We'll need to continue your training. You've grown weak,* he smirked. *There's no way you can take me now.*

Lila raised an eyebrow and smirked. *I think I just did take you—all of you. And it was a lot, but I believe I handled it just fine.*

Your present walking skills say otherwise.

Lila blushed, feeling a trickle of heat in her belly as they padded through the cave. The soreness between her thighs was unlike anything she'd ever experienced. Unlike having sore arms or legs from her training, this felt . . . powerful. Good. She remembered feeling slightly sore after he finger fucked her in the Arachnid Estate, but this was so much . . . *more.*

Yet, despite it, she already wanted him again. And again. And again.

Calm down, Little Crow.

He pulled her aside, to a small alcove, far enough away to continue speaking. Rebekkah's back was to them, at the far end of the darkness, asleep, and Lila made the mental note to speak to her in the evening when they awoke—to make sure she was okay with joining them to the Maggot Mansion. To make sure she was okay after watching her brother get murdered.

Just before Lila readied herself to lie on the ground, Ambrose shifted into the monstrous form and laid down first. He splayed his wing out on the ground, and indicated for her to lay on top of it beside him. But she wanted to be closer.

Lila crawled on top of him, her belly resting against his. Ambrose watched her with those ruby eyes, a twinkle of mischief glimmering as he quirked his eyebrow.

"All right, then," he smirked, and wrapped his arms around her waist, followed by his large wings. It was like being tucked into a warm blanket.

The things I would do to you if we were alone, he said, and she felt his cock harden below her.

You can already go again?

Darling, for you, I am unstoppable.

Lila snickered before laying her cheek against the tattoo on his chest.

"You're warm again," he said in a voice so low, it could've been a whisper.

Lila hadn't realized it, but he was right. She'd been warm since they made love. At some point, her shivers from the cold had turned into shivers of ecstasy, and the chill never quite returned.

"I hadn't felt so cold in so long . . ."

"I suspect that collar was the cause. It muted your power, your thoughts . . . it muted *you.*" Ambrose's arms tightened around her as he bit out the words.

Lila placed her palm over his heart. "It's okay. I'm here now, with you."

He inhaled sharply, then slowly released, bobbing Lila up and down on top of him. "You're right. I just—Thinking of you in that collar, that dress . . . it makes me want to—"

"Punch something? Me too."

Ambrose shrugged. "I was going to say rip their throats out with my teeth. But punching something works too."

"When did you become so violent?" Lila scoffed, knowing fully well he'd been violent long before he pushed her out of a window after making a bargain with her.

He chucked his forefinger under her chin. "Darling, I'm the monster of Malvania. I'm always violent."

As Lila smiled, he cupped her cheek, then tucked those

lilac strands behind her ear. "Speaking of, I seem to remember *you* are rather violent too, love. I know you were still training at the Morada. What happened to your stake?"

Lila gulped, leaning into his palm. "When they—" she swallowed hard at the memories. "When they whipped me, just before putting the collar on, they threw it into a fire and made me watch as it burned." She felt tears sting her eyes but fought to hold them back. It was silly to cry over it, but Lila felt like it was more than just another piece of wood, more than just a weapon. It *meant* something to her. Many somethings. Her trust in Ambrose, her trust in herself, her ability to fight back—and they stole that from her, made her watch as they destroyed the symbol of her power.

Ambrose caressed her cheek. "You are so much more than a wooden stake, and you know it. If it's about the fact it was mine, *you* are mine as well, and I'd much rather it burn than you."

"It's also that you made it. That it made me stronger—"

"It did no such thing. You were already strong without it, and stronger now again after it. Your power—the power not connected to warmth and the sun—it didn't come from the wood, it comes from you. Your resilience, your heart, your stubbornness. And now, love, based on what you've told me of these new abilities of yours, I believe *you* can be the weapon." He paused, cupping her cheek once more and guiding her to look at him. His void-like eyes bore into hers, breaking through every wall she'd created these last three months in a heartbeat. "If your heart mourns for something I've made, I will make it again and again and again, until my hands fail to make any more. If your heart mourns for something because it was mine, you already have all of me, body, heart, and soul. I am yours — and I'd like to believe I can do much more for you than a piece of wood. My greatest possession from now until the rest of my days is already yours, resting in your chest." He placed his hand atop hers, over his chest. "And if your heart mourns the loss of your strength — you are the strongest person I have *ever* met, Little Crow. Stronger than you could even believe."

Tears welling in her eyes, Lila snuggled her face into his chest. "I love you, Ambrose."

"And I love you, darling. But," he chucked her chin up once more to look at him, "I need you to know I am not saying these things *because* I love you. These are all facts I would believe if you were mine or not. Do you understand me?"

Lila nodded. *I really wish we were alone right now . . .*

He tucked her against him, raising his wings so they rested against her shoulders. *Oh yeah? What would you do to me if we were?*

From the moment I saw you like this, I knew you'd be a challenge I wanted to conquer.

You think you can handle me, darling? You could barely handle my human cock inside of you.

He was right, the amount he stretched her was just on the edge of too much, she wasn't sure if it would be anatomically possible to fit *that* inside of her. But she wouldn't let him know that.

I can always try. She shook her hips just enough to rile him up, to feel him pressed between her thighs. *And if all else fails, I can use you as I used that stake and grind against your cock till* you're *seeing stars.*

Lords, what a filthy mouth on you. Who taught you such a thing? She could hear his chuckle in her mind, and it sent that familiar wave of heat to her core.

A vampire with a silver tongue and voice like liquid gold who says the naughtiest things imaginable.

Well, he said, *I'll have to thank that vampire for teaching you to be so vulgar. Now, before poor Rebekkah is awakened by your lustful need for me, we both need to sleep. It's been such a long night, and for you even longer. We need our strength tomorrow.*

Are we walking the rest of the way to the Maggot Mansion?

It all depends on how quickly the strigoi army has spread before we awake at dusk. If they're on a tail again, yes. We'll stay below the trees—better coverage that way. If they're not, then we'll fly. It would save a lot of time.

Lila looked around the cave. The sunlight was slipping through, but they were far back enough to remain in the shade.

A prickle rose at the base of Lila's spine. What if the strigoi rallied and came once more? What if Hektor or Drusilla came to steal her again? What if—

"Lila," Ambrose called, "You're safe with me. *Here* with me. Nothing will harm you while you're with me. I won't allow it. Tonight, I will remove the venom from your body and heal your wounds. But now, you need to sleep."

"Promise you'll stay with me?"

He gently scratched her scalp with his long nails, soothing her, as he wrapped his arm around her waist once more. "Lila, I'm never letting you go again. Ever."

21

Before the sun was even setting, Ambrose eased Lila awake. She slept through the day, dreamless and unmoving and purely, utterly, exhausted. As she saw the rays of light poking at her vision, Lila knew it was a rest she definitely needed, as Ambrose had said. She'd felt as tired as when she first escaped the Viper Morada, when Ambrose whisked her away, saving her from Hektor.

Only, replace the comfortable and massive bed with the comfortable and massive monster below her.

"It's time to wake up, love," Ambrose cooed.

As Lila looked around, she noticed Rebekkah remained asleep, and the sun was just falling behind the horizon line. "Why? Rebekkah isn't up yet," Lila huffed as she pushed herself up, straddling him.

"Rebekkah doesn't have to get venom removed and train to compensate for the three months she's been inactive." Lila pouted, but Ambrose simply smirked, lifting Lila up with him as he stood. "Plus, I want to see this new power of yours."

She laced up some of the stolen boots Ambrose had gotten for her in Asterim, and followed him out of the cave, deciding she would properly dress in the clothes he'd pillaged once they were done with their training and continued to wear the coat from last night. They rounded the mouth of the cave, and instead of heading straight past the trees toward the flowing river once again, Ambrose made a hard turn, following the outer wall of the cave. He stopped them in a spot where the trees made a small circle for them to stand, and the tall wall of the cave—which looked more like a small hill from here—was at Lila's back.

"All right, love. You know how this works. It'll hurt, but we need to do it."

Lila nodded, already eager to get the rest of the Viper venom out of her. "I don't know which bites are which, or which their last ones were."

Ambrose took a small step back and studied her.

"I assume the one here," Lila pointed at her inner thigh, "was Hektor."

Ambrose's eyes flared red. "That fucker." He took a deep breath, closing his eyes. "Okay, fine. And Ciro?"

Lila couldn't remember. "I'm not sure."

Scratching the back of his neck, Ambrose took a step forward, studying her body. "Are there any hidden by the coat?"

"My arms," she said, rolling the sleeves up.

Ambrose studied her neck, her chest, and then his gaze drifted to her wrist, where she had a mark. He gingerly lifted it closer to him.

"This one, I think. It looks fresher than the rest." He turned it back and forth, and the red, inflamed puff of the wound with the small spots of dried blood proved he was right. "Are you ready?"

Lila bit her lip and nodded. She would never be ready to voluntarily give herself to this kind of pain. But it was this, or keep their venom inside of her. "I'm ready."

Ambrose cupped her wrist in his hands, one supporting the back of her palm, while the other rested gently—comfortingly—over the wound.

And then the fire tore through her. She knew what to expect, but it never quite made it easier. She felt her knees buckle right as the last of the fiery thorns ripped from her veins, exploding from the skin at her wrists. Ambrose caught her as she swayed, keeping her upright.

"All right?" he asked, eyeing her.

Lila nodded, too weak to speak, as sweat pooled on her forehead from the short moment of pain.

Taking her wrist, Ambrose carefully examined the wound on her arm. "You said you'd been practicing with your warmth more and more, correct? And discovered it could heal when prompted?"

Lila raised an eyebrow and then nodded.

"I want to see it. Heal your wrist."

With the aftereffects of pain still raking her body, Lila was finding it difficult to concentrate on love or any emotion near it. She tried to focus her attention on her wrist, but the more she did, the more she felt the pain still radiating from the throbbing wound.

"It's hard when I'm in pain or upset," she explained, remembering the night in her village. "It's hard to *force* feelings of love and joy, when other feelings are dominating."

"Don't I know it," Ambrose huffed under his breath. "Unfortunately, love, we don't have the ointment that can heal your wounds, and out here, getting an infection on the slash marks on your back would be too easy. You need to heal yourself. Now."

He watched her for a moment, and Lila saw something cross his eyes. Something . . . mischievous.

"I've an idea . . ." Ambrose pulled Lila into him carefully, his hand at the lowest part of her hips. He leaned down, his long hair tickling her neck, her shoulder. Whispering in her ear, he said, "I'll bring love and joy to you."

With swift hands, Ambrose unbuttoned the coat Lila wore, and pulled it from her shoulders, leaving her nude in the open yet again.

Immediate heat welled in Lila's core, as Ambrose's hands trailed her body. They caressed down her shoulders, over her hips, and then up her thighs. In a swift move, Ambrose's hands were cupping her ass, lifting her. She instinctively wrapped her legs around his waist, her core pressed against his hardening length. He eased her against the rockface behind her, careful not to press any of her wounds into the cool surface.

"What are you—"

Ambrose brought his lips to Lila's neck, softly kissing the sensitive skin there, before trailing up to the spot she loved behind her ear. As his tongue slipped from his lips, his hand slipped to the bite mark on her thigh. Just as pain erupted through her yet again, Ambrose took her mouth and devoured her scream. His tongue was hot on hers, demanding, needy, desperate. He sucked her tongue, taking it into his own mouth before playfully biting at her bottom lip.

But still the pain tore through her and all she could do to escape it was kiss him. Lila threw her arms around his neck, pulling closer.

She groaned into his mouth, "Ambrose," and then the groan turned into a scream, "show me my sunlight."

Lila held on, as Ambrose slipped his free hand between them, unbuckling his pants swiftly, pulling his cock free.

He wasted no time as he pushed his bulging head between her wet folds.

The hand at her thigh tightened as another wave of pain hit her. Every nerve ending was electrified and it felt like a thick worm was trailing under her skin, inside her veins, moving throughout her body toward the bite on her thigh.

But just as the pain seemed like too much, Ambrose plunged into her.

She screamed his name as he groaned into her mouth. She was still so sore from their night before, but it felt so damned good. Lila took him to the hilt, squeezing so tightly around him, as she felt every inch of him conquer her. With his hand gripping her ass, Ambrose slowly pulled all the way out, and drove back into her again.

Lila moaned so loud, she was sure Rebekkah would hear. But right now, she didn't care. He thrust into her, again and again, as the venom wormed through her toward the wound.

"Focus on me, love," Ambrose grunted as a whimper escaped Lila's lips. "Focus on my cock inside of you. Focus on how well you take me, how fucking tight you are for me." He bounced her on his length, and each thrust felt like he was plunging deeper and deeper inside of her. Her walls fluttered around him, feeling *everything*.

"You're so fucking hot, Lila," Ambrose groaned. And Lila felt it then too. Her body radiated heat, and the pain on her arms, legs, and back were slowly ebbing, as was the pain from the venom.

Ambrose pulled his hand up, high enough for Lila to see the sickly green ooze coalescing in his palm. Hektor's venom made her sick to her stomach, and made her violence surge. She stared into Ambrose's ruby eyes, shining

THE SUN CHILD

so bright with lust and passion, and power. She imagined Hektor could *feel* them ridding her body of his venom as she healed and fucked her monster. Her eyes blazed back up at Ambrose, and she met each of his powerful thrusts with her own, riding his cock.

He smirked, "That might be my new favorite expression, right after seeing your face when you come for me." He thrust deep again, and then he took his palm with the venom in it, and smashed it against the rock wall next to Lila's head.

As he wiped his hand on the rocks, Lila smiled, knowing all that was left of Hektor was destroyed, nothing more than a stain on dirt. Fitting, to be filthier than the dirt she walked on.

She used her need for violence on his body. She rocked her hips in time with his thrusts, meeting each and every one with just as much force, love, and emotion he showed her. The heat spread along her skin, healing all signs of small wounds Ambrose had from his battle with Ciro, and every mark and slash on her own body—all save for the two tattoos she had from her bargains with Ambrose. "You love to see my face when I come? Then do it, Crow Lord, make me come for you."

Ambrose groaned. "Fuck, I love when you tell me what to do. Ride my cock, darling." He thrust into her over and over, her breasts bouncing against his chest as he fucked her against the wall.

She felt the orgasm building and building, ready to explode. Her toes curled and her entire body went taut.

"Come for me, baby."

And with another thrust, she became liquid as she moaned her release. She felt herself come all around Ambrose's cock, and it made everything feel even hotter.

Ambrose thrust into her, feeling her cum slide down his length, and in a matter of seconds, he erupted inside of her, filling her till their orgasms were fused together, dripping from her core down her thighs.

The two remained embraced for a moment, breathing each other in. All they could hear were their heavy breaths and the birds and crickets singing their evening songs as their sweaty chests pressed against one another, heart to heart.

Ambrose ran his hand up and down Lila's spine, soothing her as he eased out of her. Lila twitched from the remaining sensations, but slumped into him. "And just like that, love, you're fully healed."

Lila eased up, looking down at herself. She felt all the wounds close, but there wasn't even so much as a scar on her.

"We need to practice it more. While I'm not opposed to making love to you every time you need to use your powers, I feel it might be a bit cumbersome. Especially if we were in the middle of a battlefield."

"Are you kidding me?" Lila scoffed. "That sounds like the best time to make love. Think of all the lives we'd save by having sex on an open, dangerous, death-infused field."

Ambrose chuckled and rolled his eyes. "Are you saying fucking me is lifesaving?"

"I'm saying, fucking *me* is lifesaving."

For the first time since they'd reunited, Ambrose let out a loud laugh—a *real* laugh—and it filled Lila's heart so much, she felt warmth course through her all over again.

After washing off in the river from the night before, Lila and Ambrose returned to the cave. She finally exchanged the coat for proper clothes, a simple green dress perfect for spring, and fresh undergarments. She missed the feeling of normal clothes, of not feeling exposed at all times.

The moon was fully in the sky, and Rebekkah sat, brushing her fingers through her hair. The black dress she wore from the Morada was torn, and Lila took the bag of clothing toward her, leaving Ambrose at the edge of the cave as he watched through the eyes of his crows.

Before even looking up, the vampire cooed, "Hello, Mousey."

"How are you?" Lila kneeled down, resting on the backs of her heels as her knees were pulled to her chest. With Rebekkah still resting against the cave wall, the two were at eye level.

Rebekkah shrugged. "It's bittersweet, my situation. My enemies have become my allies and my allies have become my enemies. My own brother was murdered yesterday by a man I have always thought was our biggest adversary—and here I am, traveling with him and conversing with his lover."

Lila mimicked her shrug. "And that same brother had you tied and gagged in a carriage yesterday to act as a decoy for him to wage war on another vampire lord who ended up saving you."

Rebekkah sighed. "My point exactly. Everything feels...so turned around. I'm not sure if I just haven't started grieving but...I don't even feel sorry for Ciro's demise. I feel sorry he became the way he was, but not sorry he is no longer around. I believe I grieved him long before he met death. Even more so, I wish Hektor were in that battle as well...I saw Ambrose do a nasty number to him before he escaped. In the last moments, Ciro asked for his help, and Hektor ran—abandoning him."

Lila wished she'd seen it. Maybe her scheming hadn't been totally in vain after all. "Ambrose helped me heal the wounds," she said and Rebekkah immediately grinned.

"I heard, Mousey. You sounded like a wild cat."

Lila immediately flushed. The need to hide behind a rock, bury herself in the dirt, or scream to the heavens overcame her in a wave of embarrassment. "Oh nonononono—"

Rebekkah laughed, cackling, "Don't worry, once I heard your first love cry, I excused myself deeper into the cave and didn't hear a thing. We might be friends now, but I do not need to be hearing any of your love making with the Crow Lord."

Lila swallowed the waves of embarrassment, still wanting to bury her face behind her hair at least, and met Rebekkah's eyes. "Do you have any wounds you need healing?"

"Can you manage without Ambrose's cock filling you?"

Lila groaned and actually *did* hide behind her hair this time, as Rebekkah once again cackled, her laughs turning to breathless snickers. "I'm kidding! I've seen what you could do." She held out her arm, still giggling, and Lila took it.

She focused that new sensation of warmth she felt hearing Rebekkah laugh and joke with her and channeled it outward. Lila felt heat radiating off her skin, and within moments, the bites on Rebekkah's neck, the old marks on her face from her brothers' fists, and the burns on her wrists from where the ropes bound her too tightly all were cleaned away.

Rebekkah looked at her arm, mystified. "It's amazing. And . . . the feeling. It's really like touching sunlight." She opened and closed her palm, flexing her fingers. "My brothers were fools. They never even knew what they had. The Sun Child—real, and right under our noses all along."

Lila balked. "This is the third time I've heard someone

refer to me as that. Hearing it again and again, it sounds like an official title?"

Rebekkah stood, changing into a new dress from the bag, also black, and said, "Well, that's because it is. The Sun Child has been a passing theory—almost a prophecy even—since vampires came to be."

"With the original vampire and his first wife?" Lila sat a bit closer.

Rebekkah nodded. "The wife is said to have been the Sun Maiden, and eventually there would be a child to take her place—to finish what she could not."

"And what's that?"

Pressing her lips together in thought, Rebekkah rubbed her hands together. "All I know is the old wives' tale. *A child of man, with hair like day meeting night, will guide the vampire back into the sunlight.* The wife had tried to save the original vampire, but was unable to do so completely. She turned him from a strigoi into what we now know as vampires. Maybe you're meant to 'heal' vampires the rest of the way—whatever that means."

Lila thought about it for a moment. She *could* change strigoi back into whatever they were originally. But it hadn't seemed to work the same way with vampires. Maybe . . . they were as they were meant to be, and "healing" them meant something different.

Coming up behind her, Ambrose lightly tapped on her shoulder. "Ladies, we should move out if you're ready."

Rebekkah smirked awkwardly and stood, brushing her skirts off, and Lila followed.

"Um, Ambro—Lord Draven . . . Should I be here? With you both? I fully understand if you'd prefer—"

"Please, Ambrose is fine," he said, lifting a palm. "What you've done for Lila has not gone unnoticed. If *you* are comfortable traveling with us, I would be glad to have you, Rebekkah."

Lila grinned. "You can't leave now, *friend.*"

Rebekkah wrinkled her nose. "I'm going to regret this, aren't I?"

"Probably."

Within the hour, they were soaring through the night sky toward the Maggot Mansion.

Lila loved flying, she loved holding Ambrose as the wind blew through her hair, loved feeling safe while so high up in the sky. Flying with him was just what she needed—it was what she loved. His arms wrapped around her tight, an excuse to hold her body to his, and experience the same freedom they both shared.

Tell me what Gustov is like, Lila mused.

A corner of Ambrose's lips lifted. *He's . . . he's something. He was old as a corpse when he was changed—also by the original vampire—so though he's been a vampire for slightly less time than myself, he has a few years on me. I believe he was miraculously ninety-eight.*

Oh lords. Being changed at that age sounds a bit awful, no? Being old forever?

Ambrose shrugged. *He doesn't have any of the issues old men face. He's not senile, doesn't hobble, his memory is intact, and he's actually incredibly spry. I almost don't want to say more and let you experience him for yourself. He's quite entertaining.*

Lila tried to imagine it. A man with hair as white as

snow, a hunched back, limbs skinnier than a twig. And fangs. It just didn't look right.

The three of them flew through the night, stopping in another cave and sleeping through the day, before setting out the next evening. As they crossed from the Crow Court to the Maggot Mansion, Lila watched the small villages like tiny sculptures below her. She wondered if they'd been plagued by Drusilla and her strigoi as the other vampire manors had been.

Gustov Nostro will likely ask for a demonstration, Ambrose said to her once they were nearing the manor itself.

A demonstration? Of my powers?

The powers of the Sun Child, yes.

Lila blew a breath from her lips and rolled her eyes. *You still haven't told me everything about being the Sun Child. I had to hear from Rebekkah that it was a proper title and not just another nickname you made for me. Am I walking into the dark on this?*

He glanced at her. *No. I heard what Rebekkah told you, and she knew pretty much everything I know. Besides the fact I saw, firsthand, the monster the original vampire was before the first wife changed him, and after. But I am just as unsure what "guiding vampires back into the sunlight" refers to, if it is literal or not, or if you could "heal" us in any way beyond the obvious. As far as I'm aware, that's all anyone knows. Because of this, some—like Drusilla—see you as a threat to us, while others—like myself—see you as a savior.*

This is why you wanted me to travel with you to the different manors? As a bargaining chip to show your hand? Lila knew her words were harsh, but a pang ran through her at the memory of that bargain in the Arachnid Estate, the feather still on her collar.

Yes, he replied.

Lila didn't answer for a long moment, lost in the memory, and trying to figure out how she'd show this vampire what she could do.

Remember the circumstances in which we made that bargain, Ambrose bit back.

I'm aware.

He sighed and then said, *I'm not using you, Lila. Surely you know that by now?*

She balked at his reaction. He could always read her emotions, but now he seemed to confuse them for something else. *Of course I do. I'm just processing. Won't the bargain end once we arrive? We've already been to the Arachnid Estate and, technically, the Viper Morada together when you came to visit me.*

Taken aback, Ambrose said, *I suppose so, yes. Marcus is safe, and we've visited the four vampire manors together.*

I hope he is staying safe. I cannot wait to see him already. Lila sighed. *It's also a shame. I like the crow feather.*

We can always make a new bargain, love, Ambrose smirked.

Lila tightened her grip around his neck. *We still have favors to ask for too.*

Remember when you asked if they'd be sexual favors? I think I'm liking that idea more and more.

Scoundrel. She huffed a breath, but a smirk was threatening to spill over her lips.

Lila knew she could handle whatever Gustov Nostro decided to throw at her, but the fact that they hadn't had a chance for even one more training session before arriving worried her. She hadn't practiced her *other* power, the scalding heat that could scar even a vampire. Even her healing needed help. She seemed to understand how they worked, but she struggled switching from offense to defense with no more than a thought. Would she know, when the time came, how to activate which was needed for the circumstance?

Fuck, she should've trained more.

But it was already too late—the Maggot Mansion was in sight.

Ambrose? What the heck am I looking at?

A chuckle escaped his lips. *That, love, is the Maggot Mansion. Quite a sight isn't it?*

Before them loomed a building unlike anything Lila had seen, even odder than the manor of the Arachnid Estate. Clad with mismatched pieces of rock, metal, stone, grass, crystal, and every kind of natural source imaginable, stood the tallest tower—the tallest *thing* Lila had ever seen. It stood so tall, it seemed to sway in the wind, its peak reaching as high as the clouds. It looked like it reached the stars! But the oddest aspect was just how thin it was. It looked like it should snap right in the center.

For three centuries, the tower has stood tall and strong, Ambrose explained. *The mansion has 204 floors, and 3,672 steps from top to bottom. Each floor has a different "theme," as Nostro likes to call it, and while many are residential, there are also ballrooms, entertainment lounges, markets, theaters, libraries, dungeons, arenas, fighting pits, menageries, and so much more. It's possible I visited fifty floors the last time here, and maybe fifty the many times before that—not even half and what was inside will forever blow my mind.*

Lila felt excitement run through her. It was like its own little world within, and she couldn't wait to explore it all—even if the structure looked absolutely terrifying.

Due to its size, many in the land of the Maggot Mansion reside in the manor itself as well. All nobility live here, as do the entirety of the capital's army, which is dwindling more and more by day, as they lose numbers to strigoi, Ambrose explained.

Lila turned from the tower and glanced up at Ambrose, *The strigoi are that big of a threat here?*

Ambrose nodded solemnly. *This is where they were first a problem. It's worse here than in the other three manors combined. The maggot venom makes addiction to blood—of any kind—a real problem. Any vampire untrained or weak struggles against it. And because of such, so many of those in the Maggot Mansion become strigoi, either because they give themselves over, or because they're in the wrong place at the wrong time.*

Which is exactly why you'll be staying very *close to me, Rebekkah, or Nostro as long as we're here. And you must keep up Concord communication anytime we're apart. Not to mention, I'm sure Nostro will want to try your mass healing on some of his people who've turned, to see if you could. But I refuse to let you burn out, refuse to allow you to be used as nothing more than an object. If* you *want, you could help to the extent* you *see fit. No more, no less. Understand?*

Lila loved when he took that demanding tone, it made her toes curl and her thighs press together with a mind of their own. More than that, she loved that even though he *sounded* demanding, in truth, Lila could do or say or be anything, and Ambrose would let her. If she wanted to heal the entirety of the Maggot Mansion, and be nothing more than a weapon in the eyes of Gustov Nostro, he would let her.

It was the power he gave her to say no that thrilled her, and the power of knowing she could command him much more than he could command her—and they both knew it.

But as they approached, Lila knew, just because she *could* say no to Ambrose, didn't mean she ever would.

22

As Ambrose, Lila, and Rebekkah descended onto a small platform jutting out from the tower, Lila saw a small group of people huddled at the floor's entryway. She saw the familiar facade of Bogdan, whose sharp teeth were gleaming in a horrifying yet endearing smile. Behind him were two young women, who looked much more like herself or Rebekkah, but both had large, nearly buggish eyes that seemed to be glowing that pale blue she saw in Bogdan at Sanktus Pernox.

But none of them surprised her as much as the man in the center of the entourage.

Ambrose was right, the man was beyond comprehension. He was incredibly tall—taller than Ambrose, maybe even nearing the height of Darius Maronia's strange butler, Balzar. He was completely bald, with two long gray eyebrows that seemed to shoot from his face. His ears were large and pointed and his nails were long claws on even longer fingers. His eyes were a blue so pale, they almost looked white, and his skin was the color of eggshell.

But what truly surprised Lila wasn't the fact this vampire looked like he'd been permanently stuck between his monstrous and humanoid form, nor was it that he looked like a walking corpse ready to fall over. It was something else . . . maybe the way he held himself, Lila guessed.

But she knew, without a doubt, this was Gustov Nostro, the Lord of the Maggot Mansion. He wore all black, a coat with a high cowl, black pants, and black shoes, all melting into one another. And on his head sat a pair of glasses . . . only, the frames and glass were also a black color. How was he supposed to *see* out of them?

What really sent the entire image off, however, was the drink in Nostro's hand. His long-clawed fingers were wrapped around a funny-shaped glass that held what she only assumed was blood, but it was thick. Almost as if it had been mixed with snow or ice. And springing out of the cup was a hot pink straw that managed to curl around itself before pointing toward Nostro.

Lila withheld her balked expression, the fits of giggles that wanted to spring forth after. Ambrose was right, Gustov Nostro was beyond explaining.

"Ah, the lovely Crow Lord and Sun Child," Nostro flourished a long arm and gave a small bow. His voice was so thick with an accent Lila had only heard from Bogdan, and just a tad bit shrill. "Welcome to the Maggot Mansion. Your arrival has been long anticipated, dear friends. In fact, we're throwing a revel right now, in your honor."

More like, using our arrival as an excuse to continue their party, Ambrose harrumphed in her mind, and Lila once again had to fight the urge to laugh aloud.

I don't know about you, but I desperately want to revel with this man.

Trust me, love. You'll regret it for a full week after any of his revels. I wouldn't wish a Gustov Nostro hangover on anyone. It is too awful a punishment.

Before Lila could burst, Ambrose stepped forward. "Nostro, it's so great to see you."

The two clapped each other on the back—or, Ambrose did. Nostro kind of just wrapped an awkward arm around Ambrose's shoulders and squeezed once before letting go completely. But his smile was unquestionable.

"Rebekkah, you're looking fantastic, especially without the two sacks of meat that always followed you around."

Lila guessed the news of Ciro's death hadn't yet made it to the Maggot Mansion then.

A pained smile slid along Rebekkah's lips. "Likewise, Gustov. I see you still fancy your blood in the form of cocktails."

He smirked, his jagged fangs peeking through his lips. "Want one, dear?"

"Desperately."

Rebekkah patted Lila on the shoulder and sauntered off, kissing Bogdan and his daughters hello as she entered the tower and disappeared.

Nostro's eyes landed on Lila's. "And this lilac-haired fox must be Lila Bran? I've heard so much about you, child." He reached for her hand, and at their first touch, a wave of static shock sparked up Lila's arm, and she felt how cold and clammy his palm was.

"It is great to meet you," she said. It wasn't her first time meeting an oddity and being surprised later when they became her favorite person in the room.

Speaking of, Bogdan stepped forward and threw cold arms around Lila. "Miss Bran, I am so pleased you're here! I want you to meet my daughters—"

"Ah, Bogdan!" Nostro hissed. "That can wait! First, we

revel!" He grabbed Lila's hand again, and dragged her into the sprawling tower before her. Lila had no idea what to expect, but she was immediately filled with a rushing sense of wonder.

The moment Lila walked into the tall tower, her mind just couldn't pick a spot to focus on. Everything was so dazzling, like something she'd see in a children's picture book. The candles lining the room were of all different colors, producing flames that matched the color of the wax. Greens, pinks, blues, and purples engulfed every corner, and instead of blending together or looking muddy, the colors sparkled all on their own, like sunlight peeking through a stained-glass window.

The room was circular shaped, and massive—Lila assumed the room alone took the entire floor.

Fabrics of every color were draped from the ceilings, creating a cozy effect, and tables were propped about with glass that twinkled in her eyes as the candles shined off of them. Below her feet, the floor was bedecked in *real* grass, with tiny pink flowers springing from the emerald-green blades.

Lila started when something lit up in her face, right between her eyes. The tiny light pulsed and shimmered a neon green, and then flickered out.

It was a firefly. The room was full of them, roaming around the real trees lining the edges of the room.

"I like to call this room the Hidden Spring," Nostro says, admiring his own home. "A friend from my youth inspired it. From what I hear, she was much like you actually."

Lila watched the man for a moment. Could he mean the first wife? The Sun Maiden?

Nostro, seeming to understand Lila's thoughts as Ambrose always had, nodded sadly. "Yes . . . I was already old when the Sun Maiden was a child. We were neighbors in a tiny, decrepit village. But she was always a ray of sunlight. When she first began to notice me, I was a widower, my children had grown and left, and all I had was myself and my dog." His eyes gleamed, and a smile tilted his lips. "She found Bear injured, attacked by another animal. She brought him to me, and took care of him—took care of me. The Sun Maiden nursed the poor hound back to full health, and made a friend of a lonely old man. I met her in the spring, and this room is for her."

At that exact moment, a firefly landed on Lila's arm, pulsing its dazzling light, its tiny feet tickling as it walked.

"It's gorgeous," she breathed. "Beyond gorgeous—beyond words."

"It's one of my favorites. It's why I made this one of the entryways to the mansion. I hoped everyone would see it." Nostro held out his arm, and the firefly flew off. "I'd like to show you more, if you'd like? Preferably *before* we start consuming our spirits."

Lila took his arm. "I would like that very much." She quickly looked over her shoulder, back at Ambrose. He was just behind her, smiled and nodded.

Go, I'll be around if you need me.

Lila grinned back, and then followed Nostro's lead as he stepped into the hollow of a tree.

Ten floors. Ten floors that were all incredible in their own way, things like she'd never seen. There was an entire floor dedicated to a hot spring, full of steam that smelled minty and immediately relaxed every muscle in her body, flowing with waterfalls and fountains. She saw people swimming within, while others leaned back and relaxed, wrapped in towels or completely nude. But no one seemed to mind, as the air was utterly relaxing. Another floor held a massive menagerie. There was a small caged walkway in the center, and all around them animals wandered freely. Big cats and birds of every color, small weasels and deer species she'd never seen before.

Lila felt like her head would screw right off her neck at the rate she was turning to ogle at everything in sight. It was all so... *spectacular.* That was the only word she could think of.

"Which is your favorite floor?" she asked, turning to face Nostro. The man was watching her with a prideful gleam in his eyes.

"Hmm. You know, everyone has always been too preoccupied choosing their own favorite—I don't believe anyone has ever asked for mine." He sheepishly grinned, revealing scraggly sharp teeth.

Lila put her arm through his. "Well, I want to see it. I'm sure it's the best in the mansion."

He patted the back of her hand and guided her to a bronze grate with a set of buttons next to it on the wall. Nostro pressed one of them and, after a *ding,* shoved the grate open. "Have you been to any of the major cities in the vampire manors?"

Lila shook her head. "Small villages, towns—and now the four manors. Not really the world traveler. Not yet, anyway."

Nostro smirked. "Well, then, you'll never have seen one of these. Much better than stairs, I fancy." He held his hand out to her, and guided her into a tiny room behind the grated door, before sliding it shut again. The entire room jolted up, and Lila grabbed onto Nostro.

"It's an elevator. They were invented just before the climax of the Mass Death," he explained.

"What do they do?"

"They're attached to pulley systems and travel up and down. Traveling the tower by stairs is exhausting for this old man, so I had an elevator installed, and can go to any floor I please."

Once again Lila was left awe-struck. The ride was quick and carried them from the hundredth floor to the 147th floor.

As Nostro unlatched the lock and pushed the bronze grate open once more, he said, "Now, the floors in which I hold the majority of the Maggot Mansion's revels are some of my favorites, of course. I thrive on hosting and I promise the party tonight will be unlike any other you've been to—but *this* room is my favorite for *me*. When I like to just think or be alone or reminisce, this is where I come. I hope you enjoy it as much as I do."

He led her out of the elevator and into a wide circular room. It was dark, with no windows, but small lights were set into the stone all around, only illuminating the floor to see where to walk.

"Come, the center is best."

The room was silent, but Lila followed him, and as they stood in the center, she waited. Maybe standing in the dark for him was the same she felt when she was in a coffin the first time: relaxing and—

An array of colors lit up the walls, lavender melded into a golden yellow that became brighter and brighter till it illuminated white. Lila gasped, and Nostro chuckled in response. Then the white morphed again, as it spread throughout the entire room, turning into tiny white specks. Not specks, Lila realized . . . stars. And the dark walls were breathing color—dark blue.

It was the night sky.

"This room shows you your favorite memory—not the actions, not the words, not the people, but how it looked. Almost so you can relive it once again. The flashes of color were the room reading you."

The night sky. She knew exactly what night this was. A special night on the roof of the Crow Court manor, Ambrose's tongue on her body as he told her to watch the stars.

"I see a field in the middle of spring," Nostro said softly. "It's daytime, just after noon if I remember correctly. The flowers—sunflowers—are swaying in the wind. But I know—I know because I was there—the wind isn't what's pulling them."

"Pulling them?"

Nostro nods. "Did you know sunflowers stretch toward the sun? They reach and reach, trying to get as close to it as their delicate little bodies can."

Lila pulled her gaze from the night sky and watched Nostro's expression.

"In this memory, however, they're not reaching for the sun. They're reaching for *her*."

Realization dawned on Lila. The Sun Maiden, the original vampire's first wife.

"She was with me that day. I believe we were having a tea party. She was still so young, yet even then her power— her warmth—it radiated. The sunflowers knew it, I knew it." He sighed. "I wonder . . . would they stretch to you as well?"

Lila didn't answer, but then again, she got the sense he

wasn't really asking *her*. His gaze was fixed on his own illusion, eyes misting, so Lila turned to give him a moment of privacy. She watched the stars, as Ambrose had once told her to do, and wondered . . . Ambrose had shown her the beauty of the night. Could she ever show him the radiance of the day? How his white hair would be blinding under the sun, his dark skin would glow with such warmth. Suddenly, Lila had the violent need to see his eyes in the daylight. To see the sun brighten them, reflect her, and radiate with such vibrance.

Watch the stars, love, he'd said once. But now Lila wanted to reciprocate, wanted to tell him, *Feel the sun, Ambrose.*

23

After spending a few more moments in the quiet of the Memory Chamber—the name Nostro had given the room—he led Lila down the elevator, past the landing floor they originally entered through, and all the way down to the tenth floor of the tower.

"Lila, love, welcome to your first *true* revel." He pushed the grated door open, and Lila was smacked with sound and color and light and voices.

It truly was like *nothing* she had ever seen before, and standing only a few paces away, watching the elevator door open as if he sensed her coming, was Ambrose Draven. He was dressed in form-fitted black pants that hugged his waist, and a sheer black shirt—buttoned only halfway—was tucked into them. His fingers were bedecked in rings, his neck covered in golden necklaces, and a long earring with a small sun hung from one ear. His hair was smoothed back behind the ear with the earring, while his bangs loosely fell over his smoldering eyes, drinking

Lila in. The sexual deviancy was oozing off of him, and it immediately made Lila's toes curl just by looking at him.

With one hand in his pocket, he lifted a ringed finger and crooked it at her, beckoning her to him.

"I think the Crow Lord wants your attention now, love," Nostro chuckled. "I'll find you later, we'll have a drink together—a cocktail I'll make in your honor." And just like that, Nostro *literally* jumped into the crowd and disappeared.

She suspected there were two sides to the Lord of Maggots. One, a sad and lonely old man, and the other, a loud and boastful immortal who loved spirits, parties, and debauchery. She spotted him only a moment more, putting those blackened glasses over his eyes, and immediately grabbing two drinks, both amber in color, and joining in the fun.

Lila walked up to the sex god before her, and his smirk was as sharp as a knife.

He leaned in, speaking into her ear as music and voices boomed all around them, "Had fun with Nostro?"

"I did," she said, realizing her voice got lost in the noise, and then repeated it after leaning in. Ambrose wrapped a hand around her waist, and kept her close.

"Come with me."

He took her hand, guiding her through the throng of the crowd. There were so many vampires all around her, lost in their own conversations or to the rhythm of the music. It was nothing like Sanktus Pernox. No one cared there was a human there, no one cared what they were doing, or about being judged. People danced, and ate, and drank—and Lila barely even saw any blood. It was all human food, human drinks.

She saw people of all genders grinding on each other, jumping with their hands above their heads, laughing vivaciously, and *living*.

As they neared the back wall of the massive room—so big, Lila was sure the room was actually two floors, with balconies lining the upper floor—she saw a wall of curtained rooms.

Scooching up to Ambrose, and pulling his hair so he'd know to lean down, she yelled in his ear, "What are those for?"

He immediately smirked, and she knew she shouldn't have asked. "Do you want to find out?"

Something in Lila felt bold, maybe it was the thrilling environment, or the burst of life all around her, but she *did* want to find out, no matter how scandalous it may be.

She nodded.

Ambrose's eyes shone like those beautiful rubies she loved, and he tightened his grip on her hand, guiding her to the closest one.

Ready? he asked through the Concord, and Lila was. She took a breath and stepped forward just as Ambrose pulled an edge of the curtain back.

And she held back a gasp with all her might.

She saw naked bodies—*many* naked bodies. Moans and groans, breasts and cocks, men fucking men, women eating out women, all in a chain, all making love, all enjoying each other to the fullest.

Do you want to see another?

And Lila did. All she knew was *their* love, what she felt inspired to do, what Ambrose guided her through. But she wanted to know *more*.

The next curtain was a male couple—a man tied at the wrists to the barred back wall of the room, while the other lifted his legs over his shoulders and thrust into his ass. The one tied had a gag in his mouth, and a bar stretching his ankles far enough apart to comfortably sit on the other man's shoulders.

These are some of the toys I mentioned before, Ambrose said, watching Lila.

And—is everyone supposed to partake in these rooms here?

Not if they don't want to. Many find freedom in dancing, others in fun, but some find freedom in sex. Nostro wants his tower to be like a sanctuary for any and all. Pleasure, fun, romance, deviancy, and—most of all—safety.

And the curtain?

The only policy is anyone can watch if they want. They can't join unless permission is granted. But there are enough bedrooms in the tower that if they don't want to be watched, they could occupy a room. The people in these rooms are making love here by choice.

Lila understood that a bit. She knew many found pleasure in being watched, or in being caught.

I want to try it, she decided, riding the bold energy she was feeling.

Watching? Ambrose fully turned to her, closing the curtain on the lovers.

No, I want to use a room—but only with you. Unless . . . you wanted others? Lila suddenly felt insecure. What if they were better than she was? What if Ambrose realized that?

Darling, if anyone so much as tries to touch you, I think I couldn't help but bite their hand off. If you are okay with just us, I will happily obliged. But I want you to be sure about this. People might watch.

Ambrose, this place is like a fantasy. She grabbed his hand. *Three months. Three* agonizing *months of a horrible, horrible life. I want you and I want this. I feel so . . . alive. I haven't felt like this since the rooftop.*

Ambrose caressed her cheek, *And I will give you anything you desire, Little Crow. Anything.*

He pulled her with him, slowly taking steps back, into

a room with an opened curtain. It was unoccupied. Ambrose turned a small knob and a dim light illuminated the red room—just as red as his eyes. The room was mostly bed, with deep carmine sheets, but there were chains with cuffs, ropes that matched the bed, gags, and so much more Lila had no idea what they'd be used for.

Ambrose pushed Lila onto the bed, closing the curtain behind him, and spun her around so her back was flat on the mattress.

Slowly—so damned slowly—he unlaced her boots. He propped her foot on his thigh, and watched *her* as his fingers slid under the threads, pulled each knot until they were loose enough to slip off. He tossed the boot onto the floor, and delicately put Lila's foot down, then he repeated the agonizingly slow process on the other.

Once done, his hands drifted up her body, untying the simple green dress, slowly pulling the straps from her shoulders before he slipped the dress down her body. It pooled at her hips for a moment as she felt his gaze warm her breasts where her stolen bra covered her. Lords, that stare was intoxicating. He pulled the dress the rest of the way off her and dropped it to the floor.

"There is *so* much I want to do to you, Little Crow. So much I want to try."

Anticipation was eating Lila alive. Every touch felt electric, every breath felt explosive. She was so desperate, she felt like she needed to jump from her skin.

"Ambrose," she whimpered.

"I need a word, love. When you say it, I will stop no matter what. I need a word that will be my limit, *your* limit." His thumb stroked her ribs, toying with the underwire lining of the stolen bra.

Lila pouted. He would *never* be enough, she couldn't imagine a limit.

Sensing her hesitation, he continued, "It's for both of us. If things become too much, if you decide you want to make our moment private, if you decide you simply want to stop—I need a word. The things I want to do to you . . . they could be dangerous. And I need to know it's pain you *like*, not pain you tolerate, not pain that actually hurts."

She thought about his hand around her neck, about his teeth digging into her neck. That was good pain, pain she liked. But then her mind raced to Hektor, to the ropes he tied around her wrists, and the harsh bites on her thighs. His eyes as he fucked Drusilla underneath her.

Lila nodded. "Okay. How about sunflower?"

Ambrose grinned, his thumb dipping under her bra and grazing the bottom of her breast. "Sunflower's our word. I love it." He leaned over her, planting both hands next to her head, and kissed her.

In less than a breath, their kiss deepened, his tongue dipping between her lips. He dragged his hand through her hair, removing the ponytail and letting it fall free around her. At the sight, he groaned into her mouth, drinking her in, before he hiked her up the bed in a sitting position.

"Ready, love?"

Lila nodded, and in a heartbeat, Ambrose unclasped her bra, throwing it to the floor. She felt so exposed, her nipples hardening, but she sat straight, keeping her eyes on Ambrose.

He grinned, revealing those delicious fangs, and reaching into a small basket resting next to the bed.

"Ah, I hoped they'd have some of this." Ambrose pulled out a bottle filled with clear liquid, and then he turned back to Lila with a devilish grin. "Hands on the headboard, love. Don't let go."

Lila reached behind her, and built into the wall of the

room, were bars wrapped in a soft fuzz, comfortable to hold onto.

Ambrose straddled Lila, squirting the clear liquid into his hand first, then rubbing his palms together. "I'm going to give you a little massage first. Loosen you up a bit."

Lila bit her lip. She knew the vampire was plotting something wicked. At least the liquid smelled good—like mint, cooling the air around them.

He groped her breasts, sending fire down Lila's spine, and squeezed. The liquid in his hands felt warm and almost sticky but he started focusing on her nipples, plucking and twisting them between his fingers. Lila yelped when a sudden warmth spread over them, hot and tingling. But just as fast as they warmed, a sudden coolness rushed to their peaks, a stark contrast to her own rising temperature. Her nipples felt like they were buzzing in Ambrose's hands, and she arched her back, pushing them against his calloused palms. She needed him to touch them, to grab them.

Lila whimpers at the sensation tingling all over them.

"The liquid heightens your sensitivity. It's edible too." He leaned down and took one of her breasts in his mouth, coiling his tongue around the hardened peak. "Mmm." The hum vibrated on her sensitive skin, and she could feel the apex of her thighs damp with need.

As he sucked her nipple between his teeth, Lila jolted up, ready to unbutton his shirt, but he pushed her back. "No, love. Hands on the bars. Let go again and I'll have to punish you."

I like it when you punish me, she said through the Concord.

He smirked, but instead of acting, he just sat there, watching her almost-nude body. He'd deliberately left her underwear on, and she knew it would be more of a torture device than anything else.

"You're mine. You know that, right?" His voice was hoarse, and his eyes were greedy, like they couldn't focus on a singular part of her—only wanting to consume *all* of her.

"I'm yours."

Ambrose fell onto her again, kissing her hard, and she instinctively let go of the bars, wrapping her arms around his neck. He kissed her, driving the kiss with his tongue, moving down her chin, her neck.

And then Lila felt rope brush against her arm.

In a distracted flash, Ambrose grabbed Lila's wrists, gripping them in one hand, and sat back. He straddled her hips, keeping her pinned under him.

"You disobeyed me," he grinned. "You know what that means, love." He jerked Lila up, pressing her against his body, and yanking her wrists behind her back. "I'll make you regret not listening to me." He began circling her wrists with the red rope, and though the rope was incredibly soft, and *Ambrose* was the one tying her, her body jolted at the memory of the last time her wrists were bound. Of her being pulled across the snow, whipped, and collared.

She must've straightened because Ambrose pulled back. "Sunflower?"

Lila's eyes shot to his. "No. Just . . . memories. I'm yours. I need you to make sure I know it." *I need you to reclaim me,* she didn't say, *reclaim me* for *me.*

Ambrose swallowed hard, but his eyes darkened. He pulled her wrists from behind her back and brought them to his lips.

"I will make sure you never forget it, love."

He kept his eyes locked on hers as he kissed one slowly, continuing to tie the rope around her. She inhaled sharply, but something about the way he was looking at her only filled her with warmth and desire. As he pushed that one back, he licked the other wrist languidly, just above her pulse, and then pressed a number of soft kisses along it.

As he pulled both of her arms back and tied them together, his thumb ran between her skin and the rope, massaging her. "I'm going to tie you up and keep you all for myself," he whispered over the boom of music on the other side of the curtain—a fact Lila had completely forgotten about. She peeked around Ambrose's large shoulder and saw two sets of eyes. The way the room's lighting was situated, she couldn't make out their faces, nor any distinguishing expressions. Just eyes.

We have viewers.

I know, Ambrose said. *Just ignore them. Eyes on me, love.*

His words thrilled her, and the fact people were watching sent a new wave of ecstasy to the warmth between her thighs.

With her wrists bound, Ambrose continued his descent down her body. He bound her arms with a ton of little knots, then crossed the ropes between and under her breasts, squeezing them, and down her hips. When he got to the apex of her thighs, he ran his finger along the seam of her panties.

"What to do with these . . . should I leave them on?" He snapped the waistband, her sensitive skin bursting in flame. Lords, she wanted him to fuck her already. "Or should I rip them off?" Ambrose tucked his middle finger between her thighs, running it along the seam of her lips. "Fuck, baby. You're already so wet and we haven't even begun."

"Ambrose," she moaned.

"You've been a bad girl. Bad girls don't get to come so fast." He left her panties on and tied the rope between her soaked lips, the coils rubbing roughly against her pulsing clit.

Lila threw her head back, desperate for the friction, desperate to get these damned panties off. But, instead, Ambrose grabbed Lila's leg, bending it back so the knee sat close to her chest, then he tied her calf to her thigh. He repeated the action on the other, and with her legs like this, it left her core completely exposed.

"Lords, look at you. Absolutely delicious."

Ambrose stood from the bed, and took a step back, admiring his handy work. There were so many more people now in the curtain way, just watching. Lila felt embarrassment flooding her cheeks. But the more she fidgeted in her restraints, the more she realized how little she could actually move.

"They're being drawn by your warmth, love," Ambrose called over the music now that he wasn't mere inches apart. "And the gorgeous sight of you, of course."

Lila felt the familiar feeling of vampire gazes heat all over her body. Some eyes were staring at her dripping, cum-stained panties, others were staring at her purpling breasts and pink nipples, others stared at the ropes, at her feet, at her neck. Everything was on display for them, almost as if she were just another exhibit in the menagerie.

Eyes on me, Ambrose repeated. When she shifted her gaze, Ambrose was unbuttoning his shirt. *Eyes.* He dropped it to the floor. *On.* He kicked his boots off and pulled his pants down. *Me.* And finally, he pulled his hard cock from the snug black briefs he wore, and slid them off.

Lila made sure to keep her eyes on him, and a sinister smirk spread on his lips just before he slowly, torturously licked his lips.

He pulled the end of the rope, and tossed it above his head, to where a hook Lila hadn't noticed before jutted out from the ceiling. The rope wrapped around the hook, and once secured, Ambrose pulled it down. Lila shrieked as the pull also lifted her off the bed.

The rope bit into her skin, but damn did it feel good. It pressed against her core so tight, she thought she might come from it alone. Ambrose tied the rope off to a small bar on the banister by the floor, and then stood up straight.

"You're perfect, Lila. Fucking perfect."

Her head started feeling light immediately, but damn did she want him. She wanted him bad.

"Get these fucking panties off of me, Ambrose, or I'll use the safe word and get myself off right here."

Ambrose chuckled. "So demanding."

With her pussy exposed to the viewers, to Ambrose, he lifted one of the many knives he seemed to have hidden in his gorgeous outfit that had been sitting on the floor. Lila felt the steel slip under the panties at her crotch, the cold grazing against her hot, dripping folds. It was too much, cold and hot, as the mint on her nipples still tingled every part of her chest. It was danger and pleasure in one. The flat of the knife pressed against her, and then cut right through her panties.

"Fuck," she moaned.

"Not yet," Ambrose teased.

Lila's head lolled back, and she felt all the blood rushing to it. Could the vampires feel it too, desperate to stick their teeth in her? She was already tied up like a hog for dinner.

Ambrose returned in view with a . . . thing. Lila didn't really know what it looked like, a knob on the end of a handle maybe? It was long and purple, and when he pressed a button, the knob started to vibrate.

"H-How?" she balked, squirming in the ropes.

"Remember I told you a charmist made that ointment I

used on you in the Crow Court to heal your wounds? Well there are many witches like her—some that specialize in other things besides herbs—that can do all sorts of things. One of them made this."

He stepped forward, grabbing one of her thighs. And with that same sinister grin, he placed the vibrating head on the rope pressing into her clit.

Immediately, Lila's world exploded.

"Fuck, *fuck*," she hissed. "Lords, that feels so good."

"Want to feel it on your clit, love?" Ambrose took another step, closing the distance between them, and pushed the rope between her folds aside. She let out a sharp exhale, which was immediately followed by a sharp inhale as the vibrating tool was pressed against her. Shock waves burst through her. She screamed and her head fell back as all the sensations rushed from her desperate clit to her curling toes and the constricting rope tying her up. It was almost too much.

Almost.

"Don't come yet, love."

But Lila couldn't wait. Her entire body wound tight, and she knew she wouldn't last much longer, not with the vibrations driving her body wild.

"Lords," Ambrose groaned. "You're going to heal the entire fucking Maggot Mansion at this rate."

Lila suddenly opened her eyes, turning to the people watching. More had come, more faceless eyes, drinking her in. Was she . . . healing them? She *definitely* was feeling all new levels of love and pleasure from Ambrose—so much so, she hadn't even recognized her warmth from the heat of her body's desire.

"I said, eyes on me. If you're gonna disobey, Little Crow, then I'll just have to take your eyes away." Ambrose lifted the shirt he'd been wearing, and walked around, behind Lila's head.

"What are you doing?"

He placed the shirt over her eyes, folded enough to make it impossible to see through the sheer material. "Shh. I think you'll like this."

With her vision blocked, Lila felt everything one hundred times more. Each touch, each caress, each tug of rope, and each kiss Ambrose placed as he traveled back around her.

"Ah—Ambrose," she called.

"I'm right here, Lila. You're safe. Remember our word." Though the room was still so loud, his voice sounded as though it was pulled from reality, pulled to be only in her ears. His voice like liquid gold, his voice that made her melt.

Lila was ready for him.

But Ambrose seemed to want to play more.

He took the vibrator again, and pressed it into her entrance, leaving it pushing the slightest bit in. Lila threw her head back, pleasure pounding through her.

And in only a moment, she realized it was *nothing* compared to when he surprised her and sucked her clit into his mouth.

Lila shrieked—*actually* shrieked—as Ambrose pressed the vibrator into her and drew his tongue in a lazy circle around her throbbing bud at the same time. He did it more and more, lapping at the juices slipping down her thighs, her ass, and he then returned to her clit.

The orgasm had been building in Lila for a long time, but it was all too much. Her entire body was shaking, the ropes were making her head spin, and she was sure if she came right now, she'd likely pass out. But, as her toes curled and her legs stiffened as far as the ropes would let her, she didn't care. She would *die* for this orgasm.

"Fuck, Ambrose, can I come? Please?"

He drove his tongue all over her, scraping her with his teeth. "Please, please, *please,*" she moaned, lifting her hips into him. He moved to her thigh, kissing her and leaving hickeys all down his path. Kissing and sucking and biting and—drinking.

Ambrose drove his fangs into the back of her thigh and drank her blood.

24

Fuck, she tastes so good, he thought as he lapped at her soaked pussy. He loved her. He loved this. If he could, he'd eat her out for eternity, for every meal. It was almost better than sex. Almost.

But it wasn't enough. He wanted all of her. She tasted so fucking good, he refused to waste even one drop of her. He licked her dripping cunt again and again until he'd had all of her, and then he moved to her thighs, her ass. Lords, she was perfect. More than she knew.

He gently kissed her inner thighs. He'd let her come soon, and then he'd fuck her till she saw double, fuck her until everyone watching them got off and fucked off, and then he'd fuck her some more.

Her thighs were so sweet, so smooth, he didn't even notice when his fang nicked her. Didn't even notice when he'd bitten her. Didn't even notice when he'd injected her with his venom and started gulping her blood just like he'd done to her cum seconds ago.

"Ambrose?" she called, and it was like a moan and a cry. She continued through the Concord, *Ambrose*—she moaned again, louder—*I'm going to come, your bite . . . ah, it's too much.*

My bite? he thought. And that's when he realized what he'd done.

Just as he pulled his fangs back, Lila screamed and she came all around the vibrator pressed into her pussy. Ambrose's senses dulled again, and with her blood dripping down his chin, he just couldn't help it. He tossed the vibrator and devoured her hole, licking and sucking every part of her like a starved pup. Her blood, sweat, and cum all mixed together to be the perfect cocktail, a cocktail Ambrose would die for.

Ambrose, it's too much. Too much.

She wasn't saying the safe word.

He kept going. He'd go until she was clean, then keep going until she came again, and repeat the process over and over.

Amb—

His head snapped from between her thighs. Lila's head was lolling back, her body limp, for only a moment before she snapped up again.

She'd blacked out.

"Sunflower," he said.

"What? No, I can—"

"I said sunflower, Lila." And there was no more question about it. He swallowed hard, forcing himself to calm down as he took deep breaths through his nose. He needed to untie her. He needed her to get her circulation back.

Before he did anything though, he needed some damned privacy. He stood and, with his cock still out and hard, he shut the curtain, forcing the onlookers away.

Ambrose turned back to Lila, climbed up onto the bed, and untied the rope from the ceiling hook, easing her into his arms.

"We need to get your circulation back to normal." Without letting her speak, he removed the makeshift blindfold from her eyes, wrapped the carmine bed sheet around her, lifted their belongings, and carried her from the room. Ambrose felt the partygoers' eyes on him—on them. Thankfully, he had *some* modesty as Lila's sheets covered all the important bits, but he was still walking through the crowd, butt naked. Lila had definitely called attention with the warmth spreading throughout the entire tower too. If there had been any strigoi Nostro had holed up, he wasn't sure they'd be the monsters they once were after the experience he'd just felt.

"Ambrose, I'm fine, truly."

"Of course you'd say that. You have my venom running through you."

He was thankful the party was still bustling, thankful the music was loud, the beat echoing through the bodies all around them.

In the back of the room, behind the small curtained sex dungeons, there was a pathway that led to two sets of stairs, one up and the other down. Ambrose took the stairs up, climbing and climbing until he'd gone from the tenth floor, to the fourteenth, where Nostro had set up his and Lila's living quarters for the duration of their stay. The stone hall was deathly silent compared to the booming noise of the room only a few flights down. And all Ambrose could hear were Lila's needy whimpers.

He shoved a dark wooden door open, the door to their room, and kicked it closed behind him. The room was smaller than Lila's room in the Crow Court, but suited the two of them well. The fire was lit, the rug below his feet was soft, and the coffin in the center of the room was large enough for both of them.

Lila wiggled in his arms. "My shoulders hurt," she squeaked. Her cheeks were practically stained red, an effect from his venom, or the hanging, he wasn't sure.

"Let's get these off of you," he whispered gently. Instead of taking her to the coffin, he walked before the fire and placed her on the plush white rug. Her expression lit up, and he knew the soft fuzz was doing wonders to the parts of her that were numb from the ropes. He knew how much Lila loved soft things.

Tucking a pillow under her head, he slowly began untying each knot running up her legs. The rope came undone, and Ambrose cursed himself when he saw the imprint the binds had left on her skin. He knew they'd happen, but *seeing* the marks of his love still unsettled him. He would always be too much for her, no matter what he did.

He was a monster, after all, and she was a human.

Once one leg was free, he carefully unbent it, massaging all along her thighs, calves, knee, and ankle, to make sure the circulation returned. It was a slow process, but one that seemed to be driving both of them wild with need. He could smell Lila's sex, hungry for him—so much so, he could practically taste it on his tongue still. And her eyes. They were watching him with so much love and adoration, but more than that—the heat in her blood was reflected in those gorgeous brown eyes, begging him without words.

His cock twitched.

Ambrose bit his lip, and as he did, he remembered the feeling of biting into her thigh, her blood still on his chin, and his heart felt like it'd been squeezed dry. So much shame and guilt flooded his system—the last time he'd bitten her during a moment of intimacy, he'd been *such* an asshole. This time, he wanted to be different. But was it Lila that wanted him right now? Or the venom? And, regardless, he'd hurt her—again. What if next time, he bit through her neck, through her veins? What if next time, he kept drinking? What if next time, he couldn't stop himself?

"Ambrose," she whispered. "What's wrong?"

He schooled his expression, and continued onto her other leg. "Nothing."

Untie, massage, untie, massage, untie massage. When he got to her breasts, Lila's moans filled his ears, and he had to do everything in his power to stop himself from coming just to the sound of her. Her nipples were so peaked, she'd pushed them into his hands, her back arching, as she begged for him to touch them, to rub them, to taste them.

"They're so numb," she breathed. "Please!"

And he tried his best to abstain.

By the time Lila's arms were freed, her entire body was slack on the rug, marked everywhere with the ropes' imprints, and the purpling skin slowly turned back to red and finally to her usual pearly white.

"Better?" he asked.

A small scowl formed on her face. "What do you mean? That was incredible." Lila forced herself up, and Ambrose put his hand on her back, guiding her. "*You* are incredible."

She looked at him again with those steamy, sparkly eyes.

"I bit you," he said bluntly.

"So? You're a vampire. You bite."

"I drank your blood."

"Again, vampire."

"I couldn't stop." He clenched his fist against her back,

his long nails softly scratching at the tattoo of crows he'd left on her.

"But you did. You always will, even if you doubt yourself."

"I didn't when I was a strigoi."

Lila flinched. "That was—"

"What? Different?" Fuck. He was being an asshole again. He opened his mouth to apologize, but Lila pressed her finger against it.

"Yes. It *was* different. Bloodlust and being a strigoi *are* different. And you just proved that by not only pulling away, but stopping the moment, using our safe word, and getting me out of there. You proved it by untying the ropes and assuring I was okay, even when I was begging you to touch me. To fuck me." Lila crawled forward, crawled over him on her hands and knees. "You love me, Ambrose. You would never hurt me. Not really. Remember, I *like* pain—if *you're* the one causing it."

She wrapped her small, delicate hand around his length, and pumped it, bringing it back to its full length.

"Now, if you'll still have me, I'm not done with you yet. *I* want to be in charge, Ambrose."

"But the venom—"

She gripped a little harder, and Ambrose moaned.

"So? I already wanted to fuck you. This changes nothing. If anything, it'll be a fun toy to use. I wanna see what it feels like when you're inside of me." She stroked his cock again, and Ambrose bucked his hips, shoving it in and out of her palm.

"Lila," he whimpered.

She abruptly stopped, and stood before him. "You—You liked when I danced for you, right?" Her cheeks were stained red, and he could tell she was embarrassed by her words, but the golden color of her boldness outshone everything else.

Ambrose helplessly nodded. "Yes."

Lila began to sway her hips back and forth, moving to a silent rhythm Ambrose felt in his soul.

She spun and shook her ass in his face, swaying her hips as her hands ran over her body. Suddenly, he felt a deep desperation for those to be *his* hands. He grabbed her hips and brought her closer, but she didn't stop dancing. Instead, she danced over him, dropping her hips till her wet pussy grazed his cock, then springing back up again.

"I didn't know you were such a tease," he huffed a laugh.

Lila smiled, her teeth showing. She pushed him back, swaying her hips lower and lower until she was on her knees right above him.

Her warm palm splayed over the crow on his chest, and as she gazed into his eyes, she shoved him to the floor, his back falling to the fuzzy rug.

She shimmied over him, straddling him as his cock smacked against her dancing ass. Ambrose wanted to touch her, was desperate to feel her. He cupped her breasts above him, pinching her nipples, and he knew it drove her wild as she started grinding his cock through her folds. She was so wet, so hot, and it took everything to not plunge into her to the hilt. When she rubbed her throbbing clit over his rosy head, they both threw their heads back.

"Fuck." It was so . . . sensual. He feared he'd come before he even had the chance to enter her. But then, he guessed, they'd be even. After all, he made her come downstairs.

Lila put her hands over his, still cupping her breasts, and focused her heady gaze on him.

"I want you. All of you. Now," she demanded.

Ambrose reached between them, and adjusted himself at her center—but she was in control. She took his hand again, and brought it to her lips, licking his thumb into her mouth as she lowered herself over his head.

She moaned around his thumb and he slammed his head back against the floor. She felt so fucking good already and he was only barely in.

Lila slowly dropped herself lower, and inch by inch he felt himself stretch her walls. He made a tiny thrust up, but Lila plopped his thumb from her mouth and placed her hand on his chest.

"No, I'm in control," she reminded him, a look of warning in her eyes. She wanted to fuck him, wanted to lead. Fuck, would he let her.

Lila rocked her hips on Ambrose's cock, taking him completely as she moaned his name. Then she pulled herself off and slowly repeated it all again. After a few slow thrusts, Lila quickened her pace, and soon she was bouncing on his cock, her breasts matching each movement above him. She took his hands and guided them to her hips, and it was only when she uttered, "Help," did he take over.

Ambrose gripped her hips and pressed her as far down as she'd go, eliciting a scream to erupt from her throat.

"Oh, lords, do it again," she moaned.

So he did, he pushed her all the way off, and then pulled her down, fast and hard, meeting her hips with his. Lila's eyes rolled to the back of her head, and he knew he had her. He did it again, again, and by the fifth time, she was screaming incoherently, and burst all over his cock. He quickly moved his hand to her neck, pulling his venom for her as the orgasm washed over her. She screamed in a mix of pleasure and pain as he thrust into her. Her orgasm was hot and slick, and he knew with it wrapped around him, he wouldn't last much longer.

"Hold on, love."

Lila flopped down onto him, her chest flush with his, and grabbed onto his shoulders as Ambrose pounded into her. It was fast and rough, and he was chasing the high he knew only came from fucking her.

She was so hot pressed against his skin, wrapped around his cock, and he felt every aspect of her body against his. Ambrose couldn't hold himself off any longer. He thrust deep into her as he came, his cock spurting so much, he thought it'd never end.

Lila moaned and he grabbed her cheeks, bringing her lips to his, moaning into her mouth as he filled her up. Thrusting into her a final time, he felt their combined orgasms completely engulf them both and as they both came down, they slumped. Lila went limp on his chest, her cheek pressed against his collarbone, and her legs limp at his sides.

"That was . . ." he tried, breathless, but gave up halfway. All he could do was nod as he tried to catch his breath again.

Amazing? she finished through the Concord.

He huffed a breath, and threw one arm around her back. *She* was amazing.

Ambrose felt her heart racing, could hear it thump so loud, if she hadn't been laying on top of him, he'd think she was sprinting. He gently pulled out of her, and they both hissed from the movement.

"Should we get up?" he asked, but she leaned up onto her elbows, her hair brushed over her shoulder as she looked at him and bit her lip.

Her cheeks were still red, so red.

"Wait," she breathed.

Ambrose lowered his eyebrows, a crease forming between them. "What is it? Are you hurt?" He began to sit up to inspect her, but she pushed him down again.

"N-no. I just have something I want to say."

Now Ambrose's heart was pounding.

"You-you know I love you."

His eyebrows lowered even more. "Yes?"

Lila bit her lip, and he knew she was struggling to get whatever it was out. Her emotions were unclear, something Ambrose wasn't used to. She seemed to still be coming down from the orgasm, but she was also so filled with anxiety and fear, but above all—she was filled with love.

"I want to make a new bargain."

Ambrose's eyes darted to her collar bone. He had been too busy to notice before, but the feather was gone, that bargain was completed.

"You know you can ask me for anything. You don't need to bargain with me . . ." he ran his thumb over her collar, stroking her skin.

Lila took a shuddering breath. "Still, I want a bargain."

An idea circled his brain. A vision, maybe. Or a dream.

"What do you want?" He was trying to hold himself back, to wait until she made her desires clear. He didn't want to assume—not this.

"I want you. All of you. Forever."

His heart stopped. Or maybe it was moving too fast. He stared at her a moment, taking in her eyes, her quivering lips, her rosy cheeks. Her heart quickened in his silence.

Ambrose swallowed hard. *Forever.* "And what will you give me for it?" He barely recognized his voice, it was as light as a feather. But he knew the words slipping from his lips. They were *their* words. And he would do *anything* to give her what she wanted.

Lila bit back a smile, but couldn't stop herself. Her smile burst and it felt like his entire being would go up in flames, melt at the sight of that gorgeous smile reserved for *him*.

"Anything." Tears brimmed in her eyes.

He couldn't hold it in anymore, couldn't contain the love that was threatening to consume his very being. In a burst of movement, he pulled her close, brought his lips to hover over hers.

"I want you. Forever. Marry me, Lila Bran."

25

Lila threw herself against him, kissing him deeply. "Yes, yes, please. Yes."

Ambrose smiled against her lips, and kissed her, holding him tightly to her. He interlocked their left hands, rubbing her ring finger.

"Then consider it a deal. My forever for your forever."

Lila's heart swelled, and she couldn't help but kiss him again. When they pulled apart, she lifted their hands, feeling a tingling sensation where he'd caressed.

Around her ring finger, by the base, was a new tattoo. Lila gasped at the sight. A small crow, with its wings flared to the sides, wrapped around her finger. But in the center of that crow, was a tiny ornate sun. It was an engagement ring. It was . . . them.

"The bargain . . . it's between both of us. So it fused the Crow Lord and the Sun Child." Ambrose moved their hands, showing her his ring finger, where he also had the crow and sun tattooed around his ring finger. "I gave one to myself too. And I'll get you a real ring—one of gold and jewels—but these are *ours*, to remember this moment when we bargained our hearts away."

Lila was shocked into silence. She couldn't speak as the words caught in her throat. She loved him, she loved their rings, she loved their combined symbols—the crow and the sun—and most of all, she loved *their* forever. Even if his forever were longer than hers.

At the thought, doubt settled in.

"You don't like it?" Ambrose asked, concerned. Finally, he sat up, pulling her into a seated position on his lap, with his arms still wrapped around her waist.

"No, I love it! I just... I just realized I said *forever*, but... my forever is much shorter than your forever. Does that—" she paused, remembering what he'd told her of bargains. If either end isn't upheld, the promiser will die. "If my forever ends, but yours continues... will you die when I do?"

Ambrose considered for a moment. "I'm not sure." She saw a nerve in his jaw tick, as he clenched his teeth together. "But let's not worry about that now." He took a deep breath and smiled, tucking her hair behind her ear. "I think we should clean up, get dressed, and go enjoy that party. Nostro knows how to throw them, and it'd be a shame to miss it completely."

There was something behind his smile, Lila almost thought it was fear. But she let it go, not wanting to ruin their joyous moment. As he said, they had forever to figure it out. Right now, she just wanted him.

Lila smirked, and climbed in his lap, straddling him once more. "Mmm, yes to your plan, but not just yet. I plan on fucking you forever, and I want that forever to start right now. Fuck me again, Ambrose Draven." And with a devious grin, she kissed him.

The Sun Child

Washed and dressed, Lila and Ambrose returned to the booming floor of the party. Ambrose put on the clothes he wore earlier, the sheer top tucked into the high-waisted black pants. He looked absolutely divine, and Lila had to fight herself not to jump his bones for a third time.

She decided to wear a matching all-black outfit. She wore a dress with a snug corset, hugging her ribs and curves in all the best places. The long sheer skirts pooled from her waist, revealing her bare legs, and the bodysuit under the skirts covered her modestly, while still leaving her feeling completely sexy. It didn't help that Ambrose seemed to be having a hard time taking his eyes off his future wife. Before they left their room, Ambrose buckled black heels onto her feet, and gave her a set of mismatched earrings—one was the pair with his long sun earring, while the other was a small stud of a moon.

You look like a goddess, his voice sounded husky through the Concord—the same voice he used when he was hungry for *her*. It seemed he was having an equally difficult time not taking her again as well.

Would you worship me? she teased, as they made their way through the booming room.

I would be on my knees night and day, worshiping you, praising you, giving you everything you want. In fact, that is exactly how I plan to spend our marriage.

Lila smiled, pressing her lips together. For now, she wanted to keep this joy to herself and Ambrose.

"There you two are," called a voice getting close to

them. "We've been looking for you." It was Rebekkah, and behind her were Bogdan's two daughters.

"Well, looking for you is putting it strongly. We've glanced around the crowd whenever we got a drink." The older one—Alyssa, Lila thought—smiled.

Ambrose grinned, "It's good to see you, Alyssa, Elizabeth. And your father?"

The younger one, Elizabeth, looked around the room. Her big blue eyes were like saucers as they scanned the crowd. "He's around somewhere, probably trying to keep Uncle Gustov in check."

Uncle? Lila thought briefly.

He's not related by blood, Ambrose said to her, reading her mind as always. *But they're close enough to be family. Like us with Kaz and Constance.*

Lila smiled at the mention of their names, of the familiarity in her heart. She missed them desperately and couldn't wait to see them and Pollock, and to be reunited—finally—with Marcus.

Rebekkah turned to the girls, "Alyssa, Elizabeth, this is Lila Bran. Lila, as I'm sure you've already figured out, these are Bogdan's daughters.

"The reason he's bald, as he always says," Alyssa giggled.

"Sorry, if our father's a bit . . . intense," Elizabeth huffed. "He looks scary, but he's not really—well . . . vampires, right?"

Lila smiled. "No worries, he was a perfect gentleman. You want to talk about intense vampire meetings? Do you know Ambrose pushed me from a window the first time we met?"

"He did *what?*" Rebekkah gasped. "That first night you went to his manor?"

Ambrose dragged his palm down his face. "Not my finest moment."

Lila giggled, "Definitely not."

"Ah! Why if it isn't the finest group of ladies in all of the Malvania!" Nostro appeared next to her, grabbing her arm and spinning her. "And Draven. Why are you all standing around? I haven't seen you on the dance floor all night, darling!"

Lila spun and spun, and when she finally stopped, Nostro held up a frozen drink for her. It was a light lavender in color and had a lemon wedge on the glass. "I think you'll like this, it's sweet while still packing a good punch."

"What is it?" she asked, taking it anyway.

"Alcohol, of course. A drink I've made just for you! I'm calling it the Sun Child." He winked. "It's sweet lemons and a special, sweet pea blend of gin. Drink some of that, and then you and I are going to dance, all right?"

Is it safe? she asked Ambrose.

He reached over her, took the drink from her hand, and sipped it. "Mmm. Delicious, Gustov. A Sun Child you say? I would *love* to drink one of those." He winked at Lila. Then, Ambrose took a breath in her mind. *I think so. He'd never do anything to actually harm you, but if you start to feel odd let me know. Cute drink, though.*

He handed it back to her, and as Lila sipped she let Nostro guide her to the center of the dance floor. The crowd of people moved for him, creating a pathway of dancing, smiling bodies. It wasn't regal dancing like on Sanktus Pernox, and Lila was so ready to experience the jumping and jiving. She sipped her drink and turned to Nostro. He smiled at her and slid his shades over his eyes.

"Get ready for this, my dear." And immediately after, he popped his arm, flicked his wrist, popped his chest, and bobbed his head back and forth. It took a moment, but Lila realized the man was dancing. She burst into laughter before copying his movements, and jumping along whenever she felt it. The rhythm was a heavy beat, and as Lila sipped her drink, she felt herself care less of how she looked, and care more about the freedom she felt from swinging her limbs around.

You two look like fools, Ambrose chuckled through the Concord. *The two happiest fools in the entire room.*

Lila's laugh came from her chest, and then she told him, *Well, make it three fools. Get out here! I want to dance with my future husband.*

Ambrose didn't hesitate. He sauntered up to Lila and Nostro—who was still spinning in circles with his hands above his head—and took her hand.

Ask me for anything, love, and I will do it.

Lila blushed as she started dancing with him—though, it was still much less dancing and much more jumping. Eventually, another hand touched her waist, and Rebekkah was by her side, red faced and smiling as she joined the small crew, all following Nostro's strange lead. And soon after, Bogdan's daughters dragged their father behind them and joined their small jumping, dancing, bundle.

Lila thought, as she snapped her arms to and fro, shaking her hips, and spinning whenever she had the chance, this was *fun,* and Lila had been in desperate need of fun.

Nostro took her arm and called in her ear, "See, I told you I knew how to throw a good revel." And damn him, he was right. Though, she thought more than once he'd pop a hip or break a bone with the moves he was doing.

Lila had no idea how long they'd been dancing for, there were no windows throughout the floor to indicate daybreak, but Lila was sure it should be well into the morning by the time the music began to quiet and the bodies of revelers slowly dwindled. She spotted some still using the curtained rooms for pleasure, but most now had vampires passed out, laying on top of each other. Others seemed to have gone to the many rooms Nostro had available, and others—she assumed—left the Maggot Mansion tower altogether.

Bogdan and his daughters said their good mornings, and disappeared up the staircase, and only a few moments later, Rebekkah excused herself, stumbling toward her room with a lazy smile on her lips.

Shall we retire too, love? Ambrose asked, as a slow song came on.

Yes, maybe after this—

Nostro turned to her, gently grabbing her hand. "I'm afraid this old man is officially worn out. Lila, dear, will you honor me with one last dance?"

She grinned and nodded, following Nostro's lead.

I'll be right back, she told Ambrose.

Take your time, love. And she could feel his eyes watching every sway of her hips.

As the song played slowly, Nostro spun Lila, his hands gently guiding her as they rested high on her back and the other holding her hand with those incredibly long and decrepit fingers.

"What do you think of the Maggot Mansion so far?" he asked.

"Honestly, not what I expected."

"Oh?" he spun her again. "And what did you expect?"

She shrugged shyly. "Before meeting Ambrose, my entire knowledge of vampires came from my time with the Reinicks. Lord and Lady Reinick weren't awful per se, but they still kept murine, and then my encounters with the brothers—it led me to believe *all* vampires were like that. That all had murine and were just awful monsters. Even when I met Ambrose, I thought the worst of him."

"And then?"

"Then I *met* him. He saved me from that place, and though he pretended to do it only for his benefit, I quickly learned it was . . . more. Then I met Constance, and some of the vampires of the Crow Court, then Darius Maronai, the Cambrias, and Bogdan at Sanktus Pernox. At first, I thought everyone treated me well because of Ambrose. But the Crow Court nor the Arachnid Estate employee murine, and while I'm not sure of the Maggot Mansion, you have been nothing but kind to me, Gustov."

He smiled bashfully. "We do not have murine in the same sense the Morada holds them. Here, they are murine in name alone. Like the Crow Court, we pay for blood. Murine come and work in the tower for as long as they please, and are paid. They do more than just give us their blood. They cook, clean, build, and live here. Murine here is just another word for servant or maid." He paused, watching her. "In fact, the word murine originated in the Maggot Mansion four hundred years ago, during the Mass Death. We gave work to those cast out by society for sympathizing with the vampire cause. The Reinicks took the word and exploited it, mistranslating servant for slave. I know you are not unfamiliar with what they made you become, but the vampire manors of Malvania had been very against the murine blood bags. Has Ambrose told you of the eight manors?"

She nodded, remembering the other four manors that hadn't made it.

"Many of them believed in murine. Thought themselves better than humans. From what I'm told, it is very similar to what Drusilla Reclus currently believes in and is fighting for. With Ambrose Draven having been a slave of man, myself a peasant, and Darius Maronai a romantic, we fought to protect that line in the sand. To protect that which feeds us. After all, if humans went extinct—"

"So would vampires."

He spun her again. "Precisely. I think at some point, Lorent Reinick just chose the winning team, and of course his wife, Cassandra, and their children followed. The other manors fell, and murine as slaves were all but extinct. Until, they suddenly weren't." He watched her for a moment. "I truly am sorry for all your brother and you have been through, Lila. Truly. And please know, humans are treated very differently here."

She smiled softly, and stopped swaying. "For a time, the Reinicks stopped using murine, when they preferred my brother and me over the starved citizens of their lands. It didn't last long, though. In fact, the last *revel* I attended was one of theirs."

"Let me guess, mine looks like flowers budding in springtime in comparison?"

Lila giggled. "You could say that. The bodies . . . they weren't even drained. It was all just for the pleasure of killing them—killing *us*."

Nostro studied her for a moment before extending his arm out to her. "Can I show you one more thing before we retire for the day?"

Lila nodded and took his arm.

I'll meet you in the room, she told Ambrose.

Call if you need me. Remember, he's still a vampire. And I'm sure he still wants a demonstration—be on guard.

Always.

She felt Ambrose leave, and as she followed Nostro back to the elevator, she saw they'd been the last in the room.

26

"What if you could do something about it?" Nostro said as he punched the button on the elevator. They were going to the 204th floor—the *top* floor.

"Do something about what?"

"The murine residing in the Viper Morada."

Lila contemplated. "I would like to free them. To show them the world beyond the Morada, to show them that vampires and humans can and *should* coexist."

She saw Nostro nod from the corner of her eye before he turned to face her.

"I will stop playing coy. I want to make a bargain with you, Miss Bran. And I mean *with you*, not Draven. I have the utmost respect for him, but this is only something you can give me."

Lila lifted an eyebrow, turning to him. "I'm listening."

Nostro smirked and turned back to the grate. "I will tell you when we arrive. For all I know, your lover is still eavesdropping. He's head over heels for you, you know."

Lila smirked. "I know."

"I've known him since before he was first changed, and I have never seen him as he is now," he chuckled. "Love radiates off of him, his eyes practically melt anytime they land on you—which is always, by the way. He has been looking at you every moment I've seen him since your arrival."

Lila blushed, remembering the feel of his eyes on her, the hot trace running along her back like his fingers grazing over her skin.

"I'm happy the both of you have found a love like that."

The elevator dinged, and Nostro pushed open the door. "Now, Miss Bran, will you, um—" he rubbed his hands together. "Will you take my arm again, please?"

Nostro's demeanor had changed. She wasn't sure what it was, but he seemed . . . nervous. Lila took his arm, and Nostro took a deep breath.

"Gustov, what's—"

He pushed the final door open to reveal the stone rooftop of the tower, blindingly lit with sunlight.

With his free hand, Nostro pushed the blackened shades onto his eyes with a small hiss.

Then he took a step forward.

"What are you—"

"Testing a theory, Miss Bran, a theory I have a really good hunch about." Another step, dragging Lila with him.

"A theory? You'll *die*!"

"Not if my theory is correct."

"Gustov!"

"Tell me, do you love Ambrose Draven?"

Another step.

"I—What? Of course I do."

"Tell me about it."

Another step.

But this time, Lila was beginning to understand.

She took a step with him.

"I love that he *sees* me. He knew from the moment we met, I was not the meek murine the Reinicks made me out to be."

Step.

"Go on," Nostro insisted. His feet were at the borderline of shadow and sunlight.

"I was always brave, always a bit reckless, but he made me see it in myself. He didn't give me power. He gave *my* power to me. He made me *see* myself."

They took a step, Nostro's skin touching the sunlight. And as Lila and Nostro held their breaths . . . nothing happened.

"And he's good in bed, I'm sure, right?" Nostro nervously chuckled, forcing the same nervous sound out of Lila.

"That definitely helps. But it doesn't even begin to cover it. He is just . . . everything. He has helped me at every turn, he has a heart of gold though he pretends not to. He cares *so much* and *so deeply* for those he loves. He is the kind of man who would stop at nothing to help those in need."

"Is that why you're marrying him?"

The question hit Lila like a punch. She wasn't exactly hiding her finger, but she hadn't said the words out loud yet. But leave it to senile old Gustov Nostro to be the one to notice.

She swallowed. "Yes, that is why I am marrying him. Because I love him and I know he loves me. And I want whatever our forevers will be, to be together."

Nostro smiled, and the two of them stood in the gleaming light of the early afternoon sun. It must've been just before noon, and Nostro stood, breathing deeply.

"Don't let go," he whispered. "I don't know if I need to be touching you to be here, but just in case I'd rather not turn into a crisp."

Lila cocked an eyebrow again. "Oh, *now* you'd rather not burn? Not five seconds ago?"

He waved her sass away. "I knew what I was doing, dear."

"Yeah? And what's that?"

"I was being guided into the daylight by the Sun Child. When you get this old, life becomes all about taking risks." He wiggled those caterpillar eyebrows.

Lila laughed from her belly, and copied Nostro who'd thrown his head back to embrace the light.

"It really does feel like you," he whispered. "I couldn't remember exactly if it was the same. But it is. Only, your warmth is more comforting. This is getting a little hot, and my skin is . . . perspiring," he chuckled.

"Well, you are in a long black coat. That tends to add to overall heat and sweat."

"Such a smartass," Nostro tutted behind a grin. "The sky is also a blue I didn't remember. I thought it'd be . . . darker? But it's beautiful. Like a gem."

Truthfully, Lila also had forgotten what true sunlight felt like. She'd been out only at night, dusk, or dawn, whenever the sun was still too shy to come out fully.

Now, she felt like warmth was filling her blood, her bones. She felt like the sunflowers in Nostro's memory, reaching for the source of it all.

"You're getting warmer, dear. I think you're recharging."

They stood in silence for another few moments, arm in arm, before he pulled her down to the floor, lying flat on the stone with his arms splayed out like a sunbathing starfish. Lila lay next to him, her hand holding his.

"Tell me about this bargain," she said.

He hummed, not looking at her. "Tomorrow I will make a bargain with Ambrose to test your skills in exchange for joining your endeavor against Drusilla and her strigoi."

Lila shot up. "You'll *what*?"

"Relax, dear, I'm telling you now, aren't I? I know the Crow Lord well. And while he's had his eyes on you all night, he's also kept his distance, allowing his most treasured possession to walk around a den of vampires. Seeing his faith in you, and meeting you myself—plus, now there is this," he reached a long boney hand toward the sun above them. "I will go anywhere the Sun Child tells me to. I believe in your power, Lila, but over this short evening, I've also come to believe in *you*. I am proof right now, lying in the sun, of your power and the truth to the prophecy. But I need my people to see it as well. So, tomorrow, I will ask Ambrose to have you show me your power."

"Why not just ask me directly?"

"Because it needs to be a bargain between the Crow Lord and the Maggot Lord, a union between manors."

Lila remembered the feather tattoo on Maronai's hand while they were at the Arachnid Estate—the same bargain she knew Ambrose would ask of Nostro.

She sighed, lying back once more. "You vampires and your bargains."

"It's rather stupid, isn't it?" He chuckled. "Anyway, for demonstration, I will have you complete a sort of . . . obstacle course. In what I can only assume were throes of passion, you cured half of the strigoi population in the dungeons of my tower, which I thank you for. Those were good people who shouldn't have been forced into what they were. But many strigoi, like the one I'm told attacked you in the Arachnid Estate, are beyond saving. I will throw a few at you, nothing more than you can handle. But use your judgment. Heal those you can, attack and defend against those you cannot."

"Great, so you want me to fight. You do realize I haven't properly trained in the three months I've been captive to the Reinicks, right?"

Nostro waved her away again. "Darling, you have *power* now. What use are muscles when you can incinerate a man just with a touch?"

He had a point.

"Plus, I saw you on the dance floor. I know your body is still more than capable."

And sitting out here in the sun, Lila knew he was right. Something about her didn't feel like the weakling she'd been when she first snapped out of the collar-induced haze. Nor how she felt when she first went to the Crow Court. She didn't *feel* weak.

She wondered, had she healed her body in more ways than she knew after the Viper Morada?

"Okay, then what's the bargain you want with me?"

"Simple. In exchange for your compliance tomorrow, and making sure Ambrose agrees—because I doubt he will agree to this *for* you, especially knowing there is a possibility of danger—I will help you liberate and rehabilitate the murine of the Viper Morada."

Lila felt her eyes go wide as she turned to him.

"You'd—You care that much? For humans?"

"Believe it or not, dear, I once *was* human."

Lila sat up. "I—I know. But . . ."

"I've told you. Humans and vampires must coexist in order to live. And I do not believe treating one as slaves is the way to go. Humans treated vampires like monsters who had to live in the shadows. Gather enough angry vampires and the Mass Death happened. Who is to say the tide will not soon flow the other way? It is not about right and wrong, good and evil, monster and man—it is about balance." He lifted his hand to the sun, reaching those long skeletal fingers. "With the day comes the night. With the sun comes the moon. They are not enemies, they are a cycle. A cycle that depends on the other to continue. The sun is not a slave to the moon, and the moon is not a slave to the sun, and therefore man should not be a slave to a monster and vice versa. Help me, Lila, and I will help you liberate your two worlds. Your heart and your mind. Your soul and your skin."

"All at the price of me agreeing to show off my powers?"

"I need my people to rally behind you, just as I am. I need them to see and to feel just as I do. They will not blindly believe just on my words alone. Many of my people have been affected by Drusilla's strigoi. It is a sickness long overdue for a remedy, and the Maggot Mansion has been hit by it the hardest. If they see you heal those who we've believed had no hope of being healed, they will fall to their knees for you. We believe in the Sun Child here, Lila. Children have been told her story for centuries. And they will see you and they will *know* you."

Lila didn't hesitate, "All right, Gustov Nostro—you have a deal."

He smiled a toothy grin, full of sharp fangs. "Then, my dear, it's rather hot and I think this old man will like a good day's rest."

They both stood, and as Lila glimpsed down at their still joined hands, a small sun with wispy rays sat tattooed in the flesh between Nostro's thumbs and wrists.

"Get some good rest," Nostro said, leading her to the elevator. "You'll need it. For at midnight, you'll be entering the arena."

27

Ambrose waited for Lila. It wasn't too long, but long enough he grew concerned Nostro decided to throw another party, or suddenly play a very elongated game of chess, or maybe even force her into a slumber party. Who knew what that crazy old man would be up to.

But then she delicately pushed the door open, as if he were asleep. Like he'd sleep without her there in his arms. Lila crept in, and as she saw him awake, leaning against the edge of the coffin, she smiled.

"You waited for me."

"Darling, I've waited four hundred years for you. An hour is nothing."

She smiled at that, and fuck was it heart-stopping. Each jolt of emotion he had for her made him want to run up to her and engulf her in his arms, to kiss every part of her, to squeeze her and hold her and feel her.

But he had to be the cool, collected one.

"What did you and Nostro talk about?"

"Not much. But . . . I've had a suspicion about my power, and he helped me prove it."

"Oh?"

She just grinned again. "I'll show you tomorrow. Now, I just need to take this dress off."

"Is that an invitation?"

Lila quirked an eyebrow. "Maybe. But I'll make you work for it."

"Tempting," Ambrose huffed a breath.

Lila spun, moving her long gorgeous hair to the side, "Since you're offering, can you help?"

Damned Little Crow, Ambrose chuckled. He placed his hands on her shoulders and pulled her back toward him. Beginning with the bottom lace, he started the arduous work of untying her corset. He loved doing this, loved seeing the skin of her back slowly unveil itself to him, loved undressing her—not for the purposes of more sex, but the closeness of the action.

She sighed when the corset loosened from her ribs, and soon the dress was untied completely. Ambrose pulled it down her body, letting the skirt and bodysuit drop to the floor. Then he threw his arms around her bare waist, and hugged her close. His hand drifted between her breasts and settled over her heart, feeling each thump under his palm, as she leaned back into him.

"My favorite sound," he mused. "Other than those sweet little moans, and your screams when I'm making you come, of course."

She hummed. "You're ravenous."

"For you? Always." He kissed up the side of her neck, and lifted her in his arms. "Tell me, love, can you handle me once more?" He placed her on the mattress of the coffin. It was flat and sitting on a tall stone table. Ambrose leaned his arms over the edge, his fingers trailing over her thigh as he looked down on her. "Or is that sweet little pussy too sore from earlier?"

Her cheeks immediately flushed and he saw as she ever so slightly pressed her thighs together. His heart jumped into overdrive, as he caught the first scent of her sex.

"I . . . I'm sore," she breathed.

He lifted an eyebrow. She was playing hard to get, so he could play the tease.

"Are you now? I thought your warmth would heal that. Shall I help you?" He traced his finger up her thigh, slowly, delicately. "Maybe targeted affection will force your power to give it the much-needed attention your pussy needs." He let his hand pause just before her core. "What do you think?"

Lords, he loved seeing her squirm. Especially as she lay below him, nude. It was absolutely maddening, he'd never have enough of her. He thought of their month-long hideaway they spoke of while she was in the Morada, and wished they had the time for that.

But now they were at war, and tomorrow he'd ask Nostro to join him. Then, they'd fly south, to the Arachnid Estate, rejoin the others, and solidify their plan to take back their home and bring Drusilla and Hektor to their knees.

"We can try," Lila squeaked, a bashful grin spreading over her lips.

The war could wait till nightfall.

For now, Ambrose planned to spend every moment cherishing and worshiping the woman he loved. He tore off his clothes and snuggled in beside her, spooning her and he pressed his cock against her ass.

"Remember my fingers inside of you, love?" he whispered in her ear. "In the Arachnid Estate, when I first touched you?"

She huffed a laugh as he cupped her breast. "How could I forget?"

"Well, I plan to do that again—but this time, I *will* give you anything you ask, for as long you ask." He thrust his middle two fingers into her. "And I will have you coming on my fingers till your perfect little pussy is nice and healed."

Lila bit back a moan.

"No, Lila. I want to hear it all." He plunged his fingers into her, and the room echoed with the sound of his name on her lips.

She'd been so warm, he didn't even need a blanket, but the soft furs on their bodies made the coffin even more comfortable.

Lila, against him, tucked herself into a little ball against his side. He didn't want to move her, didn't want her to wake just yet, but he knew their day should begin—especially if he was going to train her before going to chat with Nostro.

He planted kisses all along her cheek, her arm, the curve of her side, and the roundness of her hips.

"Lila, love—"

She groaned and turned away from him, pulling the blanket over her shoulder. He huffed a laugh, and scootched closer, climbing over her. But she stayed hidden under the heap of blanket, so Ambrose decided a *better* way to wake her up.

Remembering their first morning together in a coffin, when she sucked him off so fucking well, he often found himself fantasizing of her lips on his cock in idle moments.

And rousing her from sleep by devouring her sweet pussy seemed like the perfect way to waken her.

He inched down her body and pushed the blanket around her waist, shifting her leg so it rested bent over his shoulder. She wasn't wet yet, but he'd soon change that.

He took a lazy lick up her center, coating her in his tongue. She breathed and shifted a bit, but barely stirred, so he did it again, flicking his tongue against her clit.

A small gasp escaped her lips, and he smiled against her as he fully took her. He sucked her clit into his mouth, flicking his tongue against it, until she was moaning in her sleep. Her pussy dripped for him, and he let nothing go to waste as he lapped it up.

Suddenly, her hand shot into his hair.

"Good evening," she mumbled, pressing him against her sex.

He chuckled. "Needy Little Crow, you like my wakeup call?"

She lazily nodded, eyes still closed as she turned on her back and spread her legs for him. "More."

Ambrose drove his tongue into her entrance, sending her back arching against him.

"Grind your pussy on my tongue, darling."

"Ah—this fucking tongue," she hissed, but she did as she was told, like the good girl she was.

"Lords, you taste divine. Always." He withdrew his tongue, focusing again on her clit, flicking it back and forth with his tongue and sucking it into his mouth, nibbling on her till she moaned. "Watch me devour you, love."

Lila peeked her eyes open, and those gorgeous golden-brown orbs watched him, heat filling her everywhere as he felt it radiate off of her, radiate from *inside* of her.

"Magic pussy," he chuckled, dragging his tongue from her entrance to her clit.

"Magic tongue," she moaned. And he loved how much she loved it. He would feast on her for every meal if he could.

A knock rang on the door, and before Ambrose could yell at them to disappear, Lila screamed, "Go away!" and moaned, throwing her head back and bucking her hips into him.

As he said—needy little thing.

He pulled his tongue away, letting her have a moment of respite, and lifted a hand. "For being such a good girl, I'll give you a reward." Lila lifted her eyebrows. "Tell me what you want, love."

Lila grinned, and leaped up, turning so her ass was in his face again and her hands and knees were on the coffin mattress. She looked at him over her shoulder.

"Anything?"

He grinned and nodded.

"Just one thing?"

Ambrose tapped his chin, knowing full well he didn't even need to contemplate his answer.

"That depends on how nicely you ask for the others."

She grinned at him, and if Ambrose hadn't known her heart, he would think it was a smile of the wicked. "Spank me. Hard. Spank my pussy, leave your mark, and then make it feel better with your tongue."

Ambrose blinked, long and slow, and then he felt the corner of his lips tilt into a smile that he could only imagine matched Lila's.

"Yes, my love."

He rubbed his hand on her ass, and spanked it hard, leaving a red print pulsing. She moaned at the impact, and he saw her pussy clench as more dripped from her.

"Again," she breathed.

His hand landed a little lower this time, slapping the

lips between her thighs. She moaned so loud, Ambrose thought she may wake the entire tower.

"Again!" she moaned, shaking her ass.

"Isn't spanking—" the plump lips were stained red "a form of punishment?" he asked.

Between moans, she huffed, "Not when—you do it—*so good*." He spanked her pussy again, and she nearly convulsed, it rocked her so hard.

"Are you going to come already, love? I thought there was more you want—"

The knocking picked up again.

Lila whimpered, "Not now." She let her front half fall to the mattress, just sticking her pink ass in the air.

Ambrose could tell she was so close to coming, the look in her eyes, the pink to her cheeks. *Crack.* He spanked her again, and just as she moaned, the knocking picked up louder and faster. But Ambrose only caressed the spot he'd just smacked, as Lila pushed into his touch.

"Master Draven! Miss Bran! You are needed." The voice called. "We were instructed to bring you no matter what, even if we have to bust down the door and take you as you are."

Lila whimpered again, and Ambrose cursed, seeing red. But he ignored it and spanked her again. At Lila's answering moan, he pressed his face into her sex, licking and kissing her red, swollen lips. His nose pressed into her ass cheek, and the moment his tongue was on her, she melted.

Fuck, she was delicious. Perfect. He wanted more, more, more. Ambrose reached for those lilac strands, fisting her hair between his knuckles and pulling her back. She moaned again, a guttural sound, with her neck pulled taut.

His mouth moved, his tongue circling that tight, puckered hole as he spread her cheeks as far as they'd go. Lila stiffened and made a noise he'd never heard her make before—throbbing his desperate cock, already impossibly thick—just as she pressed her hips back, begging for more.

His tongue toyed with her ass, pressing into her as he smacked her again. She moaned so loud, it was all he heard. He wanted to own this ass, to shove his cock inside of it till she came. It was so round and perfect—so biteable and *so* fuckable.

Ambrose! Lila yelped through the Concord as another moan slipped from her lips. *We have a viewer again, just so you know.*

Mine, mine, mine.

Immediately, his tongue stopped in their tracks. Turning to the open doorway, he roared, "What the *fuck*?!" and shifted into the large monster from anger alone. "*What?*" he hissed.

Someone was watching, and he hadn't even realized. He hadn't heard the door open or felt another presence. It was only Lila and her sweet moans, Lila and her sweet ass, *Lila, Lila, Lila, Lila, Lila, Lila, Lila, Lila, Lila.*

A small man stood just inside the doorway, eyes focused on his feet, and though Ambrose could've easily doubled him in size, the man didn't even flinch. He wore the billowing dark gray and black of the Maggot Mansion and his features were schooled into utter indifference— even as Ambrose growled before him, a savage monster completely nude.

"Master Nostro wishes for your audience on the grand floor." And without waiting for a response, the man turned, took a few steps down the hall, and called over his shoulder, "Now."

Ambrose bit his tongue from cursing the man out, and instead slammed the door, shaking the walls around him.

He felt his body shake, the anger rising over their ruined moment.

"I guess we'll have to continue later," Lila sighed. But her voice sounded . . . fine. Not upset at all, maybe a little disappointed. But no anger. So why was he? Why was he *so* easily angered now?

He pressed his lips together and rolled his shoulders, shifting back into his humanoid form before turning to her as she crawled down from their coffin. Her ass and pussy were *bright* red. Almost welting. Not completely unlike the lashes on her back from Drusilla's whip.

Ambrose clenched his fists, knuckles white.

She tilted her head. "What's wrong?"

He wanted to scream.

"Nothing. You weren't bothered he saw?"

She shrugged. "We had viewers yesterday, so . . . not really. I'm more upset we had to stop. I liked that, by the way . . . a lot."

"A gentleman would have asked for permission before doing something like that," he grunted. But Ambrose was glad she enjoyed it. He fucking loved it. Maybe too much.

Lila smirked. "And what would I do with a gentleman?"

Ambrose turned back to her, and faked a smile. A part of him wondered if she could see through it, but instead of addressing it, he walked to the leathers he'd worked with Nostro to get. "I don't know what Nostro has planned. Better go prepared in case."

Lila grabbed his arm, forcing him to turn back. "You've been . . . on edge. Or . . . I don't know." She looked up at him, tilting her head. "Did something . . . change?"

Ambrose paused.

He was so incredibly happy. He'd made love to the woman he wanted to spend his immortal life with, proposing and promising to love her forever.

But fear and anger and a dirty, filthy kind of hunger had been spreading over his bones. He wanted to ravage her. To bite into her again as he fucked her like an animal. Not a single drop of him cared for her safety at that moment. He could have broken her and not even noticed.

But instead of saying any of that, he swallowed it all down his throat. Ambrose gently kissed her on the forehead, smiling that same, fake grin, and said, "It's nothing. Let's talk later." And without letting her pry more, Ambrose handed her a pair of black leather pants.

28

Lila knew something was off, he'd been so tense the night he'd rescued her, and she saw that again now—saw it earlier when he'd bitten her as she dangled from ropes. Ambrose wasn't *different* exactly, just... changed. Charged. But, after the three months she'd had, maybe she had changed too.

The smile he faked hid something behind it, and she *would* find out what it was, but Lila knew her mind needed to be focused right now as they descended the tower to the first floor—the grand floor as the servant had called it.

Lila was going to face a challenge, and she needed to be ready. The leather Ambrose had given her was a bit thicker than what she'd worn in the Crow Court, and the sleeves ended at her wrist to protect every inch possible. Every part of her was also strapped with weapons—daggers, stakes, even a small crossbolt. Ambrose even requested a new gorget, fastening it around her neck before they left their room.

She hadn't trained in combat in months, not properly, but she felt invigorated as they descended the stairs, with the weapons strapped to her back. While her time with the Reinicks maybe made her physically weaker, she grew stronger in a different way. She learned about her powers, and she felt more prepared now—for anything—than ever before.

Maybe the sunlight had healed more than her wounds, maybe it healed all of her, eliminating the effect the viper venom had on her completely. She felt strong, powerful, and unafraid.

"I wouldn't be surprised if Nostro has something up his sleeve," Ambrose said behind her. "Keep your guard up."

She hadn't had a chance to tell him of her deal with Nostro, so instead of lying to him or word vomit now, she nodded and stayed silent. Lila hated hiding things from him, but it would all come out in just a moment anyway.

As they descended the final level, Lila heard the boom of voices, and something within her rattled. The last time she'd heard voices like this was right before the collar was put on her.

The last time she'd heard voices like this, she'd killed them all.

"Hey, are you all right?" Ambrose gently placed his hand on her back, startling her from the memories of flesh melting to the ground.

She studied him then, studied him as he studied her.

He'd dressed for war as well, and together they looked like two agents of Death, ready to take their marks. The black leather snuggly hugged Ambrose's chest and biceps, the sleeves stopping just above his elbows. The high neck would delay—not stop—a bite from an enemy vampire or strigoi. There was a cutout in the top, over the crow tattoo

THE SUN CHILD

on his chest in the shape of an upside-down triangle—something Lila has continuously referred to as his "boob window" before the panic set in. The leathers were meant to withstand shifting between his human and monstrous form, and he would be ready to swing into action if Lila ever needed it.

"Ye-yeah. I have . . . a lot to tell you," she sighed. "But not now." Ambrose knitted his eyebrows together, and looked ready to argue, but Lila stopped him. "And *you* have a lot to tell me." Ambrose's throat bobbed. "Don't think I haven't noticed, vampire. You've been holding yourself back, like you're afraid you'll break . . . something. Like you'll break me."

Uncharacteristically, Ambrose bit his lip, drawing a small droplet of blood the moment his fang pressed into it. "We do have much to discuss," he agreed. "Let's get this over with, and then I'll tell you everything."

As Lila and Ambrose entered the grand floor, the cacophony of noise burst through the doorway. It was so disarming, so disorienting, it took Lila a moment to focus on the room before her. As she followed behind Ambrose, she noticed they were exiting onto an elevated platform at the far end of a massive colosseum-like room. There were people all around in their seats, and at the other end of the room was another elevated platform in which Nostro, Bogdan, his family, and a number of other vampires of the Maggot Mansion resided in ornate seats.

But what made Lila dread her bargain more than anything was the pit below the platforms, in the center of the colosseum.

It was a damned battle arena.

"What's the meaning of this, Nostro?" Ambrose said, and the crowd in the stadium silenced immediately, as though they, too, were drawn to his voice.

"You have a bargain for me, don't you, Draven? Well, I came prepared."

"You already know what I want?" He stepped to the edge of the platform, and as Lila followed, she noticed stone walls rising from the stone floors of the pit, leading in all directions and coming to a center point. Nostro hadn't told her there'd be a *maze*.

Act surprised! Nostro said into her mind.

I am surprised! she whisper-yelled back through her mind.

Fuck, they had a Concord. She forgot her communication from mind to mind came with a bargain, not just something she intently had with Ambrose. She wondered if the Concord links would cross, but before she could ask or test it, Nostro responded to Ambrose.

"I have an idea. I'm assuming you asked the same of Darius Maronai while you were in his manor on Sanktus Pernox?"

Ambrose crossed his arms over his wide chest. "You'd be correct. I want the Maggot Mansion to ally with the Crow Court and the Arachnid Estate in fighting off Drusilla and the Viper Morada." He paused. "What's left of it, at least. I know your manor has been affected by the rising numbers of the strigoi—if we unite the manors once more, we have a higher chance of fighting them off than we do apart."

"Sounds promising," and Lila swore she saw a smirk flash over his mouth.

"Now, what do you want in return?"

Ready for the show, Sun Child? Nostro asked.

Stop teasing him, she retorted.

"I want a demonstration—"

"Fuck," Ambrose cursed. *I knew it,* he said in her mind, and keeping up with both Concords, and the verbal conversation the two men were having was slowly giving Lila a headache.

"Of the Sun Child's power."

"This is a bargain between you and me, Nostro. Don't bring Lila into this—"

"I want to prove to my people she is who you say she is."

Ambrose bristled again. "Can you not *feel* who she is?"

"*She* can speak for herself—" Lila began, but immediately was spoken over by Nostro.

"Of course I can. But I need definitive proof if I am to rage war for you. For her."

"For *you* as well. You think you are safe here if Drusilla takes the other manors?"

Now, Lila, Nostro beckoned.

"Ambrose," Lila demanded, "If this is what it takes, I'll do it."

He turned to her then, reading her face. *Are you sure? I don't want to speak for you.*

Lila nodded. *I can do this.*

He studied her a moment longer. *Okay. But if* anything *becomes too much, I swear to the crows, I will rip his head off.*

Lila couldn't help but smirk. He was always so quick to threaten murder for her.

Ambrose took her hand in his, gripping it tight, and turned back to the other platform. "All right, Nostro. A bargain made with me is a bargain made with Lila, and vice versa. *She* can choose to accept or not."

He looked at her through the corners of his eyes, watching her. *I guess I was wrong. Ambrose Draven, the bargain king, is leaving it up to you. I guess it doesn't need to be between vampire manors.*

A smirk spread over Lila's lips. *It is between manors. He's just giving me the power to speak for this one.*

"Gustov Nostro, on behalf of the Crow Court, we accept the bargain. What will you have me do?"

Lila really regretted saying yes to this.

She stood in the pit, so far below, she only saw the speck of Ambrose on the raised platform above at the entrance to the maze. The stone below her booted feet was damp and smelled like earth. If the elevated platforms were the ground floor, the pit had to be below the first level, *below ground*.

The thought of maggots worming through dirt underground sprang to her mind, making her cringe.

"Deep breaths, Lila," she told herself. "Deep breaths."

It's a labyrinth, Ambrose stated.

What?

A labyrinth. Not a maze. It took a moment, but from here I can see the winding path doesn't break. Meaning there is no wrong way to go, it all leads to the center. So don't think about it, and just follow the path, keep your powers on standby, and let me know if you need me. Lila knew he'd swoop down in less than heartbeat if she needed him, so she took a shaky breath and stepped forward.

That helped. Thank you, she said, and passed the first wall to the labyrinth.

As Lila continued through the long, winding path, she realized the sound from above wasn't echoed here. It became so silent between the stone walls, Lila nearly forgot the crowd of vampires sitting in the stadium seating, all eyes on her. All she could hear were the sounds of her steps and the deep breaths she was forcing herself to take. Her fingers nervously flicked back and forth as they rested by her side, ready to conjure the power coursing through her.

A screech bounced off the wall to her right, and suddenly a hand wrapped around her ankle, nails digging into her flesh, as they pulled her down. Lila threw her hands up, stopping her face from colliding with the floor, and used her strength to flip herself onto her back as she drove her foot into her attacker's head.

That was . . . Ambrose began, *amazing. How—Why . . .*

Ambrose, Lila began, but he continued stuttering through her mind.

It's as if all the training we had done was just yesterday. As if three months and heaps of viper venom hadn't happened. How—Is it your power?

The strigoi buckled off of her, releasing her ankle as they hissed, their three-pronged jaw stretching wide.

Yes. I think. I'll explain everything, but right now, I kind of need to focus.

Right, sorry.

Lila nearly gagged as she saw tiny signs of maggots crawling through wounds on the creature's skin. A half strigoi then, from the Maggot Mansion—one to save.

Pop.

The phantom sound echoed through her ears, freezing her to the spot, as the memory flooded her.

Little Crow? Ambrose called, but Lila was shaking.

What if she killed this one? Trying to save them? What if her heat wouldn't heal—

Lila!

The strigoi lunged at her, and Lila reactively threw her hands up, grabbing the jaws to avoid their venomous fangs. With them locked in her grasp, Lila drove her knee into the strigoi's gut, knocking them over, and giving her a moment to think, to *focus*.

Tell me you love me, she begged Ambrose.

I love you. I love you, I love you, I love you. I cannot wait to call you my wife, Lila Bran.

The words filled her with a joy she wasn't expecting, not in the face of a strigoi. But he'd managed to still make her swoon, still warm her heart—and therefore, her power.

Lila ran at the creature, with no doubt in her mind, no second guessing, no hesitation. She ran at them and shoved her hands against their chest, feeling the warmth leak from her onto them.

Heal, she begged. And to her surprise, the strigoi did. The vampire before her still looked half dead, like Nostro or Bogdan, but the maggots fell from the open wounds, shriveled up, and died before they hit the floor. Immediately, the strigoi's white eyes turned a pale blue, their jaw restructuring to normal, their bones cracking back into place.

The creature before her was once more a vampire, a very confused vampire, but no longer a blood-crazed strigoi.

The crowd above ruptured into the loudest cheer Lila had ever heard. Cheering for *her*.

A small, hoarse voice came from the vampire before her. "Where—?"

Lila smiled at them calmly, placing a gentle hand on their shoulder. "Follow the path back that way. Someone will be waiting for you and will explain everything."

The vampire nodded, confused, and with the gentlest push, they began walking back to the labyrinth's exit.

Nostro, Lila called in their Concord, *have someone there to comfort and care for the vampire when they exit.*

Already done, dear. That was truly marvelous by the way.

Lila smiled at the praise and kept on.

The Sun Child

The labyrinth was longer than Lila had assumed from above. It felt like she'd been winding along its path for hours already, with a handful of strigoi popping out at various times. She'd healed all of them, instructing them to find their way back toward the exit.

Do you see me? she asked Ambrose.

Always.

How much longer do you think I have till the center?

She felt him sigh in her mind. *You're not going to like the answer . . .*

That far?

You're about halfway through, love.

Lila sighed, stretching out her neck as she walked. *How long has it been already? Isn't the audience bored by now?*

Bored? They're on the edges of their seats. They've been starring since your first strigoi.

Taken aback, her step faltered for just a moment. *Really?*

Yes, they seem—watch out! As soon as Ambrose's voice echoed in her mind, another strigoi sprang down on Lila. He'd climbed over the tall stone wall, and dropped himself directly onto her.

"Ahh," he hissed, "I've been waiting for you." Other than the first strigoi she ever encountered, none had ever spoken. But this one . . . he retained his intellect or . . . got it back?

Lila wiggled under him, already feeling the burning sensation on the elbows she landed on. She knew in a moment, she'd feel the blood trickling down her arms.

"I saw you defeat the other strigoi, Sun Child—so I brought friends." The creature above her split his jaw open, screeching in her face as his legs tightened around her waist where he pinned her. Lila tried to force the healing onto him, tried to surround him in her warmth... but it only seemed to make his grip on her stronger.

"Thanks for the boost, *murine*." The word came out like a curse. Like a stab to the heart. The words took it back, making her spiral through old memories with the Reinicks. She'd become so much more than a blood bag, so much more than a slave to her captors.

But not to this monster above her—to him, she was nothing but a meal.

"It wasn't for you," she hissed, feeling the warmth coarse through her blood, rejuvenating every sore muscle, every winded breath. "It was for me."

She bucked her hips, hard enough to force one of his legs loose. Lila tucked her knee in, pressing it against her chest, before she used her shin to force the strigoi to roll off her. But as he rolled, Lila followed, and she shoved her heat-slicked hands hard into his face. The monster burned underneath her, his skin bubbling under her touch, boils bursting around her fingers, quickly turning from melting skin to blackened, charred flesh. It should've disgusted her, but it only made her feel more invigorated.

Lila knew she was more than a murine. All humans were. And these powers that came from her ancestor, it didn't make her *more*, it just validated her belief.

As the strigoi crisped away to nothing more than a husk, Lila stood, facing down the "friends" he'd brought with him. All growled and snapped their bisected jaws at her, the empty gleam she'd come to recognize as the sign of a mindless strigoi was gone. Which meant one thing.

She was going to watch them all burn.

29

Ambrose watched Lila absolutely destroy the strigoi atop her, watched as his skin melted from his bones, before hardening into nothing more than a blackened carcass. Her power—it made his cock twitch. She was so incredibly fierce and powerful, and she was slowly realizing what he'd known all along.

Once she stood, Lila took a step toward the surrounding strigoi, ready to show them the power she'd just unleashed on their leader. She was still far from the center of the labyrinth, but Ambrose could only hope this little test Nostro was conducting would be over with soon.

As Lila's knuckles made impact with the first strigoi's gut, a rumbling under the grand floor threw her off balance, knocking her to her feet. But she wasn't the only one—all the strigoi had been thrown down.

Another rumble, and the entire room shook, the stone walls vibrating as though they'd crumble at any moment. The crowd surged, screams echoing all around Ambrose, just as an even louder *boom* ruptured the room.

Without thinking, Ambrose dove from his perch. He shifted midair, splaying his wings out just shy of hitting the dirt-covered labyrinth floor beside Lila.

What is that? she asked as he lifted her to her feet and held onto her arm.

Nothing good...

Take me to Nostro.

Ambrose did as she asked—he would *always* do as she asked—and pulled her into his arms just as his wings flapped like thunder in a storm.

"Is this your doing?" he asked the Maggot Lord as they softly landed on the platform. Nostro, too, had shifted into his monstrous form, a gangly beast of all teeth and claws. Somehow, it was even more terrifying than his regular appearance.

"You think *I* would destroy my own tower, ruin the spectacle I hosted, and terrify my people enough to run for their lives in pandemonium?"

Ambrose thought, then shrugged. It wasn't something the Lord *wouldn't* do.

"If not you," Lila said, not letting either of the men answer each other, "then who—or what—is coming?"

As if summoned, another rumble shook the room, and Ambrose held Lila tighter, keeping her in his grip.

A vampire ran up to Nostro, and as he said something in his ear, Nostro's eyes widened.

"Here?"

"Yes, Lord Nostro. She's coming from the top and working down."

She? Fuck.

Nostro turned to Ambrose and Lila, his bushy eyebrows scrunched in concern, but Ambrose already knew what he'd say. "It's Drusilla. She's here... and with an entire strigoi army at that."

Another rumble shook the hall, as more screams echoed.

"I need to attend to my people—"

"Of course," Ambrose rushed out. "What do you need of us?"

"I need you to get the Sun Child out of here, Draven. I will meet you shortly."

"How will you find us?"

He turned to Lila and smirked, before lifting up his hand. Under his thumb was a small tattoo in the shape of a sun. "Lila and I have a Concord. I will communicate with her once I leave here to find you."

Another rumble echoed throughout the room, and dust began falling from the ceiling just as Rebekkah soared onto the platform.

"Are you all right?" she asked Lila, grabbing her by the arm to steady herself. "I was in the stands, I tried to get here sooner but the crowds pushed me to an exit. Nostro, it's bad out there. The strigoi are rushing the tower, turning so many, and Drusilla is leading them here. Now."

Lila bit her lip and turned to Nostro. "Do you want me to try—"

Nostro lifted his hand, cutting her off. "No, dear. I want you to leave. We don't know the state of these strigoi. Hurting them may be hurting innocents, and healing them may be healing monsters like the one you just fought. Until we know more, you cannot help us."

Lila tightened her hand on Ambrose's and he knew how she felt—defenseless, useless . . . all feelings he had felt so many times. Once they were out of there, he would make sure she knew she wasn't.

Boom!

Ambrose tucked Lila into his wings the same moment

the entire room erupted. He crashed to the stone below him, his ears ringing, as dust cascaded from above, making it hard to breathe, hard to see.

Lila, Lila are you all right? he feverishly asked.

Yes. But I can't hear anything. Even through the Concord, the ringing is just so loud.

He needed to get her out of there, needed to—

Someone tugged on his arm. Ambrose growled and tightened his grip around Lila as he readied to swing at the person, but thankfully, before he did, he saw the dark cranberry hair, as Rebekkah reached for him.

She was coughing, and probably couldn't hear just like he couldn't.

Tell Nostro we're leaving, he ordered and he felt Lila nod against where her head pressed into him. He rose to his feet, bringing Rebekkah up with him, and held her next to Lila, splaying his massive wings.

He said—

But just as Lila began speaking, an eerie, familiar cackle rose above the ringing in his ears.

Drusilla was here.

"Draven? I thought crows ate maggots. What a splendid surprise for me."

Ambrose huffed a laugh. "In my experience, crows prefer the taste of spider blood as they rip off their legs—one by one."

As the dust cleared, Ambrose found himself looking up at the hag of the Arachnid Estate. She stood in a circular hole she'd torn through the stone at the top of the room, strigoi crawling in all around her, attacking everyone they came across. Drusilla smiled, her wickedness oozing off her red painted lips. "I heard you took something from my dear friends at the Viper Morada yet again. Crushed the collar I worked so hard to get."

Ambrose bared his teeth. Just *thinking* about the band of gold around Lila's neck made him want to rip someone's throat out. Preferably Drusilla's.

"But I guess we traded," she continued. "You may have killed Ciro, but in exchange for your little whore, we got the entirety of the Crow Court. Now, my babies will take over the Maggot Mansion, and guess where's next?" Another wicked grin. "Isn't baby Bran hiding out in the Arachnid Estate with that fool, Maronai? I think that'll be the next stop before returning *home*. I miss having him as one of my loyal strigoi."

Lila flinched in his arms, and Ambrose immediately felt her skin heat as he hid her behind his wings. The more Drusilla spoke, the hotter Lila got, to the point Ambrose felt like he was actually getting sunburned.

"He behaved so well when he was enthralled, and brought me all the best meals. He was such a good pet."

Lila pushed herself from Ambrose's wings, flaring with heat.

"*You fucking witch*," she seethed, radiating, her anger burning through the room.

Ambrose felt his flesh begin to sizzle, small pieces crisping.

"Draven, get her out of here!" Nostro called, flinching back.

Rebekkah winced, but she took a step toward Lila.

"She's not worth it, not now, mousey. We need to go to the Estate. We need to go to Marcus and Constance." She took another step toward Lila, grabbing her hand and whirling her toward her.

"Fucking traitor," Drusilla spit from above.

But Rebekkah ignored her, keeping her eyes locked on Lila's, even as her skin began to steam. "Mousey, we need to go save those you love. We need to *leave*."

Lila, Ambrose said into her mind, and his voice seemed to snap her out of her fury. The heat surrounding her immediately cooled as she blinked back angry tears. In front of him, Rebekkah took a deep breath of relief.

Ambrose turned to Nostro quickly and looked the man in the eyes. "Find us." Then he stepped forward, took both the women in his arms in one swoop, and flew as Nostro soared and collided with Drusilla, creating the perfect opening for their escape.

Ambrose flew as fast as he could, even as he heard the screams echo from the Maggot Mansion in the open sky. Once they left the tower, Rebekkah got her bearings and soared next to him, eyeing their backs every so often.

Lila remained quiet in his arms, he could see the emotional turmoil on her face.

You didn't hurt me, love.

She met his eyes. *You're not just saying that?*

He shrugged a shoulder. *It sizzled, but it didn't hurt. Just as you've told me, you could* never *hurt me, love. Even if you were simmering in rage and ready to set it on the world. Remember what I said, love. You could tell me you were about to destroy the entire universe, and I would ask to be the last in line, only so I may watch you as long as possible.*

She smirked then. *You set the fire in me ablaze.*

And I want to see you burn the world down. Lila nuzzled against Ambrose's chest, finding comfort in his arms as she so often did.

But now, as they flew away from yet another attacked

vampire manor, Ambrose couldn't help but feel defenseless. On edge. Fear struck him as he watched the flood of strigoi storm the tower, fear that he would be bitten and changed again, that he would crave nothing but Lila's blood, that he would covet her until he bled her dry.

His grip around her thigh tightened, his nails pricking small cuts into her skin—thankfully, not deep enough to bleed. She flinched, and he snapped back to himself.

"I—I'm sorry," he uttered. Shame rocked through him, guilt curled up his lungs, his neck, making it hard to breathe. But Lila kept her eyes on him, wind whipping her hair.

"We still need to talk. Something is up with you, and you need to tell me."

He swallowed the lump in his throat.

"And we will. But right now, I need your mind on the Arachnid Estate. We're fast approaching, and if Drusilla's words mean anything, we need to get everyone out as fast as possible. We need to—"

"Ambrose!" Rebekkah called over the rush of wind. "Look!" She pointed to the horizon, past the dark trees and starry sky, past the village they flew over and past the small settlements in between.

In the far horizon, Ambrose could see the spider-like shape of the Arachnid Estate, could see the legs hold the body of the building up.

Only, there weren't eight legs like the Estate usually had . . . there were only five.

A cloud of smoke billowed in the air above the Estate, the fallen legs leaving behind rubble and dust as they collided to the ground.

Rebekkah voiced what he was realizing, "The Arachnid Estate . . . It's under attack."

30

Through the debris, Lila saw pale figures climbing along the exterior of the Arachnid Estate.

Strigoi? Already? Lila felt her heart jolt. Marcus was there... Constance, Kaz, her friends—her family.

Ambrose didn't respond. Instead, he tucked his wings in before flapping them hard. They sped through the sky, the smoke growing closer and closer as Rebekkah kept pace.

Lila felt her warmth at the ready, she was prepared to drop in like a sun bomb if it meant saving her brother. But for now, she could support. She closed her eyes, feeling everything she needed to feel in order to heal, to rejuvenate, and spread her warmth like an energy current to Ambrose, Rebekkah, and herself. Wounds, cuts, scratches—all healed. But more than that, so did their stamina, so did their sore wings, their sore muscles. It was like they were brand new.

"When we get there," Ambrose called, "we need to split up. Find anyone you can, but we have priorities."

"I'll find Darius," Rebekkah said.

"I'll find Marcus, Constance, and Kaz—they're bound to be together, right?" she asked, hoping with all her might that for once, luck would go her way.

Ambrose nodded hopefully. "And I'll find anyone else. As soon as we pull everyone out, we meet back at the foot of the manor stairs."

"Assuming they're still there," Rebekkah quipped.

"And then we'll figure out where else to go. Where else is safe."

Lila hadn't realized it till then, but he was right. Without the Crow Court, Maggot Mansion, and now Arachnid Estate, what other land was there? Where would they go? Another cave to hide away in until they came up with a plan?

Ambrose cut her thinking short as he dived toward the Estate. It was . . . a madhouse, completely in shambles. Strigoi were everywhere, chasing people—vampires and humans alike—biting and turning anyone they could. So many bodies lay on the floor, and Lila couldn't tell if they were dead or just paralyzed from the arachnid venom.

As Ambrose landed, she held him tight, refusing to leave his arms as she focused on his tender embrace, even in the mix of chaos and bloodshed. She focused on his love as another burst of warm aura spread from her body to the area around them.

Some strigoi turned back, dazed, some only seemed to grow more feral. The paralyzed bodies on the floor remained, as nothing but a vampire lord removing the venom—or it eventually wearing off—would work. Lila promised herself, *We'll come back for them.*

"Keep the aura up, if any strigoi tries to attack you, switch from your defensive warmth to your offensive heat. Burn the place down if you have to, Little Crow, and *stay alive.*" The order coursed through her as she nodded.

And if so much as a single hair on your beautiful head gets pulled, you call me. Understand?

Ye—

Lila, I mean it. You undertook enough damage to yourself at the Morada. You call *me if you need me.*

An ounce of shame rolled through her. She'd thought not telling him then would hurt less. Now she knew, not telling him hurt him so much more.

I promise to call. Immediately. You call too.

He nodded and tossed her something from his pocket. She caught it just as it glimmered in the sky. It was a small, pocket-sized dagger. A knife really. The hilt was a silver so clean and shiny, it mirrored her own reflection back at her—making it seem like no one was around her at all as none of the vampire reflections bounced from it—with a small, raw amethyst stone in place of the pommel, perfectly fitting her hand. But the blade wasn't made of metal like the ones she'd been fancying as of late—it was made of a white wood. White *oak* wood.

It was a tiny, bejeweled stake.

Lila smiled at it, trying to figure out when Ambrose would've had the time to find it for her—

I made this while awaiting you to come to the room this morning after your walk with Nostro. As an engagement gift. I know it's not much, but it's all I had at the time, and this was definitely not the situation I planned on giving it to you. I wanted to slide it up your thigh and buckle it there for you as I kissed every inch of your body.

Lila's cheeks reddened and her smile widened. He'd done this for her . . . *made* it for her, not found. *I love it. I have an engagement gift for you too, but—*

Later, Ambrose said. *Give it to me later.*

Lila bit her lip, and nodded. She had to wait. For her gift would be the entire sun.

Rebekkah and Lila dashed into Darius Maronai's main hall, seeing bodies all around. Some were vampires crawling toward the exit, others were paralyzed, their eyes and mouths wide open in silent screams. As her warmth radiated, every vampire that needed healing, healed, and every strigoi that could be changed back, was. Rebekkah leaped to the rest, fighting off the blood crazed monsters as they attempted to feed on the weak.

Lila rushed to help some up, noticing the Cambrias amongst the few who were standing and aiding the paralyzed. Edward and Dianne Cambria, the couple she met the night before Sanktus Pernox, were both bleeding from their arms and foreheads, dust coating their hair. They looked up at her, their eyes widening.

"Lila!" Dianne called. "Marcus was upstairs, third floor. I haven't seen him since before the attack. Go, now!"

Lila turned to Rebekkah, who quickly nodded and dashed to fight the next strigoi. Lila focused her energy on healing all she could in the room, healing Dianne and Edward, rejuvenating Rebekkah, and then she dashed upstairs.

As she passed the first landing, a strigoi lunged at her, and she swiftly dodged, using his speed to propel him off the banister and over the stairs, then she kept moving. Strigoi after strigoi swarmed the main hall she had been in months ago, the carpeted stairs where Ambrose had thirsted for her were now covered in someone's blood, the black tile below in the main hall where Ambrose had held her for the first time as she sobbed for her brother, for fear of the Reinicks.

The room where Ambrose had first kissed her, had first slept next to her, had first brought her euphoria.

It was all in this manor. And it was currently being torn apart.

Last time she was here, she couldn't save her brother, couldn't pull him from the thrall of the Reinicks, couldn't even face him really.

This time would be different.

This time, Lila would save him.

"Get downstairs and out of the manor! Quickly!" Lila yelled at the number of vampires she'd just healed. "Carry the paralyzed!"

Lila burst through room after room on the third floor, healing those who needed it, and stabbing or burning any enemy. No sign of anyone she recognized yet, and as the adrenaline pumped through her veins, so did her doubt and worry. What if Marcus and Constance weren't here? What if Kaz guided them elsewhere? She spun around, slicing the neck of another strigoi and using the moment of surprise to stab her wooden blade into his heart. His skin charred, his eyes full of hate, as more thoughts flooded her mind. What if they'd been changed? What if Kaz was killed? She burst through another door, and a black mass flew at her head. As she felt claws at her chin and wings on her cheeks, she knew—

"Pollock!" she yelled.

The bird before her stopped his assault, and tilted his

head. After the shortest beat, he squawked loudly and vigorously flapped his wings in her face, nuzzling the top of his head against her chin, her nose, her forehead.

She giggled, "It's good to see you too, buddy. Now, where are—"

"Lila!"

That voice.

Behind the black mass of feathers, Lila saw a tall, lanky boy run at her, arms spread wide. Marcus threw his arms around her waist and spun her, around and around, lifting her into the air.

"Marcus! When did you get so tall? Are you okay? Are you hurt? I've missed you so much, I can't believe you're here. Why are you so skinny?"

After putting her down, he snickered against the top of her head. "Ask me later. We need to get Constance and Kaz out of here."

"Miss Bran?"

Marcus stepped back, and Pollock flew to his shoulder. The room before her was completely wrecked, the couches and tables were tossed over, the bed sheets were ripped, but in the center of it all, a graying head popped from behind the green velvet of an upholstered chair.

"Kaz," Lila cried, just as another blond head jumped from her hiding spot, running into Lila's arms.

Constance cried against Lila's shoulder, "Lilac, what are you doing here?! The strigoi—"

Lila hugged her fiercely, pulling her into her arms and squeezing. "I know. We need to get out of her right now. But I need to hug my friend first." She pulled back and looked Constance in the eyes. She knew the young girl was brave beyond her years, but she took her hand anyway. "I need you all to stay close to me."

Without so much as another word, she grabbed Marcus's wrist, feeling the warmth of sunlight all around her, spreading from her palms onto those she held.

"Constance, Marcus, put Kaz between you two, behind me. We'll keep him in the center, and we'll fight any vampire who tries to attack us," Lila demanded. They did as she said with no question, though she saw Marcus hesitate for just a moment, arching an eyebrow. He didn't know of her power, he had only ever seen her as a weak murine. But just as he opened his mouth, possibly to ask, Lila started forward and back down the stairs of the Arachnid Estate.

Within moments, strigoi were on them. Marcus and Constance shifted into their monstrous forms, as Lila projected the sizzling sunlight toward her enemies, careful not to touch her allies. She remained in front of Kaz, keeping him out of harm's way, but the man ripped a sconce from the wall and batted it around with all the fury and strength she'd seen in Ambrose, to protect his people.

Just as Lila was burning the face of a strigoi that got way too close, Rebekkah met them on the stairs.

She met her eyes, black ooze dripping from her fangs, from her claws. "Mouse—"

Marcus leaped from behind Lila, tackling Rebekkah down the stairs. It was all so fast, his hands at her throat, as their bodies and wings tumbled over each other down the stairs.

Lila yelled his name and hurried after them, rushing the waves of healing warmth around her.

"You vile, treacherous witch! Can't you leave us alone?!" Marcus screamed, his fangs so close to Rebekkah's face. But Rebekkah didn't fight back, she just held his wrists.

"Marcus, get off her!" Lila yelled, but Marcus didn't listen.

"You've tortured us for *years*, isn't it enough?"

Lila ran up behind him and tried to pry him off.

"Why are you defending her? Does she have you enthralled?"

Marcus whipped back and his savage gaze met hers—there was so much anger, so much pain, so much... betrayal.

"Marcus, no. A lot has happened. Rebekkah isn't our enemy, not anymore."

"Since when? Last I remember she was drinking your blood and making me her puppet," he seethed.

"Since she saved me from her brothers. Since *she* became a victim to them as well."

Marcus scoffed. "Just because she's playing the victim card means we have to forgive her? Forgive everything she's done to us? To me?"

His nails dug in deeper, but Rebekkah managed to choke out. "No. It doesn't." Marcus snapped back to her. "If you need to kill me to feel better, do it. But your friends need to get out of—"

A large, pale hand—almost the size of Ambrose's—grabbed Marcus by his nape.

"Young Marcus, now is not the time for this. Settle your differences with Miss Reinick later." Darius Maronai stood above Rebekkah, holding Marcus aloft. His long black hair seemed even longer, even curlier in his monstrous form, as it contrasted his skin that looked like fresh ash. "Ambrose is downstairs with Balzar and the Cambrias, helping those you've sent down, but the number of strigoi seems endless. We need to leave."

"You'll leave the Estate?" Constance asked, stepping forward.

He nodded solemnly. "If I must. There is a greater cause now." His vibrant emerald eyes met Lila's.

Lila stepped forward and grabbed Marcus's arm. "We'll talk through all of this later. Once we're all safe."

Marcus glared at her for a moment, then nodded, and Darius eased him back down. At the same moment, Darius helped Rebekkah to her feet, his hand lingering on hers for a moment as their eyes locked.

Constance came up beside Marcus, and threaded her hand with his. "We need to get Kaz and Lilac to safety, Mar."

His eyes locked on hers, and Lila swore something silent passed between them.

Damn, how much had she missed?

31

Ambrose threw a strigoi off his back, and slammed him to the floor, just as Balzar lifted a heavy foot, and stomped it into the monster's face. But no matter how many fell, the damned things just kept coming.

We're coming back—all of us! Lila's voice was like a saving grace, giving him hope for the end in sight. On the Estate's foyer floor, the green marble ran black like fresh paint, the scent of rot and burning flesh and death filled Ambrose's nose. It wasn't a scent he'd been so raked by since the Mass Death four hundred years ago.

Lila bounced down the stairs, her ponytail loose around her face, strands hanging free at the base of her neck. Marcus was behind her, and his simmering golden eyes stared daggers into Rebekkah's back as Darius held the viper's hand.

In any other moment, Ambrose would balk at the development, study the fire in Marcus, tease Constance for how she, too, watched the boy with eyes full of worry and . . . he sighed — Constance's gaze was equally filled with teenage lust. Great.

Another strigoi leaped onto his back, reminding him of the rotting flesh all around him. He tore the monster off him, splitting its head from its body, then tossing the corpse back toward Balzar, who staked it through the heart.

Lila's eyes widened at the bloodshed before her.

"Did you . . . kill all of these strigoi?"

He shrugged. "Balzar helped."

"Fuck, Draven, there has to be three dozen here alone," Rebekkah swore.

He hadn't noticed. Not as he dashed through them, ripping them apart. Not as he bit their necks out. Not as he'd rubbed his palms raw over and over as the wood of the stakes bit into his hands. Not as the bodies piled around him.

"We need to get out of here," Lila said, hopping over a body and catching herself against his bloodstained chest. He loved the way she ran right into his arms, loved the safety she seemed to find within them, even as they were covered in gore and surrounded by bodies. "Have you seen the Cambrias?"

Ambrose clenched his fist, but nodded. "They were changed. They're both strigoi now. I locked them in the dining room."

Lila swallowed hard, her eyes trailing to the barred door. He knew she considered healing them. "Kaz, the kids—" Lila paused, glancing up, as though she heard something. Ambrose immediately followed her gaze, but there was nothing there. She quickly shook her head. "No, it's Nostro. He just told me he's coming to us, with just a handful of his people. They're flying at full speed to beat the sunrise."

Darius joined them. "Nostro? What about the Mansion?"

"H-he says it's fallen. Drusilla won."

The words echoed through him, hollowing his mind. *Fuck*. Drusilla won?

He met Lila's worried eyes, her eyebrows pinched. *She successfully took the manors . . .* she said into his mind, letting the truth sink in.

Ambrose clenched his jaw against the heaviness of the loss. "Little Crow, you need to tell him not to come here."

"Where *do* we go?" Darius paled. "The Court was taken, the Estate overrun, and now the Mansion—"

"There's still one manor . . ." Rebekkah stepped up, between Lila and Darius. "If my brother is in the Crow Court, and Drusilla is in the Maggot Mansion, and Ciro is dead"—she glanced up at Ambrose—"then there is still one place."

Ambrose felt the shades of emotion flutter the room. The vampires were muted, shut off from each other as they'd always been. Kaz's fear was palpable, but his concern for Constance and Marcus far outweighed that fear. Balzar was a familiar, a loyal monstrosity to Darius, with the only purpose to serve and care, feelings Ambrose felt permeated with each of the creature's actions.

But it was Lila he could feel most, Lila he could feel from a mile away, Lila he could decipher every shade of sorrow from, every drop of lust, every well of strength, and every cavern of fear.

And right now, it was as though the sun had been eviscerated.

"We don't have to go back," he said quickly, without thinking.

She only looked at him, startled. It dawned on Ambrose then that she hadn't been aware of the fear coiling around her entire being.

But then her eyes darted behind him, and Lila threw herself from his arms, ducking under him, and thrusting the palm of her hand into the jaws of another strigoi. "*Don't fucking touch him,*" she seethed, before slashing a body behind her and smoldering another.

A new wave was beginning.

As a dozen more strigoi flooded into the room from all over the Estate, Ambrose launched himself at Kaz and the kids, huddling them all under him. He knew Marcus and Constance could handle themselves—had seen it—but the last thing he needed right now was to be worried about them.

"We can figure out *where* later. But right now, we can't be *here*. I have a ship on the coast. We should be able to all make it, just before sunrise." Darius turned to Lila, pulling a strigoi from her path. "Tell Nostro to meet us at my docks. He knows where they are."

She nodded, but kept her guard up, her eyes shifting around the room.

Marcus shoved himself away from Ambrose, turned, and looked at him. "I'll carry Kaz. But you *must* protect my sister."

Though the boy was . . . still a boy, he sized Ambrose up. His chest puffed, his eyes were unwavering. And Ambrose couldn't help but smirk.

A memory flashed in his mind of a time long ago, a glimpse of his little brother, so young. The boy showed off nonexistent biceps before he carried something heavy for their mother. Not a single ripple of muscle or abs on his small black chest. But he always flexed for them all, even with nothing to show. Would always offer to carry the heaviest supplies, the heaviest plates.

Ambrose smirked again, seeing Lila's brother before him. "Always."

Marcus watched him for another moment, before grabbing Constance's hand. "Stay by me. No matter what happens, stay close." She nodded, squeezing his hand in return as he pulled Kaz into him.

Ambrose gave his friend a wary look. "Take care of them."

Kaz opened his mouth, then closed it, and Ambrose knew any semblance of a witty retort died on his tongue. "Of course, sir."

He turned back to Marcus, and nodded. "Go, now. We'll be right behind you."

The three began to step toward the grand entrance of the Estate, and Ambrose followed, making a path through the growing number of strigoi as Lila, Rebekkah, Darius, and Balzar followed his lead. As they neared the entrance, Rebekkah and Darius went airborne, attacking the strigoi crawling along the walls, and Balzar staked each fallen creature. Ambrose weaved through the strigoi, finding his place at Lila's side, making sure *nothing* touched her, and then he scooped her into his arms, before beating his wings against the floor. The burst of wind knocked the monsters all around them prone, but it wasn't fast enough. Some leaped and started climbing toward them, others sprouted monstrous wings, just as ragged and warped as they looked.

Ambrose hadn't seen the wings before. This was new. They were . . . mutating? No. *Adapting*. Flesh ripped, and the skin at their backs became those mangled wings.

He looked at Lila, expecting to see shock written on her face. But she only ground her teeth.

You knew?

She met his eyes. *That some are different than others? More . . . evolved?* She nodded. *The evolved ones are too far gone to be changed back. Maybe it's that they* like *being strigoi. I'm not sure. All I know is, those are the ones I'll burn.*

Her violence made his cock twitch. Wonderful timing.

"Now!" Darius yelled. He began flying toward the exit, as did the others, dodging the hissing beasts as they dropped from the ceiling, from the walls, leaped from below. Balzar ran below them, keeping pace.

We're almost there, Lila. Almost there!

Ambrose felt a tug on his ankle, and immediately Lila radiated her heat, burning the hand holding onto Ambrose. His skin warmed uncomfortably, but not painfully, and in the next moment, the hand around his ankle released.

I'll keep the radiance, you fly.

Darius and Rebekkah broke through the entryway, into the night sky, and Lila and Ambrose were just behind them.

Ambrose could hear the rapid flap of wings, the *click clacks* of their jaws, the boom of the heavy run below them. The strigoi were right behind them. How would they get to the boat, and set sail with the creatures this close?

Just as Ambrose passed through the doorway atop the long stairwell, he heard the sound of the doors closing behind him.

"Balzar!" Darius yelled, and as Ambrose turned, he felt Lila's lungs spike.

Balzar was inside, strigoi surrounding him, as he stood behind the doorway to the Arachnid Estate, pushing them closed. "Master, go!"

"Balzar," Lila whined, her voice breaking.

"Take Lady Bran and Lady Reinick away from here. I will hold them off as long as I can. *Go!*"

Ambrose caught a final glimpse at the familiar's strange visage, his eyes filled with fear, with dedication, with determination.

And then the great black doors of the Arachnid Estate were shut.

Darius was cursing. More than Ambrose had ever heard his friend curse. They caught up to Marcus, Kaz, and Constance quickly, but a number of strigoi that slipped through the door before Balzar could shut it were still racing behind them. Wings flapped as the monsters screamed and hissed, but Ambrose could see the ocean on the horizon, could see the docks ahead where Darius kept his vessel.

That's . . . the ocean? Lila asked, and he felt her astonishment, her wonder.

It is. I've planned on showing it to you. This feels disappointing compared to what I imagined.

She remained silent for a moment, studying it as she radiated her healing warmth, keeping the energy high for all around her.

I didn't picture it quite so . . . dark. I thought it would be more blue.

Ambrose chuckled, and he silently thanked her for allowing him that grace in a situation as dire as this. *It is very blue. Wait till you see it in sunlight.*

Darius pointed ahead of them. "There!" The ship was already far from port, already being manned by the crew Darius employed, already sailing away from the Arachnid Estate. "Once we're near it, we can kill off the rest of the bastards, or leave them to burn in daylight."

Ambrose descended toward a massive wooden vessel,

with sails of emerald and black. A spider sat in the middle, legs angling in all directions—the crest of the Arachnid Estate. The ship bobbed in the rock of the waves, as small specks of humans and vampires ran around the deck, untying ropes and changing course.

The sky was growing light with color, the sun would be up at any moment, and if they didn't make it inside, who is to say what would happen to them. Ambrose beat his wings harder against the breeze, as he felt Lila's warmth trickle through his veins, pump between his joints. He didn't feel the usual exertion that came with flying long distances, nor the familiar pull of muscle when he stretched his wings too far.

"Ambrose," Lila called, "Nostro is there!"

The old bat had flown straight from his manor, and he caught sight of him on the deck of the ship.

But that was it.

He was all that was left free from the Maggot Mansion.

He realized then, all Darius had now was himself. Constance, on a technicality. Rebekkah and Marcus were the last vipers not imprisoned or mad with power. And he, alone, was the final crow.

The vampires of Malvania were crumbling, being forced into servitude or madness or eternal hunger. And Ambrose had no idea how to stop it. No idea how to defeat this enemy.

Vampires overcame. Persevered. The Mass Death was proof of that, and then again when the eight manors battled for power.

But now, a new kind of monster was taking over. Would vampires become the next murine? If so, what did that mean for humanity?

Marcus, Kaz, and Constance landed on the deck, and

angled themselves to be ready for an attack. Kaz dashed to the captain of the ship, and Ambrose heard the man burst orders to the seaman, explaining the situation.

Hold on, Ambrose instructed Lila, and she hugged herself tighter to his chest, tucking her chin into his shoulders.

As he descended, Rebekkah and Darius were right beside him, and they could feel the faint brush of sunlight sting their eyes.

They'd make it, but the strigoi would not.

Just as Ambrose landed, he placed Lila on the deck and turned, claws bared to the strigoi. But the strigoi didn't slow. They barreled themselves into Ambrose and Darius, and Rebekkah immediately leaped on the backs of those tackling Darius. Marcus took another strigoi, tackling her before she could tackle Kaz, and wrestled her to the deck as he tore his claws through her chest. Constance also leaped forward, tiny claws digging into the shoulder of the monster on Ambrose, as he tore into the beast. Pollock cawed, and a swarm of crows flew from all around, some from the deck, some that had followed their flight. The birds became more like a cloud, as the black mass of them covered the ship from the rising sun, blocking Ambrose and his allies from burning to death.

But as all eyes were on the birds, on the strigoi attacking them, another flew from behind Lila and grabbed her from the waist. She immediately tried to shove herself away from it as it dug its jaws into her shoulder. She screamed, but it sounded more like a battle cry. The creature's arm bubbled where she touched it, boiling in white blisters before bursting in heat. But the strigoi didn't let go, and soon Lila's limbs went slack.

Fuck, Ambrose cursed. The strigoi grabbing her had to be a half strigoi, a vampire from Estate. Which meant their venom was currently paralyzing Lila as they dragged her into the sky.

Constance snapped the neck of one of the strigoi atop him, and Ambrose threw the rest off, shifting into his human form to be a smaller, lither target against the crowd of monstrous forms.

Though paralyzed, Lila's heat still burned the strigoi that held her, burned right through flesh and bone, and as the dumb creature attempted to fly back toward the land, it flew right into the sun.

The strigoi hissed, and as they tried to cover their burning eyes, they let go of Lila, dropping her right into the middle of the ocean.

Fuck, fuck. Lila couldn't swim. Couldn't swim *and* was paralyzed. *And* the sun had risen.

But his body moved on instinct.

Ambrose didn't think.

He didn't think about his flesh burning away. He didn't think about dying. He didn't think about leaving Lila in this large, scary world. He didn't think about the crows only covering the boat.

He didn't think about anything but saving her, as he ran across the deck, and dove into the sea.

32

Ambrose was right, Lila thought, *the ocean really is blue.* As she sank below the frothing waves, the current moving her body around and around, she could see the sunlight shine through the surface, illuminating the jewel-toned blue all around her.

Though she couldn't move, and her lungs were beginning to tighten, it felt almost serene. Her lilac hair flowed around her, weightless. All of her felt weightless, as she stared into the expanse of nothing. It was almost like looking at the night sky, and knowing it was endless.

Lila wondered what was in the ocean with her at that moment, what swam miles and miles away.

A rough hand clamped around the blood on her shoulder, and she felt the crawling sensation under her skin of the spider's venom being removed from her veins. She wanted to scream, but fought against the pain, fought against taking any sharp inhale, or any shallow breath.

The lack of air made it all so much worse, intensifying every sensation.

But then another hand was there, wrapping around her waist, pulling her into a strong chest. And just as quickly as the pain began it ended, and the arms around her heaved her to the surface, to the sunlight, to—

"*Ambrose!*" Lila shrieked the moment she broke through the waves. She was the only thing between him and the sun and she knew her shadow was *not enough*. But . . .

The morning had dawned, and the sun was sitting along the ocean's horizon. Ambrose's wet, ashen brown skin glistened in the sunlight, warming the tone to look like rich chocolate. He squeezed his eyes shut, expecting to burn, Lila realized. But she wouldn't let that happen.

He looked beautiful, gorgeous, in the light of day, and Lila pushed every ounce of love out of her, toward him.

"*Feel the sun, Ambrose,*" she whispered, holding herself up on his shoulders and he waded enough to keep them both surfaced.

Ambrose peeked one of his black eyes open, the sun's light reflecting in them and illuminating all the shades of dark brown and charcoal gray within. His white hair was pushed back from the water, his leather clung tightly to his skin. And Lila took in the sight of *all of it*. Took in the sight of the love of her life feeling the sunlight on his skin once more. Of seeing a sunrise for the first time in hundreds of years.

"How—" he began, but stopped himself as his eyes found hers.

"*The Sun Child will lead the vampire back into the light,*" Lila repeated. "This is what I've been meaning to show you. My engagement gift. I can bring you into the sun."

He stared at her, his lips parted in awe. "This . . ."

"You showed me the stars. Let me show you the sun."

Ambrose watched her once more, the sun behind her,

and he smiled as his black eyes grew glassy. He pulled her to him, devouring her lips in a kiss that told her just how much he loved her in return.

After Ambrose swam he and Lila back to the ship, the deck was mostly empty, save for Kaz, the captain of the ship, and a few of the crew members. He climbed them over the ladder and onto the deck, and Lila instantly noticed the vampires hiding in the shadows, watching, waiting to see if they would make it back alive.

When they saw Ambrose stand in the sun, gasps echoed, and Nostro stepped right out into the light. He turned to them with a shit-eating grin on his face. "I told you she was the Sun Child."

The others hesitantly followed his path, nearing Lila and Ambrose as the two held hands.

The moment Darius's skin touched the light, he groaned in complete satisfaction. Rebekkah yelped, Constance gasped, and Marcus—

Lila didn't have time to notice his expression. Not as she barreled herself toward him, throwing her arms around his middle. He'd gotten taller since she'd last seen him, just as thin and gangly, but his sharp chin nearly rested at the top of her head.

Marcus didn't hesitate, he threw his long arms around her, and squeezed her to him, lifting her and spinning around.

It was the reunion they deserved three months ago, before the madness of the Viper siblings, before Drusilla. Lila felt a hiccup rise in her chest, her cheeks wet with tears, as Marcus shook in her arms, his breath catching on heaves. "Lila," he whined, burying his face in the crook of her neck.

"I'm here, Marcus. I'm here." She rubbed his back in small circles, as she always had on particularly bad days, when the Reinicks' bites were harshest, or when they'd pulled the murine from their chambers more than once.

But they were safe now—both of them—and as Darius and Ambrose threw the strigoi corpses overboard, and the boat sailed onward, they were *safe*.

She pulled back and *really* looked at her brother. Marcus was . . . so different. His cheekbones had sharpened, the baby fat mostly gone, his eyes were lighter, almost a golden hazel. His fangs puckered his lips, and his brown mousey hair went from dull and muted, to having a warmth like amber or melting caramel. He was beautiful, a vampire through and through.

Marcus studied Lila with the same scrutinizing eyes. His warm gaze lingered at the tattoo on her finger, the small sun engulfed in the crow. He studied her eyes, her hair, her neck. She wondered if he saw traces of the golden collar the Reinicks put on her, or if he saw a snack he wanted to consume.

"My turn!" Constance stepped up next to the siblings, and threw her arms around Lila. The girl, too, had grown. Her body had developed and her cheeks were thinner. But she was still small, and still just as adorable. Lila hugged her friend, petting the now-loose golden locks down Constance's back. "I told you you'd be sunlight personified. I didn't realize I was speaking literally, but here we are." She beamed, then nuzzled her face against Lila once more.

The Sun Child

"You've no idea how much I've missed you all," she said to them, and Kaz, who was watching with a warm grin behind them all.

Just then, a loud, shrill, rambunctious squawk erupted above Lila, and as she glanced up, the black mass once more stormed toward her. Lila held out her arms, and let the foolish beast crash into her, taking her down to the ship's deck.

Lila laughed as Pollock hopped and danced on her chest, nipping her chin, her neck, her shoulders with affectionate crow kisses. He pushed the top of his head into her chin, cawing the entire time.

"Pol! I missed you too!"

"The damn thing claimed your bedroom as his own," Ambrose groaned, walking up to them and laying down beside her. He spread his limbs wide, basking each part of himself under the sun. "How long can we stay?"

Pollock finally calmed down enough, but stayed on her chest, tucking his legs under him.

"In the sun? I'm not sure. Nostro and I tested it for a bit the other morning. As far as I'm aware, as long as I'm here and feeling love and joy, then you all should be fine. So don't make me angry," she teased.

"I wonder how far your radiance stretches," Nostro hummed, sitting on the deck behind her before crossing his legs over each other. "If I am on the other side of the ship, would I burn?"

Lila tilted her chin back, looking at Nostro upside down. He rubbed his chin with a long-clawed finger, and stared into the horizon. Thinking out loud then.

"I feel the radius of the warmth. I have a general idea of how far it stretches, and right now it is just enough to cover this part of the deck."

"How does it work?" Marcus sat on her other side, and Constance next to him. The others gathered around, and their oddly shaped and strange circle took up half the ship's deck as crewmen ran around them.

Lila hadn't realized how tired she'd been, how tired they *all* must have been. She fought in a trial, then flew to the Estate, fought strigoi, flew to the ship, nearly drowned, and now was finally safe. Everyone had done so much in one night, it was finally—*finally*—time for rest.

She turned to Marcus and then explained to them all that with different emotions came her different powers. "I think, with all the love in my heart right now, I am rapidly healing you, so the sun has no effect. That's how I was able to keep your stamina up until we arrived on the ship."

"And if you feel anger, you could burn vampires as though it were the sun?" Marcus asked.

Lila nodded. "But not just vampires. I can heat anything. And the marks and scars stay, vampires can't heal them. Last I saw him, Hektor still had burns on his face. "

"And Ciro had the burns on his hands," Rebekkah added.

Marcus glared at her, and something in Rebekkah deflated. It was fair, but also not, and Lila felt incredibly conflicted. Marcus hadn't seen Rebekkah since she'd changed, not truly. When she was being beaten and abused by her brothers, he was under their thrall. When she helped Lila escape Ciro and Hektor, and gave small reprieves from the violence, Marcus wasn't there. He hadn't come to meet Rebekkah Reinick. He only knew the sister of the Viper siblings.

But, on the other hand, she had been part of his lifelong torture. Part of everything bad in Marcus and Lila's life. To him, she was evil, cruel, wicked.

And to Lila, she was a friend.

Nostro broke her thoughts as he said, "We need a plan. Where is this ship even headed?"

"Right now?" Darius shrugged. "*Away*. It's sailing into the open ocean, away from the coastlines of the Crow Court and the Arachnid Estate."

Ambrose groaned, running a hand down his face. "We have nowhere to go. No supplies. And no army. Just three vampire lords—"

"And the Sun Child," Lila playfully smacked his chest.

Then Rebekkah really did smack his chest. "And I would say *four* lords—lords and lady." She groaned. "Fuck it, I like Lord Rebekkah better."

"I thought Hektor was next in line?" Nostro scrunched his eyebrows.

"You want that bastard to rule the Viper Morada?" Rebekkah countered.

"Of course not."

"Plus, by being in the Crow Lord's manor, if that's where he still is—"

"He is," Ambrose interjected. "I had my crows spy before sunset yesterday evening."

He was sleeping in your bedroom, he said to Lila privately, and she wanted to punch something.

Gross.

"Since my brother is still there, no one has made a claim to the title yet. If we go to the Morada . . . it could be mine. Then the four manors will be in unison once more."

What do you think? Ambrose asked. It was a good plan . . . even if Lila didn't *want* to be there ever again.

It might be our only option. And, as long as I'm with you, I think . . . I think it'll be okay.

Just as she finished, Marcus huffed a laugh. "Yeah, right. You want *us* to go to the Morada? To be sitting ducks?"

The hostility was palpable. A hostility she didn't believe Rebekkah deserved. She'd paid for her crimes, and Marcus needed to know. Lila bit her lip, and sat up, Pollock shifting into her lap.

Ambrose placed a palm on her back as he sat up, making her jolt. He smirked at her before turning to the others. "Let's not overuse Lila's power. We don't yet know her limits," he began. "And we could all use some sleep."

Kaz turned to them all. "I have spoken with the captain. There are small quarters for all of us to be accommodated. Come, I will show you."

As everyone stood and wandered deeper into the ship, she grabbed Marcus's sleeve, making him stay. Ambrose's hand lingered on her back, tracing her spine, before he let go and joined the rest leaving the deck.

I'm going to sleep. Wake me if you need. And come find me when you and Marcus finish. You need sleep as well.

Always so worried about her.

I will, she promised, then she turned to Marcus, who was watching the small band of vampires leave—watched *Constance* leave, Lila realized—before his hazel eyes met hers once more. She bit back a knowing smile, and took his hand.

Immediately, any kind of tension broke as he gave her one of his famous goofy grins and threw his arms around her once more. "I missed you so much, Lila. I was so, so worried. If it weren't for Ambrose, I may have flown to the Morada myself. But . . . I'm still not well versed in my vampire body."

The corner of Lila's lips lifted. "I'm sure you'll get used to it. Do you . . . like being a vampire?"

He shrugged then leaned back on his hands. "It's not as bad as I thought. And Constance and Ambrose have been helping."

"Spending lots of time with Constance lately, are you?" she poorly wiggled her eyebrows, causing a slew of laughter to burst from Marcus's lips.

"Oh, no. I hoped the badass Sun Child would have dropped the wiggly brows! Please, don't *ever* make that expression again, for the sake of your reputation and my sanity—please." He chuckled, covering his mouth with the back of his hand. "You know? You haven't seen me in *three* months, and the last time we did see each other, I was trying to drink your blood and you were giving yourself back to our life-long tormentors. And the first thing you ask me, once we're heartfeltly and beautifully reunited, is about *girls*?"

"*A* girl." Again, wiggly eyebrows. Again, Marcus cringed and then burst into snickers. She shrugged, "At least I know my priorities."

Marcus shook his head, but chuckled. "I think you've got a lot of explaining to do, young lady."

"Young lady? Last I checked *I* was the oldest."

"And last I checked, *I* was the tallest. And the vampire. So, I win."

"Well, *I'm* the Sun Child!" she argued back, unable to hold back the giggles spilling forth.

"What even is that?!" Marcus threw his hands in the air. "Sun Child—this, healing warmth—who are you and what have you done to my sister?"

Lila stood then, brushing off her legs. Her leathers were still clinging to her from her dive in the ocean, still wet and uncomfortable. But she *did* have a lot to discuss.

"I will tell you *everything*, but first let me get out of this."

"Please do. You're starting to stink."

"Thanks, Marcus," she rolled her eyes.

"Didn't you miss having me around?"

She sighed. "Unfortunately."

He playfully grabbed his chest. "Lila, I'm wounded. Anyway, go change."

After meeting Ambrose in their room, he helped her find a simple white shirt, similar to the kind he frequently wore, loose and flowy, with lace around the cuffs, tucked into a pair of tan linen pants that didn't quite fit so he tied a rope around her waist. Lila opted not to wear shoes, since the sunlit cool wood of the ship felt nice under her feet. Ambrose then ran his fingers through her damp hair, tied it in a simple braid, and smacked her ass as she walked out of the room.

She shook her head at him, a grin on her face, as she walked back to Marcus, meeting him in his small quarters. The room was tiny, smaller even than what they had in the Viper Morada, with a small loft bed above a tiny desk and chair. Marcus was already seated in the seat, so Lila swung herself up the small ladder and into the bed. On top of the mattress was a thin, scratchy green blanket, the color of the forest at night, and she knew *this* was at least better than the Morada.

Marcus folded his arms over his chest as he pushed himself back to the opposite wall, and leaned the chair back to look up at her.

"All right, dear sister. Tell me everything."

And so, Lila did. She took a deep breath, and started from the beginning. "It all began when they told me you'd run away one night. I ran after you . . ."

She told him everything. Her run through the woods, her meeting with Ambrose, her bargain with him—including being thrown out the window to which Marcus gasped and said, "He didn't."

"He did," Lila confirmed.

Once she was finished catching up to date, she fiddled with her fingers and looked at him through her lashes. "Do you remember anything?"

"To be honest, I remember very little. I remember being changed. I remember being hungry. I remember that night Hektor attacked you, the night Ambrose came for you. I remember scratching your face, your neck, but being unable to help myself." The light in his eyes dimmed, his expression fell. He shook his head. "But once they enthralled me, I don't remember much of anything. I don't remember even leaving the Morada for Sanktus Pernox. It wasn't until I was made a strigoi by one of Drusilla's men that my consciousness came back. And that, I remember." Marcus looked . . . haunted. He gulped and fiddled with his hands, picking the skin around his thumb. "I remember Constance jumping in front to save you from *me*. And I remember biting her, changing her. I dream of it often."

Lila's heart panged. It must've been how Ambrose felt then. She had wondered if he remembered, but Marcus just proved Ambrose had. And if Marcus was having dreams . . . maybe that was what had been tormenting Ambrose.

Taking a deep breath, Lila stuck her hand off the bed, down toward Marcus. The boy looked up at her, eyebrow raised, but Lila just shook her hand back and forth until Marcus took it. Lila squeezed, and after a moment, Marcus squeezed back.

"I also remember you being enthralled. I remember you going back with *them*."

She pressed her lips together. "It wasn't like that. I wasn't enthralled. During the training sessions, Ambrose had taught me to break from a vampire's thrall."

"Then why the hell did you go back with them?"

She sighed, exasperated. "We needed to delay them. To stall. Sure, the strigoi I'd changed back were shifting back, remembering their old selves. But even *with* them, Drusilla and the brothers wouldn't have stopped."

"And look what good that did us."

His words were sharp, and they cut Lila deep. More so, because Marcus was absolutely right. Her "reasoning" to go back didn't matter at all. *She* didn't do anything.

No, her real reasoning for going with them was completely selfish. And she wasn't even sure she'd met her goals. She could *maybe* give herself credit for causing a *sliver* of divide between Ciro and Hektor that *possibly* led to Hektor leaving Ciro for dead. *Potentially*.

With another sigh, she admitted, "I wanted to prove to them I'd become stronger. I'd become more than their murine. I wanted . . ." she groaned. "I wanted to defeat them from within. But obviously that didn't happen."

"That didn't happen *and* you're friends with Rebekkah Reinick now."

"She doesn't deserve your hate, Marcus. She is a victim of the brothers as well."

He sat back in the chair once more, taking his hand from hers and crossing his arms over his chest. "Yeah? Let me decide. Tell me what they've done to her, tell me what *she* has *suffered*." Marcus's voice dripped with malice, a tone Lila was so unused to hearing. He was always so . . . light, joking in the face of adversity, even if he was afraid. Being a monster had changed him, and she wondered how much she'd changed since they last spoke—*really* spoke.

So, Lila told him the cruelty of the brothers, the beatings, the starvings, locking her away for days at a time. Then she told him about the stolen moments Rebekkah took, the moments she *risked*. She even told him about the tonic to prevent pregnancies, how real *that* fear had been in both Lila's and Rebekkah's minds.

And when she was done, Lila said, "Rebekkah did awful things, yes. But she had been raised to be awful. She broke through that learned mentality, Marcus. She's become my friend."

Marcus stayed silent for a long moment, watching Lila through hooded eyes. She could tell he was sulking, but her last point had gotten him.

He swallowed hard before muttering, "Fine. *You* can be friends with her. But it doesn't mean I have to be." He leaned his elbows on his knees, pushing his hands through his hair. "I—I need to process all of this, Lila. Can we talk more in the evening?"

Lila sat up in his bed, "Of course. It's been a long night. For all of us." She climbed down, hopping down the last few steps.

Marcus stood so fast, Lila barely had time to be startled, but he threw his arms around her shoulders once more, tucking her into a warm embrace.

"Let's never split apart again," he whispered.

Lila hugged him back, tucking her face into his shoulder. "Deal. I'm so glad we're finally together again."

33

"How'd that go?" Ambrose said the moment Lila stepped through the small cabin door. He lounged in the small bed, back propped against the wall.

She shrugged as she untied the makeshift belt, dropping it to the floor. "As expected, I think. There was just . . . so much to talk about."

He watched as she let the loose pants fall to the floor, then padded to the tiny bed and crawled on top of him. "And his feelings toward Bek?"

She sighed and dropped her cheek against his chest. "Not the best, not the worst. I don't think it'll cause us any problems going to the Morada with her, but it might make things awkward. There's a lot of pain for him to get past. And because I know Bek, I *know* she harbors a ton of guilt, but he hasn't seen that yet. Hasn't seen *her*. So . . . it'll just take time."

Ambrose ran his hand over her back, then unbraided her ocean-waved hair as he spoke, "You should talk to her tomorrow. Let her know the situation."

The Sun Child

Lila nodded. "I will. Anything from the other lords?"

"I've only spoken to Kaz. Darius and Nostro retreated to their own quarters, as did Bek and Constance."

"What did Kaz say?"

"The ship will take four days to arrive at the shores of the Viper Morada. Hope you're not prone to seasickness, love."

"I guess we'll find out," her voice was beginning to slur together. "I feel fine now, though. Just very, very tired."

Ambrose lifted the scratchy green blanket over them, then returned to smoothing her hair. "Then sleep, love. I could use it too." Apparently, Ambrose didn't have to tell her twice. Lila's breath was deep and steady, and each exhale warmed his chest. He huffed a laugh, then settled back and closed his eyes. "Good night, love. Sweet dreams."

The ship rocked Ambrose awake. He wasn't sure how long he'd slept, only that his head swam with dreams, his body sore from remaining in the same position for too long.

Lila was gone, her clothes that'd been on the floor were also gone, and the scratchy blanket came up to his neck. He was . . . tucked into bed.

That woman, he smirked. Ambrose rose from the bed, stretching his arms and shoulders, rotating them till each muscle felt *right* once more. The boat swayed back and forth, up and down, but other than the sounds of the wood creaking and the waves crashing, everything was . . . silent.

Tying his hair back, Ambrose padded out of the room and down the small dark hallway, climbed the steps that lead to the deck, and peered out of the crack between the hatch doors. The sun was out, shining brightly, and it stung Ambrose's dark eyes, as he hastily stepped back.

"Fuck," he cursed to himself. It was daytime. Morning maybe? Had he really slept so little?

Lila? His voice slipped through the Concord, reaching, searching. He waited, patiently, watching the beam of sunlight peeking through the crack he'd just looked out from.

You're finally up?

Immediately, he loosened a breath. All of his muscles calmed, his very bones relaxed. The sound of her voice was like a tonic, a drug, something that could ease every chaotic thought, could soothe every anxious move.

Come up, I'll keep you safe. And just like that, his heart melted. He was so utterly, foolishly enamored by this woman, he would melt at her feet if gravity would only allow it. Ambrose could hear the teasing smile in Lila's voice, and as he pushed the hatch doors to the deck, as the sea breeze blew the few loose strands of hair around his face, he turned to the smile.

That smile which lit up his entire world brighter even than the sun.

Lila stood at the edge of the port side, her elbow resting on the banister as though she'd just been looking out into the ocean. The sun was rising—or maybe setting—behind her, silhouetting her body in the loose white shirt, her lilac hair blowing everywhere in the sea-bound breeze, the salt of the air curling it to be a wild, untamed mess. Her pale skin was practically glowing, and those warm brown eyes were summer encapsulated. She looked like a tempest, like a goddess, like a being not of this world, nor the next. She looked . . .

Free, was the word that came to Ambrose's mind. She looked *free*.

He met her on the ship's edge, leaning over it as she turned back to the ocean. They stood next to one another, their upper arms pressed against each other as they both watched the bob and sway of the water.

"It is *very* blue," she said. And when Ambrose raised an eyebrow, she pointed her chin out to the horizon. "The ocean. It isn't black at all. It's the truest blue I've ever seen. Is it all like this?"

Ambrose nodded. "Mostly. Sometimes it's green, or a combination of the two." He turned to her then, watched her watching the ocean. Her eyes were dazzling, as though a thousand tiny stars sparkled in her irises.

"I want to see it. All of it."

The corner of his lips lifted, and he took her hand, entwining their fingers. "Then I will show it to you."

She smiled, and it's like every fear, every worry or concern, even the lust he'd been feeling for her very blood and the guilt that came hand in hand—it all disappeared. The only thing that existed, in that moment, was Lila and her gorgeous, perfect smile.

He stared at her, and realized, *she* was his sunset—sunrise, whatever it was—she was the painting he could never look at for long enough, the view he would always find mesmerizing. And as he felt the sunlight, the real sun, warm his skin for the first time in hundreds of years, he realized he could go an eternity without, so long as he had *her* warmth.

Ambrose didn't think for another moment. He stepped toward his Little Crow, driving his hands to the nape of her neck, grabbing fistfuls of her wild lilac hair. Her eyes met his, brown and golden and brilliant, with a questioning tilt of her eyebrows, a parting in those perfect lips. He ran his thumb over her cheek, caressing her skin and the simple shutter of her breath drove him mad.

He kissed her, pressing himself to her, as her small hands found their way over his chest. She clutched at his heart, breathing him in, and opened her mouth for him, taking his tongue in a way that showed Ambrose that Lila was equally as hungry for him as he was for her. He took her tongue into his mouth, sucking on it. Her lips were so devastatingly soft, and he desperately wished he could feel them around his cock at that moment.

Oh? Lila hummed through the Concord.

Ambrose was so caught up in their kiss, caught up in *her*, he hadn't realized he said that through the Concord, hadn't realized he'd asked, but now she was pulling away, a smirk on her lips, and dropping herself to her knees. Ambrose wanted her, wanted her lips on him, his tongue in her mouth. He tried to stop her descent, but she only sank farther. And then she untied his pants and grabbed the waistband.

What if someone comes on deck? It's nearly night, isn't it?

She giggled. *Ambrose, it's morning. You slept for an entire day and night. No one, but the human crew who are also sleeping or too busy with the ship, is here. We're alone.* And without hesitation, she pulled his hardening cock free. *So eager for me,* she teased. And Ambrose had the flittering thought of how sweet her wet pussy smelled on the salt air, thought about shoving his cock into her, just to show her how much he wants her.

Lila took his cock in her hand, and angled her lips just at his head. He grabbed the banister behind him, but Lila smirked, and scurried on the deck, putting her back against the ship's wall.

"What are you doing, love?" he asked as he turned to her, his cock still in her face. But she didn't answer. Instead, Lila took him in one, deep bob of her head. Her tongue languidly licked up his entire length, as her lips came together to suck on his head.

He cursed and slammed his hands once more on the railings, caging Lila under him completely.

With a *pop*, she freed him from her perfect lips. "I want you to feel the sun on your skin as you come in my mouth. I want you to *watch the sunrise, love.*"

Ambrose couldn't contain the emotion he felt. He drove his hand behind her scalp, fisting her hair once more, and fucked her pretty little mouth, again and again. *Fuck, she is so perfect*, he thought, as she held onto his hips, her nails digging into his skin.

"Lords, you're sucking me off so fucking well, love. Just like that," he cooed, petting her head with one hand as he gripped the railing with the other. "Are you wet from sucking my cock, Little Crow?"

Lila nodded, bobbing his cock against her plump lips.

"I want to fuck your perfect cunt." He pushed into her mouth deeper, feeling how far she would take him. He knew she might gag but he just couldn't help himself with her. He wanted *everything*.

Lila took the base of his cock in her hand, and pumped, her lips meeting her fist as though she were hungry for more. Ambrose rocked his hips in time with her movement as the wood splintered under his grip. *Fuck*, she was so good.

She sucked him deeper, deeper than he thought she'd be able to, and it nearly had him coming apart at the seams. He threw his head back, tempering his desire, and instead took a step forward, knocking her back into the ship's wall. He thrust his hips as the hand buried in her hair yanked her head back, forcing that pretty throat to slide him just that much deeper. He reached his thumb around, massaging the back of her jaw to help her relax, to take more of him.

"Do you like the taste of my cock, love?"

More than anything, she replied through the Concord.

"Such a good fucking girl. I know you can take me deeper, Little Crow. I want to feel the back of your throat."

He looked down at her, watching those beautiful brown eyes beaming up at him. Her plump lips wrapped around him. He pushed deeper and Lila's eyes rolled back, tears prickling her eyes. *Fuck, yes. Like that.*

Ambrose thrust harder, faster, and the sounds of the ocean were diminished by the sounds of her mouth on his cock, her lips sucking at his skin, the wood splintering under his palm.

Lords, her perfect mouth sucking him in was enough to shatter his mind, and he hadn't even gotten to his favorite part yet. He was going to fuck her. Right here, on the deck of this ship.

Lila moaned around his cock, as her head lightly backed into the wood behind her. Feeling her throaty, needy noises around him were enough to send him over, he was going to come.

"Don't you dare fucking swallow one single drop. Keep my cum on your tongue," he bit out, and with another hard thrust into her throat, he pulled his cock to the flat of her tongue and came.

Electric current felt like it was shorting his system as he erupted, his legs shaking. The banister snapped under his iron grip.

Ambrose breathed heavily, taking a long moment before he looked down at the love of his life, her lips still wrapped around him.

In a breathy voice, nearly a whisper, he asked, "Do you want me to fuck you, Lila? In the sunlight?"

She nodded feverishly, and Ambrose didn't wait a singular moment. He pulled himself from her mouth and lifted her onto the railing, his hands holding her thighs so she wouldn't fall into the ocean on the other side.

With his long nails, he tore the crotch of her pants, and tore the underwear underneath, revealing her dripping pussy. It glistened under the morning light, and he desperately wanted a taste. But he could devour her later, could spend the rest of their time on the ship eating her pussy as though he was starved for her—because he *was* starved for her.

"Spit my come on my cock, and let me fuck it back into you."

A blush crept to Lila's cheeks, and like the good girl she was, she did as she was told.

Ambrose nearly buckled as he watched his own hot ecstasy drip from her tongue, her lips. He watched as it slowly descended, landing on his skin that was still so covered in her saliva. His cock was hard, still hard, still wanting more. He met her sun-kissed eyes, and plunged himself into her. Lords, she was so fucking hot and wet, and with his come on his cock, it made his sheath inside of her so blissfully smooth.

She bit her lips around a moan, and something in Ambrose's mind broke. His anger bristled, and his need to hear her moan—to hear her *scream*—snapped every part of him. Every part, but the predator's.

He thrust into her, hard and fast, as he grabbed her jaw.

"Scream for me, right fucking now."

Lila raised an eyebrow.

Make me, she said.

Oh. She wanted to play? He could play.

Ambrose slipped his cock from her sopping cunt, and stepped back as he lowered her feet to the deck.

"Ambrose? Are you—"

He needed her. He needed her so bad, *it hurt*.

Ambrose stepped forward, and spun Lila around, facing the sun and the open ocean, before he tore her shirt open. He pulled her back flush with his chest, and cupped her breasts as his favorite shade of pink warmed in the direct sunlight.

"*Fuck* yes. I'm more than okay, Lila." He toyed with her, pulling and pinching as she stifled a moan, still biting her lip, refusing to scream for him. All Ambrose could see was the impression her teeth were making on her *perfect, fucking lips*. He wanted it to be *his* teeth. Wanted to bite down on those perfect plump lips, and taste blood as he sucked them between his teeth.

"Keep doing that, love, and I'll have to find a new way to make you scream," he said hoarsely, not recognizing the words slipping from his silver tongue. "I want everyone to hear, you are *mine*."

Ambrose took his hand from her nipple, and guided her chin to turn back and look at him. Then, he took those lips so obviously begging for him, and made them *his*.

His tongue stole into her mouth, hot and desperate. Dominating.

Stop biting these pretty little lips, he ordered. *I've told you before, it makes me feral.* At the final word, he nipped her with his front teeth, sucking her bottom lip into his mouth. She whimpered, *finally* making a noise for him.

But now, he wanted to make her pay for making him wait. He wanted more than a whimper. He wanted a *scream. More, more.* He nipped again, but this time, it drew blood.

Ambrose licked Lila's bottom lip, slowly, eyes open, watching her.

Lila batted those two suns open, her long lashes making his cock jerk against her ass, and met his gaze. *Your eyes . . .* she squeaked into his mind, *they look . . .*

Fuck it. He bent her over the boat's railing, her hands rushed to catch herself at the banister—even though Ambrose would never let her fall. He ripped her pants open farther, and when her gorgeous, perfect ass was just before his cock, he used her slick arousal from her dripping core and his come, and dipped his cock into the puckered tight hole.

A sharp inhale escaped Lila's nose, but she still didn't moan. Not as he felt every twitch, every resistance around his invasion.

"Have you ever had anything in this hole other than my thumb?" He thrusted deeper, pushing himself *just* inside. Lila shook her head, lips still clamped together. Good. Something else just for him. Lords, she was perfect and *his*.

Ambrose snarled, as he rocked back and then dove in once more. It felt like he was splinting her in half, and her muffled cry seemed to say the same thing. A swell of pleasure went straight to his cock at her cry. She must be liking this even more than when he took her pussy, he thought, because her cry nearly sounded animalistic, and he thrust deeper.

"Scream for me, Little Crow," he begged, pushing her back farther down into the wood. "Tell me how good it feels."

It—

Her voice was faint, and though the Concord was *always* there, it felt as though he were slipping further and further away from it. Which only made him feel like he needed to get closer to her.

Ambrose thrust into her again, his cock being milked by every pull of her ass. "You like pain though, don't you Little Mouse, only from me?" He knew she did. Not only that, she *loved* it.

Lila's ass tightened, her back straightened. But Ambrose kept fucking her. He went harder, harder, faster, faster.

A—Ambrose.

Fuck, she was so tight, and felt so good. And her *smell*, lords, he could smell a sharp, metallic tang he loved, her wet pussy, her salty skin. The only thing that'd make it better was if he could actually *hear* her moans, her pleads, her little begs he loved so much. Her screams.

Sun—

Her faint sound through the Concord was barely audible, but he knew what she wanted. He lifted her hips, and with both hands braced at her waist, he pulled her down his cock, and off again.

Absently, he felt his skin begin to prickle, a burn he shrugged off as an itch.

He threw his head back, groaning into the evening sky. The sun on his chest, igniting the crow tattooed there, and the divine heat swelling around his cock, swallowing him whole, drove him further and further into lustful madness as he drove further into his sunlight, again and again. Ambrose was thrusting so hard into her, he lost his footing under him, scrambling to keep up, scrambling to just *be inside of her*. He smacked her ass, grabbing her waist, and pulling her down to meet his hips at each hungry thrust.

It was euphoric, it was bliss.

He moaned, "Ah, *scream for me, love.*"

"Sunflower!" Lila shrieked, and with the sound of her voice, everything around him completely shattered.

34

Ambrose tore himself away, and before Lila could even climb down the banister and turn around, he dashed into a shaded part of the ship.

She was bleeding, she knew she was—she could feel the hot, sticky liquid drip down her ass cheeks, down her thighs. It burned, it hurt, but her soul felt like it was coming apart.

Little Mouse.

The words ripped through her more than his cock did. As she planted her feet firmly on the deck once more, her legs immediately gave out under her.

She was shaking, crying, desperately trying to regain her breath—and Ambrose wasn't near her.

But she could hear him.

"I hurt you . . ." he kept repeating. "I hurt you so bad, your love stopped protecting me from the sun. I hurt you so bad, you're crying. I hurt you so bad, you're *bleeding*. I *hurt you.*"

The Sun Child

Lila looked over her shoulder, and he crumbled on the deck. Sitting on his knees, his upper body hunched over itself. In any other situation, it would look as though he were begging her, on his knees for her. But now . . .

He looked like a man defeated, broken.

"Ambrose," she began, shifting to face him. "I'm sorry about the sun, I—"

"Don't you *dare* apologize. You did *nothing* wrong. I am the monster. I'm the one that does not deserve you, the one that *hurt* you. I am the one that has fucked *everything* up." His ruby, glowing eyes—eyes that were nearly all pupils just a moment ago as his arousal overtook him—were dimming to unused coals, black as the void, black as the depth of the ocean. "I am *so* sorry, Lila. I do not deserve your love."

Lila tried to move toward him, tried to comfort and soothe him. To tell him, yes, it hurt. Yes, he was too rough. But that did not mean he was unworthy. That one did not have to do with the other. Lila wanted to ask him what was wrong, what had *been* wrong, why he was always so on edge, why he was too careful and too filled with shame.

But Ambrose didn't let her ask anything. Not as he flinched the moment she crawled closer, and shifted into the white crow. He hovered for only a moment, and then swooped into the lower part of the ship, into the shadows, and away from the sun.

Not even a few moments later, Rebekkah hurried to the base of the steps, peeking her head onto the deck where Lila still lay slumped.

"Mousey, Ambrose sent me, he said—I smell blood! Is it yours?"

Lila weakly nodded. "I—*fuck*, this is embarrassing," she hissed, trying to get up. "I don't think I can walk right now."

Rebekkah inched onto the deck, but her skin sizzled the moment it touched the light. She hissed then met Lila's eyes.

"Just . . . give me one second." Her power felt akin to being out of breath. Like it was there, all she needed to do was take a few deep breaths to stutter it back into existence. But, as being out of breath, it felt like wading through weighted water, like each inhale would never bring enough air to the lungs.

She knew she would heal. She knew her strength would return, and she could bring sunlight to the vampires she loved on this ship. But Ambrose had surprised her. He was rough—rougher than usual—and so . . . demanding. It was animalistic, and the moment she felt him give in to his desire for her, something else shifted too. She felt like she'd never felt before, as if she were the prey being hunted, being chased, being toyed with, before being eaten alive.

Though his cock in her ass felt fantastic at first, the need to hear her made him aggressive, almost . . . blinded him it seemed. And when he called her *Little Mouse*, a slip of the mind and the predator/prey dynamic spreading from body to body, it crumpled something in Lila's mind. It destroyed the feeling of comfort, of safety . . . of Ambrose.

All he wanted was for her to scream. But . . . Lila wouldn't. All because of a little game *she* started.

Lila sighed. Maybe she fucked up. She had told Ambrose to use her, to take the monster out on her. But she couldn't keep her end of the unofficial bargain.

The hurt in his eyes when he came to, when he dashed

into the shade as his perfect, dark skin sizzled under the light of the sun, it was enough to make her burst into tears just at the memory.

She needed to find him. Yes, what he did was wrong. But she's known something was wrong for a while and still didn't make it a priority to get to the bottom of it. They were still so *new* at being . . . this, and they were constantly in peril, constantly on the run, and constantly testing new limits. Lila knew they were madly attracted to each other, and madly in love, they just needed to figure out how to navigate that. How to navigate being a monster and a human in love. She needed to talk to him, to find out what in Malvania was going on with him. This was just a hiccup. Something they could talk through, she assured herself.

Lila faced the sun, and whispered a silent prayer. *Give me strength.* She took a deep breath, imagining the rays of light converging, in through her nose, deep into her lungs, and spreading through her body. *I am the Sun Child*, she reminded herself.

And she loved Ambrose. She couldn't believe her power stuttered, she'd allowed fear to take over. But she *knew* she loved him.

Lila stood, despite the soreness between her thighs, the soreness of her ass. The wound healed and she could wash off the blood later. Right now, she needed clothes, and then she needed to talk to Ambrose.

She turned to Rebekkah. "It should be safe, Bek. Can you find me clothes? A blanket even?"

Rebekkah nodded and disappeared into the dark once more. Lila only waited a moment before she reappeared, dashing onto the deck, into the sunlight, with a blanket in her arms.

"I found clothes as well. Let me help," she said as she

tied the blanket around Lila's shoulders, covering her tattered clothes and bare skin. "I found a large barrel. We could fill it with water and wash the blood from your skin. It'll be sea water, but—"

Lila nodded. "That'll do. Is anyone else up?"

Rebekkah shook her head. "Not that I know of. Most only went to sleep within the last hour. Ambrose woke me to come find you. He seemed . . . scared."

Ambrose sent Bek. No one else would see her like this. In his madness, he still cared enough to ask the right person. Lila felt a sob in her throat.

"What happened?" Rebekkah asked seriously, her eyes flaring like the sunlight behind her. "Do I need to kill him?" Her fangs were bared, and in that moment, Lila knew she would if Lila asked her to.

The corner of her lips lifted at that, before falling into a flat line as she sighed. "No, I think we just need to talk. We just haven't *really* had a chance, not since we've reunited. Not with everything happening."

Rebekkah put her arm around Lila's waist, and guided her below deck, passed their cabin doors—and though Lila wanted to stop at her own, to face Ambrose immediately, she let Rebekkah guide her.

"Was he . . . aggressive?" she asked.

"*Not* like Hektor," Lila snapped.

"I would *never* think 'like Hektor.'"

Together, they descended another small set of stairs, going even lower into the ship. "I ask because I feel I maybe can provide some . . . clarity."

Lila turned to her, raising an eyebrow, and Rebekkah smirked, but it didn't reach her eyes.

"Our desires for body and blood are often entwined, clouded. It is easy to mistake one for the other, especially if we have lost ourselves to the sensations of it all. Hence, why Hektor is such a monster. He cares not for that difference.

"Sometimes, in the throes of passion, the throes of hunger come as well. The need to *taste*. In any capacity. Just like with our bloodlust, it is difficult to snap *out* of being the predator. I am not sure what just happened between the both of you, but based on your clothing, and where the smell of blood is coming from, I can only assume his need for you was blinding. His need to *have* you overlapped with his need *for* you, and it sent him into a kind of frenzy."

They entered a back room on the ship. It was dark, and down here Lila could feel the sway of the ship, the crash of the waves, at its strongest. But in the poorly lit room, there sat a large, barrel-sized tub, filled with water—salt water by the scent of it.

"It was all I could find. The water will be a bit cold now, but the salt will help clean any wound."

Though Lila knew she was already healed, the thought warmed her heart.

"A little cold water is no bother. Thank you, Bek," she said, as Rebekkah helped her into the tub. "And I think you're right. I know Ambrose would never intentionally hurt me. I *know* that. But sometimes . . . sometimes I think he is so afraid *to* hurt me that he ends up doing just that. As if, in holding back, it is actually shoving him forward."

"It's a primal need. We are animals, monsters . . . things of want and desire. Selfish beings. But also beings desperate for love. And Draven has found that with you, and—if my guess is correct—he is trying desperately to preserve that. And it is as you said. He is trying *so* hard, it is driving him mad. I'm sure there is more to it as well."

Lila stayed silent for a moment, using a washcloth between her legs, and then sighed heavily. "I will make sure to talk to him, and figure out what's going through his mind."

Rebekkah nodded. "I think . . . well, Mousey, it's not my place, but I think *you* should talk to him about what's going through your mind as well."

Lila scrunched her brows. "What do you mean?"

Running her long nails through Lila's hair, she shrugged a shoulder. "Have you told him about the last three months?"

Damn. "About my powers—"

"I mean about Hektor. About Ciro, and Drusilla. About the day they put that collar on you. About your trip to your home village."

Lila pressed her lips together and lowered herself deeper into the make-shift tub, pressing her knees to her chest.

Silence thickened between the two women, until Rebekkah solemnly nodded. "It might help get *him* to talk, if you talk as well."

She knew Rebekkah was right, but reliving those memories was the last thing she wanted to do, and reliving them for Ambrose? She couldn't imagine how upset he'd be.

After bathing and dressing in more loose-fitting clothes they found around the ship, Lila padded back toward her room, determined to right the wrong between her and Ambrose.

She stood before the closed door, damp hair dripping onto her loose white linen shirt, and hesitated. Did she knock? Did she just enter? Awkward tension gripped around Lila's throat like a strigoi's claws. It had *never* been awkward between her and Ambrose. Not like this. Not even when they argued in the Arachnid Estate the afternoon after Sanktus Pernox. But since their reunion, there have been so many moments in which she just simply didn't know what to do, how to respond, how to act.

This is Ambrose, she told herself. *I don't have to be afraid of saying the wrong thing, of making the wrong move. I just need to let him know I'm okay.*

The look in his eyes when she turned to him as he said "I hurt you," sprang to her mind, and pushed her into the room.

"Ambrose, I—"

But the room was empty, the blanket was tossed over the bed, their things were exactly where they'd left them. Ambrose had not returned here after he disappeared.

And he did not return to their room for the rest of their voyage. Though she thought she saw a ruffle of white feathers from the corner of her eye on more than one occasion, she slept alone in her bunk. She tried to call him through the Concord, but he would never respond, and it was a conversation she wanted to have face to face.

By the third morning, she'd had enough. She called his name, over and over, hoping to lure him out by sheer annoyance. It was torture, without him. Her heart felt like it was crumbling in two, and she felt like it was all her fault.

When he still did not appear before her, or answer in the Concord, Lila felt hollow. She began to feel far away.

She did not see him as she spent time with Constance, Kaz, and Marcus, hearing of everything that happened in the last three months. She did not see him as she spent time speaking to Darius, whose eyes were on Rebekkah for nearly the entire three nights remaining of their trip. She did not see him as she spoke to Nostro of their plans to tour the Morada villages to free the humans-turned-strigoi.

And through these all, she was only half there. She felt like she had been underwater. Floating, stagnant, her lungs quickly needing air. The people around her, the ship, they were the sun just above the surface.

And just like underwater, she needed Ambrose to come pull her above the water before she drowned.

Lila did not see Ambrose as the ship was docked at the shores of the Viper Morada, as she soared in Marcus's arms toward her personal hell, not as everyone gathered around and made a plan for Rebekkah to take over the Morada and have the remaining vipers follow her, not as they walked the path to the stone manor, not as she stepped through the main hall of the large doors and every sense of courage slipped from her veins, not as Rebekkah told the vipers to stand down, to follow her or be exiled into the lands of strigoi.

She didn't see Ambrose again until her first night back in the suffocating walls of the Viper Morada, until Rebekkah forced her to wash and change from her sea clothes to a flowing dress the same shade as her hair, with sleeves as thin as spider silk, until Pollock landed on her shoulder and nipped on her chin, beckoning her attention. Until she turned toward where the bird ushered, and followed the path that had led to what was once her room.

35

Ambrose stood in the tiny room in the depths of the Viper Morada. The hay bed Lila and Marcus once slept in at his back. His eyes flit to the window before him—the one he'd stared through, looking at her from the other side. He pushed it open now, letting the night air breathe into the room as the royal blue sky illuminated with a crescent moon. He'd lit a number of white candles, lighting the room in a soft golden glow—much like Lila herself.

He wasn't sure what brought him here. Maybe it was the fact it was the last place he thought Lila would venture alone. Or maybe it was to see where all of her hurt and pain had happened.

Maybe it was to feel confined himself, to punish himself in *her* pain, in a prison of the only true thing that mattered to him.

For the last three days, Ambrose had been torturing himself, blaming himself, and berating himself. And all he could think of was Lila's scream—a scream of pain *he* caused. His hands shook whenever he thought of it, as rage and guilt exploded through him so, too, did sorrow and pain. He felt his heart breaking, like he was coming apart from within.

He still remembered how the sunlight felt against his skin, unprotected from Lila's power. It stung. Almost as much as the thought, *Does this mean she no longer loves me?*

But just as his nails were beginning to mirror the moon in the sky on his palms, the air in the room shifted.

The smell of warmth and flowers and sunlight filled his senses. The sound of her breathing, her tentative steps, her heartbeat. It was what overtook his entire world, his very existence. It was a smell he'd come to associate with home, a song that had become the sound of his soul. At once, Ambrose was all too aware Lila was getting closer to him, and that he had nowhere to go. But more importantly, he knew he couldn't run and leave her to once again face the memories of the Morada alone, he knew he needed to stay.

For she was the sun of *his* universe, and he would orbit around her for as long as she allowed, even if it meant he got so close, it burned him right up.

He turned, and the air escaped his lungs as his gaze fell on her. She always took his breath away, no matter how she looked or what she wore. No matter if she was covered in dirt and sweat and gore. No matter if she were mad at him, or sleeping, or gasping for breath during training. She was *everything* to him.

And he needed to tell her. To show her.

"Lila, I—"

She jumped, her eyebrows shooting up—but she didn't run, like he feared she might. She did, however, put up a hand, her lips set in a pout and her eyebrows drew together. "Did you have Pollock bring me here? And have Rebekkah make me wear this dress?"

He looked her over, noticing now the dress in question and the pesky bird on her shoulder, jumping from foot to foot.

Ambrose took a deep breath. "I wish I could say yes. But, I fear those two have probably become better friends than we've realized." Then, Pollock cawed, and flew from Lila's shoulder, happily squawking all the way to the exit of the hall. Ambrose released that held breath. "And as for the dress, it does look absolutely lovely on you."

Her cheeks turned a shade of pink he loved, as his eyes roamed over her. He knew she could feel the heat of his gaze, as it took in the cinched waist, the deep sweetheart neckline, the straps that crossed at the hollow of her neck and draped on her upper arms, the transparent lilac sleeves.

When he finally looked up, he saw Lila taking him in as well.

Ambrose wore nothing as lovely as Lila. In fitted black pants and a flowy top he took from the ship, he looked more like a pirate than a lord. But wasn't that the way of him? A scoundrel. A rogue. A *villain*.

He rubbed his hands together anxiously, noticing not for the first time that he had not worn any rings in days. The only thing on his fingers was the matching crow and sun tattoo he shared with Lila on the ring finger of his left hand.

His gaze caught on the matching tattoo across from him, watching as she absent-mindedly rubbed her right thumb over it, as though it were a real ring. Then, those gorgeous brown eyes finally met his again.

He began, "I'm sorry I haven't been—"

"It's nice to see you—" she was saying at the same moment.

They both pulled their lips between their teeth.

At the sight of her clamped lips, a feral streak of rage and lust shot through him. But he would not give in to that. Not when he had so much to apologize for. Instead, he stared at his feet, opening and closing his fist, and heard Lila gulp.

"You go first," she said, her voice just a bit breathier than usual.

Ambrose took another deep breath—he'd been doing that so much lately—and stepped forward. He wasn't sure what he'd say, what he'd do. But he knew what he *needed* to do.

"There is so much I want to tell you, so much I want you to know, how I feel, what has happened—"

"Then tell me," she pleaded, meeting him in the center of the room. "You ran off the other day before I could say anything. And you haven't answered me through the Concord in days."

"I know. I am *so* incredibly sorry, I—I—"

She grabbed his hands. "Stop apologizing. I *love* you. Nothing you do will change that. I was just startled. And it's not like I didn't like it, but the moment you said—"

"Little Mouse," he cringed. "I know. I didn't even realize until later." He squeezed her hands. "I know you are more than that. You know that right?"

Lila shook her head. "It's not that. I *am* more than that, and I have never questioned if you see me as just a murine, or think less of me. It's not that."

"Then–"

"It's Hektor," she cut off. "He called me that while I was here. He and Ciro. As a way to get to me."

Ambrose's blood boiled and he cursed himself all the more.

"But you didn't know," Lila gushed out. "You *couldn't* have known, because I didn't tell you. I *want* to tell you."

Ambrose nodded. "I want to tell you too. But there is . . . too much to say. I'd rather show you." He squeezed her hands, waiting for the pensive expression between her lips, her brows. "There is a way I can show you through the Concord. But you have to ask me for it as part of our original bargain. A favor."

Her eyes searched his. He felt her skepticism, her concern. "Are you sure? Is it not an invasion?"

He shook his head, white hair falling around his shoulders. "I want you to know everything of me, Lila Bran. You asked for all of me, and I want to give it to you." He took a step closer and pressed his forehead to hers. "Every ugly detail. Every speck of history."

She put her hands on his waist, pulling him closer. "Then ask me the same. There are so many things that happened, in this room alone, the last three months that you need to see."

Ambrose nodded. "Deal. Ask me, love."

She pulled his head down, and stood on the tips of her toes, bringing her lips softly to his. After a gentle kiss, she whispered, "I have a favor. Show me everything."

It triggered an electric current down his spine, and as he pressed his forehead to hers, memories hit him as though he were reliving *everything*.

His childhood, his mother and father, his brothers. Joking around as they ate meals, caring for the land—joy and warmth.

Then white skin, but no more different than him. Human.

Until they wanted more. The attack, fear, pain, anguish. His mother, raped. His father, killed. His brothers, tied and bound and stolen. His home was gone, and he felt waves as he was pressed tightly in the bowels of a swaying ship to other Black bodies. Hot, sticky, stuck.

Then, the day once more, in a foreign land.

Masters, owners, repressors — his brother, gone.

Alone.

Years and years, and then — a new master. A master with a wife who felt like sunlight when she smiled at him. Who was kind to him. The couple paid him, considering him a worker, not a slave. Things were . . . better.

Then they killed her. Witch, they said. He felt the fire's heat on his skin, and he knew the evils of man.

The master went mad, and killed so many. He'd been . . . a strigoi — now that Ambrose could put a name to it. But in a flash of light, he looked human once more. Human, but hungry. Hungry for blood. Gore and screams raked the streets. People ran, and fear licked up Ambrose's legs, his arms, his throat.

Then the original vampire turned Ambrose.

In the first years, all he knew was blood. Drinking blood, shedding blood, craving blood. He needed it, more than anything, more than life, more than safety. And though years had begun to pass, he did not age.

But he was so cold.

And the sunlight he'd once craved, the sun he remembered — it was no more. And that hurt most of all.

So he continued killing. He became a nightmare to those in Europe, traveling from country to country, killing and drinking and everyone feared the murder of crows that signaled the arrival of the monster of Malvania — the monster that only came out in the dark.

He remembered the bloodshed on his hands, and he remembered the apathy he felt as he gazed down at his latest victims.

Something had to change.

The Sun Child

The world around him was falling apart. The children from the original vampire's next unions took the world, changing so many into the creatures of the night, and most humans either became prey or transformed into predators themselves.

Then, the original vampire was killed by humans, starting the Mass Death, and the eight vampire manors were formed.

One by one, four of them fell.

Ambrose, fighting, his knuckles bloodied, his teeth covered in gore. His stomach turned from the black, slick blood of other vampires. And all the while, he was alone.

He knew others, he knew Gustov Nostro of the Maggot Mansion, he was close with Darius Maronai of the Arachnid Estate, and Lord and Lady Reinick had once been his ally.

But he was so alone, as he waited in the Crow Court.

So alone as he butchered the other four manors.

Then, after their fall, years. Years and years—of nothing.

Slivers of joy, but nothing more.

Until her.

Lilac hair, flushed cheeks, and a warmth trickling under his veins at her mere presence.

Sitting on his foyer floor, bruised, beaten, bitten. But there.

A whirlwind of falling in love. Of sunlight. Of recognition, for he knew she matched his soul.

For he knew she was the Sun Child.

And he knew, he was wholly, undoubtedly, hers.

Her taste, her touch, her voice, her moans, her laughs, her lips, her hands, her eyes, her heart, her love. It was all his.

But then her tormentors returned. Returned and threatened to take her. They were hurting her, Drusilla was hurting her. Her brother, Constance, strigoi. Lila was going to be attacked, she was going to be killed by family—by those she loved. He couldn't let that happen. He wouldn't let that happen.

Teeth.

Then, shifting.

"Run," he'd said.

And she ran. And he chased. And he loved it. It made his chest pump— brought his body to life. He wanted to taste her, in more ways than one. He wanted her blood. He wanted her cum. He wanted to sink his bisected jaw in her neck, in her shoulder, in her chest.

When he bit her, it was like he was home again for the first time since he saw his family in his homeland. It was like he was eating a meal for the first time. Like he was feeling the sun again in nearly five hundred years.

And he wanted more.

He wanted her blood, he wanted to drink it from her neck. He wanted to pleasure her as he did so—wanted to feel every part of her cave for him.

He was an animal. A fucking rotten, disgusting animal.

Sunlight.

He was cured. But the taste of her still lingered on his tongue.

Still lingered on his tongue.

It *still* lingered on his tongue. And he wanted more.

And through their separation, he wanted more. His heart broke every day without her. He was crumbling like ash without her, like a vampire in direct sunlight, without her. But with her?

He was the rays of the sun. Impossible without her. Carried by her.

He was the monster of Malvania and he wanted more. He wanted his queen to fuel his power, to quench his drive, to be his sole reason for existence. So when he saw her chained and shackled, as though she could ever belong to someone other than him, someone at all, it drove him mad. The monster from his past came out.

And it never went back in.

36

Ambrose threw himself back. His breathing was heavy as his heart pounded in his chest. In his mind, 465 years had passed. His entire life. But in reality, it was but a moment. A moment of pain and anguish and joy and love. And *want*.

Sweat licked his brow, a droplet ran down his back, and tears pricked his eyes. It was . . . so much.

And he was so ashamed.

"You're *so* afraid," Lila whispered, a voice soft like the petal of a flower. As he stared at his feet, he heard her slump onto the makeshift bed, the hay squishing beneath her.

He was. He was afraid. Now that she'd seen everything, now that she'd seen the truth of him, his nature, his desires—what if she no longer wanted him? What if *she* was afraid of *him*?

Ambrose clenched his fists. This was *Lila*. She loved him. She wanted all of him, as he wanted all of her. Even if she were afraid or angry or upset, they would find a way to overcome it.

Wouldn't they?

He peeked up at her through long lashes. The colors of emotion swaying around her made him freeze to the spot.

She was . . . so sad. Tears streamed down her pink cheeks, the tip of her nose a ruddy red. She was shaking, and her fists were clenched.

But she wasn't afraid.

Not at all.

She was so . . . devastated, sympathetic. Sad and angry and resilient and protective and . . . love.

The breath knotted in Ambrose's chest came loose, and his feet moved of their own accord till he was kneeling before her.

"You have been through *so* much," she breathed as he took her hand. "And you . . . were so alone."

He placed his hand on her cheek and brought her face to meet his gaze. "Until you."

She threw her arms around his neck, falling into him. "You don't have to be afraid, Ambrose. I—" she took a deep breath, tickling his neck. "I didn't think I was strong enough for you. I didn't know if you could deal with being with someone so weak. But, your history just makes me sure now, *you* have made me strong. You have made me resilient and you have given me the power to overcome the traumas of my past. And I want to do the same for you. You can feel the sun now whenever you want. You can be a monster with me. You can drink from me—"

"I can't—I'll only hurt you," he choked out. He hadn't realized it, but he was holding her so tightly, pressing her to him. Tears spilled from his eyes, down his cheeks, a sob lodged in his throat, threatening to break free.

Lila pulled back from him, hands gripping his shoulders tight, saying *I'm here.*

"No. You won't. Look, you *did* what you were afraid of—you hurt me while being rough. And *look,* really. I'm fine—we're fine. I don't have any lasting mark, no wound. And, Ambrose . . . I *liked* it. I wanted you to take me like an animal. I was grossly underprepared, but that is *not* your fault. I want you to claim every part of me, every hole in my body, just as you've claimed every hole in my heart. I want you to spank me. I want you to torture me. To ruin me. To take me where you shouldn't. To make me scream in a room full of people. I want you to make me bleed, Ambrose Draven, and then I want you to devour me the same way you did under the stars. I am not afraid of your bite. And I never have been."

Lila pouted, letting her words sink in. Then, a streak of something powerful colored her emotions, an orange and red, so bright it was nearly blinding.

"In fact, I *want* you to bite me. Right now. In this room."

For the first time since Lila arrived, it dawned on him that they were in *her* room. In her space of trauma and fear or torment.

"Bite me as I show you my memories. Bite me, and take away the sting of this place. And then make it ours."

Ambrose swallowed. "I'll wait," he uttered hoarsely, heart beating so loud, he felt it'd burst from his chest. "I'll wait till just before you show me, and just as you come back—just as *we* come back, I'll fill you with my venom, and then we will make this room—the whole damned Viper Morada—into something beautiful. Into something *ours.*"

Lila nodded, clutching him tighter. "Does it hurt?"

"My bite? You tell me," he smirked.

Lila huffed a laugh. "No, goof. The memories. The finishing of a bargain."

His hand circled her waist. "They hurt as much as the

memories felt. But for physical pain, no. Though, the tattoo you love so much will be gone."

She smiled sadly. "I'm sure we can get me another soon."

Ambrose tentatively pulled her up from the bed, bringing her close.

"Are you sure?" But he was already breathing her in, kissing her jaw. If she changed her mind, he would respect it. He would never bite her again if she asked.

"I am. I *like* your bite. It is a part of you."

His breathing was shallow. So many fears crossed his mind. What if he couldn't stop? What if he hurt her again?

But the fear silenced when Lila cupped his face between her small hands. She forced him to look at her, and whispered, "Ask me." Then, she lifted his chin, bent down, and licked his neck.

Ambrose moaned, surprising himself. Though, it wasn't a moan of lust, but of release. Of letting the weight on his back loosen. "Bite me," she begged, and then she nibbled those blunt teeth into his skin, his pulse. Ambrose shuddered, from head to toe. She was biting *him*.

His knees gave out from under him. He slumped to the floor, head swaying. She was freeing him, breaking the shackles on his mind, on his heart, with each torturous act. Lila followed him down, crawling onto his lap and hovering over him.

You know I am yours, she began through the Concord. *I have given every part of myself to you, time and time again. Now, Ambrose . . .* "Prove you are mine," she said aloud.

Ambrose wasn't sure if it was her words, the pupils overtaking her irises, or the fact that it was a demand from his queen, but the invisible chains finally snapped.

He leaned into her, cupping the back of Lila's neck with one hand as she threw her head back, and pulling her waist to him with the other. He breathed her in, his lips grazing over the column of her neck, slowly brushing himself against her soft skin, till his lips were at the base of her throat. He kissed her, sucking her skin into his mouth. "I ask for a favor, love," he breathed, a shudder overcoming him once more, "show me, everything."

And with his lips hovering just above her neck, sitting on the floor of her old room, her cheek brushing the soft white strands of his hair—she did.

The last thing Ambrose heard was Lila's gasp as his fangs dove into her skin and his mind fell into her memories.

Pain sparked on her neck, her wrists, her arms, her feet, her inner thighs—all places she had been bitten by Hektor and Ciro. Fear for her brother, would they kill him today? Would they kill her?

She was always so cold—not her body, but her mind.

What if they took her today? What if Hektor forced himself on her? What if Ciro snapped and stole her away to his bedroom.

Days, months, years.

She went from being just a girl to a woman.

And they noticed.

Her breasts were ogled at, her ass was grabbed.

But still her neck, her wrists, her thighs were bitten.

*Fear and torment—*am I worth anything more than blood? *she'd think, over and over again. She was a murine, a rat, a* slave, *and nothing more.*

Something to be consumed.

Then, more fear. Her brother was gone. She was so alone.

She needed to find him, make sure he was safe.

The Crow Lord. He was salvation. He was the only chance.

And then Ambrose Draven walked in from the dark, hand in hand with the shadows, and he brought that darkness to her. He brought it, so she no longer had to fear it. The stars in the night sky, or the full moon—yes, he was like a moon. A beacon, a guide, a salvation.

Slashes down her back, death surrounding her, forcing her body to act against her will, and then—that voice; that voice like liquid gold.

Salvation.

Flight and magic and wonder and love and friendship and— dare she think it? Home.

He had given her everything, had given her hope once more, had given her life—a reason to keep fighting, a reason to live, a reason to be more than a murine.

She could face them. She could stop them.

Back in her prison. Back in her cell. Hektor's touch on her breasts, her bare before them. Ciro watching her bathe. Rebekkah becoming a friend. Rebekkah being her only solace. Rebekkah giving her safety from pregnancies.

Drusilla was here. Bodies. Blood and murine and Hektor's eyes watching her. She's between them, being drained and came on. Being tortured as others laugh and get off. Touches, glances, more bites, more pain, more anguish—but through it all, power. Through it all, Ambrose.

She loved him. She needed to tell him, and show him, and be with him. She wanted him to have her, to make sure he took her before Hektor did—before Ciro did.

The town she lived in, dark and eerie. Strigoi. Screams and fear and so much pain. But power. She burned Ciro. She burned Hektor.

And it wasn't enough.

Three months. Three months of constant fear. Three months of sowing doubt. Three months away from the light of her life.

Crack, crack, goes the whip. Her heart, burned in the pyre. A shimmer of gold. A collar.

And then, nothing.

Ambrose pulled his teeth from her neck, slumping back. His entire body was quaking in the mixed emotions of her dreadful fear and his horrid anger. There was so much. So much she'd endured. So much she hadn't told him. And he couldn't fault her for any of it. For if she had, he *would* have gone to kill them all. He would have stolen her from this place and forced her to come home, regardless of her plans, despite her wants.

"Ambrose?" Lila slumped into him, resting her head on his sternum.

It was only then that he realized he'd shifted. He'd become the hulking beast, too large for this room. His dark brown skin shifted into the deep charcoal gray, his size increased, his wings splayed behind him. And he held her, entrapped her, in his embrace.

Hektor had touched her. The feelings, her fear, her discomfort, her disdain, it all settled into his bones, into his heart. Ambrose had seen through Lila's eyes, saw the heady, hungry, obnoxious look on Hektor's face as he fucked Drusilla, keeping his eyes on Lila. Almost as if he were pretending he were fucking her. He'd flicked her nipple. He'd cornered her time and time again. He'd tasted her orgasm that *Ambrose* had given her through the Concord. *He fucking stole it.*

And the tonic Rebekkah had given her . . . the *fear* Lila had felt of the very real possibility of being raped. He hadn't known how dire things had become. Which was stupid. He should've known the moment he saw her in that sheer thing of a dress.

Ambrose had felt anger. He had felt violence and rage and murderous determination.

This was different.

This was so much more.

Ambrose stood up and — somehow even in his anger — gently placed Lila on the stone floor. His jaw was clenched. His knuckles felt as though the bone might burst from skin with how tightly he held his fists.

Hektor touched her.

"I'm going to fucking rip his cock off and shove it down his throat. I'm going to kill him for touching you, for touching what's mine, for touching what is *yours*."

37

Lila felt like she was still catching her breath as Ambrose stood her up, his venom just beginning to trickle through her blood, as the fresh bite stung her neck.

She was shaking, her hands out of her control, and she feared her knees would buckle under her if he let go. She held his arms, looked up—and gasped. Ambrose's dark eyes were lightning, shifting into that vibrant red she had grown so accustomed to, a shade that had sent jolts of electricity down her spine, to her core, through her mind. A shade that recognized the monster—a monster *for her*.

"I'm going to fucking rip his cock off and shove it down his throat. I'm going to kill him for touching you, for touching what's mine, for touching what is *yours*," he grumbled, taking a step past her, wings splaying.

Her heart jolted. She knew his anger—it was *her* anger. They would kill Hektor. But not tonight. Tonight, she needed Ambrose.

"Wait," Lila grabbed his wrist. Her hand was so much smaller than his. In fact, he barely even fit in her room at this size.

"I'm going to kill him," he growled.

"Not now."

"Yes, *now*."

She pushed herself against him, and—just like Ambrose after his memories—she hadn't realized she was crying, her hands and limbs were shaking from more than just the venom running through her.

Ambrose stuttered, turning to face her. As soon as his eyes landed on her, she knew he must've seen all of that. And in moments, tears, just like hers, fell from his eyes. For her, for him—for *them*.

She was *so afraid*. She wanted to be held, wanted to be cared for. Wanted *him*.

"I need you," she whispered.

It broke the spell.

Ambrose crashed himself into her, pulling her up into his arms and kissing her fiercely. His fangs poked her lips, but she didn't care. Let him bite her. Let him bite her, everywhere, over and over. Her blood still trickled down her neck, and down his chin. His bite was violent and fast, but she had *proved* it was fine. Let him drink from her whenever he pleased, so long as she could have him whenever she needed.

"Give me the monster," she breathed against his mouth, and Ambrose moved, lapping at the blood still spilling, drinking her in. His mouth, covered in her, pressed roughly back to her lips. She could taste the metallic tinge of her blood on his tongue, as he swirled it around her own, taking it into his mouth.

"And if I break you?" he breathed, his lips hovering just over hers.

You could never, she replied, lips too focused on kissing him to stop for spoken words.

And if I chase you?

I'll run, because we both like it.

His hand loudly slapped her ass, squeezing hard. *And if I want to be a villain?*

Lila pushed herself back, took a hurried step away. She glanced around her room, the hay bed, the stone floor, the tiny window. She saw the memories from her past seep in, memories Ambrose all had now too. Hektor slithering up her leg, the Reinicks coming to grab her for meals—but also, she saw her brother. She saw her life. This room, of any, was her only solace in this hell.

No, this wasn't the place she wanted to be ruined in. This wasn't the place she needed to smother with new memories, where she rewrote history.

But she knew where to go.

Lila met Ambrose's glowing ruby eyes, hungry for her, hungry for blood, hungry for her sex. He breathed heavily, his charcoal chest huffing, the crow tattoo moving as though it were flapping its wings. And she knew it wasn't his venom coursing through her that made her just as feral.

She smirked at him. *Then be a villain. Destroy me.*

And without another beat, she turned and ran from the room.

The manor halls were silent, the vampires were asleep, and the layer of dust on the floor sat undisturbed, but the silence was quickly broken as Lila ran for her life. Her feet pounded the stone floor, her thighs pumping with as much force as if she had the same body she rigorously trained months ago. She knew the path, she knew the halls, she knew where to go. Her heart raced, the beat of it pounding in her chest.

For there was a monster chasing her.

She could almost feel the claws *woosh* through her long lilac hair, could almost feel the fangs digging deep into her skin. After all, he was the predator, and she was his prey.

A smile was spread across her lips, adrenaline fueling her muscles, and a coiling heat working its way through her belly, between her legs, and settling at her core.

Ambrose chased her, growling, and he was *just* behind her. She knew she wasn't *actually* outrunning him. For this was just a game, a game of viper and mouse. A game she knew all too well.

But this time, *she* controlled the results.

Lila felt so fired up after seeing Ambrose's memories—after *feeling* each time of his life as if they were her own. Though she didn't know them, she loved his family. She loved that sunlight had been his respite throughout his life. That now *she* could be that for him. But she also felt the fierce need to protect him, from himself, his enemies, his loneliness.

She knew they were kindred now, as he'd felt every single one of her memories. Knew every dark moment. And she knew he felt just as fired up from her memories as she did for his.

Lila skidded past a corridor, turning sharply to the left, and down another hallway. The large lilac dress proved difficult to run in, its heavy skirts getting too in her way and she relished in the idea it would soon be ripped from her body.

Two rooms were at the end of the hall, and a decision in her mind cleared the last part of her path. She made another hard left, skidding into Hektor Reinick's bedroom.

Immediately, the smell of the stale air stung her nostrils, the way the dim light reflected made her skin want to peel itself off. Even the too-silent noise made her want to turn and run away.

But a hulking vampire was behind her, here for her blood.

Ambrose pushed Lila deeper into the room as she fought to catch her breath.

Lila was out of breath, but she needed him to know the game. Needed him to do as she wanted. It wasn't just the monster and his prey, she wanted him to take every memory from her, and fix it. *Rewrite this place for me. Make it ours.*

Ambrose knew too well what Lila needed, it seemed, and he was ready with the words. "What a beautiful little murine," he whispered, just before saying in her mind, *Remember our safe word.*

She smiled again, her chest still expanding rapidly. *I won't need it. Not this time.*

He slammed the door behind him, and turned. His breathing was absolutely feral as he pulled her flush against him, her back to his abdomen. Ambrose pushed her hair from her shoulder, and slowly licked the column of her neck, his hands roaming her body greedily.

I don't know if I can shift back, he grimaced, his voice wary.

Good. I want the monster.

His fangs bit into her, and her back immediately bowed, pressing her ass into his hard cock.

She reached behind her, shoving her fingers into his

hair and grabbing onto him as though her life depended on it.

Because in a way, it did.

Ambrose cupped her breast hungrily, then slipped one claw into the cleavage of the gown as he caressed her neck with tongue. With force, he sliced the dress open between her breasts, down her belly, until it fell away to reveal her to the room. Lila gasped, but still held on, even as her head grew woozy, even as Ambrose continued and continued to drink from her.

Just when she thought it would be too much, he pulled his teeth away and ripped the rest of the dress from her, leaving her completely naked in the middle of the room.

"Turn around, pet," his voice was thick with a thrall, as the lilac fog covered over her mind. She did as she was told, and she wasn't sure if it was her own choice, or his. Ambrose sauntered up to her, and—with purpose in his dilated eyes—flicked her peaked nipple, before he fell to his knees and sucked it into his mouth.

Lila moaned at the immediate contact. His tongue in his monstrous form was just so much ... *bigger*. Everything in his monstrous form was. And she wanted to feel this tongue between her legs, she wanted this tongue to devour her pussy.

He scraped his teeth against the peaked bud, then sucked till it hurt.

"Fuck. These are *mine*."

He focused on the other one, still giving the first enough attention as he twisted it between his fingers. A pool of wet at her core was ready for him and she was getting more needy, more desperate. Already wanting him inside of her. Already dripping down her thighs.

Abruptly, Ambrose stood and turned from her, leaving

her plucked and puckered nipples desperate for more. Lila began to follow but he looked over his shoulder, his eyes nailing her to the spot. *"Stay there."*

So she did. She watched his every move, his back muscles rippling, his arms and veins flexing. Lila pressed her thighs together, desperate to feel relief, desperate to run even a single finger along her clit.

And as Ambrose walked to Hektor's bed, shimmied out of his pants, and threw them aside, Lila was practically drooling over his absolutely perfect, charcoal ass.

Fuck, she thought. The venom and blood loss were making her mind spin.

But then Ambrose turned around, and she saw, for the first time, his enormous, *monstrous*, hard cock. It was even larger than she thought it'd be and it looked . . . different. Along the shaft, there were small, ridged bumps, and an extra fold just under his dark, charcoal head. His cock was so dark, in fact, it looked pitch black, and she couldn't even begin to imagine how *that* would fit inside of her tiny, tight pussy.

Ambrose smirked and Lila realized her eyes had flown wide open, staring at his cock.

"You look terrified, pet. I thought you said you'd be able to handle me. I thought," the mirth in his voice was back, especially as he slowly, languidly stroked the length of himself, "that I could never break you."

He sat back on the bed, resting an elbow over his knee as he hunched forward, still stroking himself.

"Now, pet, close that pretty mouth of yours before I think up something to do with it." Her lips snapped shut. "Excellent. I want you to get on your knees." Lila did as he commanded.

Another smirk, and she felt his gaze linger on her mouth, linger on her nipples, her curves, her soaked pussy. *"Crawl to me, Little Mouse."*

The words struck something through her, and she whimpered from the sound alone. Once, there was another voice saying those words, another situation, another time. But now, it was only Ambrose. Only him and only her.

So she crawled, on her hands and knees, drooling as she neared his cock, dripping as she imagined it pushing inside of her, heart fluttering as she wanted to be with him—this man, her betrothed. She crawled on the tainted carpet floor, and as each knee came down, each palm propelled her forward, Lila painted a new picture of this room in her mind, a new memory that clouded over the rest.

As she came to sit at Ambrose's feet—like the good fucking girl she was—all memories and thoughts and pain and fear from *this room* disappeared.

Ambrose placed his giant hand on her cheek, guiding it to look up at him. "Are you going to be my little sex doll, for me to play with as I please?"

Lila licked her lips as she nodded. For she knew, Ambrose was just as wrapped around her little finger. He would fall to his knees right now and feast on her till the next Mass Death if she only asked.

"That's my good girl. Now, get up on the bed and spread your legs wide for me." He stood from the bed, allowing her to crawl onto it. As she laid on her back, Ambrose grabbed her ankles and pulled her to the edge of the bed, flipped her onto her back, then eased her knees apart. "Wider, love."

Though he'd already seen it, devoured it, Lila felt bashful as she fully displayed herself for him, her knees apart, feet propped on the edge of the bed. Yet, Ambrose still smirked, eyes locked on hers. "I said, *wider*." She gasped as her knees leaned to the sides, splitting apart, stretching her inner thighs deeply. Ambrose stepped forward, standing over her, and pushed her knees even farther, till they lay flat against the mattress.

Lila felt the cool air rush into her overly hot center, as though it were licking up all of her heat. But just as she felt it, Ambrose's molten hot gaze fell to her pussy, to her clit, to the dripping mess she's already made of herself. The heat, mixed with her own growing warmth, made her moan. It was so much, she felt she might die if he didn't touch her soon.

"*Fucking perfect*," he groaned, inhaling deeply. "Your glistening, love. Pure, utter perfection."

Lila blushed, her whole body turning hot, as the warmth spread, heating her clit like an electric buzz that almost felt like the tool he used in the Maggot Mansion.

"Will it fit?" she whimpered, desperately hoping it would. She wanted to feel those smooth bumps rub her walls, to feel that extra fold as he plunged in and out of her. But she would be satisfied if he would only touch her, rub that monstrous cock against her clit.

Ambrose ran his hand down her body, starting at her breast, and moving slowly to her clit, to her needy pussy. "I'll need to work you up to it. But we can do that. I will take all the time it needs to have you ready for me."

The idea of waiting drove her mad. She wanted him *now*.

He traced his forefinger and middle finger along her spread lips, grazing her clit as he went. She arched into his touch, desperate for more.

A husky chuckle came from his chest, as he stroked her again, slowly. Fuck, it was torture.

And just as she was about to say so, he slipped a finger inside of her. It was so big, so thick, and so much more than she expected from a singular digit. She moaned as he cursed, slowly driving in and out of her.

"Lords, I can't wait to feel you on my cock again. I want your needy pussy fluttering around me till I have you begging to stop making you come, till you've had so much of me, you just can't go on."

Through heavy breaths, Lila reached for his free hand, bringing his fingers to her lips and into her mouth. "That'll—never—happen," she sucked, swirling her tongue around it. "I—will—*never*—have—too—much—of—*you!*" she moaned on the last word as Ambrose slipped another finger into her pussy.

"I want you to ride my hand, love. Soon, you'll be riding my cock."

Lila ground her hips against him, keeping his fingers in her mouth, his wrist bound between her breasts.

He scooped his fingers against her inner wall, the spot she loved, and then added another finger.

"*Fuck,*" she moaned. She was already so full, how was she supposed to take more?

"You're doing so well, Little Crow. You're going to take me so fucking sweetly."

She wanted more.

Ambrose read her as though he were reading his own emotions, grinning at her as he pulled his fingers free. He lifted his hand, for her to see how messy she made him, and then slowly sucked each digit, humming around his fingers.

"Fuck, you're so delicious. I haven't had nearly enough of you."

"Then what are you waiting for?"

Ambrose growled and stepped closer, like a shadow looming over her—like an eclipse blocking the sun.

He positioned his cock at her entrance, and slowly pushed the head inside.

Lila moaned at the force, already spreading her entrance so wide. He took it slow, thrust in and out of her as he only pressed the very tip of his head into her.

"Open up for me, Little Crow. Show me you want this."

Lila tried to spread her legs further apart as she took him just a little bit more.

The stretching was both painful and exhilarating, making her want more, but words were escaping her. She could feel every twitch of his cock inside of her, and only the head had made it past her entrance.

She tried to say his name, to ask him to continue, but all that came out was a gargled moan as she threw her head back, gripping the sheets below her so roughly, she felt her nails tearing into the fabric.

"You want more?"

In response, Lila bucked her hips, *forcing* more into her. She screamed at the sudden stretch deeper inside of her.

He immediately paused. *Safe word?* he asked—but it wasn't *too* much for her. It was just right.

It's so much, so big. More—give me more.

"Fuck," Ambrose hissed. "Goddess."

And then he gave her more, and more, and more, and they repeated the slow thrusting, in and out, as he rubbed her clit with his thumb, tiny circles to make her even more wet, to make her moan and thrust on his cock whenever she felt brave enough. Her eyes rolled in the back of her head, and her back was bowed as her walls fluttered around him. She could feel every vein, every fold. The bumps rubbed at her walls in the most pleasing way possible, she didn't think she would survive this orgasm. Death from pure pleasure alone.

Lila moaned and screamed with reckless abandon, not caring who heard. She screamed *for him.* Anyone who heard could leave the Morada for all she cared—but she could not hold herself back. Not now.

Once Ambrose was *finally* fully sheathed inside of her, she saw him watching where they joined, watching as he pulled in and out of her, watched as he fucked her ruthlessly.

His glowing, hungry, ruby eyes met hers.

Do you trust me?

Always.

Ambrose hiked up her legs, bringing her ankles to rest on his shoulders. The new stretch was *everything*, especially as he found his way thrusting deeper inside of her. But one of his hands lingered on her ankle, on the same spot Hektor had bitten her while fucking Drusilla.

And suddenly, Lila knew what he meant, and realized he was waiting for approval.

She gave a small nod before bucking her hips down his cock again.

"Lords, you feel so good," he groaned, as he split her apart. She felt her pussy spread for him, she felt him in her gut, as bundles of nerves were on fire. His balls smacked into her ass with each thrust, and the pounding noise was driving her wild as she ground her hips in time with each of his thrusts.

A liquid heat spread through her core, warming her pussy and her clit, and Ambrose moaned. "So fucking hot."

Lords, she never wanted this to end. She wanted him to spread her and fuck her till the end of her days. It was all so much, so *good*.

Ambrose licked her ankle as he pulled himself out to his head, letting the extra fold rub and press at her entrance.

"Ready?" His fangs hovered over her skin, desperate to plunge inside.

"Yes," she moaned, ready for it all.

Lila screamed as the pain of his bite turned into utter, complete pleasure in the same moment as he thrust fully inside of her, letting her feel the extra fold split her apart, the bumps along his cock rubbing every too-sensitive part of her, every vein plunging into just the right spots. She felt him in her belly, in her soul, and she wanted him to never stop.

He pulled his teeth free of her ankle, and sucked at the wound there, kissing and licking till purpling hickies were formed on her skin.

Ambrose rocked his hips, back and forth, focusing on the bumps pressing deep into her walls, and she felt herself flutter around his cock—which was . . . enlarging. Swelling. Fuck, he was going to come.

And as he pulled out of her, only to thrust back in, she knew she would too. Lila curled her toes, her entire body hot like livewire, ready to burst. This orgasm would shed her skin, shed her human form.

"Oh, *Ambrose*," she moaned. And still he pumped, grinding into her.

"Fuck, take all of me," he growled, and he pushed all the way in and all the way out, sawing her in half. She felt him thicken and couldn't take it anymore.

Lila screamed as she came, legs stiffening, toes curling, back arching. Her eyes rolled in the back of her head, as she felt herself spurt around Ambrose cock, milking him still.

Ambrose thrusted faster, not letting her come down, keeping her in the clouds, before he burst inside of her, filling her so deeply, so wonderfully, she was sure her pussy would be dripping with him for days.

"Fuck," she breathed. "*Fuck.*" Her entire body went slack, trying to regain her breath. Ambrose's cock still twitched inside of her as he breathed heavily.

"You are so fucking perfect." Slowly, Ambrose pulled out of her, sending new shivers all over Lila's body as the bumps pressed against her overly sensitive walls once more. She shuddered, and as he freed himself, they both looked at his massive, messy cock.

"Look what you've done to me," he grinned. "Such a messy, needy, greedy little thing you are."

Lila grinned, still trying to catch her breath. "I can be more needy."

"Oh, don't I know it."

Lila slumped all her limbs, her legs hanging by Ambrose's sides, her head lolled back, her arms out to her sides. "That was . . ."

Ambrose didn't finish her thought, he waited for her to say it.

"Otherworldly. Monstrous. *Amazing*. I'm going to have the best sleep of my life after that," she grinned.

A hand snapped to her waist, pulling her body into a seated position. Her eyes flew open and she saw a wicked grin on Ambrose's face. "Oh, love, if you think I'm done with you, you're sorely mistaken."

Lila was about to object, but the words were ripped away from her in a flurry of jerking movement. She was pulled off the bed and into Ambrose's arms, his wings spreading wide behind him.

"We're not done making this place ours yet. And you should know by now, having you come just once is never enough for me. I need you on my cock, and on my tongue."

38

The moment he pulled himself from her, he saw her leaking his cum and it was probably the most ethereal sight he'd ever seen.

He wanted more. He *needed* more. It didn't matter that he already finished. It didn't matter that he stretched her as far as she'd go. *Nothing* mattered—but pleasing her, and taming the monster within.

And the monster still wanted more of her.

Lila squeaked as Ambrose flew from the room. He already tainted Hektor's bed, the memories that came with it. He had seen her memories of this place, how haunted she was by each room, and it twisted his gut to think of the torment and pain she went through. Lila deserved so much more than the hand she'd been dealt, and he wanted to make sure she was given a life worthy of her.

A tall order, indeed.

He didn't know how he ever doubted that *she* could love *him*. It was written in her soul. Part of him wondered if they were made for each other, if that sort of thing existed. She had been through so much, her trauma matching his in a way he never thought anyone could relate. Different, of course, but similar.

She loved the monster, loved him with no qualms, loved him with no fear. And he knew he could give it to her—be that with her.

Ambrose took her to the main hall, where Lila was paralyzed and forced between Drusilla and Hektor, where she saw a bloodbath. He knew she still thought about the faces she saw then, about the woman Hektor fucked to death.

He bristled at the thought of the vile bastard. He couldn't wait to rip his head off.

But this wasn't about him. In fact, it would never be about him—everything was about *her*.

Lila stiffened as he flew through the doors, he could feel her spine straighten against where his palm held her. The last time she was in here was right before she killed so many vampires, right before she was whipped and beaten, right before she was collared into oblivion.

Don't be afraid, love, he said gently through the Concord. He was quite the gentle monster—at least, when it came to her. Lila gripped his shoulder tighter.

I'm here, and I'm not leaving. We're rewriting your history here, so whenever you think of this place, you will only remember how good I made you feel. How loved and worshiped you were. How my tongue felt against your clit.

She stiffened again, but by the smell of her, he knew it was from something else. Warmth reignited around her, warming him as well. Lords, he loved how that felt.

Walking up to the dais, Ambrose carefully put her down on the upper-most level. She looked like a queen, and he was ready to bow for her.

"Tell me what you want," he breathed, taking the few steps down to the main level and dropping to his knees before her.

Lila's perfect lips were parted, confused by his sudden position. He felt it shimmer off her, but just as confused as she was, there was also a magenta tendril of curiosity swirling around her, a sliver of boldness.

"I've told you once, I would beg on my knees for you. Tell me to beg, Lila. Because if you don't, I don't know if I'll survive. If you don't, I'll have to go over there, and *take* what I want."

Lila smirked, and leaned back on the dais, propping herself up on her elbows. "And what, my love, will you be begging for?" Her eyebrow arched, and she spread her legs, just a little wider for him to see her perfect little pussy, still covered in him.

Ambrose stared there, knowing what his glare did to her, knowing how it'd warm that needy swollen clit, that entrance dripping with their combined come. A shuddering breath escaped his lips as he saw her cunt glisten with new wetness.

"We want the same thing, love."

"And how," her hands slowly trailed down her body, "do you know what I want?"

Her thin fingers slipped between her thighs, between the plump lips, and circled her swollen clit. A breathy moan nearly had Ambrose lunging.

With her eyes still on him, Lila stuck a singular finger into her pussy.

The corner of Ambrose's lips twitched into a smirk. "Tell me, Little Crow, how does one of your tiny fingers compare to my cock?"

Her finger halted, drawing his attention between her

thighs once more. As she watched, he slowly, purposefully, licked his lips.

Lila gave a breathy laugh. "If you want me to admit this is nothing in comparison, fine. But, Ambrose Draven, if you want to touch me again—if you want me to come again—then you'll have to work for it. If not, I might just have to do it myself. *Maybe*, if you're a good boy, I'll even let you watch." She slipped her finger out, and circled her clit again, the she-devil.

Ambrose was salivating, desperate. So he lowered himself farther, pressing his hands to the floor. "Please, love. Please let me touch you. No—let me taste you. I want you on my tongue. I want to lick and suck and kiss and *feast* on you. I want to cradle your swollen clit, and take care of your sore pussy with my tongue. I haven't tasted you nearly enough, I'm starved, and I need more."

Lila focused on her clit, another whimper he was desperate to devour.

"Please. *Please*," he begged. He rubbed his hand over his hard length, each groove and bump desperate to pleasure her once more. Ambrose couldn't take his eyes off those tricky little fingers, he wanted them, wanted to *be* them. Drool pooled on his lips, desperately salivating for just a taste. "Just . . . one little taste. Please, baby. I need to know what *we* taste like."

"Get closer," she moaned. "But don't touch—just watch." The fingers circled faster.

"Lila, *please*. Don't come."

She smirked wickedly. "You asked me what I wanted," the fingers slid down her plump lips and disappeared into her waiting, desperate pussy. "I want you to watch."

Ambrose hesitantly crawled up the first two steps, his face hovering above her thighs. If he lowered himself now, he could taste her. Maybe just one lick . . .

"Watch," Lila whispered. She truly was testing his resolve to do *anything* for her and it was dawning on him more and more that where doing anything *to* her was easy, doing anything *for* her was the true difficulty.

A drop of his saliva dripped from his lips, and he watched as it slowly fell onto her clit, glistening as it trailed a hot path to where her fingers pushed in and out of her.

"Lila," his voice was so gruff, it didn't sound familiar to his own ears, but he couldn't take his eyes off the drop. "Please let me taste. Please let me lick you, let me have you. I *need you on my tongue*" He was shaking, his limbs full of untamed, unkempt energy, desperate to release it on her. His tongue peeked out of his mouth, imagining he could already taste her.

Lila gasped and slid her fingers out. His eyes tracked them as she grazed her clit, as they passed her belly and her peaked nipples—begging to be sucked—and onto her lips. His eyes went wide as she sucked her fingers into her lips, tasting herself, tasting *them*. She moaned around her fingers.

"We taste so good," she hummed.

Ambrose lost it, he lowered himself and pressed his face into her pussy, his lips already spreading her lips. But all he did was breathe her in. His tongue was desperate to lap her up, to lick from that tight little ass hole to her needy fucking clit.

"Let me lick you." His voice was now all demand, all order. If she didn't let him, he would punish her. Oh yes, he would punish her so well, it'll be everything she was doing to him and more. He'll suck her fucking clit for a week straight. He will feast on her dripping cunt till it's swollen and bruised from his tongue, his lips. His teeth. Till she came over and over in his mouth, till she was sick of his tongue on her.

His breath brushed against her hot center, adding to the heat wave hitting his face.

"*Please,*" he begged once more.

Lila's eyes were on him, and her hand tentatively tangled into his hair. She pushed down on his head, just the slightest, and it was all he needed.

Ambrose grabbed her hips, nails digging into her ass, and pulled her to his mouth, his tongue lapping like a starving animal, drinking in every bit of her, exploring every crevice of her pussy, sucking every swollen flesh from earlier. His tongue consumed her, driving into her cunt as she rocked her hips on him.

Ride my tongue, you beautiful thing. Ride my tongue till you come all over it.

It was so unlike the time under the stars. It was so much more raw, so much more animalistic. It was pure fucking need, it was messy, it wasn't tactful like last time.

And clearly, Lila was loving it. She wrapped her legs around his shoulders, her ankles locking behind his neck. He took one of his hands and pressed his palm into her lower belly, and Lila bucked back, moaning. Her voice clouded his ears, it was all he needed to fuel him forward.

More more more more more more more more more more more.

He couldn't stop begging through the Concord, and Lila's hand in his hair held him exactly where she wanted him.

"Ambrose," she moaned, and with her free hand dug his thumb into her flesh just above the mound of her pussy. "Cut me, here. Drink."

Are you sure?

More than anything. Drink my blood and my cum, I'm not going to last much longer.

The idea sent jolt to his cock. Months ago, before the

night under the stars, before she was taken, there were a bout of days he could smell blood coming from her room and knew she must've been menstruating. They were still training then, and every night she joined him in the dungeon was torture. Every night, he wanted to rip the leathers from her ass, from her cunt, throw her on the mat, and shove his tongue into her bleeding pussy.

But back then, he'd been walking a line. Back then, she had priorities, she wanted to get strong. So, he stroked himself over and over, thinking of her cum and blood on his tongue, until the week passed.

But now, their love was open. He could have her whenever, and he would.

He drew his thumb into her flesh, just enough to draw a thin line of blood, and pushed on her pelvis to give her the ultimate satisfaction.

Lila's blood trailed down onto her clit, and it was as though the world exploded around them.

"*Fuck*," Ambrose cursed over Lila's moans. "Delicious."

He drank her, licked at all of her, sucking her blood-covered clit into his mouth, sucking it till its pink shade turned into a color closer to Lila's hair.

"Ah, I'm going to come," she moaned, her back arching into his touch.

"*Not yet*," he growled, sucking her up, devouring her.

"I—I can't hold out, I can't."

His tongue ran all over her, back and forth, up and down, flicking every sensitive bundle, every soaked spot.

His mouth closed on the small cut he made, sucking a mouthful of blood, and then driving his tongue far enough into her pussy, he felt her walls push against it.

So fucking delicious, he said again, unable to think of better words, unable to speak the wicked poetry he normally conjured.

All he could speak now was blunt truth. She was fucking delicious.

Lila bucked against him, screaming out, as a fresh gush of hot ecstasy bursts around his tongue. Ambrose gripped her ass again, and lapped at it all, drinking it all in, as Lila wormed and moaned and lifted herself up, hugging herself around his soft hair, trying to wiggle out from under him before it all was too much.

"Ah!" she screamed, just as Ambrose finally pulled up. His mouth was dripping with *her* and he wanted it there forever, wanted the reminder on his skin that he was hers. They owned each other like it was their right. Because it was. He had offered himself to her, and she had offered herself to him. Neither was slave, neither was murine. But they both were *claimed*.

Ambrose looked down at his sun, watching as she took deep, hungry breaths. Her eyes were glossy as they met his. Her limbs slackened, before going completely limp back on the dais.

Ambrose finally felt his form loosen, his muscles slacken. His wings were lazily hanging behind him, the monster inside of him . . . tamed. Calmed. Ambrose shifted into his human form, and took a deep breath like it was the first one he'd taken since he'd lost Lila on the battlefield.

Slowly, he crawled over her exhausted form, till his face was above hers and his long white hair tickled her cheeks.

"Are you okay?"

She smiled, cheeks red from afterglow, as her chest still rapidly rose and fell as she tried to catch her breath. "More than okay."

He lowered his face, nuzzling her cheek. "There is still one more thing I'd like to do. And one more room I'd like to . . . cleanse. But only if you're up for it."

Lila pressed her forehead to his, breathing him in. "I need—to catch—my breath," she exhaled. "But, yes. Anything."

Ambrose smiled, and scooped his arms under her, pulling her up to press flush against him as he leaned up again on his knees. He rubbed her back, trying to help ease the oxygen back into her lungs. Then he guided her thighs around his waist, cupped her ass, and stood with her. Her head rested on his shoulder as he carried her from the main room of the Viper Morada, the room Ambrose had gotten on his knees for the love of his life, the room he gave her an orgasm so strong, she couldn't breathe.

It was rewritten.

Ambrose kicked the last door open. He knew this would be his final stop of the night the moment the reenactment idea came to him.

It was a room Lila was afraid of. Not like Hektor's, that was filled with violence and sexual assault. Not the main hall, filled with its vampire debauchery, blood loss, and torment. But this room was filled with something else. It was filled with her enslavement. It was filled with death.

Ambrose nudged Ciro's bedroom door open. He knew this room. Had seen it through the Concord when he helped Lila break Ciro's thrall as he tried to force her to kiss him.

He knew that spot was where Ciro killed his parents, knew that was where he forced her to act against her will. He would replace those memories, so every time she thought of them, every time her thoughts turned ugly, or strayed to pain, she could remember this too. Remember the pleasure, the joy, the sensations of this. Of *them*.

As he walked past the threshold, he lifted his hand to her back, rubbing her slowly.

"Are you with me, love?"

She groaned into his shoulder, half in sleep.

"Would you rather sleep?"

"No," she said, lifting her head. Suddenly, her body temperature rose, and he felt like he was standing in the sunlight once again, a warm blanket wrapped around him instead of the love of his life.

Lila pushed her body up, her arms on his shoulders helped her straighten.

The warmer she got, the more she moved.

She exhaled, and smirked at him. "Having these regenerative powers is proving to be . . . useful in more ways than I thought."

Lila was glowing. And he wasn't sure if it was still the afterglow of her orgasm or if it was the power of the Sun Child, but he felt mystified. Like he was in the presence of a goddess.

Ambrose carefully placed Lila on the floor, and then took a step back.

"So," she said, putting her hands behind her back. Her breasts swelled with more excitement. "What did you have in mind?"

Surpassing a lump in his throat, Ambrose gulped. "I . . . I want to try again. I . . . think I can control myself this time. If you give me the chance." His voice was low, almost shy. He hadn't heard this tone in years. Not since he's had nothing to fear.

Lila pressed her hand to his chest suddenly, a warmth

spreading from her palm through his chest, past every nerve and muscle of his being.

"From behind, you mean?"

He clenched his jaw and nodded. "Only if you want." He couldn't meet her eyes. His heart was pounding, and his palms were oddly clammy. Ambrose was just desperate to rewrite the pain he caused her, so desperate to show her he could do it right, could prove that she'd like it.

But Lila never responded. At least, not in words.

She dropped to all fours and turned, spreading her cheeks for him to see that daringly tight little puckered hole.

"Are you sure?" his voice was dark. But he couldn't take his eyes off the vision before him. Her cunt was like a painting, if the artist lost both hands and painted with a sopping paintbrush and his cock. Her thighs were a mess. Even the puckered hole he was desperate to be inside of was coated in their mixed juices.

In answering again, Lila drove her hand between her folds, shuddering at the sensation again, and smeared the wetness on the puckered hole.

Then, the fiery little goddess wiggled her ass at him, beckoning him over.

Ambrose dropped to his knees, and shifted forward till her hips were lined with his stiff cock. He was ready to come again, and this time, he'd fill her tight little ass after she milked his cock. He'd fill her so much, she would ooze his cum for days.

"Try to stay relaxed. It makes it feel better."

Lila nodded and whispered, "Okay. Can you . . . talk me through it?"

Ambrose dropped over her, his arms on either side of hers, caging her under him. His index finger reached for her pinky, and interlocked. "Of *course*, love. Anything."

He kissed her cheek. "It's going to feel a little uncomfortable at first, it'll feel very full. But once you acclimate, I'll be able to move in and out. There is a bundle of nerves within that you'll feel in your pussy. If it feels good tell me where, and I'll make sure you feel *really* good. If you need my hand to fuck you, just tell me."

"I love you."

The words caught him off guard. His eyebrows drew together, and a silly frown turned his lips.

"I just want you to know. You're . . . so sweet. More than you realize, I think." She kissed his cheek. "Now take me like a filthy animal, you monster."

39

Lila was ready, she could take it this time, and she wasn't afraid. In fact, her pussy was clenching and throbbing at the idea. She had already had two of the best orgasms she'd ever had that night, and she just *knew* this act would be the grand finale of their joining. She needed it. *He* needed it. It would cement all the feelings shared between them that night, would cement every rewriting they've done, even as they now rewrote their own history.

He loved her, and would take care of her, and she knew she was safe with him. Even as he'd pound into her.

Ambrose positioned his cock at her entrance, grinding his tip between her wet folds. "Such a messy little thing," he tisked, as he sawed himself between her. "Your cum will make for the perfect lubricant for your tight little ass."

Lila shuddered at his words. He always had that power over her, to make her wet from just a few syllables with that voice like liquid gold.

"There is a difference between pain for pleasure and pain from discomfort. The *moment* it hurts, you let me know. Understand, Little Crow?"

Lila nodded.

Delicately, Ambrose dipped a finger into her pussy, swirled it around, and plucked it back out again. "I'm going to get you nice and relaxed first." With the same wet finger, he massaged her puckered hole and slowly stuck it inside of her. She gasped at the familiar sensation, feeling the stretch around him. He leaned over her, his breath hot on her ear, "I've come to realize how much I love the slow, torturous power I have over you as I stretch you enough to fit me." His tongue grazed over the shell of her ear. "My own personal little sex doll." She moaned as he stuck the finger deeper, cupping it to massage her insides. "I can't wait to see my cock fill this hole again, to see it dripping with my cum." He added another finger and Lila gasped, rocking her hips back to feel *more*. Ambrose still sawed his cock between her folds, pressing against her sore pussy but grinding between her lips. She'd come so much already that night, and his spit still coated her.

Ambrose was right. She was a mess.

"I'll give my Little Crow a nice warm bath after this. How does that sound?" At the end of his words, the tip of his cock pressed into her clit.

Lila moaned again, and she knew her voice would be hoarse tomorrow.

Ambrose's hips grew more eager, his thrusts between her pussy picking up speed as his fingers in her ass matched pace, pulling apart to stretch her even more.

"Fu-fuck, Ambrose, please . . . Please." Lila rocked back, taking his fingers deeper.

"Are you ready for more, love?"

Lila whimpered, legs shaking from anticipation. From excitement.

"If you don't want this—" he began, and Lila refused to let him get the wrong idea.

"I want this. *Please*," she begged.

Ambrose kissed her shoulder, straightened, and removed his fingers. "You tell me if it's too much."

It wasn't a question, but a demand.

And then he positioned himself at her tight hole, and slowly pushed himself inside.

Lila immediately gasped, as he ever so slowly pushed into her. She felt herself squeeze around him as he rubbed her ass cheek, whispering sweet nothings. Once his head was fully inside, he paused, letting her get used to the size of him there, get used to the feeling. She never would've guessed her night would be filled with stretching. And he was right, it was a slow, pleasurable kind of torture she found she loved.

Finally, his cock filled her and a new sensation raked over her body from where he touched her within. She whimpered at the overwhelming, blissful sensation, as he bent over her, slowly, carefully thrusting into her.

"I want... to try something," she breathed, an idea hitting her.

"Anything," he said without a moment's hesitation. She felt his eyes fixated on her hole, felt the heat of his glare where he watched him fuck into her.

"I want to be tied up again."

Ambrose paused his thrusting, looking around the room. "Hmm," he hummed and eased out of her. He was only gone for a moment before she'd heard a quick ripping sound, and then he returned behind her. "Thank you, Ciro," Ambrose said darkly.

Lila looked over her shoulder to see a white rope in his hand. She balked a little but he nudged his head toward the bed.

"It's from the bed curtains." He pulled the rope taut between him, a wicked smirk on his face. "Tell me, love. What should I do with you?"

Now Lila smirked. "If you don't tie me up, I might just run away."

He raised an eyebrow. "Don't tempt me. I *liked chasing you*."

Ambrose pulled Lila up so her back was flush with his chest. "You look so pretty on your knees," he teased, kissing the side of her head. Then he pulled both arms behind her and began circling the rope from her upper arms down to her wrists. "And now that you're mine to do with as I please, I'm gonna fuck this little asshole till you're seeing stars. I'm going to fill you up with my cum. Tell me you're mine."

Lila whimpered as the ropes tightened. As his cock pressed into her ass again. As his hand reached around her, toying with her nipple. "I'm yours. I'm always yours."

He licked the column of her neck. "And I am always yours." Ambrose plunged inside of her, the fingers at her nipple trailing down to her clit, and Lila threw her head back against his shoulder.

"Lila," he moaned against her skin, and the sound was enough to make her toes curl, nearly climaxing from the tone alone.

Her arms were constricted behind her, and she felt her hands tingle from low circulation, making her head swim. She couldn't fight, not that she wanted to, but he was all that was there to hold her up, even as he thrust against her. She couldn't *do* anything. But she didn't have to.

As Ambrose's hand quickened between her thighs, she

felt the resistance from behind ebb away. He was hitting a spot inside of her that was leaving her dripping down her thighs onto the floor. Lila's back arched as much as it could with her arms bound, and the noises of his hips driving into her ass cheeks was a serenade she'd never recover from, his balls smacking her swollen pussy.

"Moan for me again," she begged. "Moan for me and I'll come for you."

He smiled against her forehead, his fangs poking her skin. "It's a deal."

Ambrose moaned her name, again and again, telling her how good she felt, how well she was doing, how she was such a good girl.

"Lila," he moaned again, "I love you, baby."

It was like the sea burst through her, her body stiffening into pure electricity as she screamed and finally slumped back against him as he still milked his cock in her ass. She came and came, her limbs twitching and she couldn't hold herself up anymore. But still, he fucked into her.

"I'm so close, love, just take me a second longer."

Lila felt her head swimming. It was *so* good. He kept hitting the spot that drove her wild, that had her already on the edge again, her insides warming as though they were being heated by the sun itself.

Ambrose groaned and bit into her shoulder as is cock swelled and twitched, filling her ass with his cum. It was hot and wet but she felt *so* satisfied. And as he took shuddering breaths against her skin, Lila slumped onto the floor, breathing deeply, utterly spent.

I could use my power to rejuvenate. Or . . . she began through the Concord, just trying to catch her breath.

Ambrose chuckled. *Just go to sleep, love. I've completely lost track of time, but I know it has to be the middle of the day.*

The moment Ambrose suggested she sleep, she took that suggestion and made it her life goal. Her eyes were already heavy, and she closed them without a second thought. Lila felt the ghosts of movements, she felt him slip out of her, his cum spilling out of her, being lifted into big strong arms, felt as she was eased into a warm bath and washed, felt as she was towel dried and dropped onto a plush bed. Then, she felt as he fucked her again, moaning in her half-sleep state as she came all over Ambrose's cock again.

She fell into deep sleep with him still inside of her, and she hoped that was how she'd wake too.

It was not how Lila woke. In fact, it was so far from how Lila woke, for the briefest moment between sleep and consciousness, she had to wonder if the previous night had happened at all.

The aching rawness of her holes told her it had.

But Lila did not have the peaceful wakeup she'd dreamt of. She wasn't wrapped in Ambrose's arms—Ambrose was nowhere to be seen.

"Wake up, child," she heard again, as the bed rigorously shook underneath her.

As her eyes adjusted, Lila saw she was still in Ciro's bedroom—fear jolting through her until she remembered the sweet night she had. Though she'd mostly healed her muscles, she still felt the sore tension in her ass, the ghost of a cock pumping into her.

She sat up slowly, holding the blankets to her chest, and saw who'd woken her.

The Sun Child

Gustov Nostro stood at the foot of the bed, kicking the mattress with a black-booted foot. His large black coat had its collar turned up around his neck, making a thick cowl, and he wore those same shaded glasses he wore in the Maggot Mansion.

"We had a bargain, dear, and I'm not letting you spend our only chance shacking up with the Crow Lord. You had your fun time, now it's time to get back to work."

Lila was eyeing the man skeptically, trying to even process what he was saying, when he threw a bundle of black at her, hitting her face. Thankfully, the bundle was soft. Mostly. It was her fighting leathers and the high-necked golden gorget (thankfully tossed *after* the leathers into her lap). "Get dressed," Nostro said. "We have much ground to cover today. And there is another theory I'd like to test."

"Always theories," Lila huffs. "What are you going on about anyway?"

Nostro turned around as Lila shuffled out of the bed and started to slide into her leathers.

"We made a bargain, Sun Child, to aid those in the Morada. You held your end of the bargain, though the trial was interrupted. So now it is my turn. Plus, we could use anyone willing to fight with us now."

"Fight with us?" She shimmied the shirt down her torso.

"Against Hektor, Drusilla, and her strigoi. To claim back the three manors lost. We'll save those that need saving."

"But the vampires here, even if changed into strigoi"—she snapped on the gorget—"I doubt they would go against their own house, against Hektor."

Nostro chuckled. "I forgot. You were . . . occupied while we discussed these matters last night. Come, dear, the others are catching Ambrose up on our decisions right now. It's better if you both are filled in, then we can make decisions together."

Nostro led Lila to the great room, a fleeting heat spreading through body in the memories of last night. Memories Ambrose was clearly thinking of too as his eyes met her across the room. The feel of his needy tongue on her, of his hands searching for purchase.

The room had changed since she'd last been in here. Now, a large table sat in the center, away from the dais, with large chairs surrounding it. Ambrose sat at the back end of the table, his eyes locked on Lila from the moment she entered. Across from him, with her back to Lila, sat Rebekkah. Darius was to her right, and then Constance, Marcus, and Kaz sat scattered between them.

"Look who finally decided to get her lazy ass up," Rebekkah cooed, turning over her shoulder.

"Be nice, Bek. Lila had a *long* night, from the sounds of it," Darius snickered, and Lila felt her face heat like the surface of the sun. But she tilted her head high, and crossed the room to Ambrose.

"I did. I'm guessing someone is a little jealous he *didn't* have such an *engaging* night." And with intent, Lila looked between Darius and Rebekkah, and made sure each of them saw, hoping she'd been picking up on the right signals.

"Yu-uck," Constance groaned, throwing her head back. "Children, the lot of you. Worse than me and Marcus, I swear."

Lila nodded. "As it should be."

She plopped down in the seat beside Ambrose—who had also been dressed in his fighting leathers—and folded her arms over each other. Behind her, Kaz scurried away, only to return a moment later with a fresh plate of food. Fruits and cheeses, breads and sliced meats. He winked as he placed it in front of her, and Lila immediately realized how hungry she'd been.

The Sun Child

"What have I missed?" she said around a mouthful of a cube of cheese.

Across the table, Marcus huffed a laugh, "Talking about you, of course. And how you are to save us all."

The cheese lodged in her throat. Or, it would've if she hadn't scarfed it down already. "Me?"

Rebekkah rolled her eyes. "Nostro has . . . a theory."

"Of course he does," Lila muttered under her breath.

But unlike the others, Gustov Nostro hadn't joined them at the table. Instead, he paced the length of the great hall, back and forth, hands clasped behind his back.

"Let's hear it, Gustov. We haven't got all night," Darius turned over his shoulder to the other Lord.

At that moment, Pollock flew from the rafters in the high-vaulted ceiling, and landed on the table next to Lila. She fed him a piece of fruit from her plate.

"She's strongest in daylight," Nostro said abruptly, his back still turned. "We've all seen it. She fights and heals better when she is in direct sunlight."

Constance sat up straighter. "She had no problem keeping up the . . . warmth that rejuvenated us during the flight from the Arachnid Estate."

"I *feel* stronger too. As if the sun recharges the power."

Ambrose turned to her, "Do you feel weak at night?"

"No, not weak. But—"

"Stronger in the sun," Nostro finished. Lila nodded.

"So, what, you want to attack Hektor and Drusilla in daylight? Can we assure Lila's power will cover us all to *be* in the daylight?"

Nostro turned to the table finally, and nodded once. "I . . . believe so."

Darius sighed. "Believing isn't really knowing, is it, Nostro?"

Ambrose drummed his fingers on the table. "Then let me be the deciding vote. I *know* she can."

Lila's eyes met Rebekkah's across the table. She looked regal, as she smirked at Lila, sitting at the head of the table—where her father sat, her brother. If the Viper Morada were hers to command, maybe it wouldn't be such a terrifying place to be.

"So you want me to attack Drusilla and Hektor during the daylight to catch them off guard? And to make our side stronger?"

"Can you separate who you protect and who you attack at the same time?" Marcus asked. "Or is it an attack all and heal all at once kind of thing?"

When Lila just tilted her head at him, he continued, "Say Ambrose was about to attack me, and I was hurt. Could you heal me, while fighting him, at the same moment? Or would you attack him, hurting me in the process, and then heal both of us?"

Pollock stole the grape from her fingers.

"Ah, the first, I think. That's what I did the morning we fought the strigoi on the ship. But I'm not as practiced in divvying up the warmth. Before, the power just came in all burning heat or all soothing warmth."

"What does it take for you to do these different forms of heat?" Ambrose asked beside her.

Lila shrugged. She felt all eyes on her, and though she wanted to cower away, she knew she couldn't. "Thought, I suppose. Concentration."

Ambrose smirked. "So we'll train."

"But for how long?" Rebekkah asked. "I hate to be the reminder of our unfortunate circumstance, but we're vastly outnumbered."

Darius turned to her. "We have *four* lords of Malvania

at this table, Bek, *and* the Sun Child." He lifted his hand to me. "Our lands may be taken, our people may be changed. But we are *not* broken. Far from it."

"And," Nostro added, "if my theory is correct, we may not be so outnumbered."

Marcus sat back in his chair, brown curls flopping on his forehead. "So what is this theory of yours?"

Nostro fidgeted with his fingers before finally taking a seat at the table between Lila and Darius. "Well, if the Sun Child is strongest in sunlight, perhaps she is even stronger thus in the longest and truest summer day of the year."

"The solstice?" Ambrose asked, folding his arms over each other.

"But that's in . . ." Constance counted on her fingers. "That's in nearly two months from now."

"Just under, if I'm keeping track of our nights correctly."

"And what? We're just supposed to let Drusilla continue her control of our manors till then? Risk her coming here?"

"She won't come here, Bek," Darius uttered. "Hektor wouldn't let her. He's too afraid of him," he pointed at Ambrose. "And, he knows he doesn't have an ally out of you. Word is, he's denounced the Morada, and claims the Crow Court is his now."

Lila bristled, and from the corner of her eye she saw Ambrose stiffen as well.

But it was Kaz who spoke. "That heathen has no right to claim it. He is but a worm for the crows to feast on. No offense, Lord Nostro."

"None taken. Any who, we wouldn't just be waiting around, Rebekkah darling, we would be . . . recruiting."

"Recruiting?" she raised an eyebrow.

"Think of it as a gift from the Sun Child, friend to the Lord of the Viper Morada, Rebekkah Reinick."

Rebekkah smirked. "And what is this gift, *friend*?"

Nostro turned to Lila then, a mischievous smile on his lips. And then Lila knew.

"We'll build the army. Not through force, like Drusilla." She turned in her seat, facing Ambrose. "The reason the Crow Lord is so popular in his land is not because he is the owner of murine, nor is it because he is the scariest monster of Malvania."

Constance stood, her chair falling back. "It's because of the give and take!"

Lila beamed. "Exactly. Something the Morada has never done. *Serve* its people, just as much as they serve the vampire Lord. In the Crow Court, that is exchanging blood for food, coexisting. In the Maggot Mansion and the Arachnid Estate, it is the exchange of blood for shelter, blood for safety. The Viper Morada has always been the odd one out, Bek. Now it's your chance to change that."

"What do we offer the muri—I mean, humans? We don't really have much right now." She pointed at the hall, the dark room surrounding them.

"You offer *me*."

40

Every day, Lila traveled to the farthest points of the Viper Morada land, with Nostro, Marcus, Rebekkah, and whatever other configuration of people wanted to attend that day, and would use her powers on the people—on the murine. Those changed into strigoi would be healed and changed back into their original forms. Their wounds would be healed as well, and together, Lila and Nostro would assist them in rebuilding.

With Rebekkah, they established new terms between humans and vampires, setting up trade and accommodation, and abolishing the murine system.

As they worked their way inland, the people of the Morada began to call upon the Sun Child, to save their loved ones and rescue those that had been forcibly changed, vampires and humans alike.

During this, Ambrose worked tirelessly with Maronai to . . . convince the vampire of the Viper Morada to no longer hold allegiances to Ciro and Hektor Reinick, but instead to follow the proper Lord of the Viper Morada, Rebekkah Reinick. Thankfully, many of the vampires had secretly disdained the brothers' rule since its inception, when Ciro murdered his parents for the title.

By night, Ambrose and the others trained Lila, vigorously. He focused on her strength, her skill, her hand-to-hand combat, now that *she* was the weapon. He taught her how to properly hold her dagger, how to plunge it into a chest after using her heat to catch the opponent off guard.

Slowly, the Viper Morada was making something for itself, growing, and becoming a proper vampire manor once more. And the more Lila healed, the more hands they had volunteering for the cause. Ambrose took volunteers and trained them how to fight, how to not only defend their land, but themselves. He'd armed them with stakes, and taught each and every soul who wanted to learn how to use them.

But Ambrose halted all of his duties the moment Lila told him she'd be going to her hometown next.

"Nostro says that's the next farthest town."

She shuddered next to him, their limbs wrapped around each other in bed as he caressed her hair.

"I'll go with you," Ambrose whispered. "Do not ask me to stay."

Lila nuzzled into him. She had been using her powers more and more lately, healing her tired and sore muscles, and recharging daily in the sun. Her pale skin had tanned in the last weeks, and what was originally red had now turned into a glowing warmth Ambrose couldn't get enough of. "Thank you. I would've felt selfish asking, but . . . I do want you there."

He kissed her head. "Of course. Asking me for things

your heart needs is never selfish. *You* are the most important thing to me. Even if the plan crashes and burns, even if Drusilla takes over all of Malvania. *You* are my eternity." He intertwined their fingers, rubbing his thumb over their shared bargain mark on their ring fingers. "You will be my wife."

"Can I plan the wedding?" she teased.

He nipped at her cheek. "As long as I can plan the honeymoon."

Lila giggled, "Ooo, what are you thinking?"

"I'm not sure, but I know whatever it is will involve lots and lots of rope." She squealed and snuggled closer to him.

Lately, the lot of them have barely been sleeping. With their new schedules of working during the day and training during the night, it had only left a sliver of hours for any real sleep to be had—let alone time for anything else.

So, no matter how badly Ambrose wanted to make sweet love to his future wife, he wanted her to sleep more. She was exhausted, and the only way to replenish that power she kept using would be to sleep. So instead of continuing to tease her, and whispering his dirty thoughts into her ear, he pulled her close to him, and combed his fingers through her hair until her breath became heavy and her back rose and fell with each inhale and exhale.

He rubbed her back as he thought of their time since they decided on a course of action, since they first came to the Viper Morada. They still had so much to do before the summer solstice but they had already come so far as well. Ambrose couldn't wait to have his manor back, his people. He couldn't wait to marry Lila surrounded by those he loved in the place he'd made with his own two hands.

Once Drusilla and Hektor were defeated, he would make sure to do just that. He would make sure to bring it back to its former glory.

As Ambrose rubbed Lila in her sleep, the familiar black crow wiggled his way into what was once Ciro's room, but was now Ambrose and Lila's.

Ah, Pollock, Ambrose said to the bird, *Lila was waiting for you.* Every morning after that first morning, Pollock has slept on the pillow on Lila's opposite side, and Ambrose has found himself enjoying the lilac sandwich he and the crow would make. Something about it filled his heart, and he thought this must've been how fathers felt when they watched upon their spouses and children.

Pollock hopped up on the bed, and nestled into the dip in the pillow he'd made for himself over the last month and a half they'd already been here.

It was already the beginning of June, and they would ideally be sneaking to the Crow Court in just a few weeks to surprise Hektor and whatever strigoi he had protecting him in Ambrose's manor. They were anticipating, and hoping, for Drusilla to come to aid her partner, then Lila could take on her whole army at once.

Which, in tandem, absolutely terrified Ambrose. He had full faith in Lila, and knew she was more powerful than the sun itself. But what if . . . what *if* her power faltered? What if it didn't reach the masses of Drusilla's army? What if something happened to her, or she got hurt before she could heal?

The idea sent a shock wave of cold through his system, as he pulled her closer just that much more. He couldn't fathom losing her. He'd let another Mass Death plague the world if it meant keeping her.

His hands tangled in her lilac hair, hair that perfectly matched the color of his venom. Even now, he didn't know the meaning of the similarity, wasn't sure if there was any actual significance, or if it was just a coincidence. But deep in his soul, he liked to believe it was a symbol. A tether. That Lila Bran was *made* for him, and he was made for her. That whatever gods and devils had cursed them to this life, had cursed them to be together. The Sun Child with lilac hair, the Sun Child with hair like night meeting day. Like dusk and like dawn. Lila was his tomorrow, his light after the darkness, his morning after night, his sun to the moon. And he couldn't live without her—not again.

Ambrose finally slept, with Lila's warmth lulling him into her embrace, surrounding him, encompassing him, bathing him in her sunshine.

As the sun rose beside them, he felt her shivering in his arms, and he knew it wasn't the cold affecting her. As they neared her hometown, Lila became increasingly stiff in Ambrose's arms, a reaction she'd hadn't had in all the trips out to save her people. But, Ambrose now knew *everything* that had happened here. Her entire youth spent scavenging for food, her mother's death, her father's hollowness. He knew of the last time she was here too, of Hektor Reinick trying to force himself on her, of Ciro acting as if he'd claimed her.

But, then, Lila had just figured out how to simply conjure her power. Now? Now, she was so much *more*.

Everything's going to be okay, Little Crow, he reassured through the Concord, rubbing her thigh with his thumb where he held her.

She visibly gulped. *I know. I'm just—I feel so bad I failed them last time. I tried to help them but . . . I was too afraid.*

He remembered how her power spurted, how the love she attempted to conjure was completely overshadowed by the fear and heartache.

You're stronger now. And you're not alone.

She turned to him, lilac hair blowing past her face and against his chest. Then she smiled at him and it almost made his wings give out.

And, if you need the reminder of how loved you are, I could also show you in the center of the town. Maybe with my tongue? Or maybe you'd like to take my monster cock again?

Lila's cheeks blushed furiously, dipping into a deep red, as she smacked his arm. *You complete, utter rake and your silver tongue,* she tutted.

Oh, you love me and my tongue and you know it.

She bit her lip. *I do love your tongue.*

He chuckled, and slowly licked his lower lip, just for her to get a glimpse of his best weapon against her.

Maybe I do need a reminder. We could take a quick pit stop and then get back to—

An actual laugh bubbled out of Ambrose's lungs, one that caused his head to fall back, and his entire body to shake. "Who's the rake now, love? Trying to seduce me out of this? I don't think so."

Lila's pout only extended his laughter, a sound and feeling that had been so foreign to him for so long before she came into his life. Now, it seemed like he was doing it more and more.

As they flew closer to her hometown, Ambrose felt Lila's resolve solidify. Her back straightened. Her shivers turned into a hard grip against his shoulder. He felt her warmth, her heat, emanate—it felt dangerous. It was a rageful surge, something threatening and protecting all at once.

But more than that, the colors of her aura had shifted.

The Sun Child

The hue of fear had ebbed away to be something . . . so much more. It was the shades of colors he had fallen for when he first saw her that night in his manor. Colors he saw again when she first took up training, when she first fought the strigoi on the way home from the Arachnid Estate, when she entered his office wearing that skimpy little dress and underthings. It was courage and determination and a fierceness for others. Her gaze was focused, her lips were set.

She was a war goddess, being sent to a battlefield, ready to conquer her enemies and protect her comrades.

As the sky pinked, then oranged, and finally became the brilliant blue of daytime, Ambrose flew with Lila in his arms, Nostro guiding them, Pollock and Constance behind them, into the town.

It was decrepit and silent. The buildings had fallen apart and dusted even more than Lila's recent memory. The courtyard was broken. Stone smashed, plants ripped apart, and not so much as a cricket chirped.

Ambrose put Lila down, and Pollock immediately landed on her shoulder.

"If they're all strigoi, then they're probably asleep right?" Constance asked, landing on Lila's other side.

Nostro nodded. "As we hoped. It's been easiest with them asleep."

Lila didn't speak. That determination was fueling through her, swirling through every limb. She walked past Constance and Nostro, past Ambrose, and into the winding veins of the town. Ambrose kept a close eye on her, keeping only a couple of steps back.

He sniffed the air, trying to sense where the monsters hid, only hearing the smallest amount of shuffling in the nearest buildings. Ambrose could feel their hunger more than anything else.

In there, he told her.

She turned in the direction he indicated, and walked right up to an old, gray door. The wood looked worn, molded, like the simplest touch would send it crashing down.

But Lila didn't even need to touch it, she just walked up to it, and closed her eyes.

An all-encompassing warmth crashed out of her, like waves in the ocean. A tear dripped down Ambrose's cheek he hadn't realized was coming. It was like . . . a blanket when you're a child, like soup when you're sick, like a parent's hug, like a first kiss, like cuddles with a pet, like a day in with the rain hitting your window, like reading your favorite book, like life, like joy.

It was like love.

Ambrose's heart was overflooded, his knees threatening to buckle under the weight of it all, while simultaneously feeling like he could float, free and weightless. He clutched his heart, breathing deeply, breathing to ground himself.

And all too sudden, the rush of warmth, the rush of *love* was gone.

He looked up, searched for Lila, to make sure she was all right. But she was already looking back at him, a smile on her face, as humans and vampires groggily stepped out of the buildings surrounding them, out into the daylight.

41

Lila rubbed her tired eyes. She hadn't slept more than two hours in the last week. It was finally the night before the solstice, and she'd been training *hard*. After her display in her hometown, Ambrose had only been training her harder. Now, he was focusing on adapting her to fighting with the crows. She may not have the mindlink with them as Ambrose did, but they listened to her just as much. And, just like Pollock, she had learned to understand them. She knew what the bobs and dips in flight meant. She knew when they'd swarm for attacks, and when they'd swarm her for cover.

She was becoming one with them. They flew to her movements, swooping around her legs as she kicked, using their strength to propel her forward. They were the dark mass blocking out the sun, and they were preparing to burn Hektor with their eclipse.

Pollock squawked loudly once, then chirped twice—indicating the crows needed another burst of juice. Lila wiped the sweat from her forehead, and kept her eyes on the aggressor as she let the warmth flood from her skin, blocking it from the him.

Ambrose made sure to come at her at that moment. He lunged, clearly aiming for her legs to swipe them from under her. Lila didn't hesitate, she ran right at him, and leaped at the perfect time to take one step on his monstrous shoulder and then jump onto his back. As she fueled the crows, and herself, she spun, letting herself land on his back as she wrapped her legs around his waist. Then she pushed her chest against him, bringing her forearm around his neck and her other wrist barring the arm in, as her palm grazed his face.

She let the smallest amount of heat pour from her palm — and like that, the fight was over.

Ambrose slackened as Lila slipped from his back, and lay on her back against the mat Rebekkah had brought in for this exact reason. She took deep breaths that burned her lungs.

"That was great," Ambrose huffed.

"Do you —" another deep breath "— think I'm ready?"

Ambrose sat next to her, his elbows resting on his knees. "If it were up to me, I would never send you to battle."

She grinned, and threw her leg over his. "If it were up to you, I'd be your pet wife?"

"My pet wife, running around in that little see-through dress, and tied to my bed every morning."

Lila closed her eyes, picturing how much easier — and how much more fun — that reality would be. But instead, she was the Sun Child. Instead, she was the only hope for the vampire lords to claim their manors once more. For *her* to claim her home once more.

"But, yes. As ready as anyone could be for war."

Ambrose stood, and held out a hand to her. Once she took it, he did all the work and lifted her to him, wrapping his other hand around her waist. "Now, the last thing to do is sleep. As impossible as it seems. You're exhausted, and you need all the rest you could have before tomorrow."

She nodded. "And you?"

Ambrose quirked one perfect eyebrow. "Me?"

"Are you ready?"

He shrugged. "I guess I have to be. It'll be nice to see that fucker Hektor die. But . . ." He placed a hand on her cheek, and guided her gaze to meet his. "But, remember, *you* are what's important. If it ever becomes more than you can bear, if there is even the slightest doubt it is more than you can handle, a moment of fear, a moment of doubt, you tell me. I will get you out of there without a second thought."

Lila nodded, knowing she'd never ask that of him, knowing she would never abandon the others or the Crow Court.

"Shall we sleep then? Take a bath before getting filthy tomorrow?"

Ambrose caressed her cheek. "Great idea." Then he pressed a soft kiss to her lips.

"I can't sleep," she said after an hour of trying. No matter how much Ambrose massaged her, pet her, played with her hair, her mind just couldn't shut off.

"Hmm," Ambrose hummed against her hair, still twisting his fingers in the lilac strands. In vampiric speed,

Ambrose untangled himself from her and hopped out of bed. He sauntered around to her side of the bed, and Lila couldn't help but drink him in; his low-hanging black silk pants, bare chest, his soft white hair freshly washed. He was such a sight to behold, and Lila wanted to lick every part of him.

He huffed a laugh. "Calm down, Little Crow." He held his hand out to her, and when she took it, he lifted her from the bed.

"Mmm." Now it was Ambrose's turn to ogle. After bathing, Lila had only worn a short nightgown and matching panties he had gotten her. Floral lavender and emerald lace covered her breasts and sheer chiffon reached her hips, leaving her legs bare.

Lila raised an eyebrow, feeling her nipples peak under the attention.

Ambrose shook his head. "No, no. That wasn't my idea," he chuckled. "I mean, we can, of course, but . . ." He turned and shuffled through a small pile of things he had on the floor. When he turned back around, a glint of gold caught her eye.

It was something she knew.

"It's not the one I'd given you in Sanktus Pernox, but I had it made again for you, to fit the dagger."

In his hand was a brown leather thigh holster, with a golden metal sun buckle—an exact replica of the one he'd given her before.

"I thought it fitting for the Sun Child when she has her moment in the sun to have her blade at her thigh." He stepped closer, and Lila felt her heart patter in her chest. "May I?" he asked around a smile.

This man. He had seen every part of her, touched and licked and sucked every part of her. Yet he still asked for things as simple as this. It made her chest flutter.

"You may."

Ambrose crouched to his knees and wrapped his hand around her lower waist, pulling her to him.

"You're going to do great tomorrow, you know." He brushed his lips over her flesh, kissing her thigh. "And I will be right there with you the entire time."

The leather was cold on her skin, but his hot breath sent waves of gooseflesh along her thigh, sending heat straight to her core. Whenever he got on his knees for her, it drove her wild with need.

"Tell me more," she breathed.

He smirked against her skin. "You're going to save our home. You're going to be rid of your demons. And we are *going* to win."

Snap. The buckle closed around her, just as he kissed the skin just above the strap.

Ambrose stood then, and reached over her shoulder to grab her wooden dagger on the nightstand.

"And you are going to burn our enemies to the ground." He forced it in, sending an erotic jolt to Lila's body. "I just hope I can watch."

Ambrose took a few steps back, marveling at Lila as though she were the night sky full of stars, as if she were the first sunrise after an endless night.

"Stunning. Perfect."

The piece at her thigh invigorated her. She was ready, she knew she was, she just needed this little extra push.

"Will you wear it tomorrow? For me?"

Lila blushed. "Of course."

After unbuckling it, kissing all along her thighs once more, and putting it aside, Ambrose pulled Lila back into bed, back into him, as he stroked her back.

"Do you want me to thrall you?"

She threw her arm around his chest, digging herself into his side. "Yes, please."

He smiled against her forehead as he kissed her. "I love you."

The words were so simple, but they warmed her heart. Her nerves were trying to get the better of her, but with those three words, she could do anything.

"I love you too."

"*Sleep, love. Sleep well, and have the sweetest dreams.*"

Lila felt the lilac haze fall onto her mind and she didn't fight it. She let the mist slowly cascade around her, as her eyes grew heavy and her limbs felt limp.

Tomorrow would be the summer solstice—the day the Sun Child had to guide the vampires back into the light.

Morning came too soon.

Or rather, the morning that should still be considered night. Lila was eased awake, fed, dressed in fighting leathers, and strapped with weapons—weapons she hoped she wouldn't need. Ambrose took a moment to strap the sun buckle and dagger to her thigh once more, reaffirming everything he'd said the night before.

Once out in the great hall, she could barely concentrate on those running around her, getting ready for the day, as her legs shook, as she fisted her palm.

Lila was nervous, yes. But a thought kept crossing her mind. The thought of her hand on Hektor's face. The feel of his flesh burning under her palm. She thought of the vampire faces, the eyes popping before her in the Viper

Morada. She had been disgusted at herself then. But now? She reveled in it. Lila couldn't wait to feel the burn of his skin again, couldn't wait to hear as his eyes liquified and boiled out of their sockets. She was going to *torture* Hektor Reinick, for all he had done to her, and there would be no mercy.

She'd thought about her home. About the strigoi currently running rampant. About her friends, Robin and Sandra and Ivan, who were either all turned into strigoi or dead. She thought about the gardens, the plants being pulled from the ground, the flowers stomped on. She thought of the books, of *her* book of fairytales, being burned. She thought of *her* bedroom being occupied by that pile of filth, of him sifting through her things, deluding himself into thinking she wanted him.

Lila cracked her knuckles. She was more than ready for this. She was anticipating it.

As Ambrose strapped the golden gorget around her neck, she met his gaze. "Are we ready?"

Her fingers were twitching, legs bouncing.

Ambrose clasped her shoulders. "Almost. Turn around." Once she did, Ambrose pulled her hair into a ponytail and tied it snuggly. "There. Now you're ready, Little Crow." Then he did the same with his own hair, only leaving a strand of white falling loose. "I won't ask you to stay close. But know, I *will* stay close to you."

She grinned at him. "Of course you will. I'll keep you safe, Crow Lord."

Ambrose smirked, rubbing his tongue over his sharp fangs. "Such a mouth on you. I might have to punish you for that one later."

"Promise?"

He grabbed her waist, pulling her flush to him. He

kissed her deeply, leading with his tongue, then trailing kisses along her jaw, till he got to the spot she loved behind her ear. "Want to make a bargain over it?"

The morning was still just waking, but the tiny army of vampires and humans alike traveled in silence to the Crow Court. They took the path Lila had taken as she ran from the Reinicks all those months ago. The path that led her to Ambrose. She knew these trees, knew the roots sticking up from the ground, even if the season was different, even if the snow had been replaced by wildflowers and bugs, even as the cold was replaced by a heat so brilliant, it rivaled Lila's own. But the sun was still hiding, and as it rose, it would only grow hotter, and she would only grow stronger.

Marcus walked next to her, eyeing her.

"You good, Lila? Nervous?"

"No. I'm ready to finish this."

Marcus looked ahead. "We'll kill him. We'll kill Hektor, and he will *never* try to touch you again."

She saw his hand fist from the corner of her eye, and knew Marcus had wanted to kill Hektor just as badly as she did, just as badly as Ambrose.

But he was hers to kill. And they both knew it.

Nostro walked between the siblings, stopping. "Do you remember what to do?"

"Marcus, Ambrose, Constance, and I will enter the manor. I will immediately activate the warmth to heal the turned-strigoi, while the others help the newly changed figure out what's going on, and fight off remaining strigoi. Once the main floor is healed, we will work our way up as you, Rebekkah, Darius, and the rest of the Viper Morada will come in to take the rest of the Crow Court once the majority have been healed."

Nostro nodded along. "Good. Remember, if anything goes awry—"

"We have the Concord."

"Yes." Nostro awkwardly put his hand on Lila's shoulder, then pulled her into him, wrapping his long arms around her shoulders. "Working with you like this . . . it is how I wished to work with *her*. If she had survived . . . Well. I'm just happy I could do it now, with you, Lila, our Sun Child." He pulled away then, and Lila grabbed his hand.

"Thank you, Nostro. For everything. For your friendship and trust."

He gave her a sharp, toothy grin that probably would've scared her a few months ago, but now warmed her heart. Then he kissed her forehead. "I followed you into the light, and I now follow you into battle, gladly."

And before she could say anything more, Nostro scurried away, between the trees, where she knew Rebekkah and everyone else waited.

It was only her, Ambrose, Constance, and Marcus now. She turned to them, and whispered, "Stay close to me."

Constance stepped forward, taking Lila's hand. "Promise, Lilac."

So they walked across the forest. The manor came into view, and with it, the decrepit images Lila imagined. In the few short months Ambrose had been away, it was like the building was caving in on itself without its lord. From what she could see of the garden, the flowers had wilted, the green had turned to brown, and the color had faded completely. The stone was falling apart. People were nowhere to be seen.

The place she had so fallen in love with, her *home*—it was abused, and scarred.

Like her.

Heat bubbled up inside of her as rage consumed every thought. This was *hers* and she would take it back.

Lila stomped from the tree line, crossing the small field she battled Drusilla and the Reinicks six months ago, across the field she ran from Ambrose. She climbed the steps to the main doors of the Crow Court, and waited for the others to be by her side. Then, as she pushed her palms into the wood—as the sun rose at her back, finally touching her skin and filling every fiber of her being with strength—she released a wave of loving warmth, hoping it would heal the manor just as much as the people within.

Lila shoved the doors open, heat pooling from her hands, as her family followed behind her. It was eerily silent within. But the sense of bodies was overwhelming. Coming in daylight hours was already proving to be a good decision.

"We should go to the dining room first," Constance whispered beside her.

Exuding heat in case there were strigoi in the main hall, they crossed the foyer and pushed the next door open. Lila's heart dropped at the sight. All around the room—the room that had once been filled with the vampires and humans of the Crow Court alike, the room that had once broken every stereotype Lila had about Malvania—was littered with bodies.

Most were alive, writhing, but some were as stiff as the table in the center of the room. Some were already decomposing, others looked as if all of the blood within them had been drained from their bodies. Constance gasped beside her, and the young girl took a step back, into Marcus, who gripped her hand tightly.

But to her other side, Ambrose was fuming.

Click, clack, click. Heads were beginning to turn toward them. New blood, new bodies.

In the crowd, Lila spotted Sandra, the maid she'd befriended during her time here. Blood dripped from the woman's bisected mouth, her eyes were large and vacant. And a new wave of anger and horror washed through Lila, as she clenched her fists, ready to heal everyone she could.

There were other strigoi in the room, similar to those Constance, Ambrose, and Lila fought on their way back from the Arachnid Estate after Sanktus Pernox. They were clicking their bisected jaws in the air, their eyes covered in a white film. Lila wondered if, like those, they would just be happy to feel the sunlight, or if they would be like those in the Maggot Mansion—too far gone.

Only one way to find out.

"As soon as they come to, get them out of here," she said over her shoulder, stepping deeper into the room as warmth surrounded her.

Lila thought of her friendships with these people, and also of the horror they must have felt when Drusilla overtook the manor. These had become *her* people, and she wanted to protect them. She *needed* to save them.

Step by step, warmth pooled in the room, feeling like a soft bath of humidity on a cold night. Lila walked toward Sandra, who hissed at her but didn't attack.

Sandra's jaw closed, and soon, the line driving down her chin slowly mended back together, mended closed. The dazed look in her all-black eyes, returned to a deep brown Lila knew, as they sharpened on her lilac hair and charcoal wings behind her.

Groans echoed through the hall, as muffled whimpers rumbled out of others. Constance and Marcus immediately darted to those healed, helping them up, and whispering words of comfort, quickly explaining where they were, what happened, and that they needed to get outside.

But Lila's eyes were still focused on her friend, as she dropped to her knees before her.

"Miss Lila?" Sandra rubbed her head. "Where—? What—"

She put her hand on Sandra's shoulder. "You're all right. Drusilla and her strigoi took over the manor, they turned everyone into strigoi as well. But you're safe now. You're back to your old self. But there are still others who need to be helped, so I need you to go outside, at least until you get your strength up."

Sandra nodded slowly, then pouted. "Why, I'd like to pull all the hair from that hag's head. I'm . . . I'm remembering that night now. She came and said the Crow Court was hers. That bitch."

Lila huffed a laugh. "We'll get her. This house is ours, and no one can take it from us." She helped Sandra up, holding her arm as they stood. For a moment, Sandra wobbled, but she took a deep breath, and started walking till she neared Ambrose, who was in the middle of assisting someone else.

"Lord Draven, I don't remember much yet, but I know Drusilla left the manor. Hektor though . . . Hektor is here. I remember him. As a strigoi, he made us go out and—" her face shifted, contorted to horror. "Dear lords," she uttered.

Ambrose quickly placed a hand on her shoulder. "I know firsthand what you are feeling, Sandra. The things I did as a strigoi . . . they haunt me still," his eyes flicked to Lila's. "But that was *not* you. You were not in control, and the strigoi had none of your will."

Sandra nodded weakly.

"I'm sorry to rush this, but we need to keep moving. Should I walk you outside?" Lila asked carefully.

"No, no. I'm all right. I'll *be* all right." She shuffled outside, slowly, others following behind. Thankfully, none in this room were too far gone. Marcus, Constance, and Ambrose had to carry the blinded ones from the manor themselves, but they would eventually be okay, Lila told herself. They would all be okay.

42

"HEKTOR!" Lila yelled as she pushed her way through the dining room doors back into the great hall. This was all his fault, and Lila couldn't let it go anymore. She knew there was a plan, knew to go floor by floor, but she just couldn't wait. She wanted to kill the fucker.

But, as she expected, her scream only woke more strigoi. They slithered from the stairs, from the vaulted ceilings where the crows usually slept, from Ambrose's office. They hissed and growled as Ambrose stepped beside her.

You ready? he asked.

Fuck. Yes.

Lila lunged into the thicket of strigoi, a battle cry bursting from her lungs. She punched and kicked bodies away from her, while forcing warmth all over the room.

It was a messy whirlwind of bodies dropping and others running at them. As Marcus and Constance guided the healed out, Ambrose stood by Lila's side, swatting away those her heat wasn't fast enough to cure. He surrounded her with his wings, keeping her in a protective shell as she conjured more warmth.

Any sign of Hektor? she asked as she tried to build herself up once more.

Not yet. But I might need your offense heat.

Gladly.

In tandem, Ambrose flared his wings out as Lila shot her hands forward. The strigoi that couldn't be cured screamed as their skin sizzled and bubbled, turning into gooey messes on the floor.

Just as the rush of bodies hit the floor, a whole new wave of strigoi rained from above. The sounds were nearly deafening as the screams and wails crashed through Lila's ears. Instinctively, she threw her hands up to cover her ears, but the moment she did, one of the fleshy bodies leaped on top of her, sending her down hard.

But as Lila fought the creature off, she realized . . . his hair fell in lush brown curls and his jaw wasn't bisected as he smirked wide with sharp fangs just above her face. It wasn't a strigoi above her, but Hektor Reinick. And the shit-eating grin on his face told her he expected to surprise her, just as he'd done.

He lowered himself over her, his fangs brushing against her ear. "Hello, Little Mouse. I'm so sad to see you without my collar," he whispered in her ear.

The strigoi were swarming around them; Constance, Marcus, and Ambrose were bombarded with the creatures all around attacking.

"Let's see how long it takes for any of them to notice I'm here," he snickered, his gross breath pungent in Lila's nose. "Lords, how I've missed your taste, Little Mouse." Lila tried to push him off in a panic, as he licked along her jaw, over her cheek.

Just as his tongue flicked off of her, a whirlwind of events cascaded around her. A swarm of maggots, writhing and wriggling, crashed into the room like a wave, knocking Hektor off of her. Lila immediately wanted to gag, but she knew these maggots were friends. Nostro was near. Like Ambrose's crows, Nostro summoned an army of the little larvae, and they devoured everything in their path, including the strigoi.

The moment Hektor was off, Lila leaped up and focused all the heat she could muster into her fist before punching him in the face. She felt a satisfying crunch as his flesh bent around her knuckles. When she pulled away, she saw a large stain on his tanned cheek—violently pink, with small white bubbles forming where her fist connected.

But Hektor, unwisely, didn't stay down. "Fucking bitch," he hissed. He shifted his body into a monstrous form, towering over Lila and bearing his fangs. But just as he lunged at her, another form swooped past her, screaming.

"You *fucking traitorous bastard*!" Rebekkah yelled, pulling at his hair and raking her claws down his back.

"*I'm* the traitor?" Hektor threw her off, but Rebekkah was up again in less than a blink. She jumped on top of him, sinking her fangs into his shoulder.

Lila used the moment to assess around her. Ambrose fought a number of strigoi, all surrounding him, but he looked like he was handling himself well. Nostro rode atop his maggots, climbing the stairs to the next floor as they attacked as many strigoi as possible. Darius was just behind Rebekkah, taking care of the strigoi trying to reach her as she fought her brother.

The humans and vampires from the Viper Morada, and now some trickling in from the Crow Court she'd already healed, were beginning to attack the rest of the hissing beasts. She spotted Robin near the kitchen, defending Sandra as she swatted at strigoi with a wooden stake, bonking them on the head, and Robin killed them as they were (surprisingly) dazed.

But, in all the chaos, Lila realized one thing. She spotted Marcus, running toward her—but Constance was nowhere in sight.

"Drusilla—" Marcus yelled, grabbing Lila's arm. "She's here. Constance ran to face her." Without another breath, he ran past Lila. She didn't hesitate, she followed him through the main hall, bursting with heat and warmth to burn her enemies and fuel her allies.

Then she saw the wisp of blond hair running into Ambrose's office.

Fuck, Lila thought. She knew *something* had happened between Constance and Drusilla when she'd first changed, but she didn't know what. She didn't know if Drusilla *was* the one who changed her.

Marcus bobbed and weaved around strigoi blocking his way, with Lila close behind. He pushed through the door only a moment later, and Lila gasped as she stumbled into him, seeing what stopped him over his shoulder.

At the far end of the room, beside Ambrose's desk, Drusilla stood, smirking wide, with her hand gripped around Constance's throat. The vampire wasn't even wearing any kind of battle adornments; no armor, no leathers—only a slimming red dress with slits high up her thighs. The only indicator she was here at all to fight, was the stake clutched in her hand, and the long, silvered nails currently digging into Constance's flesh.

Marcus dove forward, not hesitating for another moment. He swung himself haphazardly at the hag, his fists clenched all wrong, and Lila swore at herself for not taking more time to train him. But he was a vampire now. He didn't need proper form when he had raw strength.

Constance wiggled in Drusilla's grasp, clawing at the hand at her throat, but as Marcus dashed toward them, Drusilla flung Constance, hard. She smashed Constance's head against Ambrose's desk, and let her drop before throwing her hands up to fight off Marcus.

Lila didn't wait to see, she ran to Constance, forcing warmth to her hands—but fear for her friend was shooting through her. She knew Constance would heal. But she wanted her to be okay, *now*.

The moment she reached her, she saw blood oozing from Constance's forehead where it'd been smashed. She hovered her hand above the wound, shaking, but could feel the warmth pool out, and—thankfully—the gash began to stitch itself closed.

Suddenly, all the wind was knocked from Lila's lungs as a hard force was thrown into her, tossing her body back. Her body, and Marcus's. Lila's back smashed into the bookshelf, and then Marcus crashed into her gut. She tried to catch her breath, but nothing was coming.

"You just can't fucking give up, can you? Bastard brother, like bastard sister," Drusilla scoffed. Marcus tried to get up, but fell back down immediately. His elbow was bent in an odd direction and the back of his hand was flush with his forearm. "Too weak to do anything, but too stupid to just give up—" she kicked Constance's head with a heeled foot, and Constance went flying into the opposite wall.

"Stop!" Lila gasped out.

"Constance!" Marcus yelled in unison, trying desperately to crawl to her with his broken arm.

Lila focused her warmth on Marcus, whose bones began to snap back into place, as she regained her breath. "Your issue—is with us." Another deep inhale. "Leave Constance the hell alone." Forcing her lungs to accept air, she forced her warmth around the room, healing Constance, Marcus, and herself.

Marcus lunged for Constance, sliding on his knees till he reached her. As Drusilla's head spun to follow him, Lila switched gears. Heat poured from her skin, sizzling the air around her. She threw herself at Drusilla, throwing her fist into Drusilla's gut.

"She's okay!" Marcus yelled. Immediately, Lila's fear was devoured. Now, she was only angry.

Drusilla gasped as Lila's fist collided with her again, leaving a gaping hole in the red dress, and blackened scorch marks all around. As Drusilla doubled over, Lila sent a sharp upper cut to her chin, and then a hook into her opposite cheek. She didn't relent, she didn't give the vampire a moment to catch up. Each hit fused with scarring heat, leaving Drusilla's perfect skin reddened and bubbling. With the skin under her left eye turning into a black crisp, Drusilla screamed.

Lila! Where are you? Ambrose's voice broke through Lila's mind in a panic.

Your office. Drusilla's here!

I'm coming.

Lila punched the hag again and then sent a roundhouse kick into Drusilla's ribs, feeling a couple shatter at the impact. Drusilla stumbled back, catching herself against the chair in front of Ambrose's desk.

"Well, that's new," she sneered. Her face was a charred, boiling mess as black blood dripped from her nose, from her lips. Drusilla spat out black blood as she huffed for breath. "I underestimated you, murine. I knew you were the Sun Child, but . . . to be frank, I just thought you were content being a whore—for the Reinicks and Draven."

Lila bristled but remained silent. Let the hag try and antagonize her. She knew her power and soon, the bitch would too.

"If memory serves correctly, according to Hektor you're also a slab of meat."

Fury over taking her, Lila lunged at Drusilla, a yell burst from her lungs. Crashing into the chair and breaking it underneath Drusilla, Lila punched the hag over and over, feeling flesh melt and liquify against her knuckles as it stuck to her skin.

Between one punch and the next, Drusilla shifted underneath her, and in the moment Lila was caught off balance, Drusilla slashed at Lila's torso. Lila screamed as long claws tore across her chest, ripping her leather armor and leaving bleeding gashes underneath.

But with the scream, Lila focused on the sun. Focused on the day. It was the summer solstice, and she felt it course through her blood, even as she fought in a dark room.

Lila reared back her fist once more, focusing all her heat into her knuckles, hoping she would punch Drusilla with the force of the sun behind her. But just as she did, Drusilla thrust her charred arm up, wrapping those long talons around Lila's throat, just as she'd done to Constance. Lila grabbed Drusilla's wrist, ready to set it ablaze if she had to, when she heard someone force their way through the door.

"Lila!" Ambrose stood, wings flayed, scratches all over his body, in the opening of the door. Behind him looked like chaos as bodies continued to swarm. But her eyes only focused on his. Red rubies watching her, glancing between her hand and Drusilla's.

Something changed in his gaze right before her. His eyes went wide, his eyebrows shooting up, as he lunged forward.

Lila heard him cry out. Heard Marcus cry too. But she couldn't hear what they said.

Not as claws tore through her neck, tearing her open. Not as her body was flung and thrown out the only window in the room—the same window Ambrose had thrown her out of. Not as blood gushed out of her, spraying across the windowsill.

Lila was dead before she even hit the ground.

43

Ambrose halted in his tracks. Every muscle, every hair on his head, every blood cell in his body—it all stopped. Lila's blood sprayed across his face as her body was thrown from the room.

She was fine. She had to be fine.

She could heal.

She was the Sun Child, for lords' sake.

Lila would be fine.

His *wife* would be fine.

"Lila?" Marcus's voice cracked behind him, sounding so small, so . . . fragile.

Ambrose heard a resounding *thump* come from the window, and he knew it was Lila hitting the ground. He *saw* it, in his mind. Her body, mangled and broken and . . . cold.

Dead.

The word hit him harder than the knife she'd driven through his heart her first full day in the Crow Court. His eyes grew blurry, his cheeks wet, and he still wasn't completely sure why he was crying.

Not until he tried to call her name through the Concord. *Lila?*

Not until she didn't reply. And it felt how it did when she wore the collar. When the Concord between them simply didn't exist.

He didn't even realize what his body was doing. He lunged at Drusilla, his claws immediately digging into her head. He clapped his hands together, smashing her skull between his palms. Eyeballs and teeth dripped down his wrists.

But the fucking hag of the Arachnid Estate was a vampire, and a powerful one at that. She healed, just as Hektor's jaw had swiftly healed when Ciro punched it clean off of him.

"You—" Marcus's voice broke through the ringing in Ambrose's ears, stuttering, stopping . . . breaking. "You killed . . . my sister." He paused, and Drusilla's head melded together, her eyes rolling as they grew back into place. *"YOU KILLED MY SISTER!"*

Marcus lunged, and Ambrose reacted solely on his fight or flight, unconsciously moving to assist Marcus's attacks. He grabbed her and twisted Drusilla's back toward Marcus, just as the younger vampire drove his hand through her. Ripping his hand back, he did it again, and again—until he punctured her heart with his claws.

Marcus slumped to the floor, his eyes dazed as he stared at the floor. "She killed Lila. Lila." He repeated this over and over, and with each instance, the words nailed to Ambrose's mind just a little bit more.

He dropped Drusilla, and took a few steps back. Ambrose ran a hand over his face, and when he pulled away, his palm was stained in red. Human blood. Lila's blood. In a cacophony of anguish and pain and torment and hate and rage, Ambrose screamed his throat raw, he screamed his lungs out, he screamed but still felt far too much.

He needed to go to Lila, to confirm she was fine. He imagined her lying there, wound already healed, ready to fight on.

Ambrose ran to the window, ready to leap out. Ready to leap to Lila. The sun sizzled his skin as his head passed the windowsill. But it was fine. Lila was fine. This didn't mean anything.

He saw her, lilac hair surrounding a serene face, blood pooling around, saturating that color he loved so much. His heart raced, slamming his chest with each beat, yet he felt like he couldn't breathe.

Something crashed loudly behind him, but it didn't matter—he needed to get to Lila. To just . . . get to her.

But the moment he pushed from the window, a long tendril pierced his calf, driving through his flesh, muscle, and bone, before it pulled him back into the room.

Ambrose smashed into the hardwood below, his wing taking the brunt of the damage as he landed on it, snapping the bone within. He grunted, but jumped to his feet quickly, taking in the room around him.

Everything was destroyed. Marcus caged Constance, now awake, under him. And a massive spider was crawling over him as it pulled its leg from his thigh, dripping his blood all over the floor.

Drusilla struck again, this time with two long legs, stabbing toward Ambrose's chest. He spun out of the way, grabbing one of the long legs and snapping it. But Drusilla was in her prime, healing immediately. She lunged again, attempting to drive her fangs into him.

Snarling, he grabbed her chelicerae, and *pulled* them apart, waiting to hear the crunch as they dislocated. The moment they did, he puffed his chest, and summoned the crows from within as he'd done with Ciro. He pulled them farther apart, and released the murder into Drusilla's face, knowing all of his crows would be diving beak first. They swarmed as they shot from him, piercing through Drusilla. She made a shrill noise, and reared back.

"Marcus, get Constance out of here!" he ordered. The birds took up the room, and as Drusilla backed away, she crashed through the door, breaking it and the wall down, into the main hall once more. The room was wild, but they'd been winning—before Lila.

Before Lila, they were beginning to outnumber the strigoi. They were beginning to take back the power. They were beginning to *win*.

But without Lila, all it took was a single bite. One bite, and they'd be changed into strigoi once more.

Ambrose snapped his wing back into place, flinched at the pain, but forced them to move as he launched toward the ceiling. From his brief glance around the room, he saw the other manor lords still fighting, Darius and Rebekkah back-to-back, Nostro surrounding them in a swarm of maggots to shield against attacks. Fangs and claws ripped into flesh. Vampire against strigoi.

Fangs snapped behind him once more, and Ambrose's quick reprieve came to an end. He turned and faced Drusilla, the brown fuzz, snapping fangs, and large beady black eyes already focused on him. The crows of the Crow Court surrounded Ambrose, a tiny army in size, but not in number. They were just as ready.

Ambrose slammed his wings down, propelling himself forward. He threw himself onto Drusilla and let the monster of Malvania take over. *For Lila.*

He slashed and tore, digging his claws into the spider's sternum, pulling at organs as she screamed and writhed. Below, Marcus leaped onto one of her legs, climbing up it until he was next to Ambrose.

Marcus stabbed his hand, nails like knives, into the joint connecting her body and one of the eight legs. He repeated the motion, stabbing over and over until the leg came loose.

Drusilla buckled under them, knocking them both off. They caught themselves immediately, but Drusilla shifted back into her monstrous form, arm sputtering blood where it was ripped from the socket.

"You *fucking* bastards!" she screamed, then immediately lunged at them as the arm only just began to reform.

Ambrose met her midair, stabbing through her chest, slashing her neck, as her nails drove through his gut. He didn't care, he snapped her neck, but she healed, and smashed her hand into his cheek, breaking his jaw. The crows swarmed them, diving at her, and driving their beaks through her fleshy wings. Torn open, her wings faltered, and as she fell, Marcus was there. He grabbed Drusilla by the hair, swinging her body up for Ambrose to catch.

Grabbing her shoulders, and Marcus wrapping his hands under her jaw, the two *pulled*, flapping their wings toward each other.

Drusilla screamed as she was being ripped in two. The skin on her neck stretched until it tore, black blood sprayed widely, sprayed all over them, all over the floor and strigoi fighting below them. Drusilla slashed and fought, but she couldn't stop them.

"Just fucking die," Ambrose seethed, pulling with all his might. Drusilla's neck popped, her spine falling apart, and then her body fell limp in his hands.

"Marcus!" Constance called from below. She had a sconce in her hand, flame burning bright. Marcus pitched Drusilla's head at the floor below, throwing it hard. The moment it smashed the marble floor, Constance threw the fire onto it, burning her head in the middle of the great hall.

"Ambrose," Maronai flew up beside him, taking Drusilla's body from his hands. "She's my responsibility. Give her to me. I'll bury her as far south as I can fly."

Ambrose let him take her, and before he could process anything more, he flew from the room.

Lila, Lila, Lila, was all he could focus on.

He flew through the doors, the sunlight stinging his flesh, burning small holes in his wings. But he couldn't stop. Not till he reached her. The battle with Drusilla must've only lasted a handful of minutes, but that already was too much time away from her. He rounded the corner of the manor, saw the bloodstain on the ground, covering the dirt.

But Lila was just . . . gone.

Lila? Lila!

He looked all around. There was no sign that she got up and walked away from here. No blood drops, no footsteps.

Am-Ambrose. A voice, faint and weak, but a voice. *Her* voice.

Lila! Where are you?

He waited for what felt like an eternity, spinning in a circle, looking for a sign.

Room.

Ambrose dashed back inside through the window of his office. He flapped his wings as hard as they would, flew through the main hall, up the stairs, down the hall, up the other stairs, and down to Lila's bedroom. He heard crashing and cursing from beyond the door.

But as he broke through the door, nothing he saw was what he prepared himself for.

Her bed was covered in blood, the sheets were torn apart, feathers and fabric everywhere, chairs overturned, her clothes thrown about. But . . . the curtains were scorched, the balcony door was thrown open, and Hektor Reinick was hurriedly crawling away from them. His clothing had been reduced to scraps, his back was red and raw, with long, thin burn marks as though caused by a whip, his face half pink and raw and oozing, the other half a crispy, purplish black.

As Ambrose continued to survey the room, as he followed the path Hektor crawled from, he saw a figure standing on the balcony. The sun shone in his eye, peeking behind the figure, silhouetting her until she stepped forward.

A swarm of crows flew behind Lila, ready to defend her, cawing like a battle cry, as the sun fueled her. Her fiery brown eyes met Ambrose's, bursts of oranges and golds and reds shimmering. Dried blood caked her neck, but there was no wound in sight. Instead, her neck was covered by a new golden collar, much like the one on her when they first reunited. But this time, the gold was dripping. Melting down her chest.

Pure liquid gold.

Lila's light lilac hair blew in the morning breeze, the summer solstice sun at her back, and an aura of hazy heat distorted the air around her. The haze continued from her hand, like that of a whip, and Ambrose knew where the marks on Hektor's back had come from.

"He's mine," she said, her voice pure fucking satisfaction. Her pink lips tilted into a smile, and Ambrose felt his cock harden just at the sight of her.

An utterly perfect sun goddess.

44

Everything hurt. Her back, her legs, her arms—and mostly her neck. Lila winced as the sun beamed on her, warming her skin through the black leather. Sweat coated her forehead, her upper lip, between her breasts, dripping down her back—pretty much all over.

But . . . she was alive. In pain *everywhere*, but alive. She felt like she had died. She knew everything went black as she flew from the window, and she hadn't felt the impact of landing on the ground. But the gaping wound at her neck was slowly stitching closed.

There was just one problem. Lila wasn't on the ground where she'd landed, and she wasn't alone.

Lila was currently hauled over someone's shoulder, swinging with her arms and legs dangling, as she was being carried up the side of the manor. She couldn't move, couldn't turn to see *who* was scaling the shaded side of the building, as everything felt so stiff. Not like the bite from a vampire of the Arachnid Estate, but close.

Being upside down was doing nothing good for her head. She felt the blood rushing, and as she swayed back and forth, hitting the powerful back with each move, her vision doubled and clouded.

The smell of burning flesh punctured her nose, and she knew this vampire was struggling. She knew *not* to protect them.

He grunted, adjusting her on his shoulder, and the sudden jerk made everything go black once more.

She was falling, hard and fast. But just as panic ensued, she landed on something soft and fluffy, bouncing a few times before settling in. Lila was in a bed—and as she opened her eyes slowly, she realized it was *her* bed.

"Fuck, Lila, you couldn't help me out even a little?"

Cold dread ran through her, hair standing on end. Hektor's voice was like claw marks grazing down her back, like a knife pressed against her throat.

With her eyes still lidded, Lila felt a weight press into the bed beside her thigh, just before a hand—burned permanently pink and white—pushed the hair from her forehead.

"Damn. Drusilla got you good, didn't she?" He ran a finger over her neck, pressing it into the wound. Lila winced, and she saw sharp fangs as Hektor's lips split into a wicked grin. "Lords, I love the sounds you make."

Lila tried to move, but her limbs were still so stiff, as her body seemed to be focusing all its energy on healing the wound at her neck.

"I have a little present for you. I've been *dying* to give it to you ever since I last saw you."

He hopped up, and disappeared from Lila's sight. She heard him scuttling around the room, moving things, and took the moment to regroup. She focused on her neck, feeling her skin rejoin under the blood that had already gushed from her. It burned and itched and tickled, all at once, but soon her neck was mended, and Lila was able to spread her warmth through the rest of her body.

She needed to get out of here. She needed to get away from Hektor. Whatever he had up his sleeve, she knew she needed just a few more moments to be able to handle it. Moments she wasn't sure she'd get.

Lila's brain spun, working out a plan. Hektor had disappeared into the other half of her room, into the sitting area. The room was a complete and chaotic mess. Her clothes had been thrown everywhere, heaps lay on the bed. Her panties were on the pillow next to her, stiff and gross. She wanted to gag at the mere thought of Hektor in here, tainting her room in more ways than one. But she didn't have time. Hektor was out of sight, for now.

And now would be her only chance.

The balcony. If she could get to the balcony, the sun would refuel her. Then, she could fully heal. Then, she could fight him.

Lila hauled herself up, her legs not obeying, so she dragged herself across the torn covers, pulling her body behind her. She crawled down the bed, her legs thumping onto the cold floor. The noise would alert him, she assumed, but she couldn't risk looking back. Lila needed to keep moving.

Dragging herself across the room as fast as she could, her body slowly began responding to her once more. She crawled, and soon was able to push herself with her feet as well.

But Hektor was already walking up behind her, chuckling. "Where do you think you're going?"

Lila didn't deign him with a reply. She quickened her speed, gripping the wood with her nails, propelling herself like a frog climbing against a wall. She'd made it to the door, already thrown open, and her fingertips stretched into the sunlight.

And though she knew Hektor was allowing her to *try*, playing with his food as he'd always done, this small touch of light was all she needed.

Hektor grabbed Lila's shoulder, and flipped her onto her back before he straddled her waist. "I haven't even given you your present yet."

Lila's heart sank, fear gripping her throat like a hand.

"A pretty collar for a pretty pet," he smirked, twirling a golden band around his hand. It was thinner than the one they'd put on her in the Viper Morada, far daintier. It came together in a chevron shape, and at the base of the neck was a small golden hoop. "I don't think Drusilla or my brother knew this, but I had this one made for you right after the last one was made, using *my* thrall instead of theirs. It's the exact same, only this one will make you *mine, alone*. I'm done sharing."

He opened the collar and Lila bucked her hips, trying to get him off. She punched at his face, but he swiftly grabbed both her hands.

"Use that heat on me, pet. I would love for you to get all warmed up for me. Because the moment this is on you, I plan on commanding you to fuck me senseless."

"You sick fuck," Lila spat.

"You've made me this way. If you only let me fuck you,

THE SUN CHILD

I wouldn't have had to do all this to make you see. To show you how badly you want me too."

Lila was so shocked, so *disturbed*, by Hektor's words, she didn't even know how to retort. She'd always wondered what made the Reinicks so different from the vampires she'd met since her time with Ambrose. For so long, she believed all to be like the siblings, like the evil Viper family. But Ambrose and Constance, and everyone else, had proved it wasn't *all* vampires. And Rebekkah had proved the vileness didn't run in their blood. There are beings, creatures, that do bad things out of instinct and survival—but Lila finally realized, then there are creatures who do bad things for evil's sake. Creatures like Hektor, whose mind is so warped they believe their victims are perpetuating their own abuse. A relentless predator who doesn't fucking understand the word, *no*. A true monster. An *actual* monster. Not like Ambrose, who claims to be one when all he is, is a fierce protector. Not like Marcus, who was forced into this. Not like Rebekkah, who was literally bred to be. And not like Nostro, who only looks the part.

They may claim themselves to be a monster, but the true evil is right before her. The true evil is for evil's sake, and nothing more.

"What the hell is wrong with you? I don't want you, you *disgust* me." As she said this, Lila tucked her knees in as hard as she could, smashing them into Hektor's lower back. The moment he jolted forward, she swung her legs between his, knocking his knee out from under him. He fell forward farther, his hand releasing her wrists and slamming into the floor next to her in the same moment Lila rolled from under him.

She quickly scurried to her feet, and dashed back for

the door, but Hektor recovered far quicker than she expected. He grabbed her wrist, pulled her back to him, and as her body spun, he pushed the collar into her throat. Lila choked, wheezing at the sudden impact, just as her body smashed into his. It sent them both tumbling down, but once again, Hektor recovered quicker.

Lila gasped, trying to shuffle away, just as Hektor snapped the collar closed.

45

It was different this time. Everything swirled around her mind, a yellow-tinted haze falling like a mist. But Lila was still Lila.

She stumbled up the moment the collar shut closed, Hektor rising with her, taking a step forward, and causing her fall through the balcony doors—into the sunlight.

"Lila," he said, his voice thick like sludge in water. Like shoes dragging through the mud. Like pure venom. "Tell me you're mine."

And just as suddenly, her mind cleared. The mist fell, and Lila saw Hektor, burned face and all, stand before her with that same wicked grin spread on his lips—the grin that haunted her worst nightmares, both waking and sleeping.

"No," she uttered under breath. She wasn't his. Far from it. She was her own. She was Ambrose's. She was the Crow Court's.

But she was *not* Hektor Reinick's.

"I do not belong to you. I never have, and you can be damned sure I *never* will."

All of a sudden, Lila heard the loud caws of crows at her back, and knew they were there *for her*, ready to fight *for her*. Pollock swooped low, his feather brushed against her cheek as he flew. *I'm here*, it said.

Hektor took a step back before he regained his composure and clenched his jaw. *"Tell me you're mine,"* he repeated, his words dripping with the thrall. But it didn't haze Lila's mind in the slightest.

Instead, she felt angry. Instead, she felt *hot*.

"No," she hissed. The collar heated against her skin, and as she stood in the sun, the gold liquified, beginning to melt the collar from around her neck, slowly dripping over the black leather protecting her chest.

She was *done* with Hektor Reinick.

The crows flew forward, darting past Lila and swarming into the room. They knocked Hektor back, tripping him over the mess he created in her room, and stumbling onto the floor. "I am not your *pet*. I am not your murine. I am not your anything. I am not *yours*." Lila summoned all the rage within and poured it into her hand, creating a long tendril of heat so hot, it hazed the air around it. Lila snarled, bearing her blunt, human teeth. "And I *never will be*," she repeated, slashing Hektor with the tendril.

It cracked against him like a blazing whip, singing his clothes, burning his skin. Lila didn't pause, she hit him again and again, as the crows flew from the room and hovered around her — watching and waiting.

Hektor scrambled back.

"You are *nothing*. And you will always *be nothing*." She cracked the whip against him again, and he cursed, twisting to crawl deeper into the room.

Crack. Whip.
More hits.
And then—ruby eyes. Eyes that were red and tear-stained. Eyes that were *hers*. Ambrose's eyes ran over her, staring at the invisible whip in her hand, the room around them, her neck. But when they landed on hers, something in his expression changed. Softened.

She felt the rush of love hit her all at once, and every bone in her tired body felt rejuvenated—alive.

Hektor whimpered, still trying to crawl away, and Lila's eyes dropped to him. She huffed a breath at the pathetic creature below her. "He's *mine*," she claimed, lips tilting at the words. He couldn't claim her. But she *could* claim him. And she planned on claiming his life.

Ambrose's lips parted as a smirk overtook him. "May I watch you?"

"Of course." Lila strutted back into the room, the haze whip disappearing.

"Fucking bitch," Hektor wheezed. The wounds weren't healing, just like the burn she'd left him on his face. Good.

"Hey, watch how you speak about my wife." Ambrose shifted into his human form, pulled one of the ornate chairs from her sitting area, and dragged it into the bedroom, draping himself over the arms, with his legs stretched out as he used to do when he'd tease her. "This will be fun. Oh, I forgot to mention, Hektor, did you know Lila and I are to be married? I'd invite you to the wedding but—"

"I just don't think he'd be able to make it," Lila pouted. "Such a shame."

"He'll probably be quite *burned* out from all of this, don't you think?"

Lila giggled—a sound she didn't think she could make in the presence of Hektor.

"Fucking psychos!" he spat. Lila kicked him in the ribs, her foot leaving holes surrounded by burned brown stains on his shirt. He whined again, and Lila kicked him harder.

"You like breaking things that aren't yours, don't you?" she hissed. "You like breaking anything you can get your dirty, disgusting hands on?" Another two kicks. "You like torturing people, letting them hold out hope, only to rip it away as you watch?" Ribs shattered, and she smelled burning flesh, felt the skin stick to her boot.

"Who's the fucking psycho?" Ambrose gritted out. "Who thinks it's okay to touch someone without consent? Who needs a collar, an *unbreakable* thrall, that eliminates a person's ability to think freely?"

As Hektor had done to her, Lila grabbed his shoulder, and flipped him onto his back before straddling him.

"A *true* monster." Lila met Ambrose's gaze. A flicker of fear passed through his ruby eyes, but as she unshakably held his stare, an exhale escaped his lips and a lift to his chest showed Lila he'd understood her words.

Lila punched Hektor, breaking his nose under her molten fist. Black blood gushed out, but she only punched again, and again. The small stream of blood boiling on his skin, steaming and burning through the flesh like lava with all the heat exuding out of her.

"Stop. Please, please," he begged. And it was like music to Lila's ears.

He had made her this way. As much as she might hate being like this, as much as she might *regret* feeling this way later, might think the worst of herself, Lila enjoyed this.

She enjoyed hurting Hektor.

She enjoyed making him beg for his pathetic fucking life.

"Beg for me," she uttered, pulling her dagger from her thigh. She carved his face, slicing along his cheek.

"Please, Lila. Please. It hurts. It hurts so fucking bad." He coughed blood, and it hit Lila's cheek.

Ambrose leaned back, tilting his head at Hektor. "Hmm. Love, I don't think he's being very genuine."

"Shut up, fucker," Hektor spat.

The smile on Ambrose's face was like stuff of nightmares. All shiny, pointy teeth and pure malice. "You wanna know a little secret before she burns your ugly face off?" He paused, adjusting in the seat. Ambrose leaned forward, lowering his head as he propped his elbows on his knees. "I fucked *my wife* in your bed. Hard. And I made sure she came while screaming my name."

Hektor buckled under Lila, his face red for all new reasons, but he couldn't get her off. She gripped her thighs tighter around him, raising the heat.

"He knows all the perfect ways to touch me," Lila said. "And his cock feels *so good* inside of me." She shoved the wood into his ribs, careful not to puncture his heart, and twisted.

"You're supposed to be *mine*." Hektor snapped. He shifted under Lila, into his monstrous form. The burned grotesque beast hissed and kicked Lila off. Or . . . attempted to at least.

Lila threw her hands forward, dropping her dagger, and grabbed Hektor's throat. Then, she poured the entire sun into him.

Hektor writhed as his skin singed and bubbled, boiled and melted. He screamed as his monster form's white flesh turned gray, then black, charring as though on fire, as though in the sunlight.

Lila moved her hands to his face, pushing her palm into it. "Ugly fucking bastard!" She poured every ounce of hate and pain and anger, every sliver of trauma and fear and resentment, into this one touch. All the years of torment, all the years of trying to protect Marcus from them, all the years of not knowing whether she was going to be raped or killed by the next evening. She drowned him in it.

Screaming, Lila gripped the sides of Hektor's head, watching as she melted him—watching as she killed him.

"I already told you. I was never yours. Just like I was never a murine. I'm the fucking Sun Child, and I'm going to end your torment on me, and anyone else."

Her hands burned, like two suns pressed against his face. Hektor's skin charred even more, as though an invisible fire were taking him. His eyes popped, oozing from their sockets, his hair completely burned off, his wings incinerated, and soon, Lila didn't have a body under her. She had a corpse. A charred, shriveled up, blackened corpse.

The room was silent, the only noises were the deep breaths she took and the crows outside.

Ambrose stood, and as soon as he did, the caws from the balcony disappeared along with the flapping of wings. The crows were leaving.

He padded up to her, crouching before her. But she couldn't look at him. Her eyes were transfixed to the corpse.

"Lila," he whispered. "Lila, look at me."

And when she did, she saw so much love in his eyes, it overwhelmed her.

And her feelings were all over the place.

She threw herself at him, jumping into him and forcing him to fall back as his leathers sizzled from her touch. Lila pressed her lips to his, grinding her hips against his—trying to feel him, to know this was real, he was there.

The kiss quickly grew deeper. Ambrose pulled her tongue into his mouth as his hands dove into her hair.

"I thought you were dead. I thought you'd left me."

"Never," her voice cracked. "I will *never* leave you."

The kiss was hot and wet, tears spilling onto their lips.

"I need—to feel you," Ambrose declared. He pushed her back onto the floor, on top of the charred remains, kissing her deeply as he hovered over her, one hand to the side of her head, and the other pulling her waist flush to his body.

"He's dead, Ambrose," a smile broke on Lila's lips. "He's *finally* dead."

Ambrose broke the kiss and wiped the tears from her cheeks with his thumb. "He is. He's dead. So is Drusilla. It's over, love. We did it. We lived."

She kissed him. "It's not fully over. There are a number of strigoi to heal still."

Ambrose hummed. "I think I might be able to help with that."

"And Marcus? Constance?"

"Both fine, Little Crow."

He lowered himself onto Lila, kissing her once more. Kissing her like it was breathing, like he needed her kiss to survive. Something she felt too.

Ambrose trailed kisses over her chin, plucking her nipples over her leathers, as she ground her pussy on his thigh. His head dipped lower, sucking her breast into his mouth, and though the leather was between them, it still felt so hot. So real. He clumsily lowered his waistband past his hips, pulling his already hard cock free, before he ripped Lila's pants from her body.

She needed him then. She needed him to hold her, to kiss her, to love her. She needed him inside of her, to fuck her, and to help her heal Malvania.

"I fucking love you, Little Crow."

"Show me," she breathed, and he pushed inside of her, groaning at her tightness and proving every ounce of his love.

Mostly, Lila needed *him*. Always. Forever.

Lila ran down the steps, Ambrose close behind her. The last thing she remembered before Hektor was fighting off Drusilla with Marcus and Constance being injured. Ambrose had told her Drusilla was dead, and that both of them were safe. But she needed to *see* them. To hug them and hold them and feel them in her arms.

Ambrose's love had helped her heal the rest of the strigoi in the castle that could be saved, and as they ran down the steps, it became evident the others took care of those that could not. Humans and vampires sat on the floor, dazed and mumbling, while others began shifting around to help.

She saw Rebekkah, helping Nostro up from the floor. The old man cracked his back and scratched his head, and while Bek was sporting a black eye, the color and swelling were already fading.

The great hall was an utter mess, and part of her was glad Kaz stayed back in the Viper Morada for the time being. He would have an absolute fit if he saw the manor in such disarray.

Lila ran up to Rebekkah and Nostro, embracing them both in a warming hug. "I'm so glad you both are all right. Thanks for the save back there, both of you."

Rebekkah grinned against her cheek, "I've been wanting to punch my daft brother for a long, long time. Is he—" she paused, then pulled away to look Lila in the eyes. "Is he dead?"

Lila slowly nodded. "He is."

A long sigh escaped her lips. "Good. That's good."

The Sun Child

Nostro looked up at Ambrose, "Maronai left immediately, but without protection from Lila, it will take a while for him to make it as far as we want. I don't suppose he will return till late tonight."

Ambrose stepped beside Lila, placing his hand comfortingly on her lower back. "And the head?"

"Still burned. It hasn't regenerated and it shows no signs of doing so. I haven't seen a death like this in decades, but if memory serves correct—which, I know it does—Drusilla, the hag of the Arachnid Estate, is officially deceased." A toothy grin flashed on Nostro's face. "We win."

"*Lila!*" her name was yelled across the hall. The moment she turned around, she was pushed back with such a force, Ambrose was the only thing keeping her up.

Marcus wrapped his arms around his sister so tightly, Lila could barely breathe. "How? How are you okay? *Are* you okay? Fuck, Lila, *you're okay!*"

Tears fell onto her hair, soaking through. She returned the hug, burying her face into Marcus's chest.

"I'm fine, Marcus. Really."

"But . . . how?" He pulled away, keeping his hands on her shoulders, and studied her. His brown eyes lingered on her neck, on the melted gold, and then met hers again. "How did you survive that?"

"I—I have no idea," she said honestly. "I died. I know I did. Yet . . ."

"I have a theory about that—"

Rebekkah rolled her eyes, "Oh wonderful, another theory."

Nostro pinned her with a look. "She is the Sun Child, after all. Healing is a part of her. I believe if Lila isn't destroyed completely, she can heal herself to any capacity."

"But the Sun Maiden died?" Ambrose asked, turning to him.

"Yes. But she didn't really have healing. Not like Lila. Her powers were mute. A sensation rather than an existence. Only in death was she able to heal. Whereas, in life, Lila is gifted with it all."

"Shall we test it?" Rebekkah wiggled her eyebrows playfully.

"Touch her, and I'll kill you," Ambrose smirked.

Rebekkah put her palms up in mock defeat. "Say no more, Crow Lord." She left their tiny circle and disappeared into the crowd to help more.

"That said, I also believe our dear Lila will no longer age. Only time will tell, but if she could continuously replenish our energy, who is to say she also cannot heal her own mortality?"

"So," Marcus began, dumbfounded. "She's immortal? Like us?"

"Theoretically. Only time will tell."

Ambrose looked at her again. *Together . . . forever?*

Lila blushed. *I like the sound of it. Do you?*

He pulled her to him and planted a chaste kiss on her forehead. *It's all I've wanted. I didn't think it was possible, I only hoped for so much. But . . .* Again, he kissed her.

After a moment, Lila turned to Marcus. "How is Constance?"

"She's okay, startled a bit. But she is keeping busy. Would you like me to take you to her?"

Lila nodded and followed him into the dining room. The room was even more in disarray than the main hall. It looked like a sick house with all of the people lying about. But her eyes snagged on the small blond girl in the corner, her eyes unfocused as she helped another vampire up from the floor.

But the moment Lila passed the door's threshold,

The Sun Child

Constance's head shot up and she turned to Lila, her tired eyes widening and a smile growing. She said something to the person she was helping, and then ran to Lila, her ponytail bouncing with each step.

"Lilac! I knew you were okay!" She threw her arms around Lila's neck, squeezing tightly.

Marcus raised an eyebrow. "Really? How?"

After pulling away, Constance shrugged. "The manor was healed. Strigoi changed. I thought it was pretty obvious, since only one person we know could do that." She smirked at Marcus, who immediately blushed.

"Oh. Right..."

She grabbed Marcus's arm, and Lila immediately saw his skin react, gooseflesh appearing on his arms, and his cheeks pinkening even more. "Don't worry, I won't tell anyone." Constance winked.

"We're vampires, Constance, we all heard every word," Ambrose said, coming up behind her.

Pollock stood on his shoulder, a little dusty but completely unscathed. He chirped when he turned to Lila then bounced down to her shoulder, nuzzling his head into her cheek.

"If no one minds, I'd like to borrow our Sun Child for the rest of the day. Night too, perhaps."

Constance rolled her eyes. "Gross."

Lila bit back a smirk, and without a moment's hesitation, Ambrose shifted, wings splayed out, and swept her into his arms. He didn't so much as say goodbye as he flew her out of the Crow Court and into the open morning, Pollock soaring beside them.

I tried to leave him behind, but he insisted he come as chaperone, Ambrose grunted in her mind.

Good, Lila giggled. *Someone has to keep the monster at bay, because it evidently won't be me.*

No, no. You just make the monster more feral. Ambrose paused for a breath before continuing. *Back there, against Hektor. You called him a true monster.*

Lila nodded. *He is—was.*

And I am not, correct?

No. You and Hektor were never *the same.*

I feared I was but . . . you've shown me I'm not. I'd still like to be your monster though, Lila.

Oh, you will forever be my monster. I insist. What would I do without my protective beast to love and chase me?

And punishes you when you're naughty?

And rewards me when I'm a good girl with a rough spanking, Lila giggled, heat immediately radiating off her and warming her core.

Well, aren't I glad I told Nostro and Bek I'd be taking you for the rest of the solstice.

Where to?

Ambrose grinned, and it did funny things to Lila's belly. His eyes were cast forward, looking to the horizon, but Lila couldn't stop looking into those two dark pits, the black holes she loved just as much as the shining rubies. *I promised you the ocean. What better day to show you than the longest day in a solar rotation?*

He dove down, swirling in the sky, the wind rushing past them. Lila felt so free at that moment. Her enemies were dead, the last of her chains were broken, and she was bound to the love of her life forever.

As she let the wind rush through her hair, her eyes caught the horizon Ambrose had been watching. It was stunning, breathtaking. The ocean was vast and lay beyond them with the sun hovering just above the horizon line, gleaming, illuminating the ocean in a mosaic of greens and blues, and the sand at the shore looked so white, it almost blended with the foam of the waves.

I want to watch you with the waves. It's been a dream of mine.

She turned to him, and he was watching her, the sunlight gilding his face.

Will you teach me to swim?

Of course. We'll have a picnic, and then, if I can get this pesky bird away from us, I'll make love to you by the ocean.

Lila smirked. *Only if you beat me in a race. If not, Pollock and I get to have a romantic evening while you serve us hand and foot.*

Is that a threat, Little Crow? Ambrose raised one of those perfectly shaped eyebrows, voice like liquid gold in her mind, already heating her core.

No, Ambrose. It's a bargain.

hree Months Later

She rode his cock as if it were the last time she'd be able to. But he already had plans for their evening as well, feasting on her wet cunt as she lay bare for him on his dining room table, just as he'd said he'd do almost a year ago. Lila moaned, bouncing on top of him as Ambrose bruised her hips with his fingers. And he knew she loved it.

The newly blooming sunflowers were facing them—facing *her*—as they made love in the garden in the middle of the day. It would still be hours before Robin would have to come to work, and he planned to spend all of it out here with her.

"You feel divine," he groaned, throwing his head back into the grass. She always did, but taking her like this, where anyone might find them, the sunlight warming his skin—it was moments like these he'd been living for during the rest of the summer months.

Lila moaned, "Lords, fuck—I'm going to—" She screamed

as her riding hesitated, feeling the hot burst of sweet cum drown his cock. Her pussy was so hot, so tight, so perfect—each and every time.

The feel of it alone was enough to send him over, finishing inside of her, just like she'd asked.

Lila slumped down on top of him, and rolled into the grass, still resting half of herself on his chest.

The sun beamed down on them, warming their skin, though the breeze kept them cool. It wasn't fall just yet, but the first caresses were beginning to touch their skin, to turn the leaves. Lila smoothed her light pink sundress down, back over her thighs. Ambrose promised himself to properly clean her later, but for now, he enjoyed her weight on him. After adjusting himself, he rested his cheek against her head, drawing small circles on her upper back as he rubbed her.

"I could fall asleep out here, it's so nice." Lila stretched her legs like a cat then curled them toward her.

"You can, if you'd like. A nap sounds nice right now." They both had been working tirelessly to get the Crow Court back to what it was, and it finally resembled the manor it once was.

Over the months, Lila had been traveling the four vampire manors of Malvania, healing or removing the remaining strigoi. She helped Nostro in the early stages of rebuilding the Maggot Mansion tower, and helped Rebekkah establish close bonds with the villages in the Viper Morada. She'd gone to the Arachnid Estate for Balzar's funeral, and helped Maronai establish a proper system for humans and vampires to live in harmony.

Meanwhile, Ambrose had rebuilt. He joined the people of the Crow Court and traveled all around—first to Asterim and then to the neighboring towns and villages, all the way to Catacomb City and back. He worked, with his own two hands, to rebuild what once was, to build new, and to help those in need. With the help of Constance and Kazimir, Ambrose had reestablished the trade in his land between humans and vampires, and made sure everyone had plenty of food and shelter.

All the while, he began training Marcus, both in education and combat. He was teaching the young man to be a vampire, to be a warrior. And it seemed he was reveling in his newfound strength, finally growing confident in his new fangs.

Finally, after everyone else had been taken care of, Lila and Ambrose were focusing their efforts on the manor.

Lila's room was still a mess, and she hadn't returned since the summer solstice. *Since Hektor.* Ambrose's office had also been destroyed, and was in the process of being pieced back together.

The garden had been slowly replanted, and Lila requested a field of sunflowers in honor of the Sun Maiden. The field they were now laying in. At the opening to the garden, the wisteria still swayed in the wind, the lavender stalks were still used for tea, and the entire garden was abundant in lilacs and hyacinths.

Lila put her hand on Ambrose's chest, and he took it, entwining their fingers as he slowly massaged the crow and sun mark on her ring finger.

"Will you be my wife?" he mused.

Though everyone had been asking repeatedly, Lila and Ambrose felt they both had been too busy to even *begin* planning their wedding, though he still liked to tease her about it. And they wanted it to be exactly what they wanted. So, instead of rushing things, they decided to wait. Decided to give it the time it deserved. After all, they had forever.

The Sun Child

"Hmm. What will you give me if I do?"

He felt her smile against his bare chest, his shirt open. Ambrose kissed her forehead and whispered with his voice like liquid gold, "Anything, love."

Acknowledgments

Whew! Another one down! This book was such a journey for me, and was so different from when I originally planned it. Did you know, *The Crow Lord* was originally meant to end in betrayal? Lila and Ambrose quickly outgrew that notion, but this book had an *entirely* different outline than what came to be, and I am honestly so happy for that. I am so proud of our babies and how far they have come.

This book wouldn't have been possible without a very specific group of people who kept me sane during this endeavor.

Mike, my *fiancé* (he upgraded from partner *finally*), thank you for being the chief captain of the Keep-Julie-Mostly-Sane party. Thank you for all the cheese, meals, hugs, and telling me "boys don't work like that."

Maki, though you tried to stop my writing to give you pets on a *number* of occasions, I knew you were really just supporting me, keeping the vibe up. You're a real one, my fluffy babe.

To my mom, I wrote the end of the book while you were packing up the house, and I finished it while you were moving into the next. I'm so excited for the continued journeys we will have in a new home that we will make all our own. Thank you always for being the best dang cheerleader, sounding board, hype woman, and friend a daughter could ask for. And one special shoutout line to the rest of my parents and family (I know this sounds weird to outsiders, but it's not that complicated, I swear.)

Huge thank you forever to the skeleton to my ghost, Anto. You come through for me every single time, and make the most gorgeous covers and graphics imaginable. Thank you for always supporting my writing, no matter how weird it gets, and for bringing my stories to life with your art.

Brandi, you were my original sounding board for the idea of Ambrose and Lila, and thank you so much for hyping me up whenever I needed it, and for helping me visualize our hot dark-skinned vampire daddy. I don't think this story would be where it is if it weren't for you.

To my fellow Cheese Goblin, Larissa, thank you for reading and editing this whole dang book, and for constantly reassuring me it is good and I should publish it and I should *not* run away into the woods and disappear for the rest of my life.

Wren, thank you so much for being my third pair of eyes on this beast. I appreciate you so much, and always enjoy bouncing ideas off you. You've helped me make this story what it turned out to be and I am forever grateful.

To Jessi, you helped me in more ways than you think with this one, by constantly being my food buddy, encouraging pizza, and doing the layout *while super pregnant.* Super shout out to baby Connor.

To my street team, the Ghoulies, thank you so much for loving my books and supporting me along this journey! I love and appreciate every single one of you and cannot wait for you all to read how Lila and Ambrose's story ends!

And finally, to my readers. Thank you so much for reading the Vampires of Malvania series, and for falling in love with Ambrose and Lila as they fell for each other, for soaring with Pollock, laughing with Constance, and dancing with the vampires of the Maggot Mansion. I hope these books bring just a little sunlight into your life, and keep hope, for we may see Malvania again very soon.

About the Author

J. M. Failde (fah-eel-deh) spent just over one hundred fortnights rigorously studying the complexities of the English language at Florida International University. While she is not conjuring up stories, she can be found searching for *el chupacabra*, befriending the ghost in her house, or dying her hair a new color. Failde currently resides in her gothic manor on the outskirts of Atlanta, Georgia, with her fiancé, Mike, and her familiar—the round but feisty calico cat, Maki.

Follow her on Instagram @jmfailde or go to her website, jmfailde.com, for more.

J. M. Failde

WWW.JMFAILDE.COM

Milton Keynes UK
Ingram Content Group UK Ltd.
UKHW010006260624
444693UK00003B/34